Barbara Griggs

THE
FOOD
FACTOR

VIKING

VIKING
Penguin Books Ltd, Harmondsworth, Middlesex, England
Viking Penguin Inc., 40 West 23rd Street, New York, New York 10010, U.S.A.
Penguin Books Australia Ltd, Ringwood, Victoria, Australia
Penguin Books Canada Limited, 2801 John Street, Markham, Ontario, Canada L3R 1B4
Penguin Books (N.Z.) Ltd, 182–190 Wairau Road, Auckland 10, New Zealand

First published 1986

Typeset in Linotron Baskerville

Typeset, printed and bound in Great Britain by
Hazell, Watson & Viney Limited,
Member of the BPCC Group,
Aylesbury, Bucks

British Library Cataloguing in Publication Data

Griggs, Barbara
  The food factor.
  1. Nutrition   2. Food — Composition
  I. Title
  641.1   TX551

  ISBN 0-670-80201-8

**The destiny of nations depends upon what
and how they eat.**

Jean-Anthelme Brillat-Savarin
La Physiologie du goût, 1825

For Ninka

Contents

Introduction

If a plant is not watered, it dies. Human beings are far more complex organisms than plants, but in our need for nourishment to sustain our lives, we are as one with the primrose and the oak tree. Without the life-giving energy of the sun translated into foodstuffs we should perish.

But man is not nourished by bread alone, nor is malnutrition the only threat to his health. Like plants we also need fresh air and sunshine; like animals, we need exercise; and because we are a unique and extraordinary complex of mind and body, we have profound psychological and spiritual needs too. If these are not met, our bodies may suffer as well as our minds and spirits.

In offering a study of just one of the factors necessary for our well-being – the food factor – I should like to make it plain that I do not suppose it to be the only one of any importance. Heredity, environment, unhappiness and stress of many kinds can all be equally significant in ill health. But this book is not about them; my subject is nutrition and the new awareness of its importance which has developed over the last century and a half.

Until late in the nineteenth century, our understanding of the biochemical processes by which we are nourished was based largely on observation and speculation. Not until the early years of this century was the concept of vitamins first enunciated, and the first vitamin isolated and chemically identified. Not until the Second World War, of 1939–45, was it possible for a country at war to plan nutritional policies which were based on accurate scientific knowledge. And in retrospect our nutritional knowledge of this time seems rudimentary indeed. Almost nothing was then known of essential fatty acids; the word prostaglandin had yet to be coined; the brain had yielded up almost none of its complex secrets; we were at the very beginning of our understanding of hormonal function; important vitamins still remained to be identified; we knew next to nothing of the role of many trace elements and minerals.

To tell the story of how nutrition developed from its nineteenth-century roots in chemistry into the absorbing and fascinating science that it is today was the original purpose of this book. But as I traced it through medical and scientific journals, through accounts of dedicated laboratory work and brilliantly imaginative research, through biographies, letters and papers, I became aware of another story, an alternative history of nutrition as it were, running in parallel. This nutrition owed little originally to painstaking laboratory work; it was evolved as a new medical philosophy by a handful of American doctors and lay-thinkers who based their ideas on physiology rather than chemistry, and on the study of man in his evolutionary context.

Central to this philosophy was an idea as old as Hippocrates: that no doctor effects a cure: that 'cure belongs to the body, and if we put the system under proper conditions it will work its own cure'. These 'proper conditions' necessarily included the diet on which mankind had evolved to function at his best: wholegrains, little or no meat, fruit, nuts, vegetables: any diet which diverged widely from this – which featured such anti-evolutionary inventions as alcohol, tea, coffee and refined sugar – must unfailingly bring ill health in its wake. Other important conditions for healthy living were personal hygiene, aerobic exercise, fresh air and sunbathing, and a calm and well-balanced outlook on life.

Such ideas brought the Hygienists – as they styled themselves – into headlong conflict with the accepted medical dogmas of their day. And for more than a century the doctors or lay practitioners who invoked the food factor in sickness, and treated their patients by diet and regime rather than drugs, had to endure professional ostracism, the hostiity or contempt of their peers, and the uneasy ridicule of the general public.

Among these pioneers, who are the heroes of my story, were generations of Nature Cure practitioners; Dr Allinson who talked his East End patients into wholemeal bread and the virtues of exercise; Dr Henry Bieler, who told his patients – many a Hollywood star among them – that food was their best medicine; Dr Max Gerson, who treated cancer as a disorder of the entire system, to be dealt with by a programme of drastic detoxification, and a cleansing diet based on fruit and vegetables, from which tea, coffee, sugar, and refined carbohydrates were sternly excluded; and Dr Max Bircher-Benner, who cured his patients on a regime based on raw fruit and vegetables.

All of these doctors were eager students of nutrition, who would have welcomed the extraordinary wealth of knowledge which is available today. Yet it is doubtful whether more information would have caused them to modify their nutritional directions to any important degree. Today's elaborate and extraordinarily detailed studies of the human economy at work have only confirmed the truths that Graham, Trall, and their followers were already putting into practice a century and a half ago.

As early as 1915 one intelligent and well-read American journalist knew enough about nutrition to diagnose almost at sight the multiple nutritional deficiencies which had laid low an entire ship's crew – and baffled the ship's doctor: he successfully prescribed the wheat germ, the nutrient-rich fruits and vegetables, the eggs and the milk which restored the prostrated sailors to life. Nearly fifty years ago, we already knew enough to plan the high-fibre, low-fat wholegrain diet which enabled Britain to survive six years of all-out war in fine physical shape – and which is finally being officially recommended to us today in the NACNE Report and in the Health Education Council's admirable new booklet, *Guide to Healthy Eating*. And in 1946, Sir Robert McCarrison, one of Britain's most eminent nutritionists, could already predict confidently that whatever additions might be made to our knowledge in the future, it would be found 'that all elements and complexes necessary for normal nutrition – so far as food can provide them – are present in the fresh fruits of the Earth as Nature furnishes them, though not in these foodstuffs as man mishandles and mistreats them'.

The confidence of McCarrison and the pioneers was not based, however, on belief in their own superior intuitions, nor yet on blind faith in instinctive peasant wisdom. It was solidly founded on long clinical experience of patients for whom no other medical treatment had succeeded, being restored to health on such a regime; and on the observation of such diets and their consequences for the health of the races who lived on them. And it is being vindicated today by study after study, filling up the pages of a steadily growing number of journals devoted to nutrition.

Slowly we are learning to understand the role in our body's chemistry of every single one of the nutrients so cavalierly discarded in the refining of wheat, sugar and rice, and dismissed as insignificant by a dozen official committees stuffed with nutrition 'experts'. We are learning how disastrous for our health has been the mishandling and mistreatment of natural foodstuffs in the factories of the packaged-food industry. We are beginning to appreciate the damage we are inflicting on human ecology with our unrestrained use of food additives, pesticides and fertilizers.

These are painful and unwelcome truths, but they are dawning on a public that is showing itself not only ready to listen, but impatient for action too. Even within the relatively short time that I have been working on this book, there has been an explosive growth of public interest and curiosity. It is hardly possible to switch on radio or TV, or open a newspaper or magazine, without finding features planned to cater to the new public thirst for information. Parents are formally requesting that their children's schools supply genuinely nutritious food which will help build sound bodies and active brains, instead of the lifeless junk food too many of them still offer. Nurses are urging better nutrition on the hospitals where they work – for themselves and their patients alike. Housewives have given such a decisive thumbs-down to unwanted additives in their foods that all the big supermarket chains are rushing to bring in new additive-free lines. Motorway cafés and rail and airport snackbars offer salads, fruit, fresh juices and vegetarian snacks alongside the mandatory burgers, sausages and chips.

And the pages of the most solidly establishment medical journals – which even a decade ago you could have scanned for weeks on end without coming across a single reference to nutrition – are now crammed with papers, letters and editorials, testifying to its startlingly high profile in the mid-eighties.

Half a century ago, an editorial in the *British Medical Journal* paid tribute to a science then in its infancy – that of nutrition. 'There can be no doubt', it proclaimed, 'that this newer knowledge of nutrition has placed in the hands of our profession a potent weapon against disease – a potent instrument in the promotion of physical efficiency and well-being. It behoves us, therefore, to become proficient in this knowledge, to apply it in the daily course of our work, and to spread it by every means in our power.'

A little late in the day, the *Journal*'s professional readers are now ready to add this powerful instrument to their armoury. In medical circles, the science of nutrition has arrived at last, and doctors are in the process of 'discovering' truths which for years have been continuously and successfully employed in the battle against ill health by people they styled cranks, who were recommending a diet which they once denounced as faddist.

This book is no official history of nutrition; that account will be written some day, no doubt, in terms of impeccably scientific laboratory work, addressed to a professional audience. Let me call my own work an unofficial or – perhaps better still – an alternative history of nutrition. Even the doctors who feature in these pages – Trall, Tilden, McCarrison, Bircher-Benner, and Randolph and Hoffer – may never be given their full measure of recognition by official historians, while some of my heroes and heroines – Alfred McCann, Gayelord Hauser, Adelle Davis, Bernarr Macfadden, J. C. Thompson, Lady Eve Balfour – did not even have a formal medical training to lend respectability to the disturbing and revolutionary ideas they proclaimed. Moreover, they appealed to a professional audience if it was ready to listen; but many of them addressed themselves first and foremost to the general public, judging that health is a subject too important to be left to doctors alone.

It is people like these, of integrity, enthusiasm or compassion, who have not only shaped the development of nutrition: they have also done their utmost to see that it became available to all the millions of suffering human beings who needed it. This is their story: all honour to them.

———

The writing of this book was made possible by the generous help given me by many experts in fields where I was at best an enthusiastic amateur; I am deeply grateful for their encouragement, and their readiness to share their hard-earned knowledge with me. For those errors of fact or judgement which may have crept in none the less, the responsibility is mine alone.

I acknowledge with special gratitude my indebtedness to Dr Abram Hoffer, Dr Carl Pfeiffer, Professor Hugh Sinclair, and Dr Alexander Schauss, who all spared precious time to my notebook and many questions, then read through the passages concerning their work, and gave me the benefit of their constructive criticisms; to Mrs Ruth Kunz-Bircher, daughter of Dr Max Bircher-Benner, and to Charlotte Gerson, daughter of Dr Max Gerson, who read through and corrected the chapters on the work of their distinguished fathers; to Robert Rodale, who was lavish with information and material on the Regenerative Agriculture which it has been his own and his father's dream to foster in the United States. Other outstanding debts are to Mary Langman, who read through the entire manuscript and made many invaluable suggestions, particularly for the history of the Peckham Experiment; to Lady Eve Balfour, who rectified a number of errors in my account of her work and the origins of the Soil Association; to Dr Raymond Rice, who did his best to steer me safely through the intricacies of essential fatty acids; to Dr Jeffrey Bland, who read through long sections of the book and made many useful suggestions and criticisms; to Keki Sidhwa, who loaned me invaluable material on the early history of the Natural Hygiene movement and saved me from a number of errors; to Dr Kenneth Barlow, who allowed me to read through and quote from the typescript of his book, *What is Health?*; to Dr Donald Rudin, who generously sent me for study the typescript of his forthcoming book *The Omega Factor*; to Doris Grant, Lilian Schofield, Mrs Annette Dickinson, Professor Derek Bryce-Smith, Dr Allan Cott, Dr Stephen Davies, Dr Moke Williams, Dr Olav Lindahl and many others whose brains I have picked and whose time I have taken up with my questions.

Special thanks are due to my editor Tony Lacey, who bore with equanimity the succession of identity-crises through which the work passed before reaching its present form, and was unfailingly enthusiastic and involved throughout; to Richard Simon, for warm encouragement at many moments when it was badly needed; to Beata Duncan, for much diligent research; and to Monica Bryant, whose most useful contribution included an introduction to the work of her great compatriot, Are Waerland.

My grateful thanks to the library staff at the Wellcome Institute for the History of Medicine; Queen Elizabeth College; the London Library and the British Library; and to Terry Charman, in the Department of Printed Material at the Imperial War Museum, who directed me to fascinating records of war on the Kitchen Front.

A special thank you to my mother, Nina Griggs, for her continual enthusiasm and interest; to Ina Brok and Anya Maesen, who held the fort nobly on the home front while I battled through month after discouraging month of intensive work on the book; and to Mia and Ron Perren who pampered me with peace, quiet and comfort during the first difficult weeks of writing.

To my husband Henri van der Zee, and to our daughters Bibi and Ninka, finally, I should like to express my heartfelt gratitude for their love, their encouragement and the patience with which they endured for many weary months my preoccupation with a task that to all of us at times seemed neverending.

1
Animal and Vegetable

March 6. Friday . . . Mr Custance, Mr and Mrs
Corbould, and Mr Stoughton of Sparham, dined & spent
the Afternoon with us and stayed till after 9 o'clock at
Weston Parsonage. We gave them for Dinner a
Couple of Boiled Chickens and Pig's Face, very good
Peas Soup, a boiled Rump of Beef very fine, a
prodigious fine, large and very fat Cock-Turkey
roasted, Macaroni, Batter Custard Pudding with
Jelly, Apple Fritters, Tarts and Raspberry Puffs.
Dessert, baked Apples, nice Nonpareils, brandy
Cherries and Filberts. Wines, Ports & Sherries, Malt
Liquors, Strong Beer, bottled porter &c. After
Coffee & Tea we got to cards . . . All our Dinner was
very nicely cooked indeed. Mr Custance eat very
hearty . . .

James Woodforde (1740–1803)[1]

This high-calorie, high-protein, high-fat, high-sugar feast
would give a modern nutritionist a heart attack. But eighteenth-
century physicians had only the vaguest of notions about what
constituted a healthy diet, and almost no idea at all about what
happened to the boiled chicken, the batter custard pudding or
the brandy cherries after Parson Woodforde and his appreciative friends had swallowed them.

Various theories circulated. Hippocrates maintained that
all food, once digested, was somehow transmuted into a single
aliment by which the body was nourished. As late as the mid
eighteenth century, the influential Scottish physician William
Cullen suggested that after digestion all the nutritious parts of
the meal were blended in the blood into a single 'animal mixt',
which was then distributed around the body. 'In what manner
the nutritious fluid, then carried to the various parts, is there
applied . . . we cannot explain,' he readily admitted.

The great Galen, the fifth-century Alexandrian physician whose thinking dominated Western medicine for over a thousand years, held that food was first digested in the stomach and then a second time in the liver, before it was assimilated through the various organs. The process of digestion itself, suggested the Belgian alchemist van Helmont, was actually an acid fermentation triggered by a substance released into the stomach by the spleen; after this, the resulting acid mass passed on into the duodenum to be neutralized, and then passed through the walls of the gut to be converted into blood by another ferment, this time in the liver.

This theory seemed perfectly plausible to anyone who had ever suffered from indigestion, heartburn or flatulence; and since science lacked the tools for closer investigation, speculation went little further.

But however mysterious the workings of the gut might be, it was plain to any observant physician – as, indeed, to any intelligent layman – that a man's health and what he ate were closely related. Hippocrates went further than this: 'Each one of the substances of a man's diet acts upon his body and changes it in some way, and upon these changes his whole life depends, whether he be in health, in sickness, or convalescent.'[2] And starting with Hippocrates himself, plenty of advice was offered to the public about what they should or should not eat and drink, based upon personal experience as often as on general observation.

Galen was responsible for a prejudice against fruit that lasted until well into the nineteenth century. As a young man he suffered annually from fevers, until his father warned him against eating fruit. He gave it up – and thereafter suffered only a single day's fever in many years. Damned by association with Galen's summer fevers, the unwholesomeness of fruit became accepted medical dogma. During the great cholera epidemic of 1832, the Washington Board of Health actually prohibited the sale or import of virtually every fruit then in season, including melons, apples, pears, peaches, plums, oranges, lemons and apricots, as well as most fresh vegetables: such articles in their view were 'highly prejudicial to health'.

Much the most sensible advice was that of the twelfth-century Spanish-Jewish Maimonides, personal physician to Saladin, the Moslem anti-hero of the Crusades. In his *Treatise on Personal Hygiene and Dietetics*, which was translated from the Arabic and became well known in Europe, Maimonides summed up Greek and Arab teaching on the subject, and constantly quoted Hippocrates and Galen. But much of what he taught was very obviously the result of one exceptionally skilled physician's long and careful observation of his patients, and it has a curiously modern ring to it.

Unlike most doctors, Maimonides was slow to reach for his prescription pad. 'A doctor should begin with simple treatments, trying to cure by diet before he administers drugs,' was his view. 'No illness which can be treated by diet should be treated by any other means.' He told his patients to eat only in moderation: overeating was a great tax on their digestion, he pointed out. He warned against meals that were too rich or too varied, against drinking at mealtimes, against eating too much in hot weather. He was well aware of the dangers of constipation: patients with haemorrhoids were put on to a light, mainly vegetarian diet, thus anticipating modern views on fibre. He urged aerobic exercise on his patients – but not immediately after meals. And he was specific about what foods they should eat and what foods were bad for them.

Heading his list of beneficial foods were lean meat and 'well-prepared wheat bread'. The best meats were mutton, chicken and gamebirds, the best bread was wholemeal bread, properly leavened and kneaded, with all the bran left in. Refined flour, pizzas, pasta, pancakes he thoroughly disapproved: 'these foods require a strong stomach'.[3]

He approved of fresh milk, although he recognized that not everybody could digest it, and he frowned on its use in cookery; but cheese he thought poor, heavy stuff, apart from the fresh white *feta* cheese still eaten in the Middle East. And he frowned on fish, other than small sea fish such as sardines; even these should only be eaten occasionally.

On vegetables he was selective: garlic, onion and leeks, radishes, cabbages, aubergines he thought unwholesome. But although he thought fruit should only be eaten in moderation, he could not bring himself to endorse Galen's view that none at all should be eaten, and he allowed ripe figs, grapes, plums, pears, quinces, medlars.

Many of Maimonides's ideas about a healthy diet were echoed in the best-known and most popular text of the Middle Ages, the *Regimen Salernitatis*. At Salerno in Sicily, the earliest and most celebrated of all European medical schools had been founded in the twelfth century, and a long Latin poem embodying its common-sense teachings on diet and hygiene circulated throughout Europe from the late fifteenth century onwards. *The Regimen of the School of Salerno* was one of the first books to be printed and no less than 170 Latin editions followed; it was translated into a dozen languages and most educated people could quote chunks of it by heart. Addressed to a lay audience – the King of England, in point of fact – the *Regimen* was stylish, light-hearted, down-to-earth – and certainly eminently quotable, even to modern ears:

> *If thou to health and vigour wouldst attain*
> *Shun weighty cares – all anger deem profane,*
> *From heavy suppers and much wine abstain . . .*
> *Shun idle, noonday slumber, nor delay*
> *The urgent calls of nature to obey . . .*
> > *Great suppers will the stomach's peace impair:*
> > *Wouldst lightly rest? curtail thine evening fare.*

Like Maimonides – with whose writings they were certainly familiar – the authors of the *Regimen* disapproved of cheese, the richer meats such as hare and venison, salty foods, and the more luscious fruits such as peaches. Like him they held that the staples of good diet were wheat, eggs, boiled or roasted (but not fried) meat, soft cheese, and milk – for those it agreed with. And like him, finally, they urged the benefits of moderation in eating, 'the table thinly spread'.[4]

Most doctors paid lip-service to the view that gluttony led to ill health, but at least one layman took it thoroughly to heart. Luigi Cornaro was a Venetian nobleman, born in 1467, who was seriously ill by the time he was forty because of his greed and heavy drinking. Light dawned one day, and with all a convert's zeal, Cornaro forswore the good life. Instead, he adopted a regime that by the standards of the time amounted to little more than slow starvation: 12 oz (340 g) meat, bread, broth, egg yolk, and 14 oz (0·4 l) wine – a good half-bottle – daily. Within these self-imposed limits he varied the menu as much as possible, choosing from veal, kid, mutton, poultry and every kind of gamebird, while the wine he drank was young and fruity. On this Drinking Man's Diet he lived to be ninety-eight, and at an advanced age – to prove that his wits were as sharp as ever despite his sparse regime, and to convert others to this healthy life – he wrote an account of it called *Discourses on a Sober and Temperate Life*. A fascinated public has kept it steadily in print ever since.

Several other doctors preached austerity and moderation in diet, but none of them ventured to suggest that eating less meat and more vegetables might be desirable. On the contrary, there was a widespread belief that vegetables were actually harder to digest, and consequently less nutritious than meat, while meat was indispensable for strength and stamina. Real men needed meat. Even George Cheyne, whose immensely popular *Essay on Health and Long Life* (1734) revealed how he had shed several stones of surplus weight and regained bounding health on a restricted vegetarian diet, saw no reason to recommend anything of the kind to his readers. He held that animal food was much more suitable than a vegetable diet for those in normal health.

Was it even possible that human life might be sustained on animal food alone? There was some evidence that this might be so, as Dr Millman reminded his readers in 1772. In 1663 the Dutch Greenland Company had left a party of seven healthy sailors, amply supplied with ship's provisions, to spend the winter in Greenland making observations on the climate. The ship that returned for them in the spring found them all dead of the scurvy. By contrast, a party of eight Englishmen had earlier been accidentally stranded in Greenland for more than a year, with no provisions of any kind. They had survived free of scurvy on a diet that consisted almost entirely of fresh, raw animal meat – bear, reindeer, or whatever they could trap.

Comparing animal and vegetable food, one popular early nineteenth-century English medical writer, Dr Thomas Graham, instructed his readers that animal food was 'no doubt, more allied to our nature, and more easily assimilated to our nourishment', while vegetables were 'digested with more difficulty'. He found this truth slightly difficult to reconcile with the fact that the same animals subsisted entirely on vegetables, but fell back on contemporary notions of physiology to assert that 'In the stomach, vegetable food always shows a tendency towards acescency, while animal food, on the contrary, tends towards putrefaction. Hence the former is apt to produce symptoms of uneasiness, while the latter in moderate quantity is almost never felt.' Obviously, therefore, 'a mixture of vegetable and animal nourishment appears best fitted for the health of mankind in general'.

Like most other medical writers, Graham's lack of enthusiasm for fruit and vegetables – especially if eaten raw – is evident.

'All vegetables of the *pulse kind* are liable to strong objections . . . very indigestible, heating, productive of great flatulency, contain little nourishment . . . *Carrots* . . . *radishes* . . . rather difficult of digestion and unwholesome . . . *Salads, lettuce* and all undressed vegetables of this kind, contain little nourishment . . . not much to be recommended.' Galen's summer fevers were not forgotten: '*Cherries, plums, cucumbers, melons* . . . difficult of digestion . . . fit only for the strong and active . . . *Black currants* have a strong tendency to affect the bowels . . .'[5]

These medical prejudices were reinforced early in the nineteenth century when a young US army surgeon, William Beaumont, had the research opportunity of a lifetime offered to him and grasped it with both hands. Among his patients was a fur-trapper called Alexis St Martin who, as the result of a gunshot wound, had a gastric fistula which had never healed. Beaumont found that by peering through this tiny window he could observe what no man had ever glimpsed before: the actual process of digestion in the stomach. St Martin intensely disliked having his digestive processes experimented and spied upon, but for years he submitted reluctantly to Beaumont's tactful persistence, and in 1833 Beaumont's *Experiments and Observations on the Gastric Juice and the Physiology of Digestion* was published to an astonished audience. In it he presented the first complete and accurate description of gastric juice, showed that emotions could influence the digestion, and made clear the importance of the hydrochloric acid secreted by the stomach for digestion. He also concluded from what he had seen that 'generally speaking, vegetable aliment requires more time, and probably greater powers of the gastric organs, than animal.'[6]

Even Beaumont, however, still believed in Hippocrates' 'one aliment'. But why meat should make the most important contribution to this mysterious fluid, or what other kinds of food were essential to support life, had already been the subject of a number of experiments.

One of these had proved fatal. A young English doctor, William Stark, who was deeply interested in the whole question of diet decided, in the summer of 1769, to try and establish by personal experiment which kinds of food were harmful and which promoted health. He was encouraged to learn that Benjamin Franklin had lived quite cheerfully on nothing but bread and water for a fortnight, so he made this the basis of his diet. Honey, roast goose and olive oil were among the items he added one by one, and in true scientific style he kept a careful record of

changes in his weight, faeces, urine and saliva and his general
state of health. After two months this was not good; he had developed scurvy from a diet totally deficient in fresh fruit and vegetables. He gave himself a brief holiday, during which time he
ate all the meat and drank all the milk and wine he felt like, before
returning resolutely to his diet. His death six months later
proved that a diet based on bread and water lacks a certain something necessary to life.

Could it be found in gelatine? The French physiologist
François Magendie, officially requested to answer this question
nearly fifty years later, prudently carried out his experiments on
dogs rather than on himself, thus becoming a pioneer in
nutritional experimentation on animals. Along with the
pressure-cooker, gelatine had been invented by another Frenchman, Denys Papin, years earlier: he boiled down old bones in his
pressure-cooker with a little water, seasoned the resulting jelly
with a little sugar and lemon juice, and decided it was quite sus-
taining. During the lean years of the Napoleonic Wars, it was
touted in France as a cheap and nutritious food. But was it?

Evidently not; on a diet of gelatine alone, the dogs refused
their food after the first few days and eventually starved to death.
Magendie then tried feeding rabbits and guinea-pigs as well as
dogs on a number of other mono-diets. Some of the results surprised him. On a diet of the finest white wheaten bread – then
widely believed to be the most wholesome kind – they died after
six or seven weeks in a miserable condition. On the coarse wholemeal bread that soldiers ate, they not only survived but remained
in good shape. Raw bones sustained them; cooked bones did not.
Neither did cane sugar, olive oil or butter. Magendie concluded
that non-nitrogenous food could not support life. Observing his
animals carefully, he also noted that ulcerated eyes, loss of fur
and general emaciation also appeared to result from a poor diet.

Magendie's conclusions about the importance of nitrogenous, or protein-containing foods, received the widest circulation,
and aroused much interest. But his speculation that disease
might result from a lack of specific factors in food ran counter to
all received medical ideas. Food might be unwholesome in some
way – it might not suit a particular individual – or it might be
inadequate in quantity. But the notion of disease resulting from
a deficiency in the food itself lay far in the future, although every
contemporary physician was likely to have seen cases of at least
two: scurvy and rickets.

Scurvy is caused by a deficiency of the vitamin C present in fresh fruit and vegetables. In its absence, cell walls collapse, tiny blood capillaries weaken, and connective tissue – the stuff that literally holds our bodies together – breaks down. The victims of this insidious disintegration gradually become lethargic, listless and pale; their gums bleed and then rot; their bones ache as blood pools around the joints; resistance to infection is drastically lowered; even small cuts no longer heal; old lesions may open up and become infected.

Mild forms of scurvy, resulting from wintertime shortage of fresh fruit and vegetables, had been a fact of life for centuries, and country people knew perfectly well how to cure it; the condition was accurately described in a dozen herbals, together with the small vitamin-rich weeds that cured it – scurvygrass, brooklime, the cresses.

It became an acute medical problem in the fifteenth and sixteenth centuries, when the first long sea voyages were made. More than half of Vasco da Gama's men died of it when he rounded the Cape of Good Hope in 1497. And soon the first signs of scurvy – the sore and bleeding gums – were dreaded by sailors, travellers and explorers alike.

Sailors are practical men, and by a century later, it had been established by observation that orange and lemon juice were both effective in warding off scurvy. But to a penny-pinching and overspent British Admiralty, these were ridiculous luxuries for ordinary seamen, and the cost of this bureaucratic meanness was grim: in the Seven Years' War it was reckoned that some 130,000 seamen – nearly 75 per cent of the total number pressed – died from sickness rather than enemy action, and in most of these cases scurvy was the cause.

The disease was also a military problem. The Imperial troops besieging Belgrade in 1720 went down with it in their thousands, their plight made worse by the appallingly inappropriate remedies – purges and vomits among them – administered by well-intentioned army doctors. They were well aware that green plants were recommended for the cure of scurvy, and had shipped vast quantities – dried.

In the end, it was an observant and open-minded naval surgeon – the Scotsman James Lind – who established once and for all, by the most careful sifting of every scrap of available evidence, the best way both to prevent and cure the sickness. He clinched the matter by conducting his own rough-and-ready clinical trial during a 1747 cruise of his ship. Selecting a dozen patients all equally ill with the scurvy, he divided them into half a dozen pairs, and tried out on each pair one of the accepted medical remedies of the day. The lucky pair who were given the oranges were up and about in days, nursing the others. Fifty years later, the Admiralty finally accepted Lind's recommendations, just in time to give them a decisive advantage over the French in the Napoleonic Wars.

What was the active principle in acid fruits and vegetables that made them so effective against the scurvy? Lind had some ideas, and he offered them, but he was well aware that, in the then state of knowledge, they could be no more than speculation. It was far more important, he insisted, to know what worked and to use it. Never mind theories; they had done damage enough.

Unluckily for the thousands of rickets sufferers, there was no doctor with Lind's degree of observation and superb common sense. As late as the reign of Victoria, there was no accepted medical cure. The condition had been accurately described by a Dorset doctor in 1650, in a lengthy study *De rachitide sive morbo puerili qui vulgo The Rickets dicitur* – in compliment to which work it was promptly dubbed the 'English disease' all over the Continent.

In this deficiency of vitamin D, the bones of babies and children do not form properly. 'The sufferer presents the most miserable of aspects,' wrote Dr W. R. Aykroyd in 1932, at a time when every doctor could still expect to see cases among his poorer patients.

> It is irritable, sleepless and perspiring, with a white face and a slack and pendulous belly. The bone deformities develop according to the degree of stress which is laid upon the limbs. If the child is in the crawling stage its forearms are apt to bend outwards in a semicircle; if it is a toddler, it is liable to bow legs or knock-knees. The chest is drawn out of shape by the respiratory muscles, the result being a 'pigeon-breast'.[7]

Particularly perplexing to doctors was the fact that wealth offered no apparent protection against this disease. The pampered darling of the noble family, swaddled from birth, confined to a luxurious nursery, hand-fed on dainty gruels and little messes specially prescribed by the family physician, was actually more likely to develop it than the labourer's child clad in rags and tumbling about in the dirt. The labourer's child was invariably breast-fed, though, while noble children sometimes had neither mother's milk nor wetnurse, but were raised on a pap of cows' milk, flour, sugar and raisins. The upper classes, too, had a deeply entrenched prejudice against butter, which was thought to be unwholesome. And not until late in the nineteenth century was it suspected that sunshine might have any connection with resistance to the disease.

In a desperate effort to strengthen and straighten the curling limbs of these luckless little children, they were laced into stout corsets or elaborate metal trusses, they were massaged, exercised, dosed with iron and steel, bled, purged and fed on a variety of different diets. No regime could be depended upon, no cure was certain.

Not until early in the nineteenth century was a reliable treatment – and a most unlikely one – found at last. It was oil from the liver of the cod fish, for long a favourite German folk remedy for gout or rheumatism. Few adults today care for the taste of modern cod-liver oil – a clean, clear oil, steam-pressed from the fresh liver of the fish. The cod-liver oil that doctors began to use in Napoleon's time was thick and sherry-brown with a greenish cast to it, with a taste as repellent as its strong, rank, fishy smell. It came from the Bergen cod fisheries in Norway, where the livers of the cod were left heaped in great troughs until they began to putrefy and swell, at which point a clear pale oil ran off. When no more ran off, the remains of the livers were boiled for hours in huge cast-iron kettles until the darker nut-brown oil could be skimmed off. The darker the oil, the more effective it was found to be, and soon the fame of this curious remedy for gout and rheumatism was spreading across Europe.

If it helped with diseases affecting the bone joints, it might also be useful in rickets, doctors reasoned. A Dutch physician, Dr Bodel of Dordrecht, tried it on a case in 1817 – and thereafter never used anything else: the disease had never responded so completely to any other treatment. Just as astonishing as the efficacy of this remedy was the speed at which it operated: ' . . . even in the very extremity of life, when the patient appears to be sinking and death is inevitable, it affords relief as a matter of certainty,' noted Dr Bodel. Recovery thereafter was swift, a heart-warming sight to doctor and desperate parents:

> the old features become again natural and childish; the skin moist and browner . . . the eyes are again full of life and brightness . . . the childish gaiety establishes itself with a return of sound healthy sleep and removal of that anxious

nightly starting and shrieking which render the night so wretched to the infant; with the increasing strength the desire and ability to stand and to walk return . . .[8]

What could be in the oil that made it such an effective remedy? The Dutch physician and chemist Dr de Jongh, of The Hague, who devoted a whole treatise to it in 1844, had analysed it exhaustively. He found that it was composed of fats, biliary matter, iodine, phosphorus, butyric acid and a peculiar brown substance which he christened 'gaduine'. The darker the oil, the higher the concentration of biliary matter and butyric acid: but whether the oil was efficacious on account of these components or the iodine or the phosphorus, and precisely how it operated, its remarkable cures remained a mystery.

Moreover, it was not only useful for actual disease. The Dutch doctors had begun to administer it as a preventive too, for those children in their care who were particularly pale, puny and delicate. They found that after taking it for even a short while, the children improved remarkably, with a surge in health and growth which could be accomplished by no other means they knew. Oddly enough too, though adults gagged on the taste, it was found that children seemed not to object to it at all, and often reminded their parents when it was time for the next dose.

A substance that not only cured but prevented the onset of disease was a therapeutic mystery. 'How does it afford nourishment to the system?' wondered Dr de Jongh's English translator. The answer, he concluded, 'we must leave to the future research of the chemist'.[9] By the time he wrote these words, it seemed certain that the answer would not be long in coming: the name of the great German chemist Baron Justus von Liebig was already a household word. And chemistry promised to solve the riddle of life itself.

2

The Chemistry of Life

'The great and daily increasing number of researches appearing every year in . . . Chemistry and the Allied Sciences, renders it difficult for individuals to obtain . . . a complete survey of their progress,' announced an advertisement in 1849 from the London publishers Taylor, Walton and Maberly. 'The study of *one*, or even of several journals, does not suffice for this purpose, the communications of various investigators being distributed over a large number of periodicals, and many papers especially interesting to the Chemist being actually buried in publications chiefly devoted to other subjects.'[1] The solution to this difficulty was at hand: to order Messrs Taylor, Walton and Maberly's new *Annual Report of the Progress of Chemistry and the Allied Sciences*. Part I, covering the first six months of 1847, was to be ready in July.

This *Annual Report*, one of the earliest examples of the abstracts upon which every scientific researcher relies today, would have been attractive to any worker at that time in the rapidly expanding field of chemistry. But by a brilliant coup, the publishers made it almost irresistible: they had secured the services of no less a person than Justus von Liebig, Professor of Chemistry at the University of Giessen, as editor. And in 1849, the name Liebig was almost synonymous with chemistry.

A man of stupendous energy and industry, the forty-six-year-old Baron Justus von Liebig towered over his contemporaries. As a young man, he had studied organic chemistry in Paris from 1822 to 1824. And he was introduced into French scientific circles at a time when Paris was the Mecca of the scientific world – phenomenal advances were being made in the fields of physiology, chemistry, pathology, medicine and pharmacology by men like Magendie, Gay-Lussac, Laennec, Ampère, Cuvier, and Laplace. The brilliant chemist Lavoisier was dead, sent to the guillotine in 1794 by a Revolutionary tribunal that objected to his comfortable income derived from

tax-farming. But Lavoisier's concept of life as a chemical function had triggered a revolution of a different kind, in the application of the new discoveries of chemistry to man himself. And
Liebig in Paris grasped its importance with intense excitement.

After three years, a mere twenty-two years old, the young
prodigy was snapped up by the University of Giessen in Upper
Hesse, who appointed him their Professor of Chemistry, gave
him a free hand to run it how he pleased, and at his request
built him handsome and well-equipped research laboratories.
Students from all over the world flocked to a university where,
for the first time, they were allowed to handle laboratory appar-
atus, and devise and carry out experiments themselves, instead
of being passive lookers-on: Liebig thus trained for himself a
generation of eager research assistants.

One of them, Carl von Voit, later paid tribute to his professor's innovative genius:

> Liebig was the first to establish the importance of
> chemical transformations in the body. He stated that the
> phenomena of motion and activity which we call life arises
> from the interaction of oxygen, food and the components
> of the body. He clearly saw the relation between meta-
> bolism and activity and that not only heat but all movement
> was derived from metabolism. He investigated the chemi-
> cal processes of life and followed them step by step to their
> excretion products.

A practical man, Liebig grasped that the same principles
could be applied to the mysteries of plant growth; in 1840,
his *Chemistry in its Applications to Agriculture and Physiology* was
published in Germany and England, and became an overnight
sensation. In this work, Liebig proclaimed a new 'rational system of agriculture' formed according to scientific principles,
and 'based on an exact acquaintance with the means of nutrition
of vegetables, and with the influence of soils and action of
manure upon them'.[2] Vegetables, he stated, were able to convert minerals from the soil into such complex substances as
starches, protein, and cellulose for the nutrition of animals and,
in turn, man; these minerals could be studied in the ashes of
the plant when it was burned.

Until Liebig's work appeared, it was taken for granted
that plants and crops could not be grown unless the soil was
constantly renewed by the application of animal and vegetable

waste material in an endless recycling of life – an idea expressed with poetic force by Victor Hugo in *Les Misérables*:

> Those heaps of filth at the city boundaries, those dust-carts rumbling through the streets in the night . . . those evil-smelling drains of underground sewage . . . do you know what they are? They are flowering fields and the green grass, wild herbs, thyme and sage, gamebirds and cattle; they are the contented lowing of noble oxen at eventide, fragrant hay, golden grain, bread on your table, warm blood in your veins . . .[3]

Liebig poured a scientist's scorn on these notions:

> We discover . . . that the excrements of men and animals are supposed to contain an incomprehensible something which assists in the nutrition of plants, and increases their size. This opinion is embraced without even an attempt being made to discover the component parts of manure, or to become acquainted with its nature. But what does the soil contain, and what are the components of the substances used as manure?[4]

Having, as he believed, answered his own question through his experimental work, Liebig went on to propose that far more convenient, and equally effective substitutes for so much magical muck could be manufactured from inorganic mineral salts. And so that his readers could test the truth of this notion for themselves, he marketed almost simultaneously an artificial fertilizer based on the chemical composition of guano. It was expensive and not particularly successful, being too low in nitrogen. But the idea itself was so attractive as to be unstoppable; from Liebig's work, the agro-chemical industry was born.

Having initiated the industrialization of farming, Liebig next turned his attention to the subject of animal and human nutrition, and two years later, in *The Chemistry of Animals* (1842), he laid the foundations of scientific nutrition. In this work, Liebig finally buried the old Hippocratic notion of 'one aliment', and with a wealth of detail based on endless chemical analyses, he demonstrated that mankind was nourished by three classes of food: carbonaceous, or energy-building (carbohydrates and fats); nitrogenous (proteins); and the various mineral salts essential for the construction of bodies and teeth. Carbonaceous foods, he taught, were necessary for the maintenance of body heat, but growth and movement both depended upon a steady supply of the nitrogenous foods. He followed this up in 1847 with another work, *Chemical Researches on Meat and its Preparation for Food*, in which he discussed the all-important protein in even greater detail.

Liebig's fast-growing reputation and his tremendous authority at once secured for his theories an entranced and receptive audience. As Terence McLaughlin points out,

> Liebig's theories on food had immense impact on the Victorian public. Not only chemists and physiologists met and discussed his work, but amateur scientists, journalists and even housewives became familiar with Liebig's ideas and his classification of foods. 'Carbonaceous' and 'nitrogenous' foods were as widely known in the 1850s as calories and vitamins are now.[5]

Liebig's work popularized protein as the very staff of life, essential for the replacement of muscle tissue used up by physical exertion; and glorified meat as the most superior form of it: the protein contained in vegetables was decidedly inferior. In this respect, Liebig gave new scientific status to current notions that animal food was somehow more nutritious than mere vegetables, and his prestige soon endowed meat with near-magical qualities. When he marketed his instant beef-tea – Liebig's patented Extract of Meat – a few years later, it was soon a regular item on every housewife's shopping list. They believed it to be a wonder-food, a concentrated essence of pure protein, as it were – an illusion which Liebig did nothing to dispel.

Liebig's eulogies of meat protein coincided with the beginning of a steady rise in meat consumption in the Western world. The first canning factory had been set up in England in 1812, and soon the British were able to sample canned beef, mutton, stew and soup. By the mid-century, cheap canned beef from Argentina and mutton from Australia were flooding on to the market – 22,000,000 lb were imported from Australia in 1881 alone, by which time enormous quantities were coming from the United States, where the herding of Indians into reserves and the virtual extermination of the bison had cleared hundreds of thousands of acres of prairie for cattle-breeding. By the end of the century, the development of refrigerated shipping had made it possible to buy meat from all these countries more cheaply than ever before; even the labouring classes could now occasionally afford meat, while the Edwardian upper classes, sitting down to their solid cooked breakfasts and their

ten-course dinners, ate meat in quantities which Parson Woodforde would have approved and which strike us as wholly unbe-
lievable today.

By contrast, the countless thousands of urban poor,
crammed into Britain's dreadful new industrial slums, were
compelled by dire necessity to maintain both life and growth
on a menu that featured no meat protein for days at a time.
Wheat from the new prairie farms in America, tea from the
new plantations in India, cheap sugar from the sugarbeet plants
that had sprung up all over Europe since the sugarbeet was
first exploited in Napoleon's time, all these gave the illusion of
plenty without the substance. The poor filled their aching bellies with white bread, jam, and endless cups of heavily sugared
tea. Milk, butter, a heel of bacon, a morsel of cheese were for
many only occasional luxuries; fresh vegetables almost
unknown in their diet.

Not that Liebig's views were accepted uncritically by all.
Only a year later, the English-born pharmacist Jonathan Pereira published his *Treatise on Food and Diet* which recognized
the importance of the Baron's work, but took issue with his
classification of food into three types. Instead, Pereira proposed no less than twelve, including ligneous – or what we
should now call fibre – amylaceous or starchy, mucilaginous,
saline and, oddly enough, alcoholic. He concurred with Liebig's
view that nitrogenous foods were in a class of their own when
it came to promoting 'the development, growth, nutrition and
renovation of living animal parts', but he pointed out that this
theoretical approach took no account of the known realities of
diet and health. Salt meat and biscuit, for instance, supplied
both carbonaceous and nitrogenous foods: but who could
remain healthy on such a diet? Was lemon juice – without which
a sailor on a long voyage would surely develop scurvy – a salt,
a fat, a sugar or a 'protein', as he called it?

Moreover, since the human body was incapable of converting one elementary substance into another, every element
which had been shown to be part of man's physiological make-
up must be supplied in his diet, not just the all-important nitrogen. It had been shown that baby chicks could not build bone
without drawing on the calcium contained in the eggshell; other
vital elements were carbon, hydrogen, oxygen, sulphur, phosphorus, chlorine, sodium, potassium, magnesium, iron and
fluorine. Were adequate supplies of all these to be found in
animal foods? Pereira argued strongly for a much more varied

diet, and for the inclusion in it of those 'succulent vegetables or fruits which experience has shown to be necessary for the preservation of human health and life'. In planning diets, quality and variety were as important as quantity.

Other voices of dissent were heard. Two Germans took the trouble to climb a considerable mountain in 1866 after abstaining from protein for over thirty hours beforehand: they analysed their urine to demonstrate triumphantly that no nitrogen appeared in it: other foods had muscle-power too.

Liebig's own pupil, Carl von Voit, after his appointment as Professor of Physiology at Munich University, was soon launched into metabolic studies that eventually demolished the protein concept. The principle of the conservation of energy had been established in 1850, and the Frenchman Joule had by this time shown that heat could be calculated in terms of energy, and that thermal and mechanical energy were one and the same. The distinction Liebig had made, therefore, between foods supplying heat and those fuelling muscular exertion was shown to be erroneous.

Our easy modern calculations of calories and energy needs are possible today because of the painstaking work done by Voit and his disciples. In endless careful experiments, they demonstrated that bodily energy is supplied by the combustion of foodstuffs; that carbohydrates and fats burnt outside the body give off exactly the same amount of heat or energy as those consumed inside it; that different kinds of food require different amounts of oxygen for their combustion. They observed that carbohydrates produce a surge of heat and energy, that fat tends to be retained in the body as an energy store, that proteins are needed for tissue repair. From these studies an ingenious gadget was evolved by two of Voit's pupils, Max Rubner and a young American Wilbur Atwater: they christened it a 'calorimeter', a special chamber kept at an even temperature and big enough for a man to sit in, while his output of energy and his intake of oxygen were measured, and correlated with what he had eaten.

It now became possible to quantify for the first time the amount of food needed for this or that occupation; in future, it was believed, it would be possible to calculate diets on a rational physiological basis, for soldier or factory operator, workhouse inmate, servant girl or schoolchild. For the moment, however, the only way to establish the norms for these calculations was to work backwards, so to speak, and all over Europe researchers began feverishly measuring food intakes and correlating them with the energy output of their subjects.

Depending on whose diet they measured, these calculations were often on the lavish side, especially when made in Germany, where heavy meat-eating was common. Voit's favourite subject – conveniently to hand – was his laboratory assistant Pistel, a solidly built Bavarian with a hearty appetite. Accordingly, 125 g protein a day, Voit suggested, might be adequate for a man doing light work, but if he was engaged in manual labour, 145 g might not be excessive.

The sensational implications of Liebig's work for agriculture had not been lost on the Americans, and the Hatch Act of 1887 set up a string of agricultural experiment stations across the States. For years afterwards, many of the major breakthroughs in the science of human nutrition were made by men trained in or working for these generously funded research centres; man has always profited from the need of stockbreeders to rear well-grown and healthy animals. Soon, too, dietary surveys were being as enthusiastically pursued in the United States as in Europe: some 350 of these were published as Bulletins of the United States Department of Agriculture.

Useful though this approach was, those pursuing it tended to lose sight of Pereira's lemon juice: they equated calorific value with food value. The finer points of nutrition were easily overlooked. Fruit and vegetables were often seen as dietary extravagances. By the end of the century, this reductionist view dominated nutritional thinking: it was clearly in evidence when the respective virtues of wholemeal and white bread were being hotly debated. Roller milling had just been introduced, making possible the whitest-ever flour, stripped both of fibre and of many valuable nutrients. A handful of doctors, and a great many concerned lay writers on the subject, argued strongly for the superiority of wholemeal. The brilliant German chemist von Bunge, who was intrigued by the role of the inorganic mineral salts in nutrition, was one of the earliest to argue for the importance of the 'innutritious' parts of the flour discarded in the form of bran: 'We must see that the diet of human beings does not lack woody fibre, bran or cellulose,' he said. 'The excessive fear of "indigestible" foods which prevails among the wealthy classes leads to debility of the intestinal walls.'[6]

Von Bunge demonstrated in 1889 that 30 per cent of the protein in whole wheat was unabsorbed; 32 per cent of the protein in cabbage or potatoes; 39 per cent in carrots; 40 per cent in lentils. The American health-food writer Alfred McCann pointed out that if we applied the same logic to vegetables as to flour 'we would not eat lentils, carrots, potatoes or cabbage without refining them'.[7]

But whatever the nutrition experts said, most people continued to eat white bread partly because it was cheaper, and partly because of the long snob association of white bread with 'quality'. Here was an excellent field for research, and several workers in Germany and England began using Voit's techniques to compare the two. To general surprise – and no doubt to the delight of the millers – they found unanimously in favour of white bread. 'Every investigator, no matter how long or how short his experiments were, agreed that white bread contained more available dry matter and protein and provided more calories than did brown.'[8]

In the comfort of a well-equipped chemistry laboratory, working with scales and balances, it was possible to come to such conclusions. Out in the real world, working with illnesses still baffling to the medical mind, there were doctors who suspected that there might be more to nutrition than protein and calories. One of them was George Budd, Professor of Medicine at King's College, London, who had read widely on the subject, kept up to date with experimental work, and was considered an eminent authority on scurvy, now generally agreed to be due to lack of fresh vegetable food. Budd believed that the study of organic chemistry, together with physiological experiments like Magendie's work with dogs and guinea-pigs, would eventually reveal exactly what was the curative element in plants and vegetables – at present unknown.

As early as 1842, Budd was also suggesting that defective diets might be responsible for at least two other diseases. Of one of them, he noted that the most distinctive characteristic is a peculiar ulceration of the cornea – a condition known today as xerophthalmia, caused by a deficiency of vitamin A: the function of the tear gland is destroyed, tears stagnate in the conjunctival sac, and micro-organisms breed rapidly on the eye and lids. Budd had seen cases of this in the Far East, among natives living chiefly on rice, and he had noticed – very observantly – that the condition improved when fish, eggs or milk were added to the diet. He speculated about rickets too: could it be due to insufficient calcium in the child's food?

Budd discussed these ideas in a series of articles for the *London Medical Gazette*; he must have been bitterly disappointed by their failure to attract much attention.

Forty years later, a young Russian medical student came within an inch of a breakthrough. He had studied chemistry under the brilliant von Bunge, then investigating the role of inorganic mineral salts in nutrition, and was trying to think up a suitable subject of research for his MD thesis. Bunge came to the rescue: how about studying some of these interesting inorganic salts, those contained in milk, for instance? Lunin agreed to investigate milk, and fed mice on a synthetic mix of casein, fats, carbohydrates and the inorganic salts that chemical analysis of milk had revealed: a synthetic milk, in other words. The mice died. He fed them milk. They lived. Besides casein, fats, sugar and salts, milk obviously contained something else which was essential to life. 'It would be of great interest to investigate the significance of these substances to nutrition,' concluded Lunin.

Lunin's heart was in medicine rather than chemistry and, having achieved his degree, he went on to a brilliant career in paediatrics. It might have been useful to his work to know what exactly that something was.

3
Disease with a Minus Sign

'The Arabs are very hardy and resistant to disease,' noted Dr Bernard Auzimour, a French Army medical officer, in 1905. 'Abdominal wounds, with perforation of the intestines, heal without the use of antiseptics . . . [they] are almost entirely immune to typhus . . . ulcers and cancers of the stomach are very seldom met with . . . Appendicitis is very rare among the Arabs and quite unknown among the vegetarian nomads . . . Gout and kidney gravel are quite unknown . . .'[1]

What was the secret of this extraordinary resistance to disease?

Certainly not a hygienic lifestyle.

The wiry, brown-skinned, black-eyed Arabs lived in camelhair tents which the harsh desert winds blew straight through, crowded with people and animals, often reeking with smoke from their greenwood fires. The rags they wore swarmed with vermin.

Their diet, perhaps, was particularly health-building? It was meagre in the extreme. Sometimes they travelled for days into the desert taking nothing more than a bag of meal, a few dates and figs, and a skin of water. They were vegetarians by necessity for much of the time, and milk or meat were rare luxuries; they never touched alcohol.

By the nutritional standards of the day, such a diet was a recipe for disaster: nobody, surely, could remain in health on such wretched food. Certainly, it would have appalled the German chemists and physiologists who dominated nutritional thinking at the beginning of this century. The great Voit – his authority second only to that of Liebig – stressed the importance of balancing fats, carbohydrates, proteins: for a man doing an average amount of work, 56 g fat, a whopping 500 g carbohydrates, 118 g protein. To the almost equally influential Rubner, Voit's pupil, only calories counted: energy was all – the chemical make-up of food was of little importance. Protein, to

Liebig, was the noblest of the food elements. Food was fat, carbohydrates and protein – but the greatest of these was protein. Little else mattered.

There was another division of foodstuffs, commented an American critic of these reductionist views, 'to which some of them, on rare occasions, slurringly referred. They called this fourth division "ash". The division "ash" was always exasperatingly ignored and apparently had little if any meaning for dieticians.'[2]

Steak and chips, in other words, was a perfect diet. Or a hamburger and its bun.

———

At the turn of the century, though, it was the role of the protein element, rather than the balance of the meal, that mainly obsessed those concerned with diet. And for at least the first decade of the twentieth century, this was the hottest issue in nutrition.

'Whatever may prove to be good for an ordinary adult, there can be no question that in the case of children, adolescents and pregnant women, it is far safer to adopt a high proteid standard than a low one,' asserted a widely respected authority on nutrition in 1911. 'To growing children, a deficiency of proteid in the diet is especially disastrous, for the lack of building material which it entails may result in impaired growth and development . . .'[3]

A nutritionist only had to look around the streets, at the turn of the century, to see these views apparently confirmed. In Edwardian England, 'the well-to-do far surpassed the working classes in height, strength and beauty'.[4] This was hardly surprising, given the extreme contrast in their diets. Well-to-do Edwardians ate prodigiously by modern standards, with the king himself setting the pace with his gargantuan meals. Elizabeth David has described some of the dinners enjoyed by Colonel Newnham-Davis, the gastronomic correspondent of the *Pall Mall Gazette* at the time. On one occasion, the gourmet colonel and his actress companion ate their way through oysters, soup, sole, a fillet of beef cooked with truffles and accompanied by soufflé potatoes, wild duck *à la presse*, a pudding, and icecream.[5] Meals on this scale were quite common in middle-class families, too, throughout the nineteenth century, as the ample pages of Mrs Beeton make plain, while the solid protein-rich breakfast eaten daily in upper- and middle-class homes provided more nourishment than the poor could hope to enjoy in the entire day.

There was nothing new about the inadequate diet on which these millions lived: the well-fed merry peasant is more common in fiction than in history. But the arrival early in the nineteenth century of cheap nationwide transport, the proliferation of urban slums, the enclosures which robbed the poorest classes of pasturage and tillage for their own use, and the growth of the processed-food industry all conspired to impoverish and degrade the foodstuffs on which the poor subsisted. These were further debased by the adulteration which was common practice throughout the century. And the final body-blow to the diet of the poor, as we shall see in a later chapter, came with the invention of roller milling, which robbed their most basic foodstuff – bread itself – of most of its nutritive value.

At the beginning of the century, Wellington had built an army famed for its stamina and splendid spirit from what he dubbed 'the scum of the earth'. A century later, when troops were needed for the Boer war, the inspector of recruiting sent shock-waves through the country when he reported that he was having the greatest difficulty in raising an army at all: in some parts of the country as many as 60 per cent of those enlisting were found physically unfit to carry a rifle. Only by drastic lowering of standards was it possible to secure enough troops: the minimum height was at first fixed at 5 ft 6 in (168 cm), reduced almost immediately to 5 ft 3 in (160 cm) and finally fixed at 5 ft (152 cm). Shocked by this spectacle of a stunted and degenerate race, the government set up a committee to investigate the cause. It revealed that millions of the working classes subsisted on little more than white bread, marge, jam, sweetened tea, a few boiled vegetables, and occasionally some tinned meat – a low-protein diet if ever there was one. Contemporary research, too, appeared to confirm what Liebig had taught: the superiority of animal to vegetable protein. Animal protein was not only better digested, since it had none of the 'innutritious' fibre of vegetable or cereal protein: it also had the full magic panoply of the amino acids which, one by one, were now being tracked down and identified. In the view of one eminent English authority: '. . . the success of the races, their vitality and energy, might almost be measured by the degree in which animal flesh has entered into their diet. All the successful races have habitually consumed protein far in excess of the Chittenden standard . . .'[6]

Meat, fish, milk, eggs, cheese: how much of such superior protein did any individual actually need? How much, wondered Russell Chittenden, 'do we really know as to the amount of food the human body requires to meet daily needs under the different conditions of life, especially of protein food?'[7]

Chittenden had studied at Yale's Sheffield Scientific School: a pupil of such dazzling ability that when the school's – and America's – first laboratory of physiological chemistry was opened in 1874, he was put in charge of it, before he had even graduated. Immediately after graduation he went to Germany where he met Voit, Rubner and other key figures in his field, studied at Heidelberg, picked up the latest experimental techniques, and returned elated and enthusiastic to launch a rising generation of American physiologists into the most hotly debated topic of the hour – protein requirements.

Chittenden followed the US Department of Agriculture dietary surveys with deep interest. For a while he was satisfied that such surveys were the most reliable way of resolving the protein question – until he was introduced to Horace Fletcher. This affable, healthy, persuasive fifty-three-year-old man of the world had been in turn manufacturer, painter, all-round athlete, author, impresario, arts correspondent of the *New York Herald*, lecturer and globe-trotter. He lived in a palace on Venice's Grand Canal, and his name was soon to be a byword in the United States for one reason alone: 'Horace Fletcher taught the world to chew.' He had only recently learned to chew himself. In 1898, approaching fifty, his agreeable lifestyle had inflated his waistline to 44 in (1·12 m), his weight to over 15½ st (98 kg) for his 5 ft 7 in (170 cm), while he felt constantly tired, liverish and out of sorts. He consulted a variety of doctors, tried out endless diets and finally, in desperation, decided to work it out for himself with the help of Mother Nature.

The result was Fletcherism. Nutrition, he came to realize, begins in the mouth, where saliva must be thoroughly mixed with the food by prolonged mastication. Once thoroughly chewed, 'food was reduced to a creamy pulp . . . (and) flowed naturally towards the back of the mouth where, as the last bit of taste was released, it was suddenly and involuntarily swallowed, and naturally sucked into the body'.[8] Since chewing is time-consuming too, Fletcher soon found that he was eating less and less. After four months of persevering mastication, his weight had dropped to 11½ st (73 kg), his waistline was a trim 37 in (94 cm), and he had never felt better in his life – he celebrated his fiftieth birthday by going for a 190-mile spin on his bicycle.

Even more surprisingly, he found that such thorough pre-digestion at one end of his alimentary canal produced a surprising bonus the other end – small and completely odourless excreta, the result of his digestive economy. 'Healthy human excreta,' he was later to proclaim, 'are no more offensive than moist clay and have no more odour than a hot biscuit.'[9]

One way and another, in fact, he was a physiologist's dream, and Chittenden made the most of him.

What struck the Yale professor straight away was the amazingly low protein content of Fletcher's diet. According to sacred German dogma, such a regime ought to have produced a wretched specimen of humanity, but this was far from being the case: Yale's gym director put him through a four-day marathon of the university crew's punishing exercises, and the fifty-four-year-old Fletcher sailed through them without turning a hair.

Chittenden was so impressed that he arranged for a month-long trial. Between autumn 1903 and summer 1904, three groups of volunteers – Yale professors, Yale athletes and professional soldiers – lived on diets containing only half the protein that they ought to need if Voit had got his sums right. They all ended the programme fighting fit, and when they were put through their paces in the gym, they all showed appreciably higher scores for health and endurance.

Chittenden then tried out the Fletcher regime – chewing and all – himself, to find his weight going down by a useful stone, headaches and aches and indigestion disappearing, and his energy levels zooming. This experience and the trial results convinced him that the importance of protein in the diet had been greatly overrated, and he now argued for a level of 60 g daily as being closer to a real man's needs: he himself weighed 9 st (57 kg), and felt perfectly fit on a mere 36 g daily.

Equally interesting, in the view of Chittenden's colleague, Irving Fisher, was the fact that Fletcher maintained his splendid health on an almost meatless diet, not from any reforming ideas but simply because he found that, on his low-protein diet, meat had lost its appeal. Chittenden's volunteers had almost all noticed the same phenomenon. Since America's vegetarians were loudly proclaiming the superiority of a meatless diet at the time, Fisher arranged for another trial in which hearty Yale athletes on a high-meat diet were pitted against other athletes on a low-meat diet – and against a group of office workers from the stronghold of vegetarian faith, Dr Kellogg's famous sanitarium at Battle Creek. In this and in subsequent endurance tests, the vegetarians won hands down. This unexpected finding was so much at odds with contemporary dietetics that it was ignored by most workers.

Another assailant of the German protein lobby was a Danish nutritionist, Dr Mikkel Hindhede. A vegetarian himself, he had lived healthily for many years on a diet based largely on potatoes. And far from accepting the sacred importance of animal protein, he was beginning to think that meat, together with a high consumption of acid-forming foods such as bread and sugar, might be responsible for a number of diseases, such as appendicitis, gout and urinary calculi. He had studied the protein intake of the Munich brewery workers that Voit considered 'normal', and was not impressed. 'Surely it is not in accordance with nature that the greater number of men should die between the thirtieth and fortieth year of life?'[10]

Such views were unlikely to be popular in Denmark, with its important farming and dairying industry, and he was howled down by the scientific establishment, in Denmark and elsewhere, who regarded him as a dangerous crank. His views became much more acceptable – at least to agriculturists – when he argued in 1904 that by the same token, livestock could be successfully fed on much less protein than was generally thought necessary: he proposed half the quantity of oilcake laid down by German farming experts, and the substitution of cheap turnip fodder for the rest. His suggestions were at once given a trial, and proved right. The Danish Committee of Agriculture now came out solidly in favour of his work, and secured for him a state laboratory and a staff of five assistants in 1911.

The application of these ideas to human beings remained intensely controversial, however, and Hindhede – like many dietetic revolutionaries before and after him – eventually went over the heads of the scientific community to appeal directly to the people with his own novel ideas. In a book published in Denmark in 1905, he argued that stuffing children with quantities of meat and eggs so that they would 'grow strong' was positively criminal, and that health was best maintained on the simplest and most frugal of low-protein diets. It was unpleasant, he agreed, to be regarded as a crank, but it was worth it for the pleasure of a natural sense of health, well-being and enjoyment of life, and 'an appetite so perfect that a piece of black bread and butter with a thin slice of plain Dutch cheese tastes far better than the very finest delicacy known to the epicure'.[11]

So certain was he that current ideas on child nutrition were dangerously wrong, that he put his own four children on the same frugal diet while the youngest were still babies.

Chittenden's account of Fletcherism was therefore intensely exciting to him, and he wrote at once inviting him to Denmark: at Christmas 1910 Fletcher was a guest in his home for several weeks. He had hesitated to speak publicly of his own children as vindication of his views, but Fletcher urged him warmly to do so in the English translation of his work then being prepared.

The Hindhede children were certainly a delightful vindication of their proud father's beliefs. The two daughters, Karen and Anna, had sailed through their high-school exams with top marks in almost every subject. His sons Jens and Kristian were both civil engineers, and passed their exams with first-class honours – and Kristian was the youngest of his class. Nobody could keep up with the Hindhede girls on their bicycles – 'mounting their machines at half-past six in the morning, and doing seventy miles in six hours, with only a quarter of an hour rest for a wayside breakfast of bread and butter is an easy task for them'.[12] And it was well known in their social set that Karen and Anna were tireless dancers: three young men in turn had tried to wear Anna out waltzing – they all gave up before she did.

Hundreds of Hindhede's readers wrote to tell him gratefully how much their own and their children's health had improved as a result of following his advice. But few doctors and even fewer physiologists subscribed to his views, and most of them dismissed him out of hand. 'Hindhede is a fervent advocate of the simple life and a vegetarian diet, which is usually a low-protein diet, and his results have been received with a certain amount of scepticism,' wrote a distinguished English nutrition expert in 1932: the contempt is thinly veiled.[13]

In any case, the vast majority of doctors at the turn of the century thought that health or disease had little or nothing to do with diet.

The French chemist Louis Pasteur and the German Robert Koch had between them established the twin sciences of microbiology and bacteriology, while the Scottish surgeon

Joseph Lister had applied these ideas and developed the techniques of antisepsis. 'Almost as soon as Pasteur showed how infection took place, Lister showed how it could be avoided.'[14] By making once-perilous operations safe, he invented modern surgery and enormously expanded its range of possibilities at a single stroke.

By the turn of the century, the conviction was growing in the medical mind that almost all diseases would ultimately be traced to the baneful activities of either micro-organism or some form of toxin. And the medical profession as a whole – never the most enthusiastic advocates of Maimonides's diet-rather-than-drugs approach – now looked to a future in which disease would be successfully countered by antitoxins, chemical agents or vaccines, as well as by the newly safe surgery.

Even diseases which had once seemed firmly linked to diet were now being re-evaluated, and other explanations put forward. Some form of infection or other was quite often put forward to account for rickets, and environmental causes such as poor housing, lack of hygiene or insufficient exercise were all seriously examined. When the lion cubs in London Zoo developed rickets in 1888, somebody even evolved a 'domestication theory' to account for the fact – only to have it demolished when other baby lions were raised rickets-free on a diet of bones and cod-liver oil.

Towards the end of the century, some enthusiasts were even suggesting that scurvy – for long firmly linked with lack of fresh vegetables or fruit in the diet – might be a toxin-induced disease, a hypothesis buttressed by the unexpected disaster which overtook Sir George Nares's expedition. In 1875 he had set out with two ships, the *Alert* and the *Discovery*, in an attempt to find the North Pole. The two ships were generously supplied with lime juice, but by the end of the first year, severe scurvy had broken out among the two crews. When 'limejuice' first earned its medical reputation as a reliable antiscorbutic, the term actually signified the juice of lemons from the Mediterranean – rich in vitamin C. In the mid nineteenth century, West Indian lime juice was increasingly substituted, in the belief that it was equally effective. In fact, as studies published in the *Lancet* years later, in 1918, showed, this belief was erroneous: the vitamin C content of limes was significantly lower. In the meantime, great confusion resulted from this apparent overthrow of Lind's theories.

Dr Rae, surgeon to the Hudson Bay Company, giving evidence to the Scurvy Commission that sat to consider this unfortunate débâcle, told them that the inhabitants of Hudson Bay, in the Arctic Circle, lived almost entirely on fresh meat – and scurvy was almost unknown among them. There are small amounts of vitamin C in freshly killed meat. One up for animal protein. The Jackson–Harmsworth expedition in 1894–7 seemed like another nail in the coffin of Lind's theories. The land-sledging party survived scurvy-free for three years without either lime or lemon juice, or fresh vegetables, but eating huge quantities of fresh bear meat. The ship party, meanwhile – obediently knocking back their ounce of lime juice daily, and well-supplied with canned and salted, but not fresh, meat – were soon going down like flies from scurvy: three of them actually died. Could the meat have been tainted in some way? Were there specific toxins in putrefying meat?

By the 1890s, scientific thinking was strongly biased in favour of such explanations. Reviewing the development of nutrition in 1932, a Committee of the Medical Research Council noted that at the time 'it was difficult to implant the idea of diseases as due to a deficiency'. So generally was disease now associated with positive agents such as 'the parasite, the toxin, the *materies morbi*, that even expert thought turned naturally to such positive associations, and believed with difficulty in causation prefixed by a *minus* sign'.[15]

With theories like these gaining ground, it is easy to see why, when the dreadful disease beriberi spread with alarming speed throughout the Far East in the late nineteenth century, medical investigations at first concentrated almost exclusively on the search for a causative germ or toxin.

4
A Certain Something – the Discovery of Vitamins

I n 1611, the first governor-general of the Dutch East India
Company wrote of a new disease which had been observed
in the Far East. It caused a strange paralysis of the hands and
feet; the natives called it beriberi. Cases of what appeared to be
the same disease later appeared in Japan, where they called it
kakke.

Thereafter, references to it cropped up sporadically in
the medical literature. But European physicians had too many
problems of their own to interest themselves in an oddity of a
disease seen only on the other side of the globe. In 1876 William
Anderson, describing *kakke* in a London medical journal,
observed that the topic was 'almost entirely new to the European medical world'.[1] Thirty-five years later, the *Lancet* commented: 'there is probably no disease concerning which so
much discussion as to its etiology has taken place as beriberi'.[2]
In the first decade of the nineteenth century there had been
only a couple of references to it in medical journals; in the first
decade of the twentieth, there were nearly 500, some of them
whole treatises or books.

The growth of medical interest in Europe paralleled the
rise in incidence of the disease; like the plague, it travelled
faster and further each successive year. In armies and navies,
in battleships and prisons, in hospitals, in plantations, in labour-
gangs, the dreadful disease spread by leaps and bounds: soon
it was a problem that no administrator, no military and naval
command, no health authority could ignore. In 1876 11 per
cent of the Japanese army went down with it; in 1877, 14 per
cent; in 1878, 38 per cent. The main hospitals in the Malay

peninsula reported 1,206 new cases of beriberi among their Chinese patients in 1881, 3,175 in 1891, 6,767 in 1901. By 1883 it had appeared for the first time in lower Bengal, Ceylon, Africa and Brazil; in 1894 a German observer noted that it had now been seen in Siam and the Philippines, that it was spreading in Africa and South America, and was now common in Japan.

Beriberi might take one of two courses, either of which sometimes changed into the other. In the first, or 'dry' beriberi, the victims found difficulty in moving their legs, suffered from general weakness and shortness of breath, and finally from paralysis of the legs, the chest or ribs, and sometimes the arms. In the other, 'wet' form, arms, legs and stomach swelled, the liver became congested, and there were heart murmurs. In either form, heart failure might occur without warning; and the deathrate was high. Autopsies showed severe damage to the nerves, as well as dilation of the heart and congestion of the liver.

What caused it? To many doctors, it had to be an infection, one that particularly attacked the nervous system: all the signs pointed to some kind of epidemic, especially the fact that it was commonest in confined quarters such as ships, barracks, hospitals and jails.

Others felt that it must have a dietary origin. The Dutch naval surgeon van Leent noticed that in Dutch ships the Indian crew members – eating little but rice – went down in droves, while European sailors in the same ships were immune. The nutritional trinity of protein, fat and carbohydrates was well represented in the mixed European diet, but the rice-eating Indians were getting much lower levels of both protein and fat. Van Leent upped both for the Indian sailors – and beriberi rates at once dropped gratifyingly.

A similar remedy was resorted to by the Japanese naval doctor, Kamehiro Takaki. By adding a little fresh meat and vegetables, and by substituting barley for some of the rice, he eliminated beriberi from the Japanese navy in just five years. Was beriberi some kind of protein deficiency?

Others, in this age of Pasteur and Koch, felt that the fault might be in the rice itself. Some sort of toxin, perhaps, similar to the ergot in rye? Some taint in the rice-growing soil? An amoeba – a haematozoon – a diplobaccus – a polymorphous ascomycete?

There were objections to all these hypotheses. For hundreds of years, millions throughout the East had lived on diets composed largely of rice without succumbing to beriberi. Why should rice suddenly be lethal now? Moreover, beriberi sometimes appeared among men fed almost exclusively on protein: ships' crews living on salted meat and little else, for instance.

It was true that the sudden surge of cases coincided, in many areas, with the introduction of steam-powered rice mills, and the beautifully clean white rice they produced. But again, according to the most authoritative contemporary teachings, white rice ought to be more, not less, nutritious than crude unmilled rice because better absorbed – as with white and brown bread in Rubner's balancing trials.

It was a complete medical riddle.

The Dutch – commercially more involved than other European nations – made the first systematic attempt to come up with the answer. Piracy was a major threat to their colony of Sumatra, but wave after wave of troops sent to help wipe out the pirates went down with beriberi: the military barracks had acquired the most sinister reputation imaginable, since nobody there escaped beriberi for longer than three months.

In 1886 the Dutch government sent out a carefully chosen three-man commission to investigate; their qualifications indicated the lines along which it was expected that their inquiries might proceed. One of them, Professor C. Winkler, was a neurologist; the other, Professor Pekelharing, was a bacteriologist and expert in hygiene; their assistant was a young military surgeon, Christian Eijkman.

With microscope and slides, Pekelharing set to work at once, and, having quickly tracked down a microbe which might be the guilty party, gave orders for the barracks to be thoroughly disinfected, and sailed for home. But a nagging doubt troubled him: was it really as simple as that? Before he left, he asked that Eijkman should remain to continue research. Obligingly, the government provided a small laboratory attached to the military hospital in Java.

At first Eijkman dutifully followed up the infection theory, inoculating some of his experimental fowls with blood, urine or tissue from the bodies of beriberi victims, keeping other birds as controls, and scrutinizing both carefully for the polyneuritis, or inflammation of the nerves, known to be one of the earliest symptoms. He persevered for months, but his fowls continued to strut around in rude health.

One day the telltale signs appeared. Rushing tissue specimens to his laboratory, he found evidence of typical polyneuritis. But the control birds were just as badly affected – and some weeks later, all of them had recovered. He went over and over his results. Then it occurred to him to check the birds' feed and he found that for a while, just before they sickened, his birds had been fed on the luxury white rice reserved for the hospital's patients – until a new chef put a stop to this extravagance. Once the birds reverted to their normal diet, they were healthy once more.

Was it the rice, then? Eijkman fed crude rice to one set of his control birds, polished white rice to the other. The birds fed the white rice got polyneuritis; the others did not.

With the thoroughness of the born researcher, Eijkman tested all the possible explanations. He fed his birds rice that he had himself milled in his lab – they developed polyneuritis. He added to it the germ and pericarp scoured off in milling – they recovered. A mechanical effect, perhaps? He added bits of husk, minute pebbles to the white rice: they stayed sick. Was it the higher protein content? On a fresh meat diet, they remained healthy. But when he added just enough fresh meat to the polished rice to give it the protein equivalent of crude rice, they got sick. On sago, they sickened; on potatoes, they did not.

Having ruled out systematically the infection, the low-protein and the high-carbohydrate hypotheses, Eijkman was left with one conclusion: for birds, polished rice was fatal, and crude rice was not. Was it equally true for people? A friend of Eijkman's, Dr Vorderman, was medical inspector for Java's prisons, and with his help, Eijkman now studied the prison diets to see if they could shed any light on his puzzle. They did so unequivocally: in jails where the inmates ate white polished rice there were thirty times more cases of beriberi than in those where they ate unmilled rice.

Vorderman in turn became fascinated by the problem, and began detailed studies of the rice. It came in three forms, he found: the crude rice, still wrapped in its own superfine silky skin, the pericarp, and with its embryo or germ intact; the half-milled rice, which still had some of its germ and pericarp; and the polished white rice from which both had been removed. Thirty-seven jails were supplied with the crude rice – and thirty-six reported no cases at all; twelve jails had the half-milled rice –

and a very small number of their inmates were affected; fifty-two jails had the polished rice – and in thirty-seven of them, there were scores of cases.

By this time Eijkman had had ten years of beriberi, and enough of the Far East. He returned to Europe and, a few years later, rejoined his colleague Pekelharing, now Professor of Physiologic Chemistry at the University of Utrecht, where he himself was appointed Professor of Hygiene. Shortly after his return, he published his views on how beriberi occurred. Either the starchy part of rice contained some kind of toxin – or else a toxin was formed from it in the course of digestion and metabolism within the body; some substance in the pericarp either neutralized this toxin or inhibited its formation. But what was this mysterious toxin? Still determined to find out, the Dutch government appointed a young surgeon called Gerrit Grijns to carry on Eijkman's investigations.

Months later, by a number of painstaking trials, Grijns had ruled out various versions of the toxin theory to his own satisfaction. He had shown that birds could be protected against polyneuritis not only by an extract of the polishings but by substances contained in various other plant foods, too, and he was left with only one possibility, which he published in 1900 – that rice contained in its pericarp and germ organic substances essential to the maintenance of the peripheral nervous system (he called them 'protective substances'), which were present in such minute amounts as to defy chemical detection.

Grijns left the Far East in 1904 to take up a post in Holland. His new chief was not interested in the problems of some rice-eating coolies and criminals in a remote country, and he was given other work to do. But both he and Eijkman continued to be obsessed by the beriberi problem, which they certainly discussed when they met again. Equally certainly, Eijkman discussed Grijn's work and its implications with his Utrecht colleague Pekelharing.

By this time, Pekelharing himself had abandoned the toxin theory, and was following up Lunin's (see p.20) neglected work, feeding rats variations on a purified milk diet. Like Grijns, he had concluded that sickness such as beriberi could be induced by a deficiency as much as by a positive agent – disease with a minus sign – although the mysterious certain something eluded him: all his attempts to isolate and identify it had failed. In a paper published in a Dutch journal in 1905, Pekelharing stated his revolutionary findings:

> . . . there is a still unknown substance in milk which
> even in very small quantities is of paramount importance
> to nutrition. If this substance is absent, the organism loses
> the power properly to assimilate the well-known principal
> parts of food, the appetite is lost and with apparent abun-
> dance the animals die of want. Undoubtedly this substance
> occurs not only in milk but in all sorts of foodstuffs both
> of vegetable and animal origin.[3]

Physiologic chemists of the time were accustomed to turn
to Maly's *Jahresbericht über die Fortschritte der Thierchemie*, where
they could find mentioned or abstracted any paper, originally
published in a number of different languages, which might be
of significance or special interest in their field. Astonishingly,
this epoch-making hypothesis of a single vital factor in food –
which dealt a bodyblow to prevailing ideas of nutrition – was
ignored by the *Jahresbericht* editors.

It would have been of the liveliest interest to one of Pekelharing's opposite numbers, the Cambridge Professor of Physiologic Chemistry, Frederick Gowland Hopkins. Born in 1861
into solid middle-class comfort, Hopkins was privately educated and grew up with an absorbed interest in the chemical
complexities of life: his earliest research was into the constituents of the glowing pigment on a butterfly's wing. He was at
first attracted to analytical chemistry, and for some time worked
as assistant to the Home Office analyst, Sir Thomas Stevenson,
at Guy's Hospital. But living things, he found, interested him
more than pathology, and a few years later, when he could
afford to make the change, he gave up analytical work and
started his career all over again, as a medical student at Guy's.

Two diseases were at this time becoming almost epidemic –
with babies and small children their victims. One was rickets;
the other was characterized by scurvy-like symptoms – bleeding, spongy gums and swollen limbs – but since fresh meat or
vegetables do not normally figure in a baby's diet, nobody at
first suspected scurvy. Many of the babies in fact suffered from
both scurvy and rickets simultaneously – pathetic, pallid creatures who were fretful and restless, and screamed with pain
when their swollen limbs were touched.

The use of vitamin-C-deficient pasteurized cows' milk,
and the boom in proprietary baby-milks being introduced from
the 1860s onwards were together largely responsible for the
rising incidence of these diseases. Many of the patent milks
were variations on a product originally devised and patented

by Liebig; among them Mellin's Food, invented by a British chemist, and Horlick's Malted Milk, dreamed up by an ex-employee of Mellin's, were leading favourites. There were patent foods as well as milks: Prince of Wales' Food, made from potato flour, and Boaden's Food, made from barley and wheat flour, were typical cheap starchy concoctions. Most of these vitamin-deficient products were wildly unsuitable for babies. Even when they were not, ignorance, poverty and poor hygiene often made them so – as the irresponsible promotion of baby-foods in the Third World has tragically demonstrated in our own times – through over-dilution, unsterile equipment, or the use of contaminated milk or water, so that multiple infections and diarrhoea completed the havoc wrought by undernourishment.

The standard remedy for rickets was still cod-liver oil and for scurvy orange juice; both remedies were administered on purely empirical grounds. To the analytical mind of Hopkins, here was a scientific challenge demanding an explanation which conventional nutrition could not offer, and which must be looked for in the chemical laboratory rather than at the sickbed.

This medical background gave a special quality to Hopkins's work: an awareness that theoretical laboratory work related, ultimately, to real food eaten by real people – a point of view sometimes missed in the dry abstractions of the German chemists. As a young man Hopkins had seen deficiency diseases at close quarters; as he grew older he realized that dietary deficiencies, ill health and poverty went hand-in-hand, and he never lost sight of the fact.

A brilliant and original worker, Hopkins's reputation grew fast, and in 1899 he was invited to fill the newly created Chair of Physiologic Chemistry at Cambridge University. He had turned to the study of proteins, and in 1901, working with S. W. Cole, came his first great discovery, the isolation and identification of the amino acid tryptophan.

Voit's conclusions about the importance of fats, proteins and carbohydrates in diet were based on work done with these foodstuffs in their natural state, rather than with purified fats, proteins, carbohydrates and mineral salts. 'It would be possible and quite worthwhile to repeat these experiments with purified substances,' he had conceded, 'although doing so will not necessarily produce very different results.'[4] Hopkins now began to wonder. In the course of his amino acid researches, he was actually feeding animals on the very purified substances

Voit had mentioned – and finding that, contrary to Voit's predictions, the results were totally different. Normal growth could not be sustained on the known major components of diet in the purified forms he was using.

The suspicion that Voit had got it wildly wrong was startling to anyone raised in the traditions of the German physiologists. 'It seemed so unlikely!' Hopkins recalled later. 'So much careful scientific work upon nutrition had been carried on for half a century and more – how could fundamentals have been missed? But, after a time, one said to oneself, "Why not?" '[5]

'Why not?' is sometimes the most productive question a researcher can ask himself. One objection to the idea of a hidden essential something in natural foods was that it must be present in such tiny amounts. 'Again, why not?' said Hopkins to himself. Almost infinitesimal amounts of substance given as medicine could have a profound effect on the body – why not in foods too?

He returned with zeal to his rats – and the growing conviction that Voit was wrong. In 1906, addressing the Society of Public Analysts – his old colleagues – he could not resist talking of this work, and the conclusion to which it had led him: the existence of not one, but several vitamins, of factors in food as yet unknown.

> The animal body is adjusted to live either upon plant tissues or the tissues of other animals, and these contain countless substances other than the proteins, carbohydrates and fats . . . The field is almost unexplored; only is it certain that there are many minor factors in all diets of which the body takes account.
> . . . In diseases such as rickets, and particularly in scurvy, we have had for long years knowledge of a dietetic factor; but though we know how to benefit these conditions empirically, the real errors in the diet are to this day quite obscure. They are, however, certainly of the kind which comprises these minimal quantitative factors . . .[6]

Dozens of careful studies later, Hopkins felt confident enough to publish his conclusions. 'Feeding Experiments Illustrating the Importance of Accessory Factors in Normal Dietaries' doesn't sound like a revolution, but to readers of *The Journal of Physiology* (1912, xliv, 235) that's exactly what Hopkins's paper was. They pored with admiration and astonishment over the graph that accompanied it: 'The growth curves of the famous Hopkins's rats are familiar to anyone who has ever opened a textbook of physiology,' wrote a young biochemist years later. 'One recalls the proud ascendant curve of the milk-fed group which suddenly turns downward as the milk supplement is removed, and the waning curve of the other group taking its sudden milk-assisted upward spring, until it passes its fellow now abruptly on the decline. It was the prettiest experiment imaginable.'[7]

While Hopkins pored over his rats, a young Polish chemist, Casimir Funk, was beginning work at London's Lister Institute. Its director, Dr Martin, had followed Hopkins's work on tryptophan, and speculated that the beriberi missing link might be another amino acid, discarded with the rice polishings. He handed Funk the task of tracking down the elusive factor. After months of work, Funk came up with isolated fractions of the rice polishings which he administered to birds with polyneuritis. Eureka! they recovered. One of these chemical fractions was a crystalline compound which he became convinced was the wonder-working stuff – a 'nitrogenous substance', which he described as the specific answer to beriberi. (It turned out to be nothing of the kind. Later analysis showed that it was a mixture of several compounds, one of which was another B vitamin altogether, nicotinic acid.)

But if his announcement of the beriberi vitamin was premature, his predictions, in the same paper, about the future direction of nutritional research, were prophetic – a dazzling leap of the scientific imagination. His paper was entitled *The Etiology of Deficiency Diseases*, and in it he suggested that a wide range of diseases would be found to be due, not to infection, or to toxins in food, but to the absence from the diet of 'special substances, of the nature of organic bases, which we call vitamines'. (The word was coined from 'vital' and 'amino'.) It was obvious, he went on, 'that the minute amounts necessary cannot be considered from the point of view of food. It is most probable that they are used as such or are transformed into substances which are able to act in small quantities. Such substances in the body are known to be ferments, hormones and products of the secretion of internal glands.'[8]

Among the diseases caused by the deficiency of these 'vitamines', suggested Funk, were scurvy, beriberi – together with the shipboard form known as ship beriberi – rickets – and a disease called pellagra, which few London physicians had ever seen.

Twenty years of research had been necessary to establish these views, said Funk – and they were still widely rejected; but anybody who took the trouble to follow up the course of this research must be convinced of its truth.

Some years later, an undignified squabble broke out over who actually deserved the title, 'the discoverer of vitamins'. It was generally awarded to Hopkins – a fact bitterly resented by Funk. He was moved to protest in an article in the magazine *Science*; when he published his own paper, he asserted, he had not even known of Hopkins's work. This was too much even for the patient and modest Hopkins.

On 11 December 1929, Hopkins shared with Eijkman the honour of the Nobel Prize for medicine. He took advantage of this highly public occasion to put the record straight, courteously but firmly.

After pointing out that Funk's views were not based on his own research findings, Hopkins recalled that the Polish chemist – far from knowing nothing of Hopkins's work as he claimed – had actually alluded to it in his paper. Moreover, Hopkins had made his own views known as early as 1907, and his experimental results had been widely discussed in English scientific circles after he had spoken of them at a meeting of the English Biochemical Club in October 1911. Funk's assertions were, therefore, 'disingenuous'.

Even before this meeting, Hopkins's work had been widely publicized in the press. In an interview published in the *Daily Mail* on 28 February 1911, Hopkins had compared the value for growth of 80 per cent flour and of a much more highly refined white flour. The *Mail* at the time was campaigning for the coarser bread on the grounds of health, and Hopkins agreed. In the 80 per cent flour there were retained 'certain at present unrecognized food substances, perhaps in very small quantities, whose presence allows our systems to make full use of the tissue-building elements of the grain. These substances are . . . removed to a great extent from the fine white flour in the milling.'[9]

His remarks were picked up and quoted in Continental and American papers, to a public eager to know more about their daily bread.

Whoever could claim to have discovered them, 'vitamines' had arrived.

5

The Maize Mystery

If you should traverse the hills of Brianza and Canavese, you would most likely meet some pitiable wrecks of humanity, with eyes fixed and glassy, with pale and sallow faces and arms fissured and scarred as by a burn or large wound. You would see them advancing with trembling head and staggering gait like persons intoxicated . . . now falling on one side, now getting up and running in a straight line like a dog after its quarry and now again falling and uttering a senseless laugh or sob which pierces the heart . . . such are the pellagrins . . .[1]

Like beriberi, pellagra was hardly a new disease. It had first been described by Philip V's doctor, Gaspar Casal. He called it *mal de la rosa*, since one of its symptoms was the roughening, reddening and painful cracking of the skin across the face and arms of its victims. Other symptoms were weakness, lassitude, headaches, a debilitating diarrhoea, and finally, insanity. An observant physician, Casal pointed out that it occurred among the very poorest of the Andalucian populace in southern Spain, and suggested that it might be related to their wretched diet. The association was so obvious, in fact, that when in 1776 the Patriotic Society of Milan offered a prize for a solution to the pellagra problem, part of it was given to a Dr Videmar who said that the cause was poverty and malnutrition.

From Spain, pellagra jumped to Italy where it became common in the north: they called it *pel agre* – soured or rough skin. A leisurely plague, it next appeared in France and then cropped up in Hungary and Romania, before moving on to establish itself in Turkey and Greece. Soon afterwards, it was reported in Egypt, where it soon became endemic among the poor fellahin. What caused it?

A shrewd French doctor put his finger on a clue. The spread of pellagra followed the spread of maize-growing. Pellagra was unknown in Europe till Christopher Columbus

brought maize back to Spain – from which it had been introduced to the rest of Europe – and Egypt. Maize was obviously
an inadequate food. A poor man could live on little else but his
coarse wheat or rye bread. But a diet based largely on maize
killed him. Only if he was able to add eggs or milk, meat or fish
or good rich broth to his maize diet did he survive in good
health. Other French physicians soon joined in denouncing
maize, and its status in French eyes sank to zero. Who needed
the miserable stuff? By 1900 few Frenchmen were still eating
maize. To this day they look at it askance.

But in the southern states of America, and in neighbouring Mexico, millions of poor people lived on very little else. In
Mexico they ate it the way their Indian ancestors had taught
them. The maize was soaked overnight in hot lime water before
being husked and ground. In America, some people still prepared it in this traditional Indian way. But most people simply
ground it straight into a fine cornmeal – or into the coarser
meal called grits. They ate it made into a mush or porridge,
sweetened with cane-sugar syrup or molasses – plentiful and
dirt cheap. They left the mush overnight to set solid and then
carved it up into slices, floured and fried them, and ate them
with gravy or a little bit of bacon fat – and sometimes the cheapest, fattiest cuts of pork, usually salted. They ate it made up into
crude breads – corn pone and 'hoe cakes' cooked on the metal
blade of a hoe in the ashes of a fire.

As well as corn, they ate wheat-flour biscuits, a few boiled
vegetables – cabbage, potatoes, turnips – rice, dried beans.
Chicken, eggs and butter were rare treats.

The wheat flour in their diet had been fine and white for
some time. By the 1880s, any rice they ate was factory-milled
and white too. To the ingenious American inventors of these
cereal mills – now spreading civilization all over the world –
corn presented a tougher problem altogether. But they cracked
it at last, and by 1905 the Beall Degerminator was coming into
widespread use, to give American housewives the benefit of
fine factory-milled corn. As with rice and wheat, removal of the
germ not only produced a more refined article, with greater
eye-appeal for the consumer, it also vastly improved the keeping qualities of the meal, since it was the rich oils in the germ
which spoiled the unrefined meal as they turned rancid.

Almost immediately, pellagra was recognized as a near-
epidemic problem, which began filling up state hospitals and

lunatic asylums. In 1907 an Alabama asylum reported eighty-eight cases. Within two years, outbreaks were being reported in over twenty states. In 1909, there were so many cases at the Illinois State Insane Asylum that Governor Deneen appointed a commission to look into the problem . . . which turned up hundreds more cases.

American bacteriologists, based on Washington's Hygienic Laboratory, had in the past few years been mounting a sustained assault on two virulent infectious diseases, typhoid and yellow fever. With these in mind, what more natural than to assume that pellagra was an infection borne by some insect carrier? 'According to the weight of evidence,' they reported, 'pellagra is a disease due to an infection of a living micro-organism of unknown nature.'[2] The most popular candidate for the pellagra host was the buffalo gnat. Another researcher, Dr Louis Sambon, who had studied pellagra in Italy, named black flies as the guilty party. And yet another suggestion came from Kansas, in 1911: the more sandflies – the more pellagra. It must be the sandfly.

By 1912, there were thousands of cases, particularly in southern cotton-growing areas. Two philanthropists set up another privately funded study under the auspices of the New York Postgraduate Medical School. This group, the Thompson–McFadden Pellagra Commission, toiled away for two years and more chasing the infection theory, covered reams of paper with pretty little charts and statistics – and got nowhere. Maybe it was the stable fly?

By this time, the problem had reached such alarming proportions that people were demanding government action at the highest level. And in February 1914, Dr Rupert Blue, of the US Public Health Service, wrote off to the best man he knew: Dr Joseph Goldberger. Would he undertake an investigation for them?

When it came to investigating infectious diseases, there could not have been a better man. Goldberger had worked for the Hygienic Laboratory twelve years earlier, when typhoid was terrorizing Washington, and shown how it spread, how it must be checked; he had followed up yellow fever in Tampico, dengue fever in Texas, diphtheria in Detroit, typhus fever in Mexico. The most dedicated and selfless of workers, he took insane risks, exposed himself time after time to the terrible plagues he was researching. And time after time, he too had gone down with the sickness: he had nearly died of yellow fever and he was desperately ill with typhus. He caught dengue fever himself – and diphtheria. Many scientists would have stayed in the laboratories or at their desks, letting others do the fieldwork for them; Goldberger always insisted on going to see for himself.

Now they wanted him to go and look at another dreadful plague. He nearly said no. For months and years he had seen little of his devoted wife Mary. He had only just returned from six months away; their youngest daughter was an entrancing tiny baby and Mary was desolate at the thought of another investigation, lasting for years perhaps, which would take him up and down the country. And then there was the risk . . .

They both knew he would go, and he did. Years later, his wife recalled how he started his new assignment.

He went with an open mind, trusting only to his keen powers of observation. He visited orphanages, insane asylums, and hospitals all over the South . . . He studied the literature on trains and in hotels at night. Soon it struck him that those who worked with pellagra in orphanages handled the sick children but never contracted pellagra; also, that children of a certain age and babies who had milk were never known to have the disease. Why?

The Baptist Orphanage in Jackson, Mississippi, was just such a case in point. He wrote angrily home to Mary, 'Not one of the matrons or other employees had pellagra. Their diet was distinctly better than that furnished the children. A little muckraking would not hurt the poor helpless children. They are not as well fed as cattle.'[3]

Sixty per cent of the children had had pellagra that spring. Their gaunt faces moved him to inexpressible pity. When he studied the orphanage he found that they were being fed on a poor, high-starch diet. Breakfast was hominy grits with brown gravy, biscuits and syrup; at noon they had a snack – just one roll. Dinner at 3 p.m. was the main meal – vegetable soup, boiled turnips or cabbage or sweet potatoes, and corn bread or molasses. Sundays were special: they had pork for dinner. Dr Goldberger persuaded the staff to introduce some changes: the children were given an egg and a glass of milk for breakfast every day; they had another glass of milk with their midday roll and a helping of lean meat with their dinner.

'What do you think of this?' he wrote to his wife in October. 'Dr Waring and I were going over the grounds when a boy of seven or eight broke from the line of orphans that were passing by, grabbed me round the legs and said, "Are you the man giving us all the good things to eat?" I said "yes" and asked whether he didn't like them. He very quickly replied, "Oh, indeed we do. I hope you won't stop." [4]

On this diet the children thrived. A few months later, there was not a single case of pellagra in the orphanage.

He tried another experiment at the Milledgeville Asylum, where they had plenty of poor demented pellagrins. Since coloured people were believed to be more susceptible to the disease than whites, Goldberger took thirty-six white women pellagrins in one ward and thirty-six coloured women with the disease in another, and made the same sort of additions to their diet as the orphans had so much appreciated. As a control, thirty-two more women, white and coloured, stayed on the usual stodgy hospital diet featuring plenty of corn mush and grits. It was October – and most new cases of pellagra appeared in the spring. While the experiments went ahead, he travelled round observing, watching, making notes. Pellagra was overwhelmingly a problem of poverty, he found – a fact that stared him in the face in the depressed cotton-growing areas where the disease was rife.

By this time he was himself entirely convinced that the disease came with a poor diet. But convincing doctors was another matter. They clung obstinately to their infection theory. There was only one way to convince them; and that was to induce pellagra in healthy people simply by diet. Goldberger wanted to be able to ram home the message to ordinary people too – the poor people who didn't realize that it was their wretched diets that made them ill. 'I am strongly for carrying the true faith to Chap and Mrs Chap, who are living on bread and molasses and who have pellagra, than to Mr and Mrs Silk Stocking who have an interest in the subject to the extent of discussing it over their beefsteak.'[5]

The experiment he planned was straightforward – as long as he could get official cooperation. Twelve convicts were to be given unconditional pardon if they would remain on a diet he specified for not less than six months. Governor Brewer of Mississippi was cooperative and enthusiastic, and there were plenty of volunteers. Goldberger picked a dozen strapping, healthy-looking young men, enlisted the aid of a young physician, Dr Wheeler, to supervise the experiment, and by April it was set up.

The convicts all congratulated themselves on their luck – particularly when they saw the menu. Biscuits, fried mush and syrup or grits with gravy for breakfast, and coffee with sugar. For dinner, corn bread, salt pork, cabbage, sweet potatoes, grits and syrup. For supper, fried mush, biscuits, rice, gravy, corn syrup and coffee with sugar.

Six months – doing only light work – in clean, pleasant quarters – eating plenty of their favourite food? It was a pushover. They pitied the eighty convicts who were to serve as controls, eating normal prison fare. On 19 April 1915 the trial began . . .

While his colleague, Wheeler, kept a close watch on the convicts, Goldberger continued his endless journeys, checking statistics, amassing records of poor people's diets, matching dips in the price of cotton with peaks in the pellagra figures. It all added up.

As the hot southern summer set in, Wheeler's daily notes began to suggest that something was going on. The convicts complained of headaches, backache, fatigue, exhaustion. They grew thin and gaunt. Their tongues became fissured and sore, they suffered from cramps and from profuse debilitating diarrhoea. By September, they were too weak to work. One of them fell ill – but not with pellagra – and was let off the rest of the trial, with his free pardon. The others began counting the days, grimly.

Wheeler watched the weeks slipping past with an anxiety even more acute. Summer had come and gone, and his convicts were undoubtedly sick men, but until they developed the reddening, roughened, pellagrous skin, nobody would believe that it was actually pellagra. There was a strong and vociferous medical lobby for the infection theory; if they could not be silenced by overwhelming evidence, progress towards eradication of the disease could be held up for years.

Goldberger himself was confident that the telltale rash would appear weeks before the trial period was up. '. . . before long, we will be able to show that . . . pellagra may be produced in a healthy vigorous adult by an unsuitable change in diet,' he had written to his wife towards the end of June. 'You have had a mighty tough time of it for two years now, but you have the satisfaction of knowing that your sacrifice has not been without return, for the work that I have done, or rather that you and I have done . . . will be sure to save thousands of lives annually . . . not to mention the misery of many years of suffering and ill health of thousands of others.'[6]

But when the trial entered its sixth month with no sign of the rash, the strain on the two men became almost unbearable. Wheeler in desperation, suggested that he should give up two months' pay for the trial to be extended by a few weeks. Then, on 7 October, a cryptic telegram flashed the good news to Mary Goldberger. Examining the men that morning, Wheeler had found a patch of scaling redness on the scrotum of one of them. Two days later it had spread to his hands and his neck, and the red rash was beginning to show up on two of the other men. Soon there were five. Goldberger sent for leading dermatologists, who without hesitation gave him their verdict in writing: pellagra.

Even this evidence failed to satisfy the tenacious adherents of the infection theory – one of whom publicly accused Goldberger of faking the convict trial. So, beginning the following April, 1916, Goldberger, the faithful Wheeler and a handful of volunteers gave the infection hypothesis a heroic and stomach-turning trial. First, Wheeler and Goldberger drew blood from a pellagrin's veins and injected it into each other, after swabbing each other's throats with secretions from a pellagrin's nose and throat. They did not develop pellagra. Then Goldberger made up some pills as nauseating as anything concocted in a medieval pharmacy: scaly scrapings from a pellagrin's rough reddened skin, a few cubic centimetres of his urine, a few grams of his liquid and foul-smelling faeces, all mixed with a few pinches of flour to bind it together. Nobody else was allowed to take part in this particular trial; gagging, Goldberger swallowed them. For a few days he had a mild diarrhoea, but it soon abated: he did not develop pellagra.

In May and June, there were more 'filth parties' as Goldberger and Wheeler called them, with twenty men and 'one housewife' taking part. The housewife was Mary Goldberger, who had begged to be allowed to join her husband in at least one of them, but he would not allow her to swallow one of his concoctions. Instead, on 16 May, blood from a woman dying of pellagra was injected into her stomach. 'This was an act of faith,' she wrote afterwards. 'It took no courage. Not one of us ever showed, as a result, any symptoms of pellagra.'[7] Five months later – having allowed plenty of time for any latent 'infection' to appear – Goldberger published a description of these trials in a medical journal, with the volunteers unnamed. The 'infectionists' were almost all silenced.

Having established that pellagra resulted from poor diet rather than the bite of an unidentified insect, Goldberger might reasonably have concluded that his work was done. But the misery and sickness which had confronted him continually for two years – the wasted little orphans and the demented asylum inmates – continued to haunt this selfless and dedicated worker, and for the rest of his life, with the help of Wheeler, he worked obsessively on the pellagra problem.

What exactly was the mysterious factor missing from maize? Could it be found only in first-class proteins such as meat, milk, eggs, cheese? Tell that to the cotton paupers of the deep South, living in broken-down shacks, scratching a living from a few square yards of impoverished soil. There had to be another answer: were there other, cheaper foods that supplied it? Goldberger began years of painstaking research at the Hygienic Laboratory in Washington.

Casimir Funk had been sure as early as 1913 that he knew what caused pellagra. It was a 'vitamine' deficiency. Just as the fine-milling of rice had produced an epidemic of beriberi, so the fine-milling of corn was producing pellagra. QED. 'In Italy and Egypt where maize is hand-milled we find chronic cases with only about 4 per cent mortality, in the United States where maize undergoes a process of milling by highly perfected machinery we find a high percentage of acute cases with 20 to 25 per cent mortality.'[8] He had obtained specimens of corn milled to various degrees of refinement, and was convinced that – as with rice – the 'vitamines' were concentrated in precisely those parts discarded by milling. Among the substances found in the 'vitamine'-fraction in rice, he noted the presence of nicotinic acid – which years more of research would later reveal as one of the nutritional missing links in pellagra.

Funk concluded that 'it would be advisable to abandon the present mode of milling, since only the whole grain including the skin can be regarded as a complete food'.[9] But he had done no animal studies to support his assertion, and he had isolated no 'vitamine' shown to be defective in maize but present in milk, meat or eggs.

Whatever the PP factor (pellagra-preventive) as Goldberger came to call it, it was not only a maize diet that produced a deficiency. By 1913, there had been well-authenticated cases of pellagra among people who never touched the stuff, and who lived mainly on rice, on millet, or even on wheat. There had been cases in Britain, too.

Was the PP factor perhaps an amino acid?

It had been shown years earlier that the all-important nitrogen which turned protein into such a wonder-food was actually contained in a variety of different amino acids. Nobody grasped the nutritional importance of these substances, however, until in 1876 a young Swiss physician called Escher, a keen amateur physiologist, added the amino acid tyrosine to Papin's gelatine. A dog fed on this 'enriched' version survived much longer than those on the original pure gelatine. German interest was kindled, and intensive work on the amino acids now began. In 1897 Rubner showed that the value of protein varied according to its amino-acid balance; not by protein alone did man live and replace his bodily tissue: it was the specific amino acids in which nitrogen was stored and transported that made the difference between life and inanition.

This work was followed up at Yale by one of Chittenden's brightest pupils, Lafayette B. Mendel, who in 1911 began a lifelong research partnership with another graduate of the Sheffield Scientific School, Thomas Burr Osborne. One of the first fruits of their teamwork was a study published in 1911 which showed that specific amino acids, among them tryptophan, were essential for growth and tissue repair, and that the 'biological value' of a protein varied according to its amino-acid make-up.

'Biological value' was a popular phrase around physiological laboratories at this time. It had first been used by C. Thomas, who defined it as the number of parts of bodily nitrogen replaceable by 100 parts of any given foodstuff. He tested this theory laboriously on himself, living on a nitrogen-free diet for several days and then adding one protein foodstuff at a time, and measuring the subsequent surge in his output of nitrogen. At 105, ox muscle put real beef into him, milk did almost as well at 100, rice registered 88, wheat flour 39.5 – and maize a mere 30. No wonder maize-eaters got sick. Earlier work by Hopkins – who first identified tryptophan – and others, had pinpointed the deficiency: zein, or corn protein, contained no tryptophan, and dogs fed only on zein did poorly unless it was enriched with tryptophan.

Following up Thomas's work, W. H. Wilson in Cambridge had shown that pellagra victims in Egypt were getting only protein of low biological value in their diets: once this value fell below the equivalent value of 40–50g of meat protein, pellagra loomed.

That it was, in the end, a problem of poverty was emphasized by a sudden rise in the price of cotton during the First World War. As demand for it soared, the pellagra figures declined – so much so that a special hospital for pellagra cases, opened in South Carolina in 1917, closed only two years later, its beds empty. As cotton prices fell back to their normal pre-war levels, however, the figures rose again, to peak during the Depression: there were an estimated 250,000 cases in 1930, with around 7,000 deaths.

Meanwhile, an observation by Chittenden and Underhill at Yale had given Goldberger and Wheeler a most promising lead in 1917. The two Yale workers had noticed that on a diet of wheat-flour biscuits, peas and cotton-seed oil, the tongues and gums of their experimental dogs became black with gangrene, bloody diarrhoea set in, and the dogs died. Might this be the canine malady vets knew as 'black-tongue', wondered Goldberger – which had always been supposed to be infectious, a canine form of typhus? They checked: its incidence seemed to follow the same geographical pattern as pellagra. They tried producing black-tongue in dogs on the diets that gave human beings pellagra – and the tongues of the luckless dogs turned black and gangrenous. They fed them the diets that cleared up pellagra in people – and the dogs recovered too.

They tested over a dozen foodstuffs in this way. Goldberger's chief anxiety was to identify the PP factor in a common foodstuff that even the poorest could afford. To his delight, they found it – and successfully tried it out on pellagrins – in wheat germ, tomato juice and canned salmon, at this time cheap. They also discovered, quite by chance, that their dogs got better when they ate ordinary, dirt-cheap brewers' yeast. Just 30 g daily, they went on to establish, protected people from pellagra.

But just why such foods protected people from pellagra, and exactly what it was that made maize such a perilous food were questions that continued to baffle researchers for decades longer. It was eventually shown that the protein of maize is very low in the amino acid tryptophan, which is transformed inside the human body into the B vitamin niacin. It is deficiency of this vitamin which produces pellagra. The Indians who soaked their maize in hot lime water before preparing and eating it avoided this problem, it has been speculated, because the process made available to the body molecules of niacin which were normally too large for digestion.

Goldberger did not live to learn the true explanation of the misery he had set out to alleviate. Having done more for pellagra sufferers, in practical terms, than any other man alive, Goldberger himself died of cancer.

Goldberger's work brought him the respect of his colleagues, and the love and gratitude of thousands of pellagra sufferers. But as his widow later bitterly pointed out, it earned him no accolades from the medical profession, some of whom still clung tenaciously to the infection theory.

He was four times unsuccessfully nominated for the Nobel Prize. He was already on his deathbed when Harvard wrote to say that they were sending his name forward for the fifth time. 'He was too weak to reply,' his wife later related, 'so he asked me to write and tell them that no prize on earth was worth the love and honour of his colleagues.'[10]

In 1929, the Nobel Prize for Medicine was awarded to Hopkins and Eijkman jointly – the distinguished laboratory workers who had enunciated the general theory of vitamins, and confirmed it experimentally. For the passionately committed researcher who took this concept to the poor man's kitchen, and showed him how to avoid one of the West's most dreaded diseases by adding a few cheap foodstuffs to the menu, there was to be no such honour.

6
The Science
of Life

On 11 April 1915 the German cruiser *Kronprinz Wilhelm* steamed into Newport Harbour in the United States, and dropped anchor, to an instant storm of speculation. This crack ship, one of the fastest in the German navy, had been the scourge of the allied merchant fleets for the last eight months. Prowling the crowded Atlantic shipping lanes, she had sent over a dozen allied ships to the bottom, after seizing their cargoes of coal and provisions – and she had escaped every single one of these encounters without so much as a scratch. Why this undignified scurry into a neutral port? A crowd of journalists and curious sightseers besieged her.

The government health officials who boarded her soon knew why. She carried a desperately sick crew – so sick that she dared remain at sea no longer. Of the 500 men who had sailed with her the previous August, over 100 were already dead of what looked like heart failure. The rest were in dreadful shape. Weak, exhausted, lethargic, they complained of shortness of breath, of heart murmurs, of aching limbs. They were going down like flies – two more collapsed the day the *Kronprinz* docked. The ship's surgeon, a Dr Perrenon, was completely at a loss.

Was the sickness infectious? He was inclined to think not. In all probability, it was an outbreak of the mysterious disease called ship beriberi which had surfaced as a new medical problem at sea towards the end of the previous century. English and German naval surgeons were becoming familiar with it. The Norwegians, in whose ships it was rampant, had set up a special Beriberi Committee to study it in 1902. There were, all the experts agreed, striking similarities with the beriberi of the Far East, which had decimated the Japanese navy in the 1880s. And they had one and all agreed that it was probably a dietary problem.

But what could be so lethal about the *Kronprinz*'s catering? She bulged at the seams with food, enough to feed her crew for a whole year. Most of it had been seized from her luckless victims. She had hundreds of thousands of pounds of fresh or corned meat, ham, smoked sausages, salt fish; she had potatoes, cheese, oatmeal, oleo-margarine, white rice, condensed milk, tea, coffee. She had the purest white flour – and so many tins of delicious English biscuits looted from a British steamer that the crew had taken to handing them out as tips to the boys who ferried messages and papers to the *Kronprinz*. The captured ships, in fact, had offered such a glut of goodies that the German captain had ordered some of it to be sent to the bottom with them. Two cargoes of whole wheat, for instance: who wanted the coarse stuff when she had plenty of fine white flour for the ship's baker? If he ever gave the matter a thought, Dr Perrenon would probably have maintained that white bread was more digestible and nourishing than wholemeal. Had not the great Rubner said so?

As soon as the *Kronprinz*'s mystery sickness hit the headlines, a stream of doctors and specialists converged on her to offer their professional advice. Nothing worked. The crew continued to go down, two or three a day. At this moment the *Kronprinz* saga took an astonishing twist. One of the dozens of reporters desperately trying to get themselves aboard the ship was Alfred McCann, a former deputy health commissioner turned campaigning journalist, who had made a name for himself with his hard-hitting attacks on the American food industry. The *New York Globe* had equipped him with a laboratory, and *carte blanche* to be rude about the adulteration and chemicalization of the nation's food supply; few men were more thoroughly disliked by the US food industry. In two books, *Starving America* and *The Famishing World*, he had assailed doctors for their ignorance of the connection between food and health, and he had followed contemporary research on nutrition with the keenest – and most critical – interest.

From the little that McCann had been able to glean about the ship's mystery illness, it was already plain to him what had happened. And he sensed not merely the scoop of a lifetime if he could get himself aboard, but also a marvellous opportunity to vindicate the truth of what he had been preaching in print for many years. Having pulled every string he knew in vain, he finally 'borrowed' the card of an eminent New York physician, scribbled a polite message on it, and sent it on board. Minutes later he was walking down long corridors lined with photographs of the Kaiser, and into a state-room filled with ships' officers and medical men. Before he could open his mouth, one of the local health officials present jumped to his feet and cried angrily, 'Why, here is McCann of the *Globe!*'

In the moment of stunned silence that followed, McCann seized his chance. He knew exactly what was wrong with the crew, he asserted, he was an expert on nutrition, and he could tell them exactly how to cure the sick men – without any need for drugs. Rapidly he explained how – and why – the epidemic had happened. 'No man interrupted me,' reported a happy McCann. 'Their silence at the end of the speech surprised me as much as my intrusion had shocked them. Finally the ship's surgeon abandoned his seat at the table, advanced towards me, extended his hand, and smiled . . . "I will hear all you have to say after the others have departed," he said. When the others had boarded a launch and were taken ashore, he retired with me to his headquarters and after an hour's conversation sent for the ship's cook . . .'[1]

The McCann 'cure' was not only fast but effective. No new cases were reported the following day; by the nineteenth four men were so much better they were allowed on deck; by the twentieth fourteen men were discharged from the sick bay; by the twenty-seventh forty-seven men were considered cured. How did he do it?

He sent for sacks of wholewheat flour, sieved out the bran and germ and soaked them overnight: each man was given a big glass of the water at breakfast – and a teaspoonful of the bran night and morning to ease the constipation by now universal. At mealtimes they were fed on vegetable soups made from cabbage, carrots, parsnips, spinach, onions and turnips boiled for two hours: only the liquid drained off was given them, with plain wholemeal bread. Potato peelings were boiled – and the men given 4 oz of the water; and four times a day, each man drank a glass of milk with the yolk of an egg in it. Four times a day, too, they were each given a glass of fresh, unsweetened orange and lemon juice diluted with water. Finally, they could eat all the apples they wanted.

The original *Kronprinz* diet, high in refined carbohydrates, fat and sugar, was not vastly different from that of any big Western hospital today, although modern dieticians know how to avoid rampant scurvy in their patients.

But McCann put his finger on the worst of the problem when he castigated the Germans for light-heartedly dumping two cargoes of whole wheat. 'The germ and bran of that wheat . . . would have been worth more to the rapidly succumbing Germans than its weight in gold and precious stones because they contained just the alkaline calcium and potassium salts that were needed.'[2] If McCann had had the gift of prophecy, he could have added that his wholewheat and vegetable soups, his egg and milk, his fruit juice and apples together generously supplied the vitamins and minerals in which the *Kronprinz* menus had been so lethally deficient, and which had prostrated her crew with multiple nutritional deficiencies, including both beriberi and scurvy.

Since 'vitamines' were still little more than a new scientific subject under discussion, and not a single one had been either identified or named, he was unable to do so. But the nutritional knowledge which doctors, nutritionists and dieticians would wait long years to learn from biochemical studies published in scientific journals was already blindingly obvious to McCann and others, even if they could dignify their knowledge with no chemical formulae. And to many Americans the truths now being painfully elaborated in the laboratory were plain, honest, peasant wisdom which had been self-evident for centuries until the march of nineteenth-century mechanized progress and the growing industrialization of food had overwhelmed it.

McCann himself later wrote as if he had been a lone pioneer in this field. 'Prior to 1912,' he wrote – 1912 was the year in which his first book was published – 'the only thing the public ever heard of in connection with a description of food was the academic divisions made by dieticians . . . carbohydrates, proteins and fats . . .'[3]

The great American public had in fact heard rather more than that. They had heard of Sylvester Graham and William Alcott, of Dr Kellogg and the Battle Creek Sanitarium, of Hydropathy and Natural Hygiene, of Nature Cure and Vegetarianism, of Horace Fletcher and Physical Culture. They had certainly heard plenty about their food.

The birth of the modern health reform movement dates back to the early nineteenth century. Its parents were temperance and vegetarianism, and its prophet was Sylvester Graham, whose name has survived only in a cracker, and in the wholewheat flour he so ardently advocated (still known in the USA as Graham flour), but whose teachings had an impact far beyond the neighbourhood grocery store.

Sylvester Graham was born in 1794, the last child of his seventy-two-year-old father's second marriage. Graham *père* was a well-known Revivalist preacher, who had been for nearly fifty years the honoured and prosperous pastor of a solid New England community. By his two wives he had fathered an extended family of seventeen children, and the young Sylvester must have heard from his brothers and sisters glowing accounts of the warm and close-knit family life he was never to know himself. For when he was two his father died, his mother's health soon went downhill, and Sylvester spent a dreary childhood and youth being shuttled around from one relative or guardian to another. Three times before he was twenty-one his health broke down – a natural reaction, perhaps, to the unhappiness and insecurity of his personal life. And to the end of his days – he was only fifty-seven when he died – he seems never to have been very successful at forming warm, close relationships with either his family or his colleagues . . . a difficult, unlikeable man with a built-in frown on his thin face.

Audiences loved him, though. In the early nineteenth century, lectures and sermons were the only forms of public entertainment most people knew, and Graham – whose father and grandfather had both been ministers – had preaching in his blood. By the time he was thirty, he had settled to what was to be his career: preaching and public lecturing. The two were never distinct, to his mind.

His first lecture was on temperance – a familiar theme among the clergy of New England, where stills were legal, spirits dirt cheap, and drunkenness common. But his career in the ministry was brief. Even by sober New England standards, his strictures on the demon drink seemed excessive to his congregation, and when he was offered a job as agent of the Pennsylvania Temperance Society, he jumped at it, and gave up the ministry for good.

In Pennsylvania, temperance not only had the blessing of the clergy but medical backing too. Eight Philadelphia physicians – including the great Dr Benjamin Rush – had signed a public declaration that 'men in health are never benefited by the use of spirits'. Graham had studied physiology and pathology during a brief spell at college, and this aspect of the question was new and intriguing. In preparation for the lectures he was giving up and down the state, he began reading intensively in the textbooks – French and English as well as American – of physiology. More and more, he found himself questioning the conventional medical wisdom of the day on the subject of diet generally. If spirits were bad for you because they over-stimulated the system, as Rush and others argued, then other forms of alcohol – wine and ale – must be equally injurious. And by the same token, tea, coffee, spices – and, in particular, meat.

The vegetarianism with which Graham joined hands at this point had its origins in a noble Rousseau-ist concern for the lower orders of creation, rather than an aversion to meat as an article of diet. But it found itself deeply at odds with current medical thinking, which held that animal protein was essential to health as well as superior in its digestibility. Vegetarians countered these views by quoting Dr George Cheyne's *Essay on Health and Long Life*, a lively account of how he had saved himself from obesity, dyspepsia and an early grave by renouncing meat, and Dr William Lambe, who considered flesh food 'an habitual irritation', and pointed out that since man lacked the carnivore's claws, tearing teeth and short intestinal tract, he had clearly not been programmed by the Almighty for a meat-eating diet.

Just as influential on the development of Graham's thinking was his encounter with the Bible Christians who had settled in and around Philadelphia. Just before his arrival in 1830, the city had been decimated by a terrible epidemic of cholera, which the Bible Christians escaped unscathed, although they had devotedly nursed many of the victims. Their astonishing immunity was the talk of the city, and was all the more striking since according to contemporary medical views, their diet was dangerously lowering and debilitating: they abstained not only from alcohol, but from meat, milk, cheese, butter, eggs, tea, coffee and spices too, to live on vegetables, cereals, nuts and plain spring water. Their very survival was a matter of astonishment to the sturdy burghers of Pennsylvania, who ate meat two, three or even four times daily, and liked plenty of solid puddings and fried food. Had the Bible Christians survived in spite of their diet – or because of it? The latter, Graham concluded.

A lively and passionate speaker, Graham was soon expounding his revolutionary views to audiences as far afield as New York, who paid to hear his series of lectures on what he was now calling 'the Science of Life', and eagerly bought his books. 'The Science of Life' was far more than an up-to-the-minute apologia for vegetarianism. It was a plea for man's life to be lived in harmony with the laws of nature, as they had originally been laid down by the Creator, and were now being revealed in the study of chemistry and physiology.

In many of his views, Graham was far ahead of his time. He urged his followers to fling open their windows instead of living and sleeping in an unhygienic fug; he advocated regular exercise in the fresh air, sunbathing, occasional nudity, personal hygiene and plenty of baths. An early champion of women's liberation, Graham urged them to cast aside their tight-lacing, high heels and long skirts, made them particularly welcome at his lectures, and encouraged them to play an active role in public life by lecturing, writing and teaching if they had these talents. And he thought the contemporary treatment of children hopelessly misguided: instead of being pent up yawning in stuffy classrooms, he said, 'we should turn our children loose, to develop their bodies like calves and colts'.[4]

It has been a common observation of holy men, yogis and philosophers throughout the ages that fasting not only clears the mind wonderfully, but in some way also frees it to range at will in higher planes of consciousness and spirituality, untrammelled by earthly passions. Some teachers of Nature Cure have discouraged prolonged fasts for this very reason, finding that they can induce dangerously *exalté* states of mind – and so lead to dogmatism, arrogance, and a contempt for ordinary flesh-bound mortals.

To a lesser degree, a frugal diet consisting mainly of raw fruit and vegetables, without meat, alcohol, tea or coffee, produces a similar 'high', as well as a surge of unwonted clarity and energy of mind, as anybody who conscientiously tries it out will experience. And it is from this plane of conscious superiority that Graham, and health reformers throughout history, have tended to look down on ordinary people eating hearty meals three times a day, and captives of their base passions. A sense of moral superiority has always characterized the utterances of the health reformer, implicit even where it is not expressed, and strongly resented by the unconverted. It helps explain the profound antagonism which health-food shops, salad-eating and non-drinking can sometimes arouse in 'normal' people.

'Dost think that because thou art virtuous, there shall be no more cakes and ale?'[5] Not if Graham had his way. 'Every individual', he taught, 'should as a general rule restrain himself

to the smallest quantity which he finds from careful investigation . . . to fully meet the alimentary wants of the vital economy,
knowing that whatsoever is more than this is Evil!'[6] Graham
thought this statement so supremely important that he had it
printed in impressive capitals in his *Lectures on the Science of
Human Life*.

If overeating was evil, it logically followed that the general
consequences of this self-indulgence were equally to be
denounced. To Graham there could be no doubting that meat,
alcohol and other gastronomic stimulants had an aphrodisiac
effect to which nobody was immune, 'whether male or female,
married or single'. Worse still, over-indulgence at table –
'excessive stimulation' – could only lead to that greatest of all
evils, masturbation, which Graham and his followers
denounced in ringing terms as the foe of mental, moral and
physical health alike. To indulge was to lose control, whereas
even married people, following his simple diet, would 'so subdue their sexual propensity as to be able to abstain from con-
nubial commerce and preserve their entire chastity of body, for
several months in succession, without the least inconvenience
. . .'[7] Was sex even a *necessary* evil, Graham came close to wondering: 'health does not absolutely require that there should be
an emission of semen from puberty to death'.[8]

The thunderings of Revivalism and New England puri-
tanism echo in these fervent denunciations of sexual excess,
which ring strangely in modern ears – at the opposite pole of
views on sexuality. The psychologist might also speculate that
Graham's own sex life perhaps left something to be desired.

The medical profession were at one with Graham on the
subject of masturbation, which doctors denounced throughout
the nineteenth century as both immoral and a threat to health.
But they took violent exception to many of his other views. In
1842 a group of Philadelphia doctors denounced the baths then
being imported for Grahamites as 'an obnoxious toy from
England', and tried to persuade the city council to ban bathing
during the winter months, to avert 'an epidemic of otherwise
inevitable phtisis, rheumatic fever and inflammation of the
lungs, and a whole category of zymotic disease'.[9]

But the dispute between doctors and Grahamites went
much wider and deeper than this. From his own experience,
Graham was necessarily a critic of contemporary medicine,
which concerned itself little if at all with diet and regime, and
relied heavily on such draconian and unphysiological measures

as bleeding and purging. 'Whenever any of the family took a cold, the doctor was sent for, who would always either bleed or give physic,'[10] an earlier critic had noted. By Graham's time, anyone undergoing this therapy could truly be dubbed 'heroic'; the patient of the average GP could expect to be regularly bled – and the more severe his illness, the more drastic the bleeding, up to 140 oz (3.9 l) – and to be 'physicked' with huge doses of calomel, or toxic mercury, as well as violent vegetable purges such as gamboge and jalap.

As Graham's fame spread, testimonials to the success of his regime began pouring in. They told how the writers had successfully been delivered of a whole gamut of illnesses: gout, dyspepsia, rheumatism, 'general debility . . . excess irritability and weakness of stomach . . . no appetite . . . sometimes severe headache . . . at times very sour stomach'.[11]

Some of these accounts suggest the side-effects of drastic over-doctoring. Others were the inevitable consequence of a diet high in fat, protein and starch but low in many vital nutrients and almost devoid of roughage. Graham estimated that 90 per cent of the population – men, women and children – suffered from assorted digestive problems. And he noted that in almost every case of chronic disease that he saw, constipation had been the first symptom, often patiently endured for ten, twenty or thirty years. 'I cannot but feel confident that the use of superfine flour bread is among the causes of these and numerous other difficulties,' said Graham. Constipation, in his experience, never failed to disappear 'a short time after the coarse wheaten bread of a proper character had been substituted . . .'[12]

One of his earliest works was a *Treatise on Bread Making*, written to counter the evils of the white bread now eaten by all classes. Other books now poured from his pen, the ranks of his followers swelled, and soon there were even Grahamite boarding-houses, where you could either make a short stay while you learned how to adjust your life to the new physiological laws, or else live in on a more permanent basis. They were for the very faithful. A bell rang every morning at 5 a.m. (6 a.m. in winter) to allow plenty of time for exercise and bathing before an austere meatless breakfast. Dinner was equally austere, and the lights went out at 10 p.m. sharp.

William Alcott, another health reformer of the day, was even more spartan. He slept in a cool, well-ventilated room,

rose at 4 a.m. and retired to bed at 8 p.m. The son of a Connecticut farmer, Alcott had learned food reform the hard way,
when his health broke down seriously during his teens, and
the doctors came close to killing him. His faith in medicine
destroyed, he found his own way back to health through a
simple vegetable diet with spells of fasting. His heart was in
teaching, but health was soon his chief subject. He founded
the first popular health magazine – *The Journal of Health* – and
opened the first health-food shop, selling whole grains, vegetables grown on 'unvitiated' soil, maple sugar to replace
refined cane sugar, and bread like mother made it.

Unlike Graham, Alcott was not particularly keen on
salads – 'all these crude substances seem to me uncalled for,
and unnecessary. Why should the healthy stomach be filled
with such trash?' But the two men were as one on the virtues of
wholewheat bread, fruit and vegetables as principal articles of
diet, and the injurious effects of meat, alcohol, tea and coffee.
Alcott's dietary rules were firm: meals must be simple, with
plenty of roughage or 'innutritious matter'; honey, sugar and
molasses were to be avoided; the less digestible foods such as
fruit should be eaten separately; starch and protein should not
be eaten at the same meal, and all food must be carefully
chewed, a practice 'not enough insisted on'. A qualified doctor,
Alcott felt compelled to agree that animal food was a 'primary
aliment', but considered that it was only fit for babies or the
sick, and for those such as Eskimos living 'where better food
cannot be obtained'.

Like Graham, he too took a moral stance: 'I need not stop
to prove that a daily indulgence in what we know to be wrong
is of immoral tendency; nor that Christians, indeed other
people, are under obligation to get rid of every improper or
foolish habit . . .'[13]

The American Physiological Society was founded in 1837,
soon after Graham joined Alcott in Boston, where he had been
invited to deliver his course of lectures at Alcott's school. Alcott
was its President, and Graham's Science of Life its inspiration.
At its very first formal meeting, it called for a reform in medical
practice, and urged doctors to study prevention rather than
cure, a plea that sounds familiar to modern ears.

By the time of its third – and last – meeting, the society
had moved towards a headlong confrontation: 'Resolved, that
all medicine, as such, is in itself an evil, and ought not be used
except when it is the best means of preventing or removing a

greater evil . . .'[14] They went on to urge that only those 'who are thoroughly acquainted with physiological science deserve the confidence of the people'.[15]

At first these proceedings and Alcott's activities were viewed on the whole with kindly interest by the local medical establishment, which reported them impartially from time to time in *The Boston Medical and Surgical Journal*. Far shriller denunciations, scorn and ridicule were poured on them by lay critics, including the tradesmen who felt particularly threatened by Grahamite austerity.

But gradually it dawned on even the most tolerant of medical observers that the Science of Life, carried to its logical extremes, struck at the very roots of medical practice. In the Grahamite scheme of things, there was no place for doctors as they understood the word.

7
Cold Water and Physical Culture

The nineteenth century in Europe witnessed a boom in what we now call alternative medicine, to the indignation and fury of the regular medical profession. Few irritated their spleen quite as thoroughly as the water cure.

Hydropathy had been developed by a surly Austrian peasant called Vincent Priessnitz, whose wealthy patients put up with his offhand rudeness because of the astonishing cures which he effected. His *materia medica* was tap water, used at temperatures ranging from ice-cold to extremely hot, used in baths, alternating hot and cold showers, hand and foot baths, Sitz baths, icy compresses, and wet-packs, in which the patient was first wrapped in a sheet wrung out in cold water and then quickly tucked up in a blanket for a restoring sleep. As well as enduring the rigours of the water cure, his patients were forbidden meat and alcohol, and put on to a drastically simple peasant diet of coarse wholemeal bread and vegetables.

This water cure was introduced to America by Dr Joel Shew who in 1849 formed the American Hydropathic Society with Dr Russell Thacher Trall.

Handsome and heavily bearded, with kindly eyes set in a firmly authoritarian face, Trall looked every inch the great medical reformer he was to become. Born in 1812, the son of a Connecticut farmer, he was often ill as a child, and found out from personal experience how painful – and how useless – heroic medicine was. Thanks to his doctors, his health was still shaky by the time he finished schooling, so he gravitated naturally into medicine, to see if it was possible to improve on the crude methods which he had endured. The questioning scepticism which he brought to classes made an unfavourable impression on his professors. 'I never expected Trall to amount to much,' one of them later remarked.[1]

By the time he had spent his first decade in medicine, Trall had looked at and turned down most of the current fashionable

alternatives to the heroic practice, including chronothermal-
ism, phrenology, eclecticism and homoeopathy. None of them
appealed to him very much until he discovered the Priessnitz
method, began applying it in his practice, and soon made a
name for himself as a specialist in this fashionable new therapy.
A man of strong principles, Trall also became a vegetarian and
an ardent crusader against both tobacco and alcohol. Inevitably, he soon found himself rubbing shoulders with Grahamites, got to know Graham himself with whom he became friends,
and in turn adopted these new teachings in his practice.

In 1852 he was successful enough to open the Hydropathic and Hygienic Institute, a handsome four-storey brown-
stone on New York's Laight Street, which also housed the
Hydropathic and Physiologic School. A cross between
boarding-house and urban health farm, the Institute offered
plain vegetarian meals, hydropathic treatment and the use of
its gymnasium and public rooms. In the 1860s, Trall added
a health-food shop, selling whole grains, cereals and Graham
bread, as well as copies of his books on food reform, sex and
physiology.

By this time, he had thought his way out of hydropathy
since, as he came to realize, the bracing shocks it inflicted on
his shrinking patients were not much different in kind from
the bleeding, blistering and drugging of the regular doctor.
Nor was it without its dangers. Health reformers are expected
to live to a vigorous old age, in vindication of their dogma, but
Graham had succumbed in 1851 at a mere fifty-four, and Trall
was inclined to believe that the icy-cold baths to which his
hydropathic advisers had subjected him, even when he was too
weak to stagger to the bathroom unaided, might have hurried
on his death. Another hydropath, Dr Caleb Jackson, treated
pneumonia in his own son with so heroic a dose of hydropathy
that the boy never recovered, and died soon afterwards. The
incident made a profound impression in hydropathic circles.

Quietly, the word hydropathy began to disappear from
their letter-headings and brochures. What were Grahamite
practitioners to call themselves now? Various names were
mooted. Should they be 'hygeopaths' or 'sanatologists' or 'sanol-
ogists'? Was it 'hogeopathy' or 'higeiotherapy' or 'hygeotherapy'
that they practised? Trall himself plumped for the more gran-
diose name at first: when his school was chartered in 1857, he
called it The New York Hygeio-Therapeutic College. But it was
he who settled the matter in the end by publishing the definitive

description of their philosophy and methods in a small book which he called, simply, *The Hygienic System*. Soon, its practitioners were known as Hygienists.

In the mid century, there were already many of them, as well as several institutes modelled on Trall's New York establishment. And in those happy days before launching a new magazine became a hobby for millionaires, one new propaganda magazine after another came hurrying off the presses. Joel Shew began it with *The Water Cure Journal and Herald of Reform*, which Trall was soon editing. As hydropathy was phased out, its name was changed to *The Hygienic Teacher*, and later on, now owned as well as edited by Trall, to *The Herald of Health*. Two of his students then took it over and tacked on *And Journal of Physical Culture* to the title, while Trall, back in the editorial chair, launched *The Gospel of Health*, which ran for three or four years before he was invited to edit another newcomer, *The Science of Health*. The emphasis on health as a positive state to be actively achieved and sustained, rather than the mere absence of disease, was one of the most striking differences between the Hygienists and the medical profession.

One of his followers later said of Trall that he was 'investigator, missionary, crusader, scholar, thinker, writer, lecturer, professor, editor and a doctor, all tied up in one dynamic bundle'.[2] Certainly the stupendous energy which allowed Trall to carry on all these activities simultaneously until his late sixties was in itself an impressive testimonial to the benefits of the Hygienic way of life; and if Trall was its best example, he was also its moral leader; he defined the new science, shaped its course for the future, and laid down the broad lines along which it was to develop. A century of medical progress and nutrition research later, his descendants in the American School of Natural Hygiene would find little to modify or reject in his teachings.

In Trall's hands, Hygiene was hard-line, uncompromising. He placed before his disciples a vision of moderation and self-discipline, emotional and sexual as well as physical, in a way of life from which many of the creature comforts that ordinary people would consider indispensable, such as tea, coffee, alcohol, smoking, were ruthlessly banished, while the so-called pleasures of the table were denounced as so much health-threatening self-indulgence. What, after all, was cookery? It was 'to mix and mingle the greatest possible amount of seasonings, saltings, spicings and greasings into a single dish; and

jumble the greatest possible variety of heterogeneous substances into the stomach at a single meal'.[3]

His *Cook Book*, published in 1854, did nothing to
encourage this sort of messing about. Seasonings such as sage,
thyme, mint, basil, coriander, cumin were hardly to be classed
as food, and therefore best left out. So were mushrooms, ferns
and lichens – 'I do not regard the whole tribe as worth the ink
spilt in describing them.' Vegetable oils were allowed, but all
animal fats, including cream and butter, were 'difficult of digestion, but slightly nutritious, and liable to generate rancid acids
in the stomach'. Decomposed foods such as cheese, and fer-
mented foods such as buttermilk, vinegar and sauerkraut were
highly objectionable. Another Hygienist wrote of sauerkraut
with a shudder: 'if cabbage were treated this way by chance,
and not by design, it would be considered fit only for hogs to
eat; indeed the fermentation of the swill barrel is not one whit
different'.[4]

Not so much a dietary programme, Hygiene was indeed a
way of life, which rewarded its followers with vigour and ser-
enity of mind as well as bodily health. There were other fringe
benefits. They might wash themselves, for instance, without
any need for that 'unnatural irritating agent' soap, while by
contrast the meat eater, 'who has for years made his stomach a
sepulchre for all manner of animal food from the fat porker to
goose-liver pie' would no doubt need plenty of it to clear his
skin of 'the enormous deposit of oleaginous matter'.[5] Unlike
meat and cheese eaters again, those who followed the Hygienic
eating plan would soon discover – years before Horace Fletcher – that their breath offended no longer, their best friends
never needed to tell them, and their excreta were no more
offensive than hot biscuits.

The stern evangelism of the Hygienists made them a ready
target for ridicule; they made powerful enemies in the fast-
growing packaged and processed food industries, and the
medical profession was lost for words to express its fury and
condemnation of their weird doctrines, while there were always
those ready to assert that 'only the ailing and dyspeptic paid
great attention to their food, while the perfectly healthy ate and
drank everything that came before them, and remained happy,
healthy and vigorous'.[6]

But even if they found the undiluted Hygienic message
too strong, millions of Americans listened, and it is no coincidence that as the century entered on its last decades, the gigantic meals were dwindling, salads and fresh fruit were appearing

for the first time on many a table, and showering, physical exercise and personal hygiene had been adopted from coast to coast.

Another Hygienic habit now being adopted by millions of American families was the breakfast cereal. Today's granola can trace its origins back to the 'Granula' invented by the Hygienist Dr Caleb Jackson, who patented it in the 1860s. A breakfast cereal with c-r-r-runch, it was made by baking thin sheets of Graham flour and water, breaking and grinding them, and then baking them again. Granula was usually prepared by filling a tumbler one third full with the cereal, then topping it up with whole milk, and leaving it in the ice-box overnight. By morning it had a fine head of cream – and was eaten poured into a dish with extra cream and sugar stirred in. Commercially, Granula never made the grade, but patients at his health resort, Our Home on the Hillside, in New York State, enjoyed it – among them a group of Seventh-day Adventists from Battle Creek in Michigan. Their leader was Ellen White, who admired Jackson's establishment enough to copy the formula, and soon after set up her own vegetarian and hydropathic health resort, run on Seventh-day Adventist principles. Her Western Health Reform Institute opened at Battle Creek in September 1866.

It flopped dismally – until an energetic twenty-four-year-old, Dr John Harvey Kellogg, took over. Kellogg sensed its commercial potential, discreetly phased out the religious overtones while retaining the essential principles of diet and natural therapy, and gave it a snappy new name. Soon, the Battle Creek Sanitarium was famous all over the East Coast. Independently, Kellogg had evolved his own breakfast cereal when he was a hard-up medical student living on apples and Graham crackers in New York. His version added cornmeal and oats to the original Graham flour, and soon after he took over at Battle Creek he began marketing it under the same name as its rival: Granula. When an irate Jackson sued him for breach of copyright, Kellogg calmly rechristened it 'Granola' – a word which passed into the American language. It was his younger brother Will, however, who – deeply struck by the fact that Granola could be sold for ten times the price of its original cereal content – turned an asset into a major industry. And it is his confidently scrawled W. K. Kellogg, which appeared on the first boxes of another new cereal, made from paper-thin flakes of toasted maize sweetened with malt, and still adorns a billion cereal packs today.

Soon Kellogg's Corn Flakes were on thousands of American breakfast tables, and the name Battle Creek had acquired by association such irresistible commercial appeal that by 1904 no fewer than forty-two different companies making breakfast cereals and 'health foods' had sprung up in the area. Among those which survived the seven-day wonder was C. W. Post, whose 'Post-Toasties' were later to join the familiar Kellogg packs ('The Original and *Best*') on the shelves of every American supermarket.

Kellogg's breakfast cereals did more to publicize the 'bio-logic living' and vegetarian way of life practised at Battle Creek than a thousand tracts. 'Muscular vegetarianism' became a cult. And when Irving Fisher, Chittenden's colleague at Yale, needed sedentary vegetarians to pit against meat-eating athletes in high-or-low protein trials, he applied almost as a matter of course to the staff of Battle Creek for volunteers.

But it was Bernarr Macfadden who really put the muscle into vegetarianism. The son of a drunken Missouri farmer and a chronically ailing mother, Bernard Adolphus McFadden was born in 1868, and grew up a puny stripling, weakened by bouts of serious illness, including tuberculosis. At an early age he was dumped on an avaricious aunt and uncle, after his father had succumbed to alcoholism and his mother to TB, and it soon dawned on him that if he was to make anything of his life, it was up to him alone. Self-improvement was already a recognized all-American goal. He discovered a gymnasium, and went to work. By the time he was eighteen, he had developed his slight frame into a creditable mass of bulging muscle, and rebuilt his health thanks to fasting and a diet of Graham bread and vegetables. Having reshaped his person, he reworked his name to match, dropping the effete Adolphus, and smoothing out his surname, while his first name – now spelt Bernarr – was pronounced at his insistence with heavy emphasis on the second syllable, so that it came out like the growl of a tiger.

The new-model Bernarr Macfadden was unveiled to the public in a series of fairground booths, with glossy black and white photographs of his near-nude torso and bulging muscles, and circus stunts. Soon businessmen were queuing up to take his rejuvenation course, and he had launched a magazine, *Physical Culture*, which in a few years peaked at sales of over a million, and in its heyday was as popular and widely read as *Time* or *Picture Post*. There was nothing modest about Bernarr's ambition – that 'as world leader of the Men of Muscle, he might become the prophet of a new religion of health, whose complete naturalism and health would literally shove aside the mountains of superstition and "medical demonology" '.[7]

Physical Culture was at first written single-handed by Bernarr himself, but as its popularity grew many of the Hygienists were happy to write for it, and Europe's most famous vegetarian, George Bernard Shaw, contributed articles for love, not money. The magazine plugged Bernarr's 'new religion of health' with gusto. In its columns Bernarr campaigned against corsets, high heels, drugs, alcohol, meat eating, and the medical profession. He made himself champion of fringe therapies such as Nature Cure, newly arrived in the USA from Germany; osteopathy, recently developed by Andrew Still; and the Bates method of curing defective eyesight by simple exercises. Many of its readers learned for the first time of the benefits of fasting, 'natural' foods, cold baths, physical exercise, sun- and air-bathing, low heels and brisk walks. Bernarr claimed to have cured himself of serious illnesses by these methods. Fasting, he maintained, could cure anything, even cancer and syphilis.

Soon there were Physical Culture restaurants, where diners could enjoy salads, nutburgers and wholemeal bread, washed down with carrot or beet juice, or a herbal tea containing 'valuable nutrients from grass, alfalfa and clover leaves',[8] instead of those lethal drugs, tea and coffee. North of New York he built Physical Culture City, a tented town where people could stay to rebuild tired bodies and learn a healthier way of life. By the summer of 1905 125 tents had sprouted on the site. Among early visitors was a young novelist, Upton Sinclair, whose novel *The Jungle*, with its horrific revelations of Chicago's meat-packaging industry, was to give vegetarianism an unexpected shot in the arm. Sinclair gratefully claimed that he had been restored to dynamic vitality as a result of his months in Physical Culture City, and became another regular contributor to the magazine.

Later on, Macfadden opened the Chicago Healtharium where patients could be treated, and students after a few months of study were handed certificates attesting them Doctors of Physocultopathy, Kinistherapy, Hydrotherapeutics or Brain Breathing.

In his personal life, Bernarr practised all that he preached and more. Sleeping in a nightshirt, on the bare floor, he was up at dawn to do deep-breathing exercises at his wide-open window. After 200 knee-bends and press-ups, he exercised with his Indian clubs for quarter of an hour before a cold shower and a bracing breakfast of cold water. Then he walked barefoot to his office, where he often stood on his head for inspiration. Lunch consisted of the raw vegetables that he believed would cure more diseases than all the doctors put together, and a handful of nuts or berries. He was a great believer in water, and the more the better: half a gallon a day, he claimed, would not only strengthen the heart but conquer constipation too.

His wives in turn submitted to the same spartan regime. One of them, an athletic young Englishwomen chosen by Bernarr as the Perfect Woman, later told how, in the fifth month of her first pregnancy, Bernarr insisted that she jump from a sixty-foot platform into the sea, to demonstrate her superior fitness. He kept her on a programme of strenuous exercise and a sparse vegetarian diet throughout her pregnancy and refused to let a doctor attend the muscle-bound young mother-to-be during her agonizing forty-eight-hour labour; when she later developed pneumonia, he treated her himself by hosing her down with icy water and keeping her on a strict fast. When their four young daughters later developed whooping-cough simultaneously, Bernarr made them fast too; for three weeks they lived on nothing but orange juice and water.

There was little original in any of Bernarr's ideas on nutrition and health, apart from the genius for publicity which paraded them so energetically in the public eye. They were drawn from Priessnitz, from Graham and the Hygienists, from a more recent advocate of water cure, Father Kniepp, and from earlier writers such as Cornaro and Cheyne. Years before anyone had heard of Physical Culture, Trall and his followers were singing the praises of the natural life, of nudity, of fresh air, and of physical exercise. But where they had preached an ascetic self-discipline that made spiritual, mental and moral health its goal, Macfadden turned Hygiene on its head to launch the twentieth-century cult of the Body Beautiful, and he made muscular perfection, not spiritual awareness, the proof of its validity. His popular nickname – Body Love Macfadden – summed up nicely the general notion of what he was all about. His gospel was illustrated with any number of beautiful half-tone photographs of bathing beauties and near-nude males in virile poses, and his message had such lusciously sexual overtones that it was ridiculously easy for his opponents to make fun of him, laugh his ideas out of court, trump up a charge of indecency, have him jailed and fined $2,000, and close down Physical Culture City in a wave of adverse publicity.

There was still no denying that his methods often worked for sick people as medicine never did, that his vegetarian regime brought health where the high-calorie, high-protein regime currently being extolled as a perfect balanced diet never could, and that his denunciations of white flour and refined sugar as 'devitalized and emasculated food' sank deep into the public consciousness.

A showman to his fingertips, Macfadden revelled in the razzmatazz and publicity, but his friends saw another side of him: a sensitive, sincere and deeply serious man. And what his pupils learned from him was not the 'MacFaddism' at which his critics jeered, but the undiluted Natural Hygiene message that he himself had learned from Dr John Tilden, the friend of Trall. Among his pupils were Stanley Lief and J. C. Thomson, who took Nature Cure back to Britain, and Behramji Madon who became India's first Parsee naturopath.* And if 'MacFaddism' was hard to take seriously, there were plenty of others who compelled more serious attention now punching home the same message. They addressed themselves to an America where it was possible to get drunk for a few cents on cheap fake Scotch and bootlegger gin, not to mention patent Blood Bitters or Tonics which were sold by the million, and packed an alcoholic punch of up to 44 per cent; where addictive drugs such as cocaine, morphine and heroin could be freely purchased over the counter, and where chemical adulteration of food had become a national scandal. The crusading McCann and the muscular Macfadden were only two of those denouncing the American way of life.

A much more serious attack on the giant food industry came from within the Department of Agriculture itself. The chief of their Chemistry Bureau, Dr Harvey Wiley, had studied chemistry and food technology in Berlin. His eyes opened, he returned to take up his new post, and was appalled at what he soon discovered was going on in the American packaged-food business. He was equally horrified by the amount of refined white sugar the average American was now gulping down

*Travelling back to India from the United States via England, the young Madon struck up an instant friendship with another young Indian returning after studying to be a barrister in London. His name was Gandhi. Gandhi dated his lifelong adherence to the principles of Nature Cure from this leisurely voyage.

annually. 'If we flood our stomachs with dextrose,' he warned, 'we will need half a dozen artificial pancreases to take care of it . . . By reason of this increase of the amount of dextrose . . . we endanger our health in the most serious way.'[9]

William Dufty, who calls Wiley 'the Ralph Nader of his time', describes his efforts at cleaning up the industry. 'After crusading for pure food and drug legislation for decades, he finally undertook a public experiment in 1902 which caught the imagination of the populace. Male volunteers were organized into teams (which the newspapers soon called "The Poison Squad"). Young, healthy men were fed the old-fashioned American diet. One by one, the newfangled food additives which manufacturers were adding to ketchup, canned corn, bread and meat were introduced to their diet . . . For five years the Poison Squad was given regular doses of the food preservatives, adulterants and colouring matter then in general use by food processors: boric acid, borax, salicylic acid, salicylates, benzoic acid, benzoates, sulphur dioxide, sulphites, formaldehyde, copper sulphate and saltpetre. Periodically Dr Wiley issued bulletins detailing the serious physical effects of these chemicals . . . The newspapers soon made Dr Wiley's name a household word. The Poison Squad were as famous in their heyday as astronauts were in theirs.'[10]

The first US Pure Food and Drug Laws were passed by Congress in 1906, in a blaze of publicity. Wiley's Bureau of Chemistry was charged with carrying them out, and Wiley threw himself into his task with enthusiasm.

Now at last it would be possible to outlaw the dozens of dubious chemicals with which the food and soft drinks industry was poisoning the American food supply and undermining American health. In future, he hoped, 'Our food and drugs would be wholly without any form of adulterations . . . The manufacturers of our food supply, and especially the millers, would devote their energies to improving the public health and promoting happiness in every home by the production of wholeground, unbolted cereal flours and meals . . . The resistance of our people to infectious diseases would be greatly increased by a vastly improved and more wholesome diet. Our example would be followed by the civilized world . . .'[11]

This Utopian vision was not shared by the US food and soft drinks industry, as Wiley now learned to his cost. For the next six years he became the victim of a long-running smear campaign of unprecedented spite and ingenuity. He was held up to the public as a bungling, muddle-headed bureaucrat with an inflated ego; viciously anti-Wiley articles published in the food industry's trade journals were reprinted and widely circulated; and an Advertisers' Protective Association was formed with the avowed intention of discrediting him. Meanwhile the food industry successfully exerted its considerable powers of persuasion in Washington, on Capitol Hill, at the White House. In 1912 Wiley finally resigned, a frustrated and deeply disillusioned man. The Bureau of Chemistry was quietly dismantled, the Pure Food and Drug laws redrafted, and the protection of the consumer was entrusted to a new body, the US Food and Drug Administration, or FDA for short. Borax, salicylic acid and formaldehyde were still proscribed; otherwise, almost all the adulterants that Wiley campaigned against are still right there in the US food supply – plus a few thousand more. And it has been reckoned that the average American consumes between five and eight pounds of them in his food every year.

There's one small difference: they aren't called adulterants any more. 'Additives' sounds so much more innocuous.

8

The Vitamin Hypothesis

In 1907 a young biochemist called Elmer McCollum bought the complete set of Maly's chemical abstracts, the *Jahres bericht über die Fortschritte der Thierchemie*, thirty-seven fat volumes covering all the years from 1870 onwards, and lugged it back to his rooms. Night after night he pored over them, making a note here, marking a passage there. The account of Lunin's 1880s experiment with the milk-fed mice particularly fascinated him: why had nobody ever followed it up?

During the day, meanwhile, he continued his work as instructor at the Wisconsin College of Agriculture, supervising the interesting cow-feeding experiment which had been devised by the distinguished Professor Babcock. From Voit in Germany, Babcock had learned that all food is made up of fats, proteins and carbohydrates, and that the scientific feeding of man or beast was accordingly a simple, straightforward matter. Since the health and breeding ability of their livestock is of rather more than theoretical interest to farmers, Babcock had decided to put the question to a practical test. Three groups of cows had been given rations identical in terms of fat, protein and carbohydrates. But in one group, the ration was based on corn, in another wheat, and in a third, oats.

At first little difference had appeared in the condition of the cows as they contentedly munched their feed. But as the months passed, first the wheat-fed and then the oat-fed cows began to show signs that something was amiss. By the end of a year, the differences were startling. The placid corn-fed cows still looked sleek and fit, and they had carried healthy calves to full term. The oat-fed cows looked in poorer shape, and although they produced live and apparently normal young, the calves died soon after birth. But the state of the wheat-fed cows was shocking. They were wretchedly thin; they delivered stunted, premature, stillborn calves. And they had all gone blind, with thickly ulcerated corneas. Clearly, there was more to successful stock-rearing than Voit had supposed.

McCollum, trained in organic chemistry at the famous Sheffield Scientific School, had never conducted animal experiments before, and found now that chemistry seemed unable to supply the answer to this puzzle. He had dutifully analysed the milk, the blood, the excreta of the animals without getting any closer to solving the problem. And hours of poring over his chemical abstracts had proved fruitless – except that Lunin's mice nagged at him. Was it possible that they were on the wrong tack altogether, that their experiments with diets of purified foods were a dead end from which nothing useful could be learned?

Would it not be more interesting to feed animals on individual food substances – leaf, seed, root, tuber or fruit – and then, if the animals showed signs of malnutrition, start adding single known food substances to the diet, one by one? Cows were large animals too, and their reproductive cycles were lengthy. Results would come faster, and much more cheaply, if they used smaller animals which – like Lunin's mice – would grow, reproduce, rear their young and die within a short time.

At twenty-eight McCollum was in a hurry to make a name for himself as a productive scientist in what he sensed was an exciting new field. He laid his doubts about the cow experiments before the college authorities, and they reluctantly agreed that he might use the college premises for rat studies. But the work must be done in his own time, and it must be financed out of his own pocket.

McCollum made pens out of the cardboard boxes that laboratory supplies arrived in, with chickenwire fronts. At first he tried catching wild rats for his experiments, but they were so tricky to handle that he had to spend some of his small salary on store-bought albino rats. He had thought up hundreds of different diets that he wanted to try out, and he set to work with enthusiasm. Soon his rats were dying in the most satisfactory way on their various regimes. But the cost of feeding and replacing them, and the hours it took to write up his notes were becoming a real headache. A stroke of luck brought him an assistant: Marguerite Davis, a young biochemist who had recently started work in the lab. He confided to her his plans for the rat colony, and his dreams of glory – and she eagerly offered to help. Now the experiments went ahead fast.

After months and years of work they published their first paper. They had established that rats thrived on a given basic diet when the fat from either butter or egg yolk was added to it; if the fat was supplied by olive oil or lard, their condition deteriorated, their eyes became cloudy and ulcerated, and they went blind. Almost simultaneously McCollum's former mentors at Yale, T. B. Osborne and Lafayette Mendel, announced the results of remarkably similar experiments. On a purified diet containing only the protein of whole milk, their rats died: if it was supplemented with whole milk itself, they did not. They also noticed the eye condition – but took it to be an infection. McCollum and Davis now repeated their work, and found that the eye condition as well as the stunted growth and poor development could be reversed by adding butterfat, and concluded that they were looking at a true deficiency condition, probably the same as had been seen in human beings. Since the mysterious nutrient was found in the fat of whole milk, they named it fat-soluble A.

The importance of this discovery to physiologists and chemists was that it called in question the most fundamental dogmas about the German trinity of fats, proteins and carbohydrates. 'Hitherto all fats had been considered as sources of energy only,' as McCollum wrote, 'and were believed to be alike on an equal calorie basis.' Now his work had shown that some were more equal than others: quality mattered more than quantity.

He went on to look at dozens of other foods to see if they contained the mysterious A factor. In the process he found and identified another 'accessory factor', found in rice polishings, which dissolved into water: he named it water-soluble B. He also found that green leaves were rich in the A factor – and thus almost incidentally solved the puzzle of the wheat-fed cows: if they had been fed the leaves as well as the grain of the wheat they would have prospered like his rats. And he discovered that liver cleared up the eye condition faster than anything else.

McCollum's findings on the eye condition had brought a Japanese eye specialist, Dr Mori, all the way to Wisconsin to see it for himself. He had surmised years earlier that the condition in children was a dietary problem, and had treated dozens of cases successfully with cod-liver oil. The liver connection particularly intrigued the two men. One of the earliest of all medical texts, the Ebers Papyrus, written in Egypt around 1500 BC, mentions roasted ox liver almost in passing as an established cure for night-blindness. Twentieth-century fishermen in New-foundland had stumbled on almost the same remedy. On a diet which rarely contained either milk or vegetables they often suffered painfully sore eyes and night-blindness from the glare of the sun on the sea. They found they could cure themselves by eating the liver of a seagull – which was later found to be high in vitamin A.

The dairy-farmers of Wisconsin cared little about the eye problems of Newfoundland fishermen, and they were indifferent to the therapeutic value of green leaves or gulls' liver. The wonderful, the indispensable fat-soluble A was found in abundance in whole fresh cows' milk: that was all they needed to know and was the best news they had heard in their lives. McCollum became their hero overnight.

To help spread the good news, *Hoards Dairyman* – well-thumbed by stock-breeders all over the States – asked McCollum to write a series of articles for them about his findings and their significance for the dairying industry, which they published in the summer of 1916. The series caused such a happy stir that the journal re-ran them all the following year. Three years later they asked McCollum to update them and answer questions: he was happy to oblige. 'Milk,' he emphasized, 'is the greatest of all the protective foods because it is so constituted as to correct the deficiencies of whatever else we are likely to eat.'[1]

Now it was official – you'll feel a lot better if you drink more milk. McCollum himself continued to keep dairy-farmers happy for years after he moved from the College of Agriculture. In 1923 he suggested that much the best way to enrich white bread would be to add milk solids to it, an improvement 'sound from the physiological, agricultural and economic standpoint'. In the same year he wrote a series of articles on nutrition for the magazine *Hygeia*. Anyone who supposed that this was yet another journal from America's Hygienists was badly out. It was in fact a popular magazine put out by the American Medical Association, and one of its objects was to provide a counterblast to the barrage of 'faddist' notions assailing the public ear from writers like McCann, Macfadden and the whole tribe of advocates of 'natural' eating. Now *Hygeia* had the famous McCollum to put the record straight.

His recommendations were based on hundreds of animal-feeding studies he had carried out himself, and on similar work going ahead in labs all over the world, which showed that Sylvester Graham, Alcott and Trall had actually known far more about a healthy diet than Liebig, Voit, Rubner and all the scientific establishment of Germany. For what was McCollum telling America but to eat less white bread, less sugar, less meat, fewer potatoes. Eat a big helping of green vegetables every day. Eat two salads every day. And eat plenty of fruit – the more the better. The dairy-farmers were still happy, though: every man, woman and child should drink at least a quart of milk a day.

With the dairy industry now solidly behind him, McCollum's career took off. He was invited to write, to be guest at important official functions, to lecture. Finally in 1917 he was offered, and accepted, a real plum – the Professorship of Chemistry at the newly established School of Hygiene and Public Health in Johns Hopkins University, in Baltimore, attached to which was America's most famous medical school.

Soon he was America's Mr Vitamin. In 1918 he published a book aimed at the general public called *The Newer Knowledge of Nutrition*, in which he taught them how to eat for health and vitality. He joined Hoover's Advisory Committee on Alimentation, set up in 1918, and stumped the country giving talks on nutrition, while articles flowed from his ready pen. In a shrewd journalistic coup, *McCall's Magazine* signed him up as a regular contributor, and over the next twenty-two years he urged American housewives to feed their families plenty of what he called the 'protective foods' – green leaves and milk. Only the romantic short stories, somebody at *McCall's* calculated, got a bigger reader response.

During the first decade that he wrote, American milk consumption doubled, as did the demand for lettuces, while orange eating went up a whole 150 per cent, so the fruit-farmers of Florida loved him too.

McCollum made other, subtler points about food. If the public insisted on eating white bread – and he saw no reason why this taste should be disturbed – they must make sure that its defects were well supplied by other foods such as milk and green leaves: 'The idea that a variety of food sources . . . will prevent any faults in the diet from becoming serious, is no longer tenable.'[2] And in 1922, he told a distinguished assembly of doctors that what they now knew as the deficiency diseases were simply the tip of the malnutrition iceberg: 'the evil effects of malnutrition of a borderline type greatly overshadow the clinically recognizable deficiency diseases in nutrition . . .'[3]

He might have saved his breath. 'Classic' nutritionists, still faithful to Voit and Rubner, looked down their noses at the hundreds of rat studies – 'vitamin research yields results of sorts to a minimum of brains', one of them sneered.⁴ And the vast majority of doctors, specialists and medical researchers were far more interested at this time in pursuing infection theories – even for recognized deficiency states like rickets and scurvy – or complex causation theories drawn from the new field of endocrinology, than in pausing to consider the idea that faulty diet might have anything to do with disease.

By the end of 1916, McCollum and Marguerite Davis had together completed over 1,600 experiments, and – as well as the eye disorder noted – had induced what even to their inexpert eyes looked like a horrifying spectrum of disease.

> Among the effects produced . . . were strongly con-
> trasting appearance of the rats, loss of hair on different
> parts of the body, scaliness of the skin . . . dermatitis . . .
> [irregularities] of body form, posture, stunted size, sudden
> decline and death of rats which had grown well for a time;
> in some fertility was decreased, some were sterile; others
> gave birth to dead or living but non-viable young . . .

Keenly aware that he was no pathologist, McCollum took to carrying around pictures of his rats in the various stages of disease. He buttonholed pathologists, vets, doctors. Sometimes he could link the disease states with a specific diet; in other cases the connection had yet to be made. And the response from these professionals who spent their lives treating the diseases he was showing them in rats? 'None of the people contacted were interested, and they gave me little or no assistance.'⁶

So general was this lack of interest in the food factor as a possible cause of disease, that when the newly formed Medical Research Council in Britain reviewed the rickets problem at a meeting to discuss research projects in 1914, it occurred to only one member of the committee, Gowland Hopkins, that the dietary angle should be considered, and his suggestion was brushed aside. 'The discussion ranged over all the wellworn possibilities,' remembered another of those present, 'defective fat absorption, para-thyroid deficiency, infection, and some kind of dietary deficiency. Nobody . . . thought there was any evidence pointing to the last of these possibilities.'⁷

Various lines of attack were allocated for research – among them a study of the social and economic factors – and

Edward Mellanby, a former pupil of Hopkins, was asked to explore the relationship between experimental rickets and conditions of oxidation in the body. Mellanby worked part-time at the London Hospital, where the paediatric wards were filled with little rickety babies. An inquiry into their diet would have taken hours rather than months. Instead, Mellanby duly went ahead with his futile oxidation studies, and spent the next two years getting nowhere. Meanwhile Miss Fergusson, also on the MRC's behalf, picked her way through the slums of Glasgow, up dark and rotting staircases and into wretched homes which seldom saw a ray of sunlight. She found rickets in plenty – Glasgow had one of the worst rates in Europe at the time – and she found families where there was no rickets. She noted in passing that the families with rickets ate more flour and sugar, and less meat, eggs, cheese and milk than those without. And she concluded that wretched housing conditions, lack of fresh air and exercise, and poor mothering were to blame.

In the end, Mellanby almost fell over the food connection, when the puppies he had chosen as experimental animals developed severe rickets on one of his oxidation diets. Now at last he began looking at what they were eating. He found that on a diet of bread and milk they grew reasonably well, unless he skimmed the milk, when they developed the crooked and bowed legs of rickets. Hopkins had observed that rickets was more common in Venice among families getting little or no dairy products in their diet. Testing this observation, Mellanby found that the addition of butter prevented rickets. He tried adding Marylebone Cream – a patent food based on emulsified linseed oil which several hospitals were using for rickets – and found it quite useless, as were lard and olive oil. Finally he tried the traditional remedy which some doctors still relied on – cod-liver oil. No rickets appeared in his puppies. Rickets was caused, he concluded in 1919, by a diet defective in a factor similar to fat-soluble A.

For some time it was assumed that the two factors were identical, and rickety babies had puréed spinach poured into them. When they failed to improve, it was assumed that the purée had passed straight through them unassimilated.

The indefatigable McCollum, meanwhile, was also hard at work on the problem. The head of paediatrics at Johns Hopkins, Dr Howland, asked him if he had ever observed rickets in his rats. At last – a doctor who was interested! Delighted, McCollum took him straight over to his rat colonies, and was able to show him baby rats with the typical pinched chests and beaded, buckled ribs of rickets, together with details of the diets that had produced them. Four years of marvellously detailed research later, he was able to show that cod-liver oil contained not only the fat-soluble A, and the anti-rachitic factor Mellanby had found, but that the two were quite distinct. The A factor was destroyed when hot air was bubbled through the oil, but the anti-rachitic factor survived. He christened it vitamin D – since the third vitamin to be identified had already been named C – and thanks to the great authority of Johns Hopkins and its paediatricians, cod-liver oil became a standard item in every baby's diet.

Post-war Europe gave nutrition researchers a grim field-day. Vienna in particular became their unhappy hunting ground, where every imaginable disease that years of starvation or poor food could bring about could be studied at leisure. A team from London's Lister Institute descended on a children's hospital to make notes on the cause and treatment of rickets. They observed two groups of babies, one fed on the hospital diet of poor-quality milk, with sugar added to it, the other on full cream milk, with extra cod-liver oil. In the summer months, when the babies were wheeled out into the sunshine for a daily airing, there was no rickets in either group. In winter, the babies getting only milk and sugar soon developed unmistakable symptoms. Fresh air in itself offered no protection, they noted; it was sunshine that did the trick.

By 1925 three independent groups of researchers had arrived at the same conclusion. The mysterious dietary factor that prevented rickets was not only found in certain fats: it could actually be formed directly in the skin by the action of sunlight, or in fats exposed to ultraviolet radiation. At last it was clear why the children of the rich, confined in sunless nurseries, had often done worse than peasant toddlers who roamed the fields. It explained why the rickets figures always rose towards the end of winter, and sank in the summer months; it explained why the breast-fed babies of mothers who lived in smoke-darkened slums on a diet of tea and bread and marge still developed rickets.

Some of the Viennese babies suffered from multiple deficiencies. Together with one of the Lister reports, the *British Medical Journal* published in 1918 a photograph of twenty-eight-month-old twins, taken in a Vienna children's home. It was hard to believe that they even belonged to the same species.

On the right, supported by a nurse's hand, lolled Johann, a pathetic scrap of humanity with an oversized head, big soft belly and frail arms and legs that looked as though they would snap at a touch. On the left his sister Ida sat up confidently on her own, slightly cross, a gloriously bouncing toddler with fine fat limbs. Six months earlier, on the same wretched diet as her brother, she had been in the same state. Then orange juice, butter and a big daily spoonful of cod-liver oil had been added to her diet – and cured her not only of rickets, but also of the scurvy which had only just been finally established as a deficiency disease.

Scurvy had been associated with the lack of fresh green-stuffs in the diet for centuries. But after several Arctic expeditions had been crippled by the disease, despite supplies of lime juice, the scurvy question was once more wide open at the turn of the century, with theories of toxins or an infection agent being freely aired. The mystery was finally cleared up by two workers investigating what they supposed to be beriberi.

Towards the end of the nineteenth century, the crews of ships making lengthy voyages were often prostrated by a generalized weakness, with swelling in the lower limbs and shortness of breath. Many of them died of heart failure. Was it the beriberi becoming rampant in the Far East? Doctors thought not, since the paralysis and the polyneuritis of beriberi were absent. Was it scurvy? Apparently not, since offensive breath and rotting teeth were not among the obvious symptoms. A special committee set up by the Norwegians to study the problem concluded that it was most probably caused by tainted meat, and asked Axel Holst, Professor of Hygiene at Christiania University, to look into the matter.

Holst first took himself off to Batavia to meet Grijns (p. 34), the foremost expert in the field, and pick up a few leads for his own research. On his return to Norway he set up colonies of pigeons, and began feeding them a variety of diets. On polished rice he successfully produced polyneuritis, as he had expected, and he made careful studies of the nervous degeneration that accompanied it. On polished barley the same signs appeared, but not on dark rye bread. Next he fed his pigeons the peeled potatoes and the fine white bread which were now standard rations in the Norwegian merchant navy, as elsewhere, and was amazed to notice that they at once developed polyneuritis – the avian form of beriberi. This fact alone might have been thought to deserve an entire medical journal to itself.

But Holst had the tunnel vision that so often characterizes medical research. He was investigating ship beriberi – a quite different disease – and since his pigeons obstinately refused to develop anything remotely resembling it, he switched to guinea-pigs.

This was a piece of luck, because almost alone among the lower orders of creation, guinea-pigs – like man – cannot synthesize their own supplies of vitamin C. On Holst's diets, they obligingly developed brittle bones, greenish and bleeding gums and loose teeth. On post-mortem examination Holst and his new associate, T. Frölich, found the classic signs of rampant scurvy – the weak and atrophied bone tissue, the degeneration of the marrow, the irregular clumping of the cartilage cells. It was now a simple matter to work out which foods could help keep it at bay. And in 1907 and 1912, Holst and Frölich published the two definitive papers on scurvy.

Among the foods that prevented it, they found, were cabbage, dandelion leaves, sorrel, carrots, cranberries, apples and, of course, lemon juice. But the antiscorbutic factor in these foods was either diminished or destroyed by heating. Another paper, published in 1912 by one of Holst's colleagues, Valentin Furst, showed that sprouted seeds, too, could prevent scurvy. This discovery – like so many of the findings arrived at after years of painstaking research – had been anticipated years earlier. A Mr Young of the British navy had suggested it in the late eighteenth century: 'beans and barley and other seeds . . . brought under the melting or vegetating process, are converted into the state of a growing plant, with the vital principle in full activity throughout the germ and pulp and if eaten in this state without any sort of preparation . . . cannot fail to supply precisely what is wanted for the cure of scurvy, viz., fresh vegetable chyle.'[8]

Careful studies by two British workers, H. Fraser and A. T. Stanton, meanwhile, had linked beriberi conclusively with the consumption of polished rice. In their paper published in 1909, they showed that the disease developed in eighty to ninety days among a group of Japanese coolies fed mainly on this refined carbohydrate. Some carbohydrates were more equal than others, too.

The outbreak of the 1914–18 war had at least one happy consequence: it speeded up nutritional research wonderfully under the impetus of military need. After the Gallipoli fiasco, thousands of Australian and Indian troops were ferried to the

Third Australian Hospital on Lemnos in the last stages of sickness, most of them struck down by diseases, not bullets. They were suffering from fevers, from dysentery – and from a prostrating weakness marked by shortness of breath, and swelling of the limbs; heart failure and infections carried these patients off fast.

The hospital pathologist was Dr Charles Martin – in peacetime, the distinguished head of London's Lister Institute. He at once identified the disease as beriberi, complicated in many cases by scurvy. He sent an SOS back to the Institute asking for research to discover what easily available food supplies could be used to help deal with these cases. As it happened, someone had set up pigeon experiments at the Institute two years earlier, and Harriette Chick and Margaret Hume, loyally manning the fort while most of its male staff were away at the Front, followed up the beriberi studies. Working with conscientious thoroughness, often hand-feeding the capricious birds and animals to make sure they ate up every scrap of their rations, they found that the seeds of plants, the extract of yeast, and the germ of wheat or maize or rice – all discarded in milling – were rich sources of the anti-beriberi factor.

A century earlier, Wellington's soldiers had fought the Peninsular War for month after month and year after year in conditions quite as rough as Gallipoli. Wellington boasted of them that they could go anywhere and do anything, and they were famous for their health and stamina. Their rations? A pound of wholewheat grain daily. They crushed it into coarse flour and baked it if they could into the coarsest bread; if not, they chewed it raw.

Having explained the extraordinary resistance of Wellington's soldiers, Miss Chick and her colleagues moved on to the scurvy problem, setting up colonies of the now-traditional guinea-pigs. On a diet of heated milk, oats and bran, they developed scurvy. Patient work showed that it could be corrected or prevented by raw cabbage, by onion, by carrots – and particularly by orange or lemon juice. But they were astounded and horrified to find that the West Indies lime juice, on which the navy and several Arctic expeditions had relied, was almost wholly ineffectual, however carefully preserved.

The indefatigable McCollum found all this highly puzzling. His rats grew and thrived on simple purified diets as long as fat-soluble A and water-soluble B were present. What was this missing factor which guinea-pigs needed and rats could do without? He fed guinea-pigs on a diet of oats and fresh milk from good Wisconsin cows. Bafflingly, they developed scurvy. On milk – the great protective food? There must be some other cause, he reckoned. After post-mortem studies on the guinea-pigs had revealed severe constipation, he ascribed it to a bacterial infection reaching the bloodstream through the injured wall of the caecum. His paper, 'The "Vitamine" hypothesis and deficiency disease: a study of experimental scurvy', was one that he would afterwards prefer to forget.

In London, Harriette Chick and her colleagues had been appalled to find their guinea-pigs developing scurvy on a diet of heated milk, since babies being fed on little else (pasteurized milk was of course heated) were dying of infantile scurvy in the wards of every European hospital. Was it perhaps heating the milk that made it lethal? They gave guinea-pigs a diet of oats plus fresh unpasteurized milk, administered with their usual painstaking care, and watched. They found that if the animals drank less than about 50 cc of the milk daily, they eventually developed scurvy; anything over this amount protected most of them, and the more the better. On 100 cc daily they were perfectly all right.

The conclusion was plain. If babies were to be fed artificially, on heated milk, then they must be given orange juice or some other antiscorbutic – even swede juice would do.

The anti-scurvy factor was now known as water-soluble C, or 'Vitamine' C. 'Vitamine' (from 'vital' and 'amine')? Whatever it was, it was certainly not an amino acid, as the British biochemist Jack Drummond pointed out – any more than Funk's first 'vitamine', the anti-beriberi factor, had turned out to be. Drummond had a suggestion to make. The food factors should be called – vitamins.

The new word passed at once into the language.

9
Eating for Health

The Great War of 1914–18 drove home one lesson to civil and military administrations: the crucial importance to victory of the food factor. Germany was defeated as surely in her own kitchens as on the blood-soaked battlefields of Flanders; national morale could not be sustained on an empty stomach, as the British nutrition expert, John Boyd Orr, was later to point out. In 1916, the German harvest fell below expectations, and rumours of an impending food crisis provoked near-panic throughout the nation. By early summer 1917, military food reserves were being drawn on to supplement civilian rations. Even so, they had dwindled ominously by the New Year of 1918. Even munitions workers were getting only two thirds of their pre-war calories, the fat ration was down to under 4 oz (115 g) a week, and industrial output fell. According to one observer who visited Germany at the end of the war, 'the people were physically and mentally enfeebled . . . in a condition of dull depression and lassitude; they had no feeling of national honour; they had completely lost the will to victory'.[1]

The war provided other vivid footnotes to the history of nutrition. In the Far East, the British army at Kut – on military rations of polished rice and white bread – was laid low by beri-beri and had no choice but to surrender. Beriberi and scurvy together defeated the Indian and Australian troops at Gallipoli. And the Italian forces ignominiously beaten at Caporetto in 1917 were wretchedly provisioned, their poor-quality rations supplying 20 per cent fewer calories than the British, French or German rations. 'This is a level of nutrition', comments Boyd Orr, 'at which soldiers cannot maintain the physical fitness and the morale needed to fight a battle.'[2]

As well as these involuntary lessons, the 1914–18 war also offered the spectacle of an astonishing experimental study in nutrition, conducted not with rats but with human beings, not with tens or dozens, but with an entire population – that of

Denmark. By 1917 the Danes had already had their diet – formerly rich in pork and dairy products – severely curtailed. Now came the Allied blockade; there were 3,500,000 human beings and 5,000,000 domestic animals to feed, and their situation was desperate. In the circumstances, the Danish government called on the nation's best-known and most respected nutrition expert, Professor Mikkel Hindhede. Already Superintendant of the State Institute for Food Research, he was now appointed Food Adviser to the Danish Government and given *carte blanche*. Here was a golden, a unique opportunity to demonstrate the health-giving qualities of the low-protein, vegetarian and wholegrain diet he had advocated with so much enthusiasm for so long, and he seized it with both hands.

On his instructions, 80 per cent of the pigs were slaughtered and about one sixth of the cattle, to save their precious grain food, and meat became the rarest of occasional treats for all but farmers and their families. To save still more grain, as well as potatoes, the distillation of spirits was banned, while beer production – already well down on its pre-war levels – was halved again. In London and Berlin, nutrition experts were still mesmerized by the German balancing experiments which had apparently demonstrated the superior nutritiousness of white bread; as a result, extraction rates as low as 70 per cent were permitted in both countries despite shortages of grain. Hindhede, however, had long been convinced both by his own experience and from his experimental work that brown was best. So for the last year of the war, the Danes lived on traditional black *Kleiebrot* made from whole rye, to which was added extra wheat bran, and 24 per cent barley meal, milled to 94 per cent. The Danes grumbled at first about the dark bread, but at least there was plenty of it, and Danish bakers had not yet lost the art of baking it well. 'We are accustomed to the use of whole bread, and we know how to make such bread of good quality,' Hindhede boasted happily.

Thus for a whole year, from 1 October 1917, the Danish nation lived on a food-reformer's diet of wholegrain bread, plenty of greens, potatoes and root vegetables, oatmeal porridge, butter, milk, a little cheese, fruit; but little or no meat and no spirits at all.

According to contemporary ideas on nutrition, this diet, with its low levels of protein and its 'indigestible' bread, ought to have been decidedly inferior to normal Danish fare; but two years later, when all the figures were in, they were a triumphant vindication of Hindhede's views. During the lean year, the Danish deathrate had actually fallen to the lowest ever recorded in a European country: 10·4 per 1,000. In Denmark it had never previously been lower than 12·5. The difference of 2·1 per thousand meant that 6,300 lives had been saved by the austere diet. 'It would seem, then, that the principal cause of death lies in food and drink,' concluded Hindhede.[3] It was the kind of remark that earned him the reputation of being a little too simple in his views.

One man, however, would have agreed with him wholeheartedly: England's Dr T. R. Allinson. For years the name Allinson had been almost synonymous with wholewheat bread in Britain.

Thomas Richard Allinson was born in Manchester in 1858, just seven years before the invention of roller milling brought the finest white bread within reach of even the poorest. At the age of fifteen he was already determined to become a doctor, but his wealthy stepfather disagreed with his choice of career, and Thomas eventually left home with five pounds in his pocket to look for work. His mother secretly lent him enough money to pay for his studies, and Allinson took himself off to the finest medical school of the day, at Edinburgh, where the great Lister had opened a new era for surgery with his discovery of the importance of asepsis.

The young student realized that ahead of him lay long years of working to earn his living at the same time as following his studies; so he experimented with diets to find one that was not only as cheap as possible, but could sustain him through a sixteen-hour working day. He found that when he lived on plenty of fresh vegetables, fruit, wholegrain cereals, but no meat – a diet very like Hindhede's wartime prescription for the Danes years later – he was fit, alert, and full of mental as well as physical energy. He passed all his exams with honours, and became a licentiate both of the Royal College of Surgeons and the Royal College of Physicians in Edinburgh.

Over the next few years of widely ranging practice, he gradually lost all faith in the drugs on which he had been taught to rely. 'I saw that the drug system of treatment was a mistake,' he later wrote. 'I saw that not only were drugs useless, but positively dangerous. I even came to the conclusion that if a patient was left to nature he would run less risk than if treated with drugs.'[4]

His studies brought him to share the views of Graham, Alcott and Trall on the virtues of a simple diet, vegetarianism, temperance and wholewheat bread. In 1884 he published *A System of Hygienic Medicine*. 'Cure belongs to the body,' he explained to his readers, 'and if we put the system under proper conditions, it will work its own cure.'[5] Health lay in the patient's own hands: 'We must not put down illness to chance, but know that it comes from a violation of natural laws.'[6] There was nothing 'natural' about illness – on the contrary. 'I do not believe in anyone being ill,' proclaimed Allinson stoutly. 'I do not believe in death before eighty or ninety years of age, except from accident.'[7]

Allinson had seen life lived according to these natural laws, during travels in Spain and among the Arabs, whose hardiness and stamina, on their sparse diet of dates, coarse wholegrains and camels' milk, deeply impressed him – he had seldom seen a healthier race.

In stark contrast, most of his poor patients never saw fresh, whole food from one year's end to the other. They lived on little else but tea, white bread and a scraping of butter, margarine or cheap jam, with a bit of cheese or bacon as an occasional treat – often strictly for Father. The tea was brewed over and over, and heavily sweetened with white sugar; the milk they added to it often came from diseased cows, with swollen and infected udders, kept in filthy little sheds here and there in the great city. The meat they ate on rare occasions was the rich man's leavings – offal mainly, often contaminated; Allinson himself made a shuddering inspection of some of the busiest London abattoirs and learned an additional, aesthetic, reason for his vegetarianism. This atrocious diet was made worse by shameless adulteration. The milk might be watered, the tea was often the sweepings from the warehouse floor or old tea bought back from hotels and coloured with black lead, the cheese might owe its healthy country flush to red lead, while the bread itself might have alum added to make it still whiter, ammonium or magnesium carbonate to disguise the taste of old flour, or bone ash or sieved potatoes to bulk it out.

In Allinson's eyes, the bread of the poor was the greatest of all wrongs. 'If a law could be passed forbidding the separation of the bran from the fine flour, it would add very greatly to the health and wealth of the nation, and lessen considerably the receipts of the publican, tobacconist, chemist, dentist, doctor and undertaker,' he commented.[8]

Until the invention of roller milling, wheat and other grains had been ground in stone mills to produce a wholewheat, creamy-coloured flour. For the fine white bread of the rich – which the poor also hankered for hopelessly – this flour was sifted through finer and finer cloths, to get rid of the bran, and produce a flour of perhaps 85 or 90 per cent extraction, as we should say today. What was removed in this sifting was the coarse outer covering of the wheat, its bran – which we now know to be rich both in minerals and the roughage of which constipated modern man is so sorely in need. But even the most dedicated sifting never removed all of the germ of the wheat; and this, we now know, is rich in the B complex vitamins, in an oil containing vitamin E, and in essential fatty acids. Thus what was considered fine white flour at the beginning of the nine-teenth century was still relatively nutritious and vitamin-rich.

The new roller mills revolutionized man's most basic food-stuff. They split the wheat grain into a thousand fragments; with mechanical thoroughness they sifted it into a dozen differ-ent streams, so that at the touch of a button, the miller could now select for his customers only the fine starchy endosperm, to give them a flour white as never before.

The new invention met with near-universal approval. The millers liked it because it gave them two lots of satisfied cus-tomers for the price of one – the bakers and the stock-breeders, who bought up their bran and wheat germ as the most nutritious cattle and pig feed imaginable. They liked it, too, because once the wheat germ with its oil was removed the flour could be kept for weeks longer: wholewheat flour goes off quickly once the oil turns rancid. The bakers loved it because it made their most popular bread the cheapest; if anyone cared to pay more for 'wholewheat bread', they were happy to buy up a sackful of cheap bran, and add it to the white flour. And the customers were certainly happy: the bread they considered a luxury was now actually cheaper than any other kind. Even the nutrition experts and doctors were happy: white bread was widely held to be more digestible than the coarser brown. Besides, it stood to reason, didn't it, that the favourite bread of the rich must be superior in every way to the poor man's fare.

For nearly forty years Allinson ran a one-man crusade for the better health of the poor, for a diet in keeping with man's true needs – and for the wholewheat bread which was the foun-dation of this diet. Since he was also a gifted speaker, a fluent

and easy writer, and a good businessman with a flair for publicity, his crusade was strikingly effective. And since he practised all that he preached, the astonishing amount that he
contrived to cram into a twenty-four-hour day was in itself a
testimonial to the soundness of his views. In addition to the
seven or eight hours he spent daily with his patients – in his
surgery or their homes – he wrote a column three times a week
or more for the *Weekly Times & Echo*, from 1885 until his death
in 1918; endless letters to newspapers or magazines, or articles
for other publications; he answered daily – by hand and individually – up to thirty letters from patients wanting his advice
by post; he addressed meetings, wrote books and composed
pamphlets, which he carried in bundles with him to distribute
free – and still found time to marry a talented and artistic wife,
and raise three children.

A cheerfully practical man, Allinson could never be content
simply with suggestion or admonition. If the poor lacked the
spirit – or the space – to bake their own wholewheat bread, he
would see that it was still available for them: he worked out the
simplest, most basic recipe, and offered bakers a brightly coloured certificate to hang in their windows if they would make it
and sell it cheaply. When the numbers grew too great for him
to supervise any longer, he bought up an old stone flour mill in
Bethnal Green and began baking his own bread from freshly
ground flour: he boasted that it had 'nothing put in and nothing
added'. (He would certainly not recognize the 'Allinson's'
bread sold today complete with sugar and emulsifiers.) Soon
his Natural Food Company was turning out other health
foods: a cheap baby-food made from freshly ground wholegrain
cereals; a tea substitute; a packet vegetable soup; a range of oat
or wholewheat biscuits, as well as oils, nut butters, and crushed
wheat for English porridge.

Few of the poor bothered with any but the most basic
cookery: Allinson printed the recipes for dozens of cheap,
simple nourishing dishes, called it *Wholesome Cookery*, and sold
tens of thousands of copies at a penny a time.

Whatever their disease, his patients carried away a strikingly similar prescription: 'All are advised not to smoke, nor
drink stimulants; to eat plain food in moderation; to have
wholemeal bread instead of white; to exercise daily; to breathe
fresh air always; and to keep their skin pores open.' Urged on
by the bright-eyed, persuasive doctor with the fresh country

glow on his face, they allowed themselves to be talked into healthier habits – and departed clutching a leaflet of sound advice or simple recipes, reminding them that 'Health is free to all who live rightly!'⁹

For all their simplicity, Allinson's prescriptions worked. With his customary disregard for professional delicacy, he claimed happily: 'My results during the last twenty years show me that my ideas are correct; I have more old folks under my care than any doctor in the kingdom; my oldest patient is over 103.'¹⁰

The revolutionary importance of Allinson's teaching was doubtless not lost on the medical profession: that if people would 'learn how to live properly' they could dispense with doctors. Had he simply put his ideas into practice quietly and without fuss – perhaps expounding them in a modest paper for some reputable medical journal from time to time – he might have made several converts among his colleagues. But by going over their heads to appeal directly to the general public, through the medium of the popular press and penny pamphlets, he put himself beyond the pale professionally.

The Royal College of Physicians of Edinburgh grew restless at his repeated attacks on doctors and on the drugging habit. They warned him once, twice, three times; he simply printed the warnings in his next column and explained why he was paying no attention. Finally, in 1891, he was struck off their books. Thenceforth, he proudly signed all his articles T. R. Allinson, ex-LRCP.

It was thus easy for the medical establishment to dismiss him as a glutton for publicity, a businessman *manqué* who had built a tidy little grocery business in dubious foodstuffs on ideas even more dubious, a doctor who flouted every accepted canon of professional decency.

———

No such reproaches could have been levelled at Dr Max Bircher-Benner, whose professional conduct was beyond reproach to the end of his days. His discoveries in the field of nutrition, however, amounted to so total an overthrow of current thinking on this subject that when he presented them to the Medical Society of Zürich in 1900, with the request that they be subjected to experimental study, he was dismissed as an unscientific dreamer.

A lesser man might have been overwhelmed by the verdict of his peers. Circumstances, however, had conspired to endow the young Swiss doctor with a steely strength of character, as well as that imaginative open-mindedness which distinguishes the true scientific thinker.

Born two months premature, in 1867, the second son of a Swiss notary, the young Max was always a frail, puny specimen beside his sturdy brother. The doctors told his mother that his heart was impaired: he would never be very strong. The boy refused to spend his life wrapped in cotton wool: he forced himself to go climbing in the mountains, to do hours of gymnastic exercises, to swim in icy streams, to walk for hours in the fresh air. By the time he was fifteen there was no longer any question-mark over his physical stamina. There had never been any question at all about his choice of profession: he was determined to be a doctor. At the age of five he was already cutting out little paper patients and applying paper bandages carefully wrapped around their limbs.

As soon as he was old enough to start his medical studies, however, his father died suddenly, leaving his wife and five children nearly penniless. Friends rallied round eventually, and a modest loan from his godfather made his medical studies possible after all. But the intervening weeks of uncertainty turned him into a textbook case of insomnia. The family doctor prescribed drug after drug, as well as the more mundane suggestion of a bellyful of beer at bedtime. Nothing helped.

After weeks of this, his riding instructor, a down-to-earth soldier, was struck by his wan and listless looks and found out what the problem was. Try the wet-packs of Priessnitz, he suggested. Max Bircher had never heard of Priessnitz, of hydrotherapy, or of wet-packs, but he was desperate enough to try anything. That night, as the major suggested, he took his sheet down to the courtyard, wrung it out in the icy waters of the well, and wrapped it round him with a shudder before climbing between the blankets of his bed. Miracle: for the first time in weeks he dropped off almost at once, and slept sweetly and soundly the night through.

An early demonstration that natural means may succeed where drugs fail, this incident made the deepest impression on him.

At Zürich University, the classes in biology and physiology, with their emphasis on the new science of nutrition, fascinated him. By contrast, the clinical courses were a grave disappointment. Pathological descriptions and lists of drugs seemed to him no substitute for instruction in the most important questions of medicine: how people became sick or got better. 'As his disappointment became ever greater,' his son Ralph later related, 'he developed a fierce determination: to get at any cost to the real sources of disease and health and be content only when he found them.'[11] Even a term spent in Berlin, studying physiology under the legendary Max Rubner, brought him no nearer the solution of these questions.

In 1891, when he was twenty-four, he graduated and immediately set up his first practice in a busy industrial suburb of Zürich. He had plenty of patients, who had the utmost respect and affection for their conscientious young doctor, and within two years he had courted and won for himself a charming wife, Elizabeth Benner – 'lively, intelligent, strong-minded'. Following Swiss-German convention, he then coupled her name with his own. Soon she bore him the first of seven children. He seemed destined for the secure and comfortable life of the successful family doctor.

Pasteur had said that chance favours the prepared mind. As in the case of Newton, chance took the form of an apple. In 1895 Bircher-Benner lay in bed with jaundice, feeling quite exceptionally unwell. The thought of food had disgusted him for days. Alarmed by his refusal to eat, his worried wife one afternoon slipped into his mouth a sliver of the apple she was peeling at his bedside. He managed another slice, even enjoyed it. Over the next day or two, though he could face no other food, he ate his slow way through two or three apples.

A month later, in the course of a conversation with a medical colleague, Bircher-Benner mentioned a patient who was worrying him tremendously at this time. The young woman was wasting to death, totally unable to digest any food, even the most carefully and delicately prepared invalid dishes. His colleague, who happened to be an amateur of medical history, recalled reading an unusual prescription of the Greek Pythagoras for just such a case: a purée of raw fruit, mixed with a little honey and goats' milk.

They both agreed that this was the most improbable remedy. Any medical student knew that raw foods were much harder to digest than cooked foods, and thus unthinkable for a patient suffering from a disease of the digestive tract. No responsible physician could possibly order such a diet.

And yet – since nothing else worked – Bircher-Benner found himself ready to clutch at this straw. He remembered, too, the apples he had eaten at a time when he could eat nothing else, without apparent ill effects. Since his patient could digest nothing anyway, what would be the harm in at least giving Pythagoras' cure a trial? Next day, he proposed it to her – and she agreed at once. He ordered for her a small purée of fresh raw fruit. For the first time in weeks she ate with appetite, and no digestive upset followed. He ordered another – and another. After a few days, a little colour came back into her cheeks, and her appetite grew. He added a little raw vegetable to her regime. Better and better. A few weeks later she had made a complete recovery.

For the young doctor, this was mind-blowing; a doctor today, finding that an advanced case of duodenal ulcer responded magically to a course of Madras curries, would be equally at a loss. There must be some other explanation. But before dismissing the case as a medical freak, he tried out some tentative experiments, at first within his own family, and then on more and more of his patients. One conclusion soon stared him in the face. Contrary to received medical teaching, raw food was not only *more* digestible than cooked food: it actually appeared to possess healing powers which were particularly effective in any digestive disease.

Shaken, he went back to his books, consulted medical journals, hunted through medical libraries. He could find no hint of any previous treatment along these heretical lines.

Allinson would have shrugged, written columns on the subject and urged the benefits of fresh raw fruit and vegetables on all his patients. (He heartily recommended fruit and salads in any case.)

But Max Bircher-Benner could not be content simply with applying an empirical discovery in his practice. He needed to know exactly why raw fruit and vegetables could heal diseased tissue, what gave them their astonishing curative powers. Moreover, here was a discovery which – if it stood up to scientific scrutiny – could revolutionize the practice of medicine. But medical history was full of life-saving discoveries which had been brushed aside for years: Lister's discovery of antisepsis was only the most recent. The medical mind, he knew well, is hard to convince – and would certainly remain unmoved by a few case-histories, however interesting.

With remarkable understanding, his young wife agreed to take their two little boys off for a long stay with her parents in Alsace, while he hunted Europe for his answers. During months of research, he met Sigmund Freud in Vienna and was deeply interested by his theories on psychoanalysis; he took a course in hydrotherapy at Vienna University under Winternitz, who had developed it scientifically from Priessnitz's teaching; the subject had fascinated him since his own insomnia cure. He met Lahmann, one of the leading German exponents of Nature Cure, at his clinic in Dresden, and learned that naturopaths had been advocating raw fruit and vegetables for years: but they were as ignorant as he about why they were beneficial. Finally, he went to Berlin for discussions with Rubner. The distinguished physiologist received his former pupil kindly, but was unable to shed light on the problem.

In the late autumn of 1897 he came home to Zürich at last, gathered up his family, and opened a small sanatorium, where he began putting into practice his strange new ideas on diet, together with the hydrotherapy he had learned in Vienna. His family and his fame grew together. Seven years later he was able to move to a splendid five-storey house on the edge of the Zürichberg forest: the family lived modestly on the ground floor. The other floors became his sanatorium, christened 'The Life Force'. By 1911 there was a staff of five doctors – one a psychotherapist – and a dozen nurses. Patients were coming from all over the world.

Case after case demonstrated the truth of Bircher-Benner's astonishing discovery. It was no longer possible for him to doubt that raw fresh foods healed and nourished as no other foods could. And still he asked himself why, as night after night he hunted through books, papers, journals in search of the answer. Three years later he found it, in the Second Principle of Thermodynamics.

10

'Mangez Vivant!'

Years later, the usually courteous Dr Max Bircher-Benner allowed himself a little mild sarcasm at the expense of the Berlin physiologists who fancied that they had found out everything of importance about diet when they discovered how to count calories, and the physicians who had taken them at their word – including himself.

'With what *naïveté* indeed have the medical profession hitherto treated the natural nutrition products. It was actually believed that man could exist on fats, carbohydrates and proteins, and ultimately on calories.'[1]

Von Bunge's mice had starved to death on just such diets, but this warning had been disregarded. 'Again and again we tried to treat patients with a diet based on these standards. The amount of calories . . . was prescribed and protein increased. It was a hopeless failure . . . Strange to say, this was considered scientific!'[2]

The calorie approach had indeed seemed impeccably scientific, since it brought nutrition into harmony with the First Principle of Thermodynamics, first enunciated by the physicist Julius Robert Mayer in 1842: according to this principle, the amount of energy contained in a closed system remains constant. Three years later, Liebig had shown how the warmth of an animal body is generated by the combustion of the food it consumes, while the researches of Voit, Rubner and Atwater established the direct correlation between the warmth produced and the food consumed: both were forms of the same energy, which could be expressed in calories.

When Bircher-Benner first began his studies, nothing was known of vitamins. The discovery of accessory food factors lay a dozen years ahead. Nevertheless, the calorie approach seemed to him ludicrously inadequate as an account of how man was nourished. What, after all, was a calorie? Simply a given amount of energy. By the same token 'A Beethoven symphony taken altogether constitutes a certain sum of vibrations of the air. But the same sum of vibrations will never be a symphony.' What was the nature of this energy? How did it work? Why did man need food – and not coal or wood or oil – for his nourishment? And what kinds of food?

He found himself driven into the realm of pure physics – and faced a fundamental truth about nutrition: it straddles so many fields of human knowledge – among them biology, physics and chemistry – that exceptional vision and perseverance is needed to arrive at its truths. Thus when he put specific questions to chemists or physicists, they were delighted to supply him with the answers. But when he suggested that the same truths might be applied to the field of nutrition, they shook their heads: 'It is outside my department.' Soon it became clear to him that he must plunge into physics himself if he was ever to answer his own questions. He hired a tutor and redoubled his studies.

He had at least one advantage over Liebig and his followers. They had first arrived at their hypothesis and then attempted to apply it to nutrition in practice. He was doing exactly the opposite. He had begun with an observed fact about diet which was explained in no textbook: now he was trying to account for it. Any theory could be constantly tested in practice, rather than practice strained to fit theory.

After months of weary midnight studies, he was finally satisfied that he had found the answer. Half a lifetime later, in 1936, he summed up the result of years of continued thought and study, in which he had kept up with almost every development of importance in the field of nutrition as well as of physics. The modest little work was clearly – but somewhat forbiddingly – entitled *The Essential Nature and Organization of Food Energy and the Application of the Second Principle of Thermodynamics to Food Value and its Active Force.*

First suggested by a French artillery officer, Sadi-Carnot, in 1842, the Second Principle is concerned, he pointed out, 'with the existence of order and organization in the world of energy, as well as of disorder and disorganization'. It stated that all that happens in this world tends from order to disorder, from organization to disorganization. All natural processes must be subject to this law, Bircher-Benner had reasoned, passing from energy states of high organization to those which are lower. Logically, therefore, it must be equally true in the realm of nutrition, though no man before him had ever so applied it.

All energy on earth was derived directly or indirectly from the sun's radiance. Man's food was plants, or other animals. What then were plants? They could be described as a kind of biological accumulator of light. 'Nutritional energy may thus be termed organized sunlight energy. Hence sunlight is the driving force of the cells of our body.' Since the absorption and organization of sunlight takes place almost exclusively in plants, they are 'the original food of man, from which every dish including animal products is ultimately derived'. The energy of man came, literally, from 'the re-radiation of solar energy in their plant food'.

But according to the Second Principle, any alteration which affected the energy system and organization of plants must mean a diminution of this solar energy. It followed that 'in all the altered states of food in question, every later state will be poorer in organization and intensity'. The wilting of plants, the slaughter of animals, and all the diverse preparations to which both were subjected before they arrived on the dinner table – any kind of cooking, smoking, fermenting and so on – all diminished the biological value of the foodstuff in question. The babies who developed scurvy after being fed on boiled or heat-treated milk tragically proved his point.

The organized energy of foodstuffs could be disrupted in other ways – by choosing certain parts and rejecting others, for instance. The whole grain of wheat formed what Bircher-Benner termed 'a nutritional integral, complete with minerals, vitamins, proteins, fats, carbohydrates and enzymes' – its 'correlates' intact. By extracting only the starchy endosperm and discarding the rest as pig feed, we produced a food which was only a fragment of the original biological entity, and nutritionally greatly inferior. White flour, polished rice, refined sugar were no longer whole foods.

From his own experience, and from observing patients in his clinic, Bircher-Benner also concluded that meat-eating was unhealthy: anatomical studies suggested that man was designed to be a frugivore rather than a meat-eater. But the reason why meat, as civilized man ate it, was so particularly health-threatening was, once more, because of the way we chose and prepared it. Wild animals ate their prey in its entirety – 'blood, entrails, bones, fat, skin, and flesh' in an 'optimum of correlation'. Man chose almost exclusively the protein-rich flesh. 'Flesh, however, has extremely one-sided correlations,' observed Bircher-Benner.

What was animal food, in any case, but plant food at several removes, its biological value still further destroyed by the death or slaughter of the animal and the further changes and degeneration so produced? So much for the strengthening power of the meat diet.

Why should any doctor concern himself with these altered states of food energy? For the most basic reason: they produced ill health. 'My observations of the processes of disease and healing all go to prove that these altered states cause an essential loss of organization and intensity.' Could human beings afford such losses? 'A performance of Bach's St Matthew's Passion would be considerably impaired if the mixed chorus were to lose even 10 per cent of the strength and purity of its tone.' How much more true was this of the human organism: 'The food's loss of organization results in a reduction of the energy altitude and . . . a weakening of vital processes. That signifies a loss of nutritional value or strength. And this loss affects man's functional capacity, constitution and health.' Human beings who lived on inferior food must sooner or later fall ill. And whatever form this illness took there was one supreme remedy: 'food with the optimum organization and correlates'.³

'Mangez vivant!' Bircher-Benner always urged his patients. 'Eat living food! *Pas de jour sans feuille verte* – eat green leaves every day.'

Ideally, too, the whole plant should be consumed. This didn't mean that a carrot or a cauliflower had to be consumed roots, stem, leaves, fruit, and all – simply that, ideally, every part of a plant should be represented in the day's eating: carrots or potatoes for the root, perhaps, celery for the stem, lettuce or spinach for the leaves, an apple for the fruit. Such a combination would in fact supply the widest possible range of plant nutrients.

As the fame of his clinic spread, together with reports of the extremely odd diets he fed his patients, Bircher-Benner was written off as one more of these vegetarian cranks now becoming so tiresomely common. He was nothing of the kind. He was not opposed to meat-eating on principle, and once his patients had made a full recovery on his diets of fruit and vegetable juices and salads, they were permitted to eat a little meat or fish from time to time with his blessing, if they so chose. (Many of them, as a matter of fact, felt so much better without meat that they never went back to it.) Eggs, milk, cream, cheese were all good nourishing foods, in his view, when eaten in moderation, whereas many vegetarians were opposed to animal food of any kind. Vegetarians, moreover, cared little whether their vegetables were cooked or raw, whereas for Bircher-Benner this was the supreme importance of his diet.

His determined opposition to meat-eating was based on one consideration only – that it was bad for his patients, and that without it, they recovered faster. Since he would not allow on the family table dishes that he forbade to his patients, his children were all brought up vegetarians, like the Hindhede children. (Like the Hindhede children, too, they were a delight and a credit to him, most of them becoming doctors and following eagerly in his footsteps.) But he always preferred persuasion to prohibition. So he listened sympathetically one day when one of his children complained that she was never allowed this wonderful treat that all her schoolfriends were always telling her about – succulent roasts dripping with gravy, juicy steaks, tender chicken. Before lunch next day he presented her with a little parcel. Inside it, a chunk of raw red meat. She recoiled. He sent it to the kitchen to be cooked, and insisted that she eat it. Years later she wrote with a shudder: 'It remains one of my most unpleasant memories.'

As with raw vegetables, Bircher-Benner reached his conclusions about the dangers of meat from clinical observation before he looked for the theoretical explanation and, over the years, scientific support for his views has accumulated. It has been almost entirely ignored. We still believe that Bovril will put beef into us, that athletes perform best on plenty of good red meat, that real men need steak to make them big and strong, rather than a bloodless diet of pulses and greens, and that a feast hardly deserves the name unless it features a fatted calf. To most people, protein still means meat or fish, with eggs or cheese as distinctly second-best.*

Meat-eaters can call on anthropology to bolster their preference for steaks. Nineteenth-century travellers brought home accounts of many a tribe or primitive people that lived almost entirely on meat and fish – as the Arctic explorers often had to themselves. The inhabitants of the remote Faroe Islands, a Danish colony, lived almost entirely on marine animals, birds and fish, as well as a little barley bread and a few root vegetables. They

---

*In a leaflet *Good Foods for Mothers-to-be*, prepared by the Dietetic Department of Brighton Health District, pregnant women are urged to eat daily not only an egg, a pint of milk and a little cheese but *two* helpings of meat, poultry and fish, to supply 'the protein to build baby's body and to help him grow'.

were splendidly healthy, intelligent and quick-witted, and usually lived to an advanced age. In a book that rapidly became the nutritionists' bible, *The Newer Knowledge of Nutrition* (1929), E. V. McCollum gave other examples. The Eskimos living on the north-west coast of Greenland – most remote of all the Danish colonies – ate vegetables only in the brief Arctic summer. For the rest of the year they lived on sea animals, fish and seabirds with their eggs. They had wonderful teeth, excellent physique and enjoyed rude health, 'without the slightest trace of rickets, scurvy or other evidences of malnutrition', wrote McCollum in wonderment – a fact 'interesting in the light of their restricted and simple diet'.

More recent ammunition for the anti-vegetarian has been provided by descriptions of the fiery Masai tribe in east Africa, superb warriors who live on milk and meat, particularly relishing the blood.

Hindhede might have been discomfited by these apparently powerful arguments against his thesis that meat is a killer. But Bircher-Benner would have argued that these peoples ate their meat raw in the main; that they ate it in its entirety – skin, bones, entrails and all (the explorers were always very much struck by this uncivilized habit; the tough blubbery skin of the narwhal was caviare to the Eskimos) – and that the rest of their diet, however limited, was first-class: simple vegetables usually eaten raw and whole grains. And in fact, as later travellers found, once 'civilization' arrived with the doubtful blessings of white bread and refined sugar, the health of all these peoples deteriorated as fast as their once-wonderful teeth.

All his life Bircher-Benner was suspicious of nutrition dogmas based on theory and laboratory work. He found it ludicrous that years of careful clinical observations on hundreds of patients could be brushed aside as valueless, while the scientist had the last word. Give us fifty patients each, he would say, and we'll see whose patients get well soonest.

Plenty of doctors throughout this century have had their careful observations on the connection between diet and disease dismissed out of hand in exactly the same way. Clinical observation? The scientists have a name for it. It is 'anecdotal evidence', and it isn't worth the paper it's printed on – if any reputable medical journal can be persuaded to accept it, that is.

Bircher-Benner began by attempting to interest his professional colleagues in his tremendous new nutritional discovery. When he had successfully treated his patients with raw-food therapy for three years, and felt that he could also offer an explanation from the world of physics to account for his cures, he very properly approached the Medical Society of Zürich to ask if he might put forward some interesting cases and ideas to his colleagues in the city. On a January morning in 1900 the thirty-three-year-old doctor appeared before them, the very figure of a respectable physician with his gold-rimmed spectacles, beard and black frock-coat. They listened. They could hardly believe their ears. What had the Second Principle of Thermodynamics, or some such rubbish, to do with rheumatism or rickets? No meat? Raw food? Very little protein? Dangerous nonsense. Unscientific lunacy.

At the end of his hour-long account the President addressed him more in sorrow than in anger. He had exceeded the bounds of science. He would no longer be welcome at their meetings. Or at respectable medical congresses. And certainly he would not be allowed to carry out any of his ridiculous experiments on sick people in the university hospital.

Later attempts to gain a professional hearing, to have papers published, were almost all failures. Unlike Haig or Allinson, however, Bircher-Benner was still determined to be completely correct professionally. If his ideas were correct, then sooner or later they would make themselves known whatever his critics said now. Meanwhile there was work to be done, research to be continued, and above all, sick people to be healed.

One of his deepest convictions – reinforced by contact with Freud's teachings in Vienna – was that man is a totality of body, mind and spirit, and must be treated as such. Useless to patch up the body and get it strong and healthy again if the mind still inclines towards sickness. The positive will to health must also be restored. 'A cure in his sanatorium was . . . a cure for the courageous,' wrote his son Ralph, who after his father's death took over direction of Bircher-Benner publications. 'Patients were expected to learn to conquer themselves, to overcome their disease-inducing habits.'[5] Those who expected the pampered comfort, the soft beds and the delicious table d'hôte of the typical European spa of this time were in for a horrid shock.

One of his earliest patients has left an account of this rigorous cure. The delicate twenty-two-year-old daughter of a wealthy family, she had suffered every childish ailment imaginable, and had already spent an entire year in a comfortable convalescent home. Her family doctor advised against too early a return to the rugged Swiss climate where her family lived.

Her uncle took a more detached view. How about the Bircher-Benner Clinic, he suggested – from what he had heard, it would build her up.

In November 1906 the invalid arrived. After a thorough examination, Dr Bircher-Benner assured her that she would indeed be cured, but that it would take time. Meanwhile, the house rules were explained to her . . . Get up at six, wash, and go for a walk. 'But I can't,' she protested. 'The doctors say I must spend the morning in bed!'

'Not here, Mademoiselle. But you can go back to bed after breakfast.'

She got up to the dark, chilly morning, sure she could hardly stagger round her room. 'But when I had taken a few steps outside I breathed deeply and the fresh air smelt good . . . to my surprise I walked slowly for twenty minutes.' Early rising, hours of gymnastics, walks, uneatable raw food – for days she was convinced she would crack up under the strain of this terrible regime. One morning the nurse who came to wake her found her buried beneath her quilt. She couldn't possibly get up – she had terrible cramps.

After a while, Dr Bircher-Benner himself arrived in her room, and studied her with his piercing blue eyes. A broken leg? An internal rupture? Only cramps? But nothing was better for cramps than exercise . . . this way, please – out of doors would have been better still. And how lucky that she didn't belong to the working classes who were compelled to get up and go to work no matter how ill they felt. 'To make you forget your misery a little,' he added, 'I expect you in the kitchen one hour from now. There are plenty of fresh vegetables to be prepared . . .'

Complaints about the horrors of the cold showers were received with apparent sympathy. 'Poor girl, I see how badly you are in need of them. You'll have to endure them for a long time before you learn to appreciate them.'

The endless salads were boring – tasteless? 'I do understand. It's going to take a long time to learn to enjoy the food, too. But I am in no hurry . . .'

Seventy years later, alert and vigorous at ninety-two, with four happily married children and seventeen grandchildren, this patient realized how much she owed to his gentle, teasing firmness. 'He had strengthened my will to live and developed my energy by showing me that I could work in spite of being so weak. And his regime really regenerated my body.'[6] The psychological skill of his approach had been supremely important.

Unlike modern psychotherapists, however, Bircher-Benner knew that the basis of such treatment had to be correct diet. 'A person wholesomely nourished,' he maintained, 'and not intoxicated by an overcharged metabolism is best accessible to psychological treatment, for his brain is functioning more clearly and better, and so are his capacities to think and to associate, and his desire to become healthy.'[7]

He prescribed boldly for cases the doctors had given up. One of them was his own niece Dagmar, who in the middle of her medical studies caught a mild chill – and woke to find the left side of her face paralysed, and all sensation, including taste, gone. Her uncle was a figure of awe to the entire family, and not liking to bother him she went to the hospital's ear, nose and throat department to consult the professor. To her dismay, he told her after an examination that nothing much could be done for her, and that she would have to learn to live with it. Now she went straight to her uncle.

After a very lengthy and detailed examination, he told her, 'You will recover. But you will need iron discipline and all your energy.' His prescription? Two weeks in bed on a raw-food diet, hour-long sweats every day, followed by wet-packs, galvanic treatment to the facial nerves, quiet, rest.

Within four days, Dagmar felt the muscles on the left side of her face gently move, and found that she could taste the herbs in a salad on that side too. At the end of a fortnight she was completely recovered, to the amazement of her colleagues. She went on to complete her studies and qualify; years later, she became medical director of the clinic. She noticed after her cure that her health had never been better, and that she seemed immune to colds and catarrhal complaints.

Nowadays, trained to enjoy fresh fruit and salads, most of us would find the clinic food delicious, if spare. It was presented with great art. Those with excellent teeth, Bircher-Benner said drily, might eat raw food any way they chose: they were one in a thousand. The other nine hundred and ninety-nine needed it carefully grated, sliced, chopped, juiced. Salads had appetizing dressings: olive oil, lemon juice, a little cream perhaps, some grated onions, freshly snipped chives and parsley, and other aromatic herbs. Everything must be carefully cleaned, totally fresh, and it must look and taste good; if patients didn't enjoy it, they would never persevere with the diet.

In the early years of the clinic, the idea of raw food was still, however, so novel that many patients found the food almost uneatable. The one dish which they all enjoyed – and which spread the name Bircher-Benner around Europe – was the muesli served at breakfast. The doctor came across this quite by chance. After a long walk in the mountains, he reached a shepherd's hut just as the man was sitting down to his supper. He was invited to share it: a kind of porridge made from coarsely ground wheat soaked in milk, sweetened with honey and eaten with an apple. It was a family recipe, he said: everyone ate it.

Intrigued, Bircher-Benner learned that the shepherd had eaten it for breakfast and for supper all his life. He was now seventy, he had never seen a doctor, and he never got out of breath climbing up and down the mountains. His lunch? A piece of wholemeal bread. It turned out that most of the country people roundabout ate a similar simple dish, made from oats, wheat or barley, to which they added rich creamy raw milk, straight from the cow, any fruit in season, a few nuts. This was peasant wisdom indeed; blissfully ignorant of nutritional theories, these peasant people had nonetheless devised a simple and delicious dish of uncooked food which provided in perfect and happy balance the full spectrum of nutrients needed by man – vitamins, minerals, fats, carbohydrates and all.

Muesli was introduced to the breakfast tables of the clinic, where it has been served ever since, prepared with a number of variations on the basic theme. A spoonful of oats is soaked in a little water overnight, and next morning, creamy milk and freshly pressed lemon juice are added, some freshly grated unpeeled apple is stirred in and, just before it is served, a few chopped nuts are sprinkled on top.

When Bircher-Benner first proposed his heretical new ideas to the Zürich Medical Society, almost everything known up to that time in the science of nutrition appeared to contradict them, and it must have taken a quite remarkable degree of courage to persevere in face of this fact. Over the years, however, he had the satisfaction of seeing them confirmed by a growing body of research and clinical studies, among them Chittenden's experiments with a meatless low-protein diet (p. 24), the discovery that plants were rich in vitamins – many of which were destroyed by heating or prolonged storage – and Haig's experiments with meat-free diets. The discovery that plants are rich in enzymes which allow them – as it were – to digest themselves inside the human stomach, as long as these enzymes are not destroyed by heat, was another milestone on the road to scientific recognition.* And in 1935 the distinguished German scientist Dr Werner Kollath, Professor of Hygiene at Rostock, spoke publicly of the need to apply the Second Principle of Thermodynamics to every question of life and health, and actually alluded to Bircher-Benner's work in flattering terms. Today it has been recognized by the Austrian physicist and Nobel Prizewinner Erwin Schrödinger as the law that governs human nutrition.

By this time recognition was coming from all quarters. For years he had resisted the advice urged on him to take his work to the public instead of putting up with endless medical snubs. Finally in 1925 he began publishing a very unsensational monthly journal, *Der Wendepunkt im Leben und im Leiden* ('The Turning Point in Life and Suffering'). He wrote it mainly for his patients, to explain his treatments to them and help them continue his regime once they left his care. He wrote, too, for thousands of other patients, who had never been able to afford the journey to Switzerland, or the fees of his clinic. Many of his patients, however, were both rich and influential, much too important to be brushed aside by GPs or specialists when they drew one of Bircher-Benner's articles to their attention. Slowly but surely, word spread at last even in medical circles. In the thirties medical congresses and scientific journals began inviting him to contribute, and distinguished specialists arrived in the Zürichberg Clinic to watch him at work.

And at work he remained to the very end of his life. Literally on his deathbed he dictated the last two pages of a book about the Hunza tribe who enjoyed superb health on a diet very like the one he advocated. Hours later, on 24 January 1939, he was dead.

*This evidence has been reviewed in Leslie Kenton's absorbing book *Raw Energy* (Century, 1984). Among the wealth of supporting scientific discoveries she reports is the phenomenon of leucocytosis: when cooked food first enters the stomach it is regarded as alien material by the body's immune system, which instantly responds with a muster of white corpuscles. Constantly repeated, this defensive action gradually weakens the immune system. But if a meal begins with raw food, no such defensive process occurs.

11

The North-West Frontier

I n a cleft of the Himalayas, where the north-west frontier of
Pakistan meets Afghanistan, lies the native state of Hunza.
Sheer mountain precipices tower around it on all sides to
heights of ten or fifteen thousand feet. This little state stretches
for about seven miles along the floor of the valley, beside the
river. It is remote, but not inaccessible: to reach the high and
narrow Mintake Pass across the mountains into China, you
must go through the valley of the Hunzas. And over the years,
a steady stream of European explorers, missionaries and
government officials have taken this road. Some of them, in
the late nineteenth and early twentieth century, stayed long
enough to enjoy the hospitality of its ruler, the famous Mir
Mohammed Nazim Khan, in the Hunza capital of Baltit. A few
of them have described the people of this tiny state.

One has to go to the earliest settler accounts of the North
American Indians to find rivals for the superb human specimens these travellers described.

The stamina of the Hunzas was legendary. The English
climber General Bruce recorded how in 1894 he had had to
call up the one-time Hunza Rifles. They came down from the
mountains at once, collected their kit, and 'went to Gilgit in one
march of 65 miles in very bad country'. Another observer, in
1903, was surprised to see back in Baltit, one June morning,
a messenger who had only set out a week earlier to warn a
neighbouring ruler of his own coming. In just seven days, the
messenger had travelled 280 miles on foot, much of it on a track
which often narrowed to no more than two feet wide, and twice
crossing the Mintake Pass, which is as high as Mont Blanc. 'The
messenger was quite fresh and undisturbed, and did not consider that what he had done was unusual.'[1]

No amount of physical hardship or endurance seemed to
put them out of temper, or damp their high spirits. The
explorer Captain Morris spent two months charting the Hunza

valleys and glaciers in 1927, using Hunza men for porters. 'Always ready to turn their hand to anything, they were,' he related, 'the most cheerful and willing set of men with whom I have ever travelled . . . At the worst part of all we halted in order to help the porters across. They disdained our proffered assistance, however, and came over, climbing like cats, and with never a murmur at the hardships of this day's work.'[2] This cheerfulness was as famous as their stamina – one visitor after another commented on it.

Physically, they had bodies of Grecian perfection: medium in height, broad-shouldered, with full, deep chests, narrow waists, firm, flat bellies and strong legs. Superb dancers, the very way they moved was graceful, distinctive in its speed and lightness.

And even in old age they remained vigorous: in his late sixties, the Mir could still be seen energetically captaining his polo team, and flying down the field with huge enjoyment and speed.

On few visitors, however, did they make a deeper impression than on a young British doctor, Lt.-Col. Robert McCarrison. Fresh out of medical school in Belfast, this alert and charming Irishman had sailed for India on his twenty-third birthday, in March 1901, to take up a post as regimental medical officer to the Indian troops on the North-West Frontier. Eager to distinguish himself, he lost no time in identifying the cause of a nasty three-day fever which had prostrated almost everyone at Chitral, in the summer eighteen months after his arrival. It was an infection borne by sandflies, he concluded, after hours of happy messing about with slides and tabulating statistics. (Six years later, it was officially christened sandfly fever.)

In 1904 he was appointed surgeon to the Gilgit Agency: among the scattered peoples under his care were the Hunzas.

'My own experience', he later related of the Hunzas, 'provides an example of a race unsurpassed in perfection of physique and in freedom from disease in general, whose sole food consists to this day of grains, vegetables and fruits, with a certain amount of milk and butter, and goat's meat only on feast days . . . Amongst these people the span of life is extraordinarily long; and such service as I was able to render them during some seven years spent in their midst was confined chiefly to the treatment of accidental lesions, the removal of senile

cataract, plastic operations for granular eyelids, or the treatment of maladies wholly unconnected with food supply.
Appendicitis, so common in Europe, was unknown.'3

Their abounding health was hard to account for: 'When
the severe nature of the winter in that part of the Himalayas is
considered, and the fact that their housing accommodation and
conservancy arrangements are of the most primitive, it becomes
obvious that the enforced restriction to the unsophisticated
foodstuffs of nature is compatible with long life, continued vigour, and perfect physique.'4

Much more fascinating at first to the ambitious young
medical officer were the wretched group of Gilgit villages
where the hideously swollen and distorted necks of goitre were
to be seen on all sides, together with the rolling eyes and vacant
stare of cretinism, or hereditary goitre. In one of these villages
there was not a single case, but in another, nearly half the
people were affected.

In a masterpiece of careful and methodical research,
McCarrison established that the villain of the piece appeared
to be contaminated water; that when the contaminated water
was boiled, those drinking it no longer developed goitre, that
unboiled, it gave goitre to a small group of volunteers including
himself – and very unpleasant it was, too – though the condition
could luckily be reversed by doses of a bactericide. Medical
research had firmly linked goitre with iodine deficiency, but
this seemed not to be the explanation of the Gilgit goitres.

McCarrison's work so impressed his superiors that in 1913
he was officially moved to a research posting in Kasauli. By this
time he had heard of the work being done by Eijkman and
Grijns with beriberi, using pigeons as experimental animals;
and he now began to investigate the possibility that in goitre
too there might be a dietary connection . . . a line of thought
encouraged by learning of Gowland Hopkins's and Funk's
suggestions about 'vitamines' as food factors indispensable to
health.

The First World War interrupted these researches, since
he was called up for military service. But the war itself made
plain how badly his work was needed. On more than one
occasion, Indian troops had been unable to fight because they
were laid low by beriberi or scurvy. And in 1918, in an empty
room at the Pasteur Institute in Coonoor, in the Blue Mountains of south India, McCarrison resumed his studies of
deficiency disease. He had one untrained assistant borrowed

from the local post office and a microscope, and that was more or less all. From time to time, in 1919 and 1920, he submitted papers to Indian or British medical journals. Then in 1920 a spell of leave in England allowed him to catch up on the now rather daunting volume of nutritional research, double-check his own work, sort through his notes and publish the result as *Studies in Deficiency Diseases* (1921). Almost every line of it remains painfully relevant today.

Most nutrition researchers had set out to produce specific deficiency diseases in their experimental animals, and then reverse them by feeding the 'missing' factor. McCarrison did exactly the opposite. He fed his experimental animals on diets known to be disease-producing – polished and overcooked rice was the most successful of these – and then meticulously examined his victims to find out just what had happened to them. He found that almost every organ of their bodies was affected, while the digestive system never escaped. Some of the glands of his experimental pigeons – especially the thymus and the spleen – withered away almost to nothing; sexual organs shrank; so did the liver and the pancreas. Only the adrenal glands – first of the body's defence system to be mobilized in crisis – were enlarged.

In the course of his medical work, in the army, and among both the European and native population of India, McCarrison had observed and studied a depressing range of sub-healthy conditions, as well as actual disease. 'Who in the ranks of practising physicians is not familiar,' he asked, 'among the well-to-do classes, with the spoilt child of pale, pasty complexion and unhealthy appetite, of sluggish bowel . . . the "highly strung", "nervous" child of "delicate digestion". . . [the] static, constipated, unhealthy-skinned adolescent . . .? Who is not familiar with the overworked, anaemic girl . . . with . . . acne or seborrhoea and sometimes vague psychoses, who ekes out a paltry wage for teaching, sewing or selling . . . satisfying the cravings of her tissues principally with white bread, margarine and tea? . . . or with the harassed mother of children, oppressed with the constant struggle to make ends meet, exhausted by childbearing . . . worry and too little of the right food?'

Among rich or poor alike, the common blessings of civilization all too often include 'anaemia, loss of appetite, dyspepsia,

pain in the stomach, flatulence, debility, neuralgia, neurasthenia, headache, disordered action of the heart, colitis, stasis,
and visceroptosis'.

McCarrison deplored the tunnel vision so common among
nutrition researchers, and their unhesitating assumption that
gross deficiency states, such as polyneuritis, scurvy or rickets,
were the only consequences of a diet poor in 'vitamines'. Dozens
of trials with his experimental animals had shown him that this
was far from being the case. 'Long before nervous symptoms
supervene,' he pointed out, 'others, such as loss of appetite,
impaired digestion, diarrhoea, colitis, unhealthy skin, low temperature, slow respiration, cardio-vascular depression, progressive anaemia, and asthenia result from the deficient and ill-
balanced food . . . It is to my mind with these earlier evidences
of disease . . . that we as physicians are mainly concerned in
practice.'

One of the most keenly observant of all researchers,
McCarrison noticed other highly significant facts about his
pigeons and monkeys on their defective diets.

He noticed that poor high-starch diets invariably led to a
weakening of the entire digestive system and gastro-intestinal
function.

He noticed that on poor diets, resistance to infection was
drastically lowered. Of 142 pigeons who had developed polyneuritis on his heated rice diet, 94 showed evidence of septi-
caemic infections, compared to only 6 among 63 control
pigeons. There was plenty of human evidence to confirm this
finding. During the German occupation of Lille in 1917, when
the French lived on near-starvation rations, there was an actual
epidemic of glandular tuberculosis. McCarrison might have
added the great influenza epidemic of 1918, which swept
through ill-nourished post-war Europe to produce deathrates
of up to 30 per cent and kill more people than the war itself:
in Great Britain alone, over 150,000 died of it.

The ravages of poor diet were always aggravated, McCarrison pointed out, by lack of fresh air, overcrowding and poor
hygiene.

And he noticed, finally, one other significant fact: that
the effects of his disease-producing diets varied astonishingly
among his experimental animals. Of twelve birds fed on heated
white rice, the first developed polyneuritis after only four
weeks, while the last of them got it two months later. McCarrison thought this finding so important that he stressed it over

and over again. It must be realized, he said, that a degree of vitamin deficiency 'which may produce ill effects in one individual may not do so in another . . . Indeed, it may be said that no two individuals will, with respect to symptoms and time of their onset, exhibit precisely the same response . . .' In nutritional terms, there is no such thing as the average man.

McCarrison pounced on another nutrition myth rapidly taking root: that we're all getting plenty of vitamins in our diet if we're eating at all. 'It is often stated that vitamins are so widely distributed amongst naturally occurring foodstuffs that the variety of foods consumed by European people protects them – in times of peace – from risk of any deficiency in these essential substances . . .' How could this possibly be true, he asked his readers. Millions of children were no longer breast-fed but reared on heated milk and processed baby-foods 'vastly inferior to mother's milk'. Cows' milk and butter were luxuries few of the poor could afford. Fresh fruit was a rarity even on the tables of the well-off. Few people ate green vegetables – and then so overcooked as to lose all food value. White bread had largely replaced wholemeal bread – and many people ate little else. Sugar was now eaten 'in quantities unheard of a century ago'. Meat contained few vitamins – and many of these were lost in the freezing and thawing now so common. Even those who could afford to eat better seldom did so: 'prejudice, ignorance, habit often prevent the proper use and choice of health-giving foods'.[5]

This nutritional myth has proved even more resilient. Even today, in the eighties, when dozens of surveys have shown that few people get even the Recommended Daily Allowances (RDAs – see p. 172) of all nutrients in their diet, it is still echoed on all sides: 'vitamins . . . are so widely distributed that no mixed diet is seriously deficient'.

It was another British biochemist, Jack Drummond, who pointed out in the thirties that only one foodstuff was rich in the vital B complex: 'the germ of most of the cereals' – carefully removed from white bread and white rice.

From his own experience as a doctor, McCarrison had found how effective a good diet could be in treating a wide range of diseases. He gave examples, among them the nine-year-old son of a wealthy family who was pale, thin and weedy, with dreadful teeth, boils and a miserable appetite. His appalling nightmares horrified his parents. His medical history told of bouts of croup and bronchitis, and appalling stomach aches.

His endless treatments had included the removal of his tonsils and adenoids, breathing exercises to correct his hollow chest, a daily cold bath and gymnastics. McCarrison had seen his monkeys in just the same poor shape, so he asked the boy's mother what he ate. Porridge and treacle, with fried bacon and egg or fishcakes for breakfast, with boiled milk; stewed or roast meat for lunch with boiled vegetables, followed by an old-fashioned English pudding with custard or treacle sauce; bread and butter for tea; Ovaltine and biscuits for supper.

McCarrison suggested, instead, a big glass of fresh milk with egg yolk beaten up in it, followed by oatcakes with fresh butter and an apple for breakfast; freshly cooked beef or mutton for lunch with potatoes cooked in milk, a tomato and lettuce salad, stewed fruit, oatcake and cheese; no tea, and supper the same as breakfast.

The pallid little boy was transformed before the eyes of his delighted parents. 'This is delicious!' he cried, as he sat down to his new menus. He put on weight, the nightmares went away, colour returned to his cheeks. Soon he was another normal, healthy little boy.

There are millions of people who in their entire lives never feel 'extraordinarily well'. McCarrison was surrounded by them. In glowing contrast, the Hunzas returned again and again to his mind as examples of a people who seldom experienced a lesser physical condition. Among them, he recalled, 'I never saw a case of asthenic dyspepsia, of gastric or duodenal ulcer, of appendicitis, of mucous colitis or cancer.' The elegant Western complaint of a stomach 'over-sensitive' to cold, fatigue or nerves was simply unknown to them. In fact, they hardly seemed aware of their stomachs at all unless they were hungry. 'Their buoyant abdominal health has, since my return to the West, provided a remarkable contrast with the dyspeptic and colonic lamentations of our highly civilized communities.'[6]

It was often assumed that the legendary good health of the Hunzas was a piece of tremendous racial luck. Tall, lithe, fair, they didn't even look like their nearest neighbours; indeed, it was rumoured that they were descended directly from Alexander's conquering soldiers. But among the racial patchwork of India, McCarrison had noticed, there were others who came very near the Hunzas in their superb physique and health: there were, first and foremost, the Sikhs and the Pathans. McCarrison's own chief assistant, Sirdar Bahadur Mula Singh, was a Sikh who had first joined him in 1913 and followed him to Coonoor – a magnificent and commanding figure with a glossy black beard. McCarrison used to point him out to visitors to the laboratories as a wonderful example of what a good diet could do for you. For the Sikhs, as a matter of fact, lived on very much the same kind of diet as the Hunzas. They ate wholewheat *chapattis*, a little butter, plenty of raw milk, sprouted peas, little fruit, but plenty of vegetables, normally eaten raw.

The further south you went in India, however, the poorer the health and physique you saw around you, with the wretched Madrassi people coming lowest on the scale. The Madrassi lived on rice – white, thoroughly washed, boiled; they ate little or no fresh fruit or vegetables; they seldom drank milk or ate any form of dairy product, and for religious reasons, they ate almost no meat. The contrast between Sikh and Madrassi was striking.

It occurred to McCarrison that no better way of demonstrating the unique importance of diet to health could be found than by taking colonies of rats and feeding them on a number of these varied diets.

Odd as it may seem, this was a startlingly original idea.

Almost all nutrition experiments up to this time had been conducted with highly artificial diets, with a single lone nutrient either added or subtracted. But in real life, nobody eats like this. Nobody lives on boiled white rice alone – or milk – or oats. So nobody's diet is ever likely to be 100 per cent deficient in any one vitamin. The purified artificial diets looked impressively scientific, and they had produced a great deal of vital information, but what they could never reveal was what diets eaten out in the real world, beyond the laboratory, actually did to people.

This is what McCarrison now set out to do.

Seven groups of twenty young rats, all of similar age, weight and number of males or females, were kept in big airy cages, and fed seven different typical Indian diets for twenty weeks. Then they were all weighed, their weights averaged out, and the Mr Average in each group sent to join the line-up. From the plump sleek rat on the left, fed on the Sikh diet, their size and condition deteriorated with mathematical regularity down to the weedy little specimen fed the Madrassi diet. Since they all came from much the same stock, and were housed in identical large and airy cages, it could not be claimed that either heredity or environment was responsible for this startling difference.

So delightfully convincing was this experiment that thereafter McCarrison fed all his stock rats – from whose numbers came those he used for experiments – on the Sikh diet. The result was an object-lesson in nutrition. 'Never have I seen such sleek, glossy-looking furred animals,' wrote one visitor.* The laboratory staff were proud of their healthy rats. They used to show new students a litter of day-old rats from these splendid mothers, and stake the Institute's reputation on their survival till they were weaned. They never lost a bet.

McCarrison carried out a number of these whole-diet experiments. The unlucky rats fed the British working-class diet of white bread and marge, over-sweetened tea with a little milk, boiled vegetables and tinned meat, came off worst of all. Stunted and nervous, with lacklustre coats, they snapped at the attendant and took to cannibalism after three days; after they'd killed and eaten three of their number, they were segregated, to die of pneumonia and a variety of gastro-intestinal disorders.

Nothing else was needed to convince McCarrison. There was one great, all-important cause of ill health: poor diet based on artificially fragmented, processed and heated foodstuffs. (A diet, Bircher-Benner would have said, of low biological value, its solar energy dissipated, its nutritional integrity destroyed.)

Furthermore, he was convinced, no matter how much nutrition research might be carried out in future, no matter how many more letters of the alphabet might be needed to christen newly discovered nutrients, they would one and all be found to exist 'in the foods made in nature's laboratory'.

But his observations and his researches had taken him even further than this. In studying the extraordinary range of humanity that surrounded him in India, and in particular the sensational physical superiority of such peoples as the Sikhs, or the tall, athletic highland Pathans of the North-West Frontier Provinces, McCarrison had at first concluded that it was chiefly their diet, together with plenty of exercise and a hardy outdoor lifestyle, that made the difference.

But even compared with Sikhs and Pathans, there was an edge of incomparable physical perfection to the superb Hunzas. Was it their diet? Sikhs and Pathans ate very similar foodstuffs. The mountain air, perhaps, or something special in their situation? Yet neighbouring tribes – some enjoying even more sunshine – were 'sour, goitrous, dirty, devoid of all joy of life'. The only obvious difference was in their methods of cultivation.

The Sikhs and Pathans, like rural people throughout the East, cultivated their fields with manure, the only cheap and widely available fertilizer. But as cultivators the Hunzas were unique. Their valley was irrigated by the huge Berber aqueduct which their ancestors had built in an astonishing feat of engineering; it brought them an unfailing supply of water and mineral-rich glacial silt. Their fields were carefully terraced by walls built of huge slabs of stone; observant travellers were reminded of antique Inca methods. And every scrap of organic waste – animal and human excreta, vegetable scraps, the ashes from their fires – were carefully returned by them to the land, after preparation in deep byres, together with glacial silt collected from special channels in the aqueduct.

As early as 1926, McCarrison had carried out experiments that tested the nutritional value of wheat or millet grown in manured earth against that grown in artificially fertilized land: they showed a significant difference in the growth and health of experimental rats or pigeons.

By this time, too, he was certainly familiar with the work of Sir Albert Howard at Pusa.

In 1904, Lord Curzon had had set up at Pusa an experimental station for the study of India's agricultural problems. In 1905, Albert Howard, the son of an old English farming family, and a brilliant scholar – he came first in all England in the Cambridge Agricultural Diploma in 1897 – was appointed as its Imperial Chemical Botanist. For fifteen years he directed remarkable research work at Pusa, including the development of disease-resistant strains of wheat. Howard came to his post free of any notion that Western ideas and methods must infallibly be superior. On the contrary, he was ready to learn, and he had been greatly influenced by studying Eastern methods of cultivation, in which organic wastes were returned to the soil as fertilizer – a system which had allowed the Chinese to till the same soil uninterruptedly for forty centuries.

In 1925 Howard set up his own experimental station at Indore where he combined scientific expertise with Eastern agricultural traditions to evolve the Indore composting system, soon to be famous around the world. In all this time, he slowly became aware of some surprising facts.

Already by 1910, he later wrote, 'I had learned a great deal from my new instructors – how to grow healthy crops practically free from disease without any help from mycologists, entomologists, bacteriologists, agricultural chemists, statisticians, clearing-houses of information, artificial manures, spraying machines, insecticides, fungicides, germicides, and all the expensive paraphernalia of the modern experimental station.'[8]

Could this disease-immunity be transferred, he wondered, to the cattle grazing such crops? He obtained droves of oxen, kept in the most hygienic conditions, fed on compost-grown fodder. 'After a short time my oxen duly came in contact with other oxen, suffering, among other things, from foot-and-mouth disease. I have myself seen my cattle rubbing noses with foot-and-mouth cases. Nothing happened. The healthy, well-fed animal reacted towards this disease process exactly as improved and properly cultivated crops did to insects and fungi – no infection occurred.'[9]

As with man, so with animals and crops, in an unending cycle of health.

McCarrison returned to England in 1935 an advocate of all these uncomfortable truths. In his Cantor lectures, delivered in 1936 at the invitation of the Royal Society of Arts, he was eloquent on the subject.

> Agricultural practice is linked with the quality of food, with nutrition and with health . . . Out of the earth are we and plants and animals that feed us created, and to the earth we must return the things whereof we and they are made if it is to yield again foods of a quality suited to our needs . . .'[10]

12
The Standard for Health

By the mid-thirties the health of the British had become a major national preoccupation. There were certainly no grounds for self-congratulation.

The 1914–18 recruiting figures, released when the war was over, had revealed a C3 nation. Of the 2,425,184 men who had offered themselves for the service of their country, only 36 per cent were judged Grade I, while 10 per cent were found hopelessly unfit for any service at all. Even in the much less exacting Grade II – for those capable of such physical exertion as did not involve too great a strain – only 22 per cent made it. These figures were bad enough, but took on particularly ominous implications when it was recalled that those who volunteered naturally did not include the most obviously sick or unfit.

The nation's children were in no better shape. Of 2,400,000 schoolchildren examined in 1922, according to the Chief Medical Officer for England and Wales, 42.2 per cent were found mentally or physically defective to some degree, with poor eyesight, terrible teeth, and nose and throat ailments widespread; rickets, scurvy and anaemia were common; infant mortality was disgracefully high. These diseases had been supposed to be due largely to bad housing and sanitary conditions. Now dozens of careful studies by nutrition experts showed that poor diet might be equally to blame.

If poor diets make for poor health, what kinds of diet lead to improvements in health? This was the logical question to which nutrition studies then moved. One of the most interesting of these focused on milk, indicated by McCollum's work as one of the most important 'protective foods'. Large numbers of Scottish schoolchildren were given an extra daily pint of milk. It had been assumed that they were already eating fairly good diets. But with the simple addition of the milk, the difference was noticeable almost immediately. Their growth rate accelerated by about 20 per cent, and there was a very obvious improvement in general health and vitality.

As more became known about nutrition, the extent to which poor food was responsible for poor development and stunted growth in our children could be ignored no longer. By the thirties, thousands of the neediest children were getting school dinners provided for them free, and free milk.

Administrative action cannot be based on guesswork, however, and before more could be done, there was an obvious need to know exactly where the breadline could be drawn. In 1933 the British Medical Association set up a committee to make an estimate based on scientific fact rather than inspired guesswork. Their answer was reckoned in shillings and pence: on an outlay of 5s. 1d. per head per week, spent on a maximum of protective foods as well as cheap fillers like white bread, the poor could just about scrape through without actually contracting rickets, anaemia and outright scurvy.

Meanwhile, the national health was clearly not improving, as a number of surveys made throughout the thirties showed.

One of the most comprehensive of these was carried out by the Rowett Institute in Aberdeen. Its findings were published as a report, *Food, Health and Income*, by its director, Sir John Boyd Orr. This distinguished Scotsman had begun his career as a divinity student, but an irrepressible urge to help his needy countrymen in a more practical way took him into medicine instead. The pathetic victims of malnutrition that he saw in the children's wards of Glasgow's hospitals, it was said, had aroused his interest in the study of nutrition – and he returned to university to pursue it. Throughout his career he remained a practical working farmer – a fact which gave him a uniquely broad perspective on the subject of health.

In making his survey, Orr did not adopt the BMA's minimum as his standard. Instead, he used the available nutrition knowledge to construct what he called an 'optimum diet' – one which would bring about 'such a high level of health and physical well-being that no improvement could be effected'.[1]

His survey showed that such a diet was hopelessly beyond the reach of at least half the population, while only one sixth – those spending more than 14s. a head weekly on food – exceeded it in every respect.

In the big industrial conurbations of the North, the number of those below Orr's nutritional Plimsoll line rose as high as 68 per cent. In many of these families, the diet was little different to that of Victoria's poor. They still filled their empty stomachs with white bread and jam, and drank over-sweetened tea by the gallon. It was the vegetables, the milk, the eggs and the meat which disappeared from the shopping-lists of the needy, because they cost so much. The poorest families were buying 1.8 pints of milk a head weekly and 1½ eggs: the better off bought 5½ pints of milk and 4½ eggs.

Ill health was often the direct result of poor housing and insanitary conditions. A survey carried out in Stockton-on-Tees in 1936 by the city's medical officer of health, Dr G. C. M. McGonigle, showed that whereas the mortality rate among those reasonably well housed and fed was 9 per thousand, it rose to around 30 per thousand among poorly fed slum dwellers. But Dr McGonigle went on to prove that, of the two factors, diet was by far the most important. Studying a group of families who had been moved from appalling slums into a lovely new housing estate, with running water on tap, he was amazed to find that their mortality rates were actually higher than those in the slums they had left behind. The explanation was simple. The rent was much higher too, so they had less money to spend on food.

A rather different kind of survey was carried out by Seebohm Rowntree in York, in 1936. After much study, he calculated the cheapest possible diet on which a family with three children could still remain fairly healthy. His diet was dreary in the extreme – and not half so filling or so nourishing as those Allinson had contrived. He substituted marge for butter, skimmed tinned milk for fresh whole milk. He assumed, too, that his houswives would bake their own bread since it would be so much cheaper to do so. This was his menu for one day:

Breakfast: porridge with skimmed milk; bacon, bread and marge or fried bread; tea.

Dinner: beef roll, mashed potatoes and salad, steamed date pudding.

Tea: tea, bread and marge, watercress.

Supper: lentil soup (remains from previous day) and bread.

It is hard to believe that health could have been long maintained on a diet as stodgy as this; hard to believe that housewives struggling to make ends meet would have time and inclination to make their own bread as well as whipping up tasty puddings and soups; it is almost impossible to believe that the British working man would have put up with a diet so spare and unappetizing, however nutritious. The reality was much more likely to be fish and chips from the corner shop, for a tea that would at least fill a man's stomach.

Poor and unappealing as Rowntree's diet was, though, even this was beyond the reach of millions, according to his calculations. And even if the income of these millions were brought up to his minimum, approximately one third of all British children would still be undernourished for the most vital five years of their growth and development.

Much more realistic estimates of nutritional needs were made by the United States Department of Agriculture in 1933, the same year as the BMA's 5s. 1d. report. The report of their Bureau of Home Economics detailed amounts of basic foodstuffs and listed their nutrient composition as well. Two years later, in 1935, the League of Nations set up an international committee of experts to draw up dietary standards for mothers, adolescents and children. Those adopted were those of optimum health. To harassed administrators and doctors all over Europe struggling with the same problem, they must have seemed Utopian indeed: 12½ pints of milk a week for pregnant or nursing women and for children; 7 eggs a week for children and for expectant mothers.

The question of what the nation should eat was the subject of acrimonious debate throughout the thirties. On one side were ranged most nutrition experts, a handful of doctors, numbers of those involved in welfare and administration – and a number of earnest lay people who in lectures, books and newspapers told the British how appallingly badly they ate.

'On the other hand', reported Orr,

> were those who regarded food as nothing more than a trade commodity . . . Most of these people retained the old idea of food requirements and regarded malnutrition as merely a newfangled name for starvation. As there was practically no family suffering from actual hunger, demands for the abolition of malnutrition were apt to be regarded as a political stunt, and those scientists . . . who were enthusiasts for the application of the new knowledge of nutrition, as food faddists and a nuisance in the political world.[2]

In the absence of agreement between all these factions, the whole question bristled with difficulties.

The world economic crisis of 1929 had brought food gluts in all the major food-producing countries as incomes fell. Enormous quantities of foodstuffs were dumped on the world's markets at whatever price they would fetch. For the protection of their agriculture, most European countries raised tariff barriers to keep out the flood. Britain, like Holland, raised no such barriers and the cheap foodstuffs came flooding in. This met with the warm approval of the manufacturing vote, since cheap food kept the wages bill low, and thus helped British manufactured goods to be competitive in world markets. But it had a devastating impact on British agriculture, as prices for home produce fell.

The Conservative Minister for Agriculture, Sir Walter Elliot, shared his party's enthusiasm for promoting exports. But as a doctor who represented a Glasgow slum constituency in Parliament, he did not see the ruin of British agriculture, with its terrible consequences for the land itself, as being in the interests of anyone. Cheap imported foodstuffs – tea, white sugar, white flour, canned meat and fish – had made little contribution to a balanced diet for the nation. And as a first step to save British farming from bankruptcy, the Agricultural Marketing Acts of 1931 and 1932 set up a number of Marketing Boards, whose members were elected by the food producers they represented and whose object was to fix prices and production quotas. But the wisdom of this policy was soon questioned. As the evidence of widespread malnutrition became too glaring to be ignored, the government gradually changed its tune. Soon the Boards were being referred to as a purely emergency measure. A food policy, it became clear, would have to be evolved by trial and error. Perhaps the answer might be not lower production, but higher consumption. Instead of setting up the expected Meat Marketing Board, Elliot appointed a Fat Stock Commission. Instead of meat prices being allowed to rise to the point where production became profitable, the farmers were given a Treasury subsidy.

The Milk Marketing Board had already briskly raised the price of milk. Now Elliott appointed a commission to review the Board's activities. If the changes they recommended had been made, milk production and prices, too, would have ended up more or less in government control. There were violent objections from the dairying industry to swell the chorus of protest.

A new Minister of Agriculture was appointed, and nothing further was done until the outbreak of war in 1939 changed the situation overnight.

But the cumulative effect of so many surveys, revealing such misery, needless sickness and preventable death throughout the nation – particularly among children – gradually shamed even the most diehard Tory into a change of heart.

In the House of Commons politicians from all parties formed the Children's Minimum Council to publicize the facts and campaign for action. The need for action was now admitted on almost all sides. A National Committee on Nutrition, set up by the government in 1937, adopted the comparatively generous standards of the League of Nations, rather than the Scrooge-like minimum of the BMA 1933 Committee.

Gradually matters improved, thanks in large part to extra milk for children, nursing mothers and pregnant women, to extensions of the school meals scheme, to increases in outdoor relief and family allowances for the unemployed. By 1939, the consumption of the protective foodstuffs – milk, green vegetables, eggs, cheese, meat, fish – had increased by about 50 per cent over the past twenty years; blatant cases of scurvy and rickets were now comparatively rarely seen in hospitals. The number of babies dying before they reached their first birthday fell by 50 per cent. And children leaving school were 2–3 in (5–7.5 cm) taller than their parents had been at the same age.

In the eyes of many, these were solid achievements, but to others, they offered few grounds for congratulation. Orr himself was angrily aware that animals were better fed than people in Britain. The Rowett Institute in Aberdeen – of which he was director – richly endowed, lavishly equipped and staffed, had been founded to study the nutrition of people, as well as the experimental animals with which their practical work was done. The work on which the BMA's recommendations in 1933 had been based was carried out at the Rowett. But while farmers, vets and agricultural specialists studied the publications of the Rowett with the liveliest interest, doctors paid little attention to them. And while the BMA was happy to recommend the very minimum amounts of nutrients that these studies suggested as adequate for men, women and children, no stock-breeder would have consented for a minute to accept them for animals. Only the best was good enough for them. 'Their rations', commented Orr,

are planned to provide all the vitamins, minerals and protein needed for the highest possible state of health. It has
been found that this is a paying proposition. The productive capacity of the animal is raised to its highest level,
and the incidence of disease among well-fed animals is
less than among animals fed on a lower standard. The
standard for health, however, has not yet been applied to
the human race.[3]

When this standard was applied, the picture that emerged
was dark. Orr calculated that on the outbreak of war, only a
third of the population were living above this standard; another
third more or less achieved it, and the diet of the remaining
third fell well below.

In times of war, the fitness, the will to win and the general
alertness of the fighting forces and of the civilian population
become military necessities. Super-nutrition – or at least the
very best that can be done in the circumstances – then becomes
'a paying proposition' for human beings too, and obstacles melt
away.

But in pre-war Britain, these obstacles were formidable.
One of the greatest was the widespread lack of either enthusiasm or knowledge – or even interest – among doctors. There is
a great deal of evidence to show that while the British Medical
Association, through its Nutrition Committee, was officially
involved in the subject, this was by no means true of doctors in
general. Doctors are among the most conservative of people at
the best of times – hostile to innovation even when it promises
major advances in the conquest of pain or disease (one thinks
of Semmelweiss and Lister), slow to change their minds or alter
their methods. Those doctors who had reached positions of
eminence in the thirties had been at medical school before vitamins had been heard of, and when malnutrition meant either
hunger or starvation. They accepted now (some of them grudg-
ingly) that scurvy, rickets and beriberi were diseases caused by
defective food, but for the vast majority of them that was as far
as the new science of nutrition went.

Not even the astonishing success of the Hay diet – as famous in the USA and Britain in the thirties as the F-Plan Diet is
today – could induce them to change their minds and consider
how changes in eating habits might revolutionize health care.

Dr William Howard Hay had been as indifferent on the
subject of diet as any of his colleagues when he first began to
practise in 1893. Sixteen years later, seriously ill with kidney

problems, high blood pressure and a dilated heart, he embarked on a dietary revolution, undoubtedly inspired by Tilden and by Hygienic teachings. After three months of eating 'fundamentally', his health was completely recovered, he had shed nearly four stone, he was able to run long distances and he felt years younger. Putting his patients on to the same diet, he found 'many cases of supposedly incurable disease that have recovered completely', and all of his patients reporting that 'their health is now at the highest point it has ever attained'.[4]

The Hay rules for happy eating – explained in his best-seller *A New Health Era* – were simplicity itself. Don't mix foods that fight – never eat concentrated starches and proteins at the same meal. Eat fats, starches, sugars and proteins only in small amounts, making vegetables and fruit 80 per cent of your diet; and avoid refined starches and sugars altogether. *A New Health Era* was published in Britain in 1935. Among its earliest fans was a young woman in her twenties, Doris Grant, who cured herself, in just four weeks, of severe rheumatism. Astonished and impressed, she wrote a series of articles for the *Sunday Graphic* which provoked so huge a reader response that it ran on and on, for over nine months. Hundreds of letters poured into the *Graphic*'s offices, and direct to Doris Grant when she followed the articles up with a book of recipes called *The Hay Diet*. Readers told how the Hay system of compatible eating had changed their lives almost overnight, clearing their minds, banishing overweight problems, ending the urge for between-meal snacks, and improving overall health to a quite astonishing extent.*

The British medical profession remained unimpressed. The theory of compatible eating was, they were assured by nutrition experts, the greatest nonsense. And few of them were ready to believe that changes in diet might succeed where drugs and surgery had proved powerless. A striking exception was Sir Arbuthnot Lane. One of the most outstanding surgeons this country has ever produced, he had pioneered a number of surgical *tours de force*, the most famous of which was his oper-ation for the removal of the large colon. In case after case, he had found that other serious health problems, which had

*In a unique tribute to the efficacy of the Hay diet, Mrs Grant – who has remained faithful to it ever since – published another book about it, together with Jean Joice, just half a century later. *Food Combining for Health* (1984) has attracted a similar huge postbag from readers eager to tell her how they have benefited from it.

appeared to have no connection with the colon, cleared up rapidly once this offending piece of plumbing was removed. 'What can be more startling', Lane asked readers of the book he wrote on the subject,

> than the effect of colectomy upon a case of acute rheuma-toid arthritis! One sees a patient who has lain on her back in agony for many months, or even years, dreading any movement in her swollen and painful joints. Within twen-ty-four hours after the colon has been removed the patient is able to move every joint in which bony ankylosis had not previously existed, *with great freedom and with absence of pain.*[5]

In 1911 Alexis Carrel, working at the Rockefeller Insti-tute, stunned the scientific world with the news that he had successfully grown living tissue cells in a culture, and that they grew and prospered as long as they were nourished and their excretions daily removed. On a visit to New York, Lane called on Carrel, and saw the cells with his own eyes. What impressed him was the fact that the daily evacuation was as vital to their health as nourishment. 'When the drainage of these tissues is not properly attended to, the component cells do not die of starvation, but of auto-intoxication. The same applies to humanity in general . . . an immense number die from consti-pation and its innumerable consequences.'[6]

He had seen those consequences himself dozens of times on the operating table: colons which had turned into cesspools of stagnating matter, in which the normal intestinal flora had mutiplied and become virulent in the decomposing contents.

> These micro-organisms irritate and inflame the mucous membrane, causing painful spasms of the muscle wall, and this inflammatory process readily involves that little worm-like body, the appendix. Indeed, it is not unusual for the symptoms resulting from inflammation of the appendix *to be the first serious symptoms of the effects of constipation.*[7]

These micro-organisms, having multiplied in the colon, spread upwards to the small intestine – and were thence carried by the blood to every part of the body, together with the toxins they produced, to give rise to disease of every kind, including colitis, appendicitis, stomach ulcers, prostate problems, gout and eventually cancer. Lane named the condition chronic intes-tinal toxaemia.

A disease which can be cured by a masterpiece of surgery is respectable, and the condition was christened Lane's disease in tribute to the great man.

Having seen the need for daily evacuation, however, Lane, to his eternal credit, stopped removing his patients' colons and sent them away with a diet-sheet and the urgent advice to give up white bread. Taking advantage of his eminence, he founded the New Health Society and campaigned tirelessly for wholemeal bread. 'White bread is the curse of the age!' was his cry.

Not even Sir Arbuthnot's great status could win many doctors round to this viewpoint. In response to this dangerous propaganda, the millers restored to a strategic masterstroke. They polled a thousand doctors throughout the country to ask their views on white bread: 80·1 per cent replied that it was an excellent nutritious food in a mixed diet; 89 per cent replied that they ate it themselves.

Most of the British public continued to enjoy their white bread, now made even whiter with chemical bleaching agents. Their interest in nutrition was mild or non-existent, apart from a certain curiosity about the intriguing 'vitamins', discoveries of which were announced at intervals throughout the thirties. In 1937, Sir William Crawford published *The People's Food*, the results of what amounted to a massive public opinion poll on diet, for which over five thousand families, drawn equally from all social classes, in seven big cities, had been interviewed. One of the questions housewives were asked was whether they were 'interested' in magazine and newspaper articles dealing with food, recipes and diet generally. A bare third of classes A A and A said that they were, against 65·9 per cent who said that they were not. In class B, the rate dropped to 26·6 per cent who were interested; in class C to 17·0 per cent; in class D – the poorest – to 8·2 per cent. Even this interest was usually referred either to slimming, or to worries about whether they were feeding the babies and children properly. The words 'vitamin' or 'nutrition' were hardly ever used.

'To mention the question of diet then was to label oneself immediately as a crank of the first order,' recalled Stanley Lief, one of the pioneers of Nature Cure in this country.[8]

13

'The Right Feeding of Our People'

The Swedish health reformer Are Waerland, who spent some time in England in the thirties, was deeply shocked by the indifference of British doctors on matters of diet – 'the very profession whose business it should be to look after the health of the people has not only entirely neglected to watch and study these changes, but loathes and despises any attempts in that direction'. Into this vacuum had swarmed numbers of ill-informed and absurd cranks who damned the whole subject by association. These fanatics, in Waerland's view, 'obscured the importance of food reform in the minds of most onlookers, actually scaring away many who in their choice between ridicule and ill health prefer the latter'.[1]

Some of these 'cranks' were perfectly serious and intelligent exponents of Nature Cure, imported into Britain from the United States at the turn of the century. Others were vegetarians who denounced meat-eating on a number of grounds – often quasi-religious: some believed that 'their improved health is conferred upon them by unseen ethical powers as a reward for not eating the flesh of slaughtered animals'. When they were ill-informed about nutrition – as many of them were – they simply dropped meat, and sometimes eggs and cheese as well, from their diets, while continuing to eat the standard British fare of vegetables boiled to a pulp, stodgy puddings and white bread. Their pallid faces and dire digestive problems made them the butt of many a meat-eater's wit.

Then there were those – distantly inspired by Bircher-Benner – who would touch nothing but 'unfired food'. They gave up cookery as well as meat, and munched nuts, raw turnips and carrots, endless salads, and cereals soaked but not cooked. Yet another set of cranks banned yeast from the kitchen, and ate their bread not just wholemeal but leaden and unfermented; while others again refused to touch bread in any shape or form – 'a clogging article of diet'. These odd ideas on diet often went hand in hand with an unrestrained enthusiasm for Greek gymnastic dancing, handweaving, nudism, free love, New Thinking, and more esoteric therapies such as Ehretism or Plombière's colonic irrigation.

Whatever school they belonged to, however, all cranks were unanimous on at least one subject: that the average British diet was appalling – 'artificial, denatured, devitalized'. 'Museum foods', a rare food-reform wit styled them: 'the more museum foods you eat, the sooner you will be history'.² Much more often, though, the joke was at their expense, and the British public had endless fun contemplating food-reform meals with their lentil rissoles, nut cutlets, heavy wholewheat bread and dandelion coffee.

Among this shrill chorus, it was at first hard for the hand-ful of intelligent and serious exponents of Nature Cure to make their voices heard. By the late twenties there were two acknowl-edged leaders of this strange transatlantic cult in Britain. There was Stanley Lief, established at Champneys, the disciple of Bernarr Macfadden, who after a few years spent astounding the British public had now returned to the United States. And there was J. C. Thomson, disciple of the Austro-German Henry Lindlahr of Chicago, now established with a clinic in Edin-burgh.

Between them, the two could claim a few hundred adher-ents. There were some fifteen or twenty practitioners. Patients could stay for treatment at one of four residential clinics, to be fasted, fed on fruit and vegetable juices, salads, and a vege-tarian diet, and treated with sunbathing, hydrotherapy, gym-nastics and manipulation. In 1927, Lief started a magazine *Health for All* to carry his message to a wider public. There were articles on 'Ice Cream: the Gastronomic Graveyard', 'How Fasting Saved My Life', 'Does Modern Food Kill?'.

The popular press occasionally took up their cause: in 1927 the *Daily Express* ran a series of articles on Nature Cure, written by 'Our "Better Health" Specialist'. And from time to time they encouraged each other by proclaiming that doctors were rapidly coming round to their views, and that there was a definite trend towards the new natural methods. This was optimistic. To the medical profession, they were simply ignor-ant and often dangerous quacks. Soon after he set up in Edin-burgh, Thomson learned that local doctors were claiming that he 'was broadcasting a pernicious technique, not only advising seriously ill patients to stop eating for considerable periods of time, but worse still, telling others to eat raw vegetables'. Doctors went out of their way to caution former patients against this dangerous practice. Current medical belief was that uncooked vegetables were the cause of dysentery and that wholewheat bread, which he also advocated, would add to the tragedy.[3]

There were already a number of shops catering to vegetarians up and down the country – the first had opened in Birmingham in 1898. They were low-key, stocked with meat substitutes, dried beans and herbal remedies. But by the thirties there was enough demand – some of it now coming from the general public too – for a new-style health-food shop, the prototype of a thousand such establishments today, selling foodstuffs specially manufactured or chosen for their uncontaminated, health-giving properties. In 1933 the London Health Centre opened in Wigmore Street to sell 'Vital Foods of Quality'. It stocked not only the staple sundried fruits, wholemeal bread and biscuits and nut meats, but a range of attractive new products specially formulated by the health lecturer Edgar Saxon, who was one of the shop's co-founders.

Saxon, a lively and popular lecturer, edited his own health magazine and wrote books teaching the principles of natural eating. He realized that it was no good simply denouncing the gastronomic sins of the flesh: 'for one person willing to be led solely by reason, there are hundreds who can be persuaded solely by the palate'. So the Health Centre, and other similar shops now beginning to spring up in other cities, stocked such lines as his 'Gathered Sunshine Nature-Food Confections, Made Without Commercial Sugar, to persuade the sweet-loving palate to forsake destructive sugar-sweets and clogging chocolate'. Other Saxon Food-Craft Products included 'Integrity Health Coffee made from dandelion roots – a real help to health and inner cleanliness', 'Sylvan Savoury, a tasty and nutritious ready-to-serve luncheon savoury', and 'Sylvan Sandwich Pastes, made from creamed nuts and piquant vegetable flavourings . . .'[4]

Some of the best-known pre-war athletes were vegetarians and proud to proclaim the fact. Eustace Miles went one better – he endorsed a range of meat-free high-protein foods, forerunner of the sports supplements which have become a mainstay of health-food-shop business in the eighties. The Eustace Miles range included EMprote bread, Proteid Soup and EM Training Biscuits.

Saxon himself also ran The Vitamin Café behind Oxford Circus, 'famous for the best salads in London'. London had at least heard of salads: Thomson reported that no Edinburgh restaurant knew what the word meant.

The adherents of Nature Cure were few in number, but their ideas were adopted by a slowly widening circle of people, many of whom had been restored to normal health after years of futile treatment by regular doctors. And many of the healthy habits being urged on us from all sides today were first advocated by them in the teeth of violent opposition and ridicule from the medical profession: sunbathing, ultraviolet treatment, the benefits of fresh air and aerobic exercise.

Their favourite therapy, the long, supervised fast or 'physiologic rest' as they call it, has never found favour with the medical profession, who still regard it as a desperately hazardous procedure. Many Nature Cure ideas on diet, on the other hand, are today on the brink of becoming conventional medical wisdom. They insisted on conservative cooking of vegetables to preserve vital 'organic salts' – and drinking vegetable water rather than throwing it down the drain with these important minerals; on the importance of 'roughage'; on plenty of fresh raw vegetables and fruit; and on the excellent protein in nuts.

In their demand for fresh, unadulterated food, they were far ahead of their time. One of their practitioners, Mrs Milton Powell, described some of the commonest ways in which food of doubtful or poor quality was given eye-appeal and flavour. Milk was often skimmed and watered, with yellow colouring matter and boric acid as a preservative added to it. Cream was artificially thickened with gelatine and starch paste. Butter might be coloured white fat, margarine made from solid paraffin and fish oils, suitably coloured and flavoured. Cheese had margarine added to bulk it out cheaply. Jam was often made from rotten fruit pulp, crudely coloured, with tiny wooden seeds added. Salicylic acid was added to bacon, ham, sausages and tinned meats. Fish was sprayed with formaldehyde, pickles had sulphites added to them, white rice was polished with paraffin wax shavings and flour was bleached with a variety of chemicals.

An enormous amount of insidious disease or poor health certainly resulted from these practices.

But when two physicians set out to buy fresh vegetables and milk in a London suburb, for the purposes of an experiment, they found that reliable supplies were unobtainable.

The physicians were Dr G. Scott Williamson and his wife Dr Innes H. Pearse, and the revolutionary question which their experiment was designed to answer was: what is health?

Medical schools never even posed the question; much less did they supply answers. Medical students saw only sickness, were trained only to recognize pathological conditions. Carrying out infant welfare work in the East End of London after the First World War, Dr Pearse realized that she had no idea what a healthy baby looked like – she had never seen one.

If doctors were not taught to recognize health as well as disease, how could they identify the first subtle deviations from this state which were the forerunners of serious illness?

Health and disease, argued these two doctors, were not sharply divided states: there was a vast grey area in between.

> During the war the number of youths entering the army who had to be classed in the C category of physical and mental fitness gravely disturbed the nation. They were not sick, nor were they healthy. They were 'invalid' for work or fighting – devitalized. Thus we now know that there are two menaces to health – disease and devitalization.[5]

Why did this occur, they wondered. Could it be prevented – and if so how – and at what point in the individual's life? What environment permitted the human being to come to full physical and mental flowering?

To answer these questions, Dr Williamson and Dr Pearse devised a revolutionary study, which was to become world-famous as the Peckham Experiment. It was not, they emphasized over and over again, yet another medical experiment. It was a biological study of living beings in their normal environment.

In 1926 they opened a small family club in Peckham, and invited local families to join. Family meant husband and wife, with their children if they had any. Each member of each family was given a periodic 'health overhaul'. They found that in the impoverished lives of many of these families, the conditions for true health and self-fulfilment could never exist. They found exhausted, anaemic women with two or three small children who seldom stirred from their cramped homes except to go shopping. They found children with nowhere to romp and play. They found fathers whose only social life was the pub.

They also found a quite astonishing amount of ill health.

After three years it was clear that the quality of the family environment – in every respect – was vital to physical and mental health. In order to study this in depth, money was raised and the new Pioneer Health Centre – a beautiful, ultra-modern building, 'more glass than wall', rose and was opened. It was intended as a place where families could spend their leisure time, while the two 'biologists' observed them.

The Centre was designed for easy movement and visibility within its window-walls, with no corridors or closed doors. It was open to all families who lived within pram-pushing distance, on payment of a small weekly fee – but families had to join as a group, even if some members never went near the place. To its members the Centre became their life, and the whole family used it. The mothers brought their babies along in the afternoon to be left in the supervised nursery to romp and crawl, while they themselves could relax and enjoy a chat with other young mothers. The children gloried in the wide open spaces where nobody shouted at them to be quiet, in the swimming-pool, the gym, the flat roof that could be used as a roller-skating rink. And at the end of the working day, the men joined their wives for a drink and a little social life. If medical attention was needed, or simply information, it was easy to have a quick word with the two doctors – biologists who moved about, hailed as friends by the members; and people who hesitated to consult a harassed GP found it easy to buttonhole 'Scottie' for an informal consultation.

At first classes and activities for both adults and children were carefully organized. But it was found that members hung back, resisted regimentation. So Scott Williamson abolished the classes, tore up the timetables and watched, while the children organized their own games and learned to use the Centre's marvellous facilities under their own initiative.

What impressed the two doctors – and a stream of visitors to the Centre – was the joyful vitality, the new confidence and sense of purpose that came into the lives of its members. 'We found', reported Williamson and Pearse, 'that not only were a much greater number now free from disorder and disease but that each one individual in the family – children and their parents – were living a much fuller life than before he joined the Centre.'[6]

In the first eighteen months of the new Centre, 500 families – 1,666 individuals in all – had had at least one examination, and some, two. At their first overhaul, only 151 of these had been free from actual diagnosable disorder – and many of these mentioned headaches, or aching joints, or constipation, or catarrh. Ear infections, decayed teeth, rickets and infected tonsils were common. More than half were iron-deficient. Many who believed themselves to be quite fit, and indeed said they felt perfectly well, turned out to have conditions needing medical attention which they were not getting. Of 62 cases of heart disorder, only 4 had been to their doctor about it; of 17 cases of cystitis, only 7 realized they had it. And 200 had clinically diagnosable conditions of malnutrition or vitamin deficiency.

To Williamson and Pearse, good nutrition was an essential quality of the balanced environment in which the human being could thrive. But unlike many experts – then and now – they realized that the problem of malnutrition was not simply a question of money. They would recommend fresh vegetables and eggs, for instance, to a family who were all iron-deficient – 'only to be told that the father was a great gardener and that they grew all their own vegetables and kept hens and that the mother was particularly fond of liver, which they had not less than twice weekly'.[7]

The problem, they found, was often not just one of supply but of utilization as well. Bodies in poor shape could not absorb nutrients as efficiently as healthy ones. Cases of iron deficiency were often only cured when the individual took up regular exercise – like a swim in the Centre's big pool. But such a functional breakdown – as McCarrison's studies had shown – was often itself caused by poor food: a vicious circle.

To control this biological variable, they set up a nearby Home Farm to provide what they called 'vital fresh food' – raw certified milk from tuberculin-tested cows, and fruit and vegetables grown in soil gradually revitalized by the Indore composting system. These could be bought at the Centre by pregnant or breast-feeding women, and for just-weaned babies, at no more than prevailing market prices, while the wholewheat bread, made from compost-grown wheat, was available to everybody. Some of the members had never tasted this before. They grew to like it.

As part of the Peckham research, direct nutritional studies were carried out – mainly on the effects of improved nutrition on the next generation – made possible by close contact with young couples both before and after a baby was conceived; the studies continued as the child grew. The notion that the health of their young is directly influenced by the health of both parents is taken for granted by stock-breeders, but it was new in human nutritional studies and is still widely disregarded today. It was certainly grasped by the Peckham members, and soon young couples planning to start a baby would ask for a special family consultation, when they could have their general health and diet checked. At these consultations, the directors found, members were ready, often eager, to learn about the importance of nutrition for their own and their children's health.

This Peckham concept of nutrition went much further than the question of food and drink. The spirit, the mind, the emotional life of an individual call for nourishment as insistently as his body – a truth that common language recognizes when we speak of being 'starved of love', 'hungry for affection', 'thirsty for praise' or 'dying for company'. Thus the whole experiment could be seen as research into nutrition in its widest sense – physical, mental and social: of the whole man.

The Peckham message was so complex, and addressed itself to such a wide spectrum of specialists – doctors, welfare workers, sociologists, biologists, administrators, town-planners – that at first the nutrition aspect, which was little stressed in the writings of the two doctors, tended to be totally disregarded. In their eyes it was highly important, and was one of the main reasons why families who had done badly in their first overhauls often turned up looking ten times better at their third or fourth.

The members themselves were conscious of an extra dimension of vitality. Years later, one of them recalled '. . . the wonderfully healthy children the Centre produced, marvellous kids, all blooming, healthy, super children . . .'[8]

But to scientists and doctors at the time, words like 'whole', 'vital' and 'natural' rang little warning bells. Here was the language of the crank, almost grounds in themselves for dismissing the Peckham Experiment as a piece of high-minded day-dreaming.

Such ideas, inevitably, attracted strong opposition.

Advocates of wholemeal bread merely found themselves up against the big milling and baking interests – David against Goliath. When they began insisting that the wheat be compost-grown instead of raised with artificial fertilizers, the opposition swelled into a legion of Goliaths: most of England's farmers, numbers of people engaged in agricultural research, and a huge agro-chemical business turning out fertilizers, fungicides and insecticides.

Hardly surprisingly, Howard was coolly received when he reported his findings to the Royal Society in 1933, and again when he lectured about them to the Farmers' Club four years later. Finding the fruit of years of patient research dismissed as crankery – not a single British experimental station had taken the trouble to try out his composting process – Howard gave up the attempt to persuade by making speeches. 'I will write my answer on the land!' he declared.

McCarrison addressed the Royal Society three years later than Howard, but when he echoed Howard's themes – when he spoke of the impoverishment of the soil leading to poor-quality foodstuffs, and thence to faulty nutrition – his audience must have stirred restlessly in their seats.

In thus aligning himself with the advocates of wholemeal bread, of muck and magic, McCarrison certainly did nothing to improve his professional status in Britain. Even admirers like Orr were careful to distance themselves; in alluding to the famous Coonoor trials in his *Food, Health and Income*, Orr added, 'Such experiments, of course, do not carry the same weight as observations in humans.'

McCarrison's reputation was still high enough to guarantee him a respectful hearing. His flair, his originality, and the brilliant and methodical work he had done on subjects as varied as goitre, the stone and beriberi, earned him the highest of places in nutritional circles.

Back in London, he was invited to lecture, to sit on important committees, to advise distinguished bodies. He was knighted for his services in India. Yet no post of importance was suggested for him although he was in his vigorous fifties; no use was found for his outstanding qualities when war broke out in 1939. And the honour of Fellowship of the Royal Society – far more significant than a knighthood – was never offered him. Few doctors gave any signs of having been influenced by his work.

It must have been particularly heartening to both McCarrison and Howard, therefore, to find themselves invited in 1938 to address a large public meeting at Crewe as honoured guests of the County Palatine of Chester Local Medical and Panel Committee. Every county had such a committee, set up by the 1911 Medical Insurance Act which had as its noble object 'the prevention and cure of sickness'. The Cheshire committee was

a little unusual. Its hard-working secretary was a Dr Lionel
Picton, who not only had an enthusiasm rare in a doctor for
nutrition – he had followed McCarrison's work keenly – but an
interest in compost too.

He had applied McCarrison's ideas in his practice over
and over again, and he found that they gave excellent results.
For years he had been running a particularly successful child-
welfare clinic in a village where most of the mothers were his
patients. On his advice they lived virtually on a Sikh diet when
they were pregnant: they had plenty of good raw milk, oatmeal
porridge, salads, eggs and vegetables conservatively cooked.
Herring twice a week, a little meat, plenty of fruit. For supper
they ate thick vegetable soups, with raw carrot grated into them
before serving, and potatoes baked in their jackets. Pregnant
and would-be pregnant women were advised to eat bread specially baked to his directions from wholewheat flour with half its
weight added of wheat germ still warm from a Liverpool mill.
The village christened it the Fertility Loaf when a woman who
had been trying for a baby for eleven years conceived soon after
she began to eat it regularly. Thereafter those who wanted no
more children shunned Picton's special loaf!

The babies were breast-fed till they were nine months old.

Everyone agreed they were lovely babies, no problem at
all. They slept like tops and never seemed to be sick or fretful,
and they grew up into sturdy, healthy children with beautiful
skins. Perfect sets of teeth – as rare as a four-leaved clover
throughout Britain by now – were becoming common here.
The good humour and happiness of the children were particularly striking.

As part-time medical officer for health as well as secretary
of the committee, Dr Picton drew attention to these matters in
his annual reports. In 1938 the committee had just completed a
three-year study of maternal mortality in their county. Picton's
village compared particularly favourably with the anaemic
mothers, ailing babies and high incidence of childbirth fever
found elsewhere. The vice-chairman of the committee, Dr
Boswell of Runcorn, felt that these matters ought to be publicly
aired and such important knowledge disseminated. In the
meantime, Dr Picton had also learned of Howard's work, so
strongly endorsed by McCarrison.

Invitations were sent out to a public meeting in a Crewe
theatre hired for the day, with the Lord-Lieutenant of the
county, Brigadier-General Sir William Bromley-Davenport

presiding, to be addressed by Sir Robert McCarrison and Sir Albert Howard. With the invitations went an astonishing document, signed by the entire committee.

Even today, nearly half a century later, it is impossible not to be stirred by the eloquence and the urgency of the 'Medical Testament'. Constituted under the 1911 Act, the committee asked 'How far has the Act fulfilled the object announced in its title – "The Prevention and Cure of Sickness"?'

> . . . it is not possible to say that the promise of the Bill has been fulfilled . . . We feel that the fact should be faced . . . Our daily work brings us repeatedly to the same point: 'This illness results from a lifetime of wrong nutrition.'
>
> The wrong nutrition begins before life begins. 'Unfit to be a mother' – from undernutrition or nutritional anaemia – is an occasional verdict upon a maternal death. For one such fatal case there are hundreds of less severity where the frail mothers and sickly infants survive.

Poor teeth, rickets, anaemia, constipation – it was a devastating picture that the committee painted. The 'Testament' went on to stress the extreme importance of McCarrison's and Howard's work.

> No health campaign can succeed unless the materials of which the bodies are built are sound. At present they are not.
>
> Probably half our work is wasted, since our patients are so fed from the cradle, indeed, before the cradle, that they are certain contributions to a C_3 nation. Even our country people share the white bread, tinned salmon, dried milk regime. Against this the efforts of the doctor resemble Sisyphus . . .
>
> We conceive it to be our duty in the present state of knowledge to point out that much, perhaps most, of this sickness is preventable and would be prevented by the right feeding of our people . . .[9]

With these defiant words ringing in their ears, an audience of farmers, county councillors, representatives of local government, doctors, school teachers and the general public crowded expectantly into the Crewe theatre.

Sir Robert impressed them deeply. Sir Albert, tilting at the agro-chemical industry, brought them to their feet gasping with surprise and admiration. Revolution was in the air, that night in Crewe.

The meeting was reported at length in the Cheshire press.

Having lobbed their grenade, the Cheshire committee, meanwhile, held their breath and waited for the explosion: the public debates, the editorials in the serious press and the medical journals, the outcry in popular newspapers, the debates in Parliament, the invitations to address other meetings on these important subjects.

They waited for a long time. Only slowly did it dawn on them that nobody, really, was very much interested.

14

'Food is Your Best Medicine'

I n 1927 Gloria Swanson was one of Hollywood's hottest properties.

To her millions of adoring fans, the young $1,000-a-day star symbolized Hollywood at its most glittering. They filled her suite at the Ritz with flowers, mobbed the car taking her to film premières, where a hysterical audience pelted her with orchids, and lined the platform of remote railway stations to catch a glimpse of the star as the train bearing her steamed through. They devoured every detail of her private life – the fairy-story romance and marriage with the French Marquis de la Falaise, the palatial Beverly Hills home, the troops of servants, the cocktail parties, the grand dinners for fifty or sixty guests at a time.

Now on the eve of shooting a major new film, *Sadie Thompson*, she was sick. Agonizing stomach pains convinced her she was developing an ulcer.

Since the only doctor she trusted was thousands of miles away in Paris, a friend suggested a Pasadena doctor who had been treating her own mother. He's good, she told Gloria. He's the best. His name is Henry Bieler. Doubtfully, she went to see him. She met a little man who 'looked more like a book-keeper than a physician: no white coat, no stethoscope, no smell of medicine or disinfectant about him'. He asked her to sit down and pulled a pad of paper towards him.

'What did you have to eat last night?' he asked her.

Years later, she recalled her astonishment at the question. 'I was shocked when Dr Bieler asked me what I had been eating. What had my eating and drinking to do with how I was feeling?'

But the doctor persisted. Item by item, ingredient by ingredient, he took her through every single thing she had eaten and drunk the previous evening. The canapés. The champagne. The soup, the fish, the egg, butter and cream of the sauces, the white flour and sugar and raspberry jam and egg and sherry and almonds and whipped cream of the trifle.

The fine vintage wine. The list covered three pages of foolscap paper. Then item by item he read it back – while a wave of nausea mounted in her – asking her to imagine spooning them all on to one huge plate. Matter-of-factly he asked her, 'Tell me, what animal, including a pig, would eat that combination of things in less than two hours?'

If she wanted to get better, he told her, she must learn to eat in an entirely new way. Naturally.[1]

Gloria Swanson became America's most sensational advertisement for the simple life. Years later, when half her contemporaries were sinking gracefully into old age, she still looked maddeningly dynamic, sexy and bright-eyed.

Gossip columnists retailed her diet-sheet with awe. Breakfast was rolled oats with a few raisins steeped in hot water – a transatlantic version of Bircher-Benner muesli. A salad for lunch. For dinner, steamed vegetables – courgettes, squash, young green broccoli, buckwheat. At cocktail parties, she shook her head at the Gibsons and Manhattans and sipped mountain water instead.

William Dufty, who became her sixth and last husband, recalled his first meeting with her at a Fifth Avenue press conference. Lunch arrived from the local delicatessen – pastrami on rye, salami on pumpernickel, coffee. 'Miss Swanson . . . wasn't having any of our picnic. She had brought her own – a piece of tree-ripened unsprayed something. Of course we had all heard the legend about Swanson's exotic health regimen. Poems have been written about her age-defying presence. Seeing her close up, eyeball to eyeball, it was impossible to doubt that she must be doing something right.'[2]

Not all Dr Bieler's patients were as enthusiastic – or as cooperative – as Gloria Swanson. 'I admit mine is not an easy or pleasant cure, as is popping pills into your mouth. Complete bed rest, while fasting on diluted fruit juices and vegetable broths, isn't particularly appealing even for a few days. And living thereafter on a diet restricted in starches or proteins or fats or salt . . . is even less appealing as a way of life.'[3]

It was a way of life to which he was a fairly recent convert himself.

Medical school had turned him out a perfectly conventional doctor, with a serene confidence in all the wonderful drugs they had taught him to use. 'As an eager medical school graduate, I stuffed my patients with pills, potions and panaceas.'[4] Then the doctor fell sick – gross obesity, asthma, kidney troubles – and the pills and potions let him down. Five minutes' chance conversation with a medical colleague was the road to Damascus. This colleague, far from being one of the fringe practitioners proliferating in America at the time, was a fully qualified physician with a specialist interest in pathology. But he opened Bieler's eyes to a new way of viewing health and disease: what you eat can make you ill; what you eat can make you better.

Bieler cured himself first. He gave up a junkie's addiction to salt, to heavy starchy food, to rich puddings, to milk drunk a quart at a time. He began eating, instead, salads, lightly steamed vegetables, fruit, whole grains. His weight dropped from 15 stone to a trim 11 stone, his asthma vanished and his kidneys functioned normally. Over the next few years he read avidly everything he could lay his hands on in the new field of nutrition, and deepened his studies in the equally new field of endocrinology. McCarrison's researches on the effect of poor diet on the adrenals and other glands confirmed many of the truths to which he was groping his way.

Now he gave no more drugs. Instead, he told his patients: you are making yourself ill. You are filled with toxic wastes caused by the terrible, artificial, over-processed food you eat. You can't start your day without mugs of steaming coffee – but all you're doing is whipping your adrenal glands to give you a false sense of exhilaration – a moment's uplift. Sooner or later they will break down under the strain. Germs do not cause your disease: they have multiplied in you because the tissues of your body are sick. If you want to be well – really well – I can help you. But you must be ready to change the eating habits of a lifetime.

Food, he told his patients, is your best medicine. It is the only one I will give you.

As he had once written prescriptions for drugs, so now he scribbled individual diet-sheets for his patients, for every single meal or drink of the day at first, from the time they got up to the time they went to bed. No two diet-sheets were exactly the same – just as no two cases were exactly the same: every patient needs a programme custom-tailored to his unique needs, he said.

One of the earliest patients he treated with his new dietary approach was a woman with a large fibroid tumour in her neck, which a surgeon had tried in vain to remove. What did she eat? She and her husband, Bieler learned, ran a turkey ranch and for many months now, she had been eating turkey three times a day. Her urine was loaded with sulphur proteins. Bieler put her on a high alkaline cleansing diet of fruits and vegetables, omitting the sulphur-rich cabbage and onion family, as well as animal and seafood protein. A year later the tumour had disappeared.

On successful cases like this Bieler built himself a high reputation, and a practice that numbered many of Hollywood's leading stars, among them Greta Garbo. These stars could not afford to look anything less than their best – clear of skin and bright of eye; they could not afford to be ill when an expensive cast and film crew were hanging around waiting for them to get better; and the reality behind Hollywood glamour was a working life that demanded every ounce of energy and stamina. They went to Bieler for help. One of them later recalled being so faithful to her Bieler diet-sheet that during twelve weeks of location filming, she regularly used to cook courgettes and string beans over a little Bunsen stove in her bathroom.

After weeks of making a film, irregular meals or a string of public engagements designed to keep them firmly in the public eye, these stars would get home exhausted. Bieler taught them to go on a one- or two-day cleansing regime of what became famous as Bieler broth – a vegetable soup made from lightly cooked string beans, celery, courgettes and parsley.

What Bieler was practising, of course, was virtually pure Natural Hygiene. And in fact the greatest single influence on his medical thinking, as he acknowledged, was Dr John Tilden, at that time America's most forceful champion of Hygienic ideas.

Born in 1851, Tilden had trained at the Eclectic Medical Institute in Cincinnati, Ohio, where he equipped himself with the lengthy list of herbal, homoeopathic and conventional drugs the Eclectics were then using. For twenty-five years of practice, he plied his prescription pad with a will. But the Hygienists Trall and Page were his friends, and as he gradually lost faith in his drugs, he came to rely more and more, as they did, on the healing powers of nature. Nevertheless their system seemed to him to be incomplete.

The most hotly debated question of the day in medical circles was what caused disease? What caused gout – or rheumatism – or cancer? Why did a child get tonsillitis – or diphtheria? The germ theory was eagerly seized on to provide answers in the case of the infectious diseases – but what of those in which no microbe could be considered the villain of the piece? It seemed to Tilden that modern medicine had no answers for this question; they confused symptom with disease. What 'caused' migraine, for instance? 'The head does not cause the pain. Then we find that there are symptoms of hyper-aemia – too much blood in the head. The pressure from too much blood in the head causes the pain. Then pressure must be the disease? No. Then too much blood is the disease – hyper-aemia? Certainly: too much blood in the head was a cause. What is it that causes congestion?'[5] and so on: merely following along a chain of symptoms could give no indication of the true cause.

A powerful and original thinker, over years of study Tilden gradually evolved his own unified explanation for all disease – one so simple that any child could understand it.

'All symptoms of so-called disease', he proclaimed, 'have one origin. All diseases are one.'

This one cause, he christened toxaemia.

In the process of metabolism which sustains human life, cell tissue is constantly being broken down. The breakdown material is toxic, and when the body is strong and healthy, it is eliminated as fast as it is formed.

But when the body's nervous energy is dissipated by any cause, the body itself becomes enervated, toxins accumulate and disease results. Disease is nature's own cleansing effort to remove these toxins from the blood. All so-called diseases are crises of toxaemia.

What were these enervating habits which weakened the body? Gluttony and wrong-feeding, certainly. Tilden was stern in his denunciation: 'Perverted appetites are built by overeat-ing, eating rich food until enjoyment is lost for staple or plain foods; use of stimulants – alcohol, tobacco, coffee, tea; use of butter, salt, pepper and rich dressings; eating without a real hunger . . . eating when sick or uncomfortable; eating at off hours or between meals . . .'

Lack of poise, lack of self-control, sexual excess – these, too, were enervating. But so too were anger, grief, shock, dissat-isfaction. And here Tilden was far ahead of his time, anticipat-ing Hans Selye's important research on the role of stress in disease. Such negative emotions, warned Tilden, could be just as potent a cause of disease as any physical factor.

How, then, was disease cured? There was no such thing as a cure – not even diet – as modern medicine understood it. Only when the toxins were eliminated – by fasting and bed rest – and after rational habits had been adopted, could the body slowly return to health.

These ideas were instilled into a generation of young practitioners in the school Tilden had opened in Denver, Colorado. It was attached to a sanatorium which became almost as famous as the Bircher-Benner Clinic in Zürich, attracting patients from all over the world for a treatment very similar in the uncompromising demands it made on them. Almost all treatment began with a fast: 'It is a crime to feed anything to the sick,' was Tilden's view. 'No food should be given until all symptoms are gone.'

Tilden had little sympathy with human frailty. A man who had given up smoking because Tilden had told him that it was a chief cause of his wife's migraine headaches, congratulated the great man on curing her without drugs. Tilden replied coldly, 'Your smoking and the drugging were responsible for her unnecessary suffering during nearly a quarter of a century.'[6]

In 1924 – seventy-two years old and long past the age at which most men retire – Tilden sold his school and clinic to the Hygienic practitioner Dr Arthur Vos. In this venture Vos was backed by the makers of Jergens Lotion, who no doubt felt that the world-famous clinic must be a gilt-edged investment. But without Tilden's powerful personality behind it, the clinic was soon in difficulties – not helped, perhaps, by the fact that Tilden immediately opened another school and sanatorium in the same city. He continued to run these, with daunting energy, until his death in 1940, at the fittingly advanced age of eighty-nine. He had by then been editing his own magazine for forty years. It was called *Tilden's Health Review and Critique*. He wrote most of it himself, between the hours of 3 a.m and 7 a.m.

Tilden had little respect for the medical profession, apart from the handful he had trained himself, or those who based their practice – like Bieler – on the application of his toxaemia theory.

He preserved a grudging regard for the Hygienists, and continued on fairly friendly terms with them. Hygiene had lost Trall, but it had found a new leader in the person of Dr Herbert Shelton. Another phenomenon of intellectual energy, Shelton has been the driving force of the movement for most of this century. At the health school he opened in San Antonio, Texas, in 1928, he trained dozens of Hygienic practitioners as well as treating patients from the United States and Canada, from

Latin America, from South Africa and Australia and Europe. A prolific writer, he has given the movement a vigorous modern interpretation of its philosophy and ideas. His *Human Life, Its Philosophy and Laws* first appeared in 1928; Shelton later expanded it into a seven-volume work which rivalled Graham's *Science of Life* in its vision and scope. Perhaps Shelton's most significant service, however, was to weld the movement together into a single body, the American Natural Hygiene Society, which has presented a fairly united front to the world ever since.

Nobody could have accused the Hygienists – or Tilden – of commercialism. It is hard to see, in any case, how they could have cashed in on their public standing. They manufactured no foodstuffs – unlike the Battle Creek Sanitarium, now in Macfadden's hands; they ran no restaurants; the fees of their sanatoriums were always modest – as they are today, with no high-tech equipment and fancy drugs to be paid for. Even their magazines must have barely paid their way, for who cared to advertise in a magazine that denounced all drugs, vitamin supplements, gadgets, patent foods and herbal remedies as equally useless or pernicious? In this high-minded purity, the Hygienists were soon exceptional.

One of Shelton's earliest works, published in 1922, was a slim volume which he called *Fundamentals of Nature Cure*. He was soon bitterly regretting the choice of title. To the American public, Nature Cure had come to mean one of the two schools of thought regarded by the Hygienists as misguided rivals: either the great Macfadden bandwagon, or else the system of natural healing pioneered by Priessnitz and now being presented as Nature Cure by the German Henry Lindlahr at his school and sanatorium in Chicago. Both schools practised what Shelton tersely called 'the irritative use of the elements' – hydrotherapy, sunbathing, ultraviolet lamps, electricity, herbal remedies, saunas. And both schools enjoyed such a huge success that they soon had any number of imitators practising imaginative variations on the natural theme – a lunatic fringe which maddened genuine practitioners like Tilden and Shelton quite as much it drew the scorn of the conventional physician.

There was Chromotherapy, Electrotherapy and Thermotherapy; there was Aerotherapy, Autotherapy, Poropathy and Vita-o-Pathy. There was Vibration, Biodynamochromatic Diagnosis and Therapy, Limpio-Comerology and Naturology. There was Physcultopathy, Sanatology, and Kensipathy. There were New Thought practitioners, and purveyors of vito-chemical remedies. 'Dr William Freeman Harvard, one of its most brilliant practitioners, well described it when he said it is 'a case of where one thing fails, try another",' quipped Shelton acidly. He was equally contemptuous of the numerous manipulative therapies that had sprung up since Andrew Still had evolved osteopathy in the late nineteeth century – including Chiropractic, Naturopathy, Spondylotherapy, Naprapathy. 'Since spine-tickling became so popular, the osteopath, the mechano-therapist, the masseur, the electro-therapist, etc., are all giving more and more attention to the spine,' he grumbled. 'It is a sort of fiddle upon which they play any old tune they desire.'

Even the worst and most unprincipled of the quacks, even the most ludicrous forms of charlatanry, had some kind of following, although Shelton was obliged to concede that, however futile their treatment, they seldom did their patients a lasting injury, other than in their pockets.

Modern America, it seemed, was ready to try anything, to the great fury of the American Medical Association. And as it happened, orthodox medicine in the shape of this powerful organization had at this time reached a crisis in its own affairs. The Flexner Report, a survey of US medical education, funded by the Carnegie millions and carried out in close cooperation with the AMA, had appeared in 1910. It disclosed such an abysmal state of affairs in many medical schools – particularly in those training what we should now call alternative practitioners – that in the public outcry that resulted, the AMA was able to have many of its rivals quietly eliminated. Medicine in the United States has been a virtual AMA monopoly ever since.

The surviving schools were to be shrines to modern scientific medicine, with the laboratory sciences – bacteriology, pharmacology and pathology among them – accorded pride of place. Published two years before Gowland Hopkins and Funk announced the importance of vitamins, the Flexner Report had no time at all for nutrition in its scheme of things – the very least of the adjunctive therapies – 'baths, electricity, massage, psychic suggestion, dietetics, etc.'

But loss of confidence in the nation's medical schools was not perhaps the best foundation on which to build an admiring trust in the physicians they turned out. And although the future of scientific medicine might be rosy, the reality – in the twenties and thirties – was still dismal. A huge new pharmaceutical industry was pouring out new drugs on to the market. But not until the development of the sulphonamides in the late thirties did medicine have an answer to acute infectious diseases such as TB and meningitis. Meanwhile, doctors experimented with a dizzy variety of drugs – vaccines, antitoxins, glandular preparations, serums, and highly toxic compounds of mercury and arsenic. Few of these were consistently effective, and many produced an appallingly high rate of side-effects.

The incidence of the killer infectious diseases – chief among them TB – was already beginning to decline, thanks largely to improving hygiene and housing conditions. But other diseases hitherto rare or unheard of were increasing alarmingly. The US heart specialist Paul Dudley White said that he found no heart disease among his patients until the early years of this century. Now it was rising steadily. So was rheumatism. So was cancer. And so was diabetes.

Diabetes mellitus is not a new disease. It was described in an ancient Egyptian medical text, the Ebers papyrus, and by the eighteenth century physicians were familiar with its ominous cluster of symptoms: fatigue, excessive thirst, weight loss, constant need to urinate and sugar in the urine. With no clues to its treatment, the prognosis was grim: perhaps five years more of life. In the nineteenth century, suspicion homed in on the pancreas – and finally, around 1921, the discovery of the hormone insulin, secreted by the pancreas, and its function, not only cleared up some of the mystery surrounding diabetes, but also offered a fairly effective means to control it. Diabetes, we now know, is a malfunction of the body's ability to metabolize carbohydrates. In a normal person, the pancreas produces insulin to regulate the process of converting sugars and starches into heat and energy. For a variety of reasons – some of them still not understood – this process is disordered in a diabetic: he cannot produce any insulin at all; or not enough; or its function may be inhibited by a variety of other factors.

Until the discovery of insulin, the only treatment was by diet, and the first successful diet was devised by a British military surgeon, John Rollo. His patient, the thirty-four-year-old Captain Meredith, was put on a diet excluding sugar and consisting largely of animal foods. He breakfasted on milk diluted with lime water, and on bread and butter; he lunched on blood puddings made only of suet and blood; he dined on game so high that it stank, and on rancid old beef and fat pork. He supped as he breakfasted. As he gradually improved, he was allowed to add such luxuries as cabbage, lettuce, boiled onions and radishes: all useful sources of fibre. And if the diet was revolting at least he never went hungry. The same could not be said for the low-calorie Allen diet or for the daunting diet of Dr Cantani, who locked his patients up to stop them getting at anything beyond the bare pound or so of meat he allowed them daily – on days when they were not fasting. And until insulin came along, most diabetics spent their time miserably longing for a good square meal.

Once the processes of diabetes began to be understood, treatment by insulin injections, and by severe restriction of carbohydrates in the diet, made life more bearable for diabetics – of whom the numbers were already rising. But although the condition responded to dietary manipulation, there was little understanding of the nutritional factors at stake: from the point of view of the diabetic specialist, carbohydrate was carbohydrate and that was that: wholemeal bread was no better than white, and no attempt was made to distinguish between the biological value of one carbohydrate and another.

Doctors might be sceptical about the importance of diet as a factor in health or disease. A significant number of Americans thought otherwise. Within recent memory, doctors had said that scurvy – and pellagra and beriberi – had nothing to do with diet. They had been wrong about all three. What other diseases might they not be wrong about?

McCollum's articles on diet in the *Ladies' Home Journal* were already having an influence on American eating habits among at least a section of the population. But even those who wanted to eat healthy, natural food found it dismayingly difficult to track down. In Germany, the Reformhaus movement had by this time brought beautifully run, clean, modern shops selling natural products like wholewheat bread, vegetable oils and herbal remedies to the big cities. After the war, German emigrants to the States started opening similar shops. The idea caught on.

The Hygienist doctor Arthur Vos had a Cincinnati patient called Louis Parks, who had been forced by illness to close down his prosperous manufacturing business. Vos had told him that if he wanted to get better he must eat plenty of natural foods – including wholemeal bread. There was none to be had. He decided he had spotted a commercial opening, made up a special small burr-mill, ordered some sacks of wheat and set up the Parks Milling and Baking Company in 1919. Stanley Phillips, a Macfadden fan, joined him and took over on Parks's death in

1934. By the end of the thirties it was a lively business with a couple of bakeries, two natural-food restaurants, three shops and a mail-order department.

By this time health-food stores had sprung up in cities right across America, with names that rang all the changes on the theme of eating for health: Pasadena had Health Food House, San Diego had a House of Nutrition; La Jolla had Diet Foods, and Pittsburgh had General Nutrition. Others plumped for the simpler Health Foods or Natural Foods. Either way, the public soon got the message. The range of goods stocked looked much more alluring, too. There were the Happy Thought fruit juices and concentrates; Karoth – an all-vegetable broth; Melvite soy and malt drink; Betena – a dietary supplement; and Steep-a-Lax, a laxative tea-bag. There were herb teas with names like Herb Garden Dinner Tea, and Moon-Glo Bedtime Tea. For breakfast there were Fig and Bran Flakes, Vidaneal, Jolly Joan Toasted Wheat Germ or Niblack's Wheat Bran. The snack market was looked after with Carque's California Health Bars, sea-salt cookies with honey; and wheat germ, molasses and stoneground wholewheat flour were already standard items.

Several of these small stores evolved into full-scale wholesaling businesses. Hain's Pure Foods – one of the biggest names in the market today – started out as a modest store opened by Harold Hain in downtown Los Angeles in 1926. Ten years later, the firm's catalogue was advertising Hain's Potassium Broth; Vege-Jell – a vegetable gelatine; 100 per cent honey; Garlic Parsley Tablets; and black-cherry and strawberry juices.

The spectacular rise to Western fame of the soya bean can be traced back to a globe-trotting British doctor, Charles Fearn. Keenly interested in nutrition, he had been intrigued during a visit to China by this cheap and nourishing plant-protein food, so widely used by the Chinese. It was an American President, Wilson, who invited Fearn to the States at the outbreak of the First World War. But it was the health-food industry that made the nation soya-bean conscious with products like Fearn's Soy-O-Pancake Mix – one of the earliest convenience health foods.

By 1936 the industry had its own trade paper – *Health Foods Retailing*. In 1976 it carried reminiscences of forty years in the business by some of its pioneers. One detects a certain note of nostalgia for those small-time, high-minded days. 'The operators of health-food stores were visionaries – idealistic – and few of them were merchants.' Customers were 'mainly elderly people who were medically disenchanted, diabetic, vegetarian or wholefood dedicated people'.[7]

But thousands of Americans who never found their way into one of these unpretentious, earnest little establishments were already keenly interested in the health-building qualities of their food. Alongside columns by nutritionists like E. V. McCollum, women's magazines in the twenties were already carrying ads aimed at this market. Readers were urged to put their families on to Fleischman's Yeast – it helped correct 'clogged intestines, skin and stomach disorders'. The New Pettijohns Wholewheat had 'all the natural bran of the wheat . . . the health-giving vitamins . . . and the valuable mineral salts, protein and energy . . .' 'Decide now to correct faulty elimination through your diet' suggested another ad: 'Begin now to eat Post's Bran Flakes regularly.' With a certain ingenuity, anybody could get in on the act. 'You will eat more fresh vegetables and fruits this summer, and thus give your body the vitamins and mineral elements which build health and vigour, if you are particular about the salt you use . . . Diamond Crystal on fresh vegetables and fruit . . .'[8]

A convention at Chicago in 1937 gave the young industry a chance to take stock of its prospects. Progress had been steady if unspectacular, and with the first vitamin products coming into their shops, the future looked rosy. Over a dozen wholesalers exhibited in booths at this convention – among them the famous Battle Creek Scientific Foods range, so exclusive that retailers had to pass an exam before being allowed to stock it – and some 150 retailers attended. Bernarr Macfadden sent Mr Englehardt, director of Physical Culture Publishing, to urge on everybody the need to form a trade association so that they could present a strong united front to the world. A committee was elected, worked till the small hours with an attorney to draft a constitution and by-laws. And the National Health Foods Association was born. Dr John Maxwell, who ran a health-food cafeteria and store in downtown Chicago, was elected its first president.

Even this modest progress could not have been achieved if the health-food industry had not been able to call on a number of popular lecturers to arouse public interest and cry their wares for them. Lectures were popular in those pre-TV days, and the most successful and best-advertised of these lecturers drew huge crowds, sending their audiences away vowing to follow a nutritional new life – and often loaded with products they had bought on the way out.

Lecturers like E. V. McCollum – whose features in *McCall's* had turned him into a household name – had no commercial axe to grind, but others were blatant cheerleaders for the industry, and brilliant salesmen of their own line of products. No holds were barred in advertising terms. There was nothing to stop lecturers – or follow-up newspaper ads, for that matter – from claiming that some wonderful new food concentrate would prolong people's lives, cure their constipation, strengthen their arteries and improve their digestion. Particularly for those lecturers who were plugging their own products, reticence was not an asset.

One of the most sensationally successful was Paul Bragg, who had worked with Luther Burbank in California to produce healthful organically grown fruits and vegetables. And it was he who had opened America's first modern health-food store, in which he retailed a range of products called Bragg's Vital Foods. By the thirties he was presenting them nationwide with a travelling roadshow of lectures and demonstrations. Tall, good-looking and clearly fizzing with health, Bragg with his year-round California tan, his wide boyish grin showing off wonderful teeth and his entourage of young enthusiastic salesmen, made an overwhelming impression. 'He packed the largest auditorium in Cincinnati night after night,'[9] remembered one grateful retailer. The day after, there would be lines of customers queueing up for the wonderful products.

Everyone agreed, though, that Gayelord Hauser, of Hauser Modern Products, was in a class of his own. 'Dignified' was the word that sprang to mind. When Hauser lectured, even the carriage trade turned up.

The Hauser story began with a childhood darkened by disease:

> A boy lay dying in the Evangelical Deaconess Hospital in Chicago. Despite many operations, his tuberculous hip refused to heal. One of Chicago's best surgeons told the nurse, 'Send this boy home. Just make him as comfortable as possible. There's nothing more that we can do.'
>
> So the unhappy and discouraged boy was sent back to Europe, to die in the serenity of the Swiss mountains. There, high up among the snow-capped peaks, a miracle happened. One morning, as he was eating his usual breakfast, an old man who was visiting his family told him, 'If

you keep on eating dead foods, you certainly will die. Only *living* foods can make a living body.'

'What are living foods?' asked the boy.

The man described them vividly. 'Fresh, young, growing things, especially the green and yellow vegetables saturated with the earthy elements; lemons, oranges and other tree fruits, full of sunshine and living waters' . . . the boy started to eat enormous amounts of the designated foods and, wonder of wonders, the hip which had defied all sorts of treatment now slowly but surely healed. Through this amazing recovery, I discovered for the first time what diet can do . . . for I was that boy . . .'[10]

Resuscitated by this Bircher-Benner regime, Hauser became understandably fascinated by the newly disclosed possibilities of nutrition. His Swiss-German origins later gave him a decided advantage over every rival in the States – he was able to study at first-hand much of the remarkable pioneer work being carried out in the field of nutrition in Germany and Eastern Europe.

A jetsetter long before the term was invented, Hauser travelled endlessly throughout his career. He met experts and came to know all the great names in his field – among them Dr Bircher-Benner and Mikkel Hindhede. He visited spas and Nature Cure clinics, he met Ragnar Berg – then doing some of the earliest work in analysing foods for their nutrient content. He familiarized himself with the technical jargon of the nutrition laboratory, and read widely and intelligently in his field.

Back in Chicago, a new man in every sense of the word, Hauser opened a dietetic school which was soon crowded with people coming for nutritional advice. 'The dejected faces of these poor men and women became radiant after they took on a new lease of life, simply because they were taught to eat sensibly.'[11]

After months of gazing at dejected faces, however, Hauser began to feel that his talents could be more usefully employed. He had by this time evolved a line of dietary products – including a powdered Alkaline Broth based on the cleansing vegetable bouillons served in the Bircher-Benner clinic. He took to the road and began a new career in lecturing.

In big cities all over the United States, he announced courses of lectures on nutrition. As his confidence grew and his style developed, he pulled bigger and bigger crowds. Audiences loved him. He was so positive, so inspiring, so upbeat. Instead of the grim denunciations of the Hygienists – the near-biblical warnings of dire retribution for gastronomic self-indulgence – Hauser told them that they too could be happy, healthy, full of dynamic vitality, eating an exciting new kind of food. He gave them diet-sheets, demonstrated recipes, composed wonderful colourful salads before their eyes. Soon the Hauser message was going out in book form, too. *Eat and Grow Beautiful* was its irresistible title.

The medium was as attractive as the message. Hauser had film-star good looks, an interesting face with one quizzically lifted brow. His lean, trim figure was set off by exquisite tailoring. And his effect on women was devastating. Throughout his career few of them – rich or poor, aristocrat or typist – could resist the great Hauser charm.

To one woman in particular, he was always grateful: Adele Astaire, the sister and first dancing partner of Fred Astaire, now Lady Cavendish. She was his entrée to the world of the Beautiful People.

In pre-war London, she introduced him to Mayfair society. He met the Duke and Duchess of Kent, and dined at their home – 'delicious broiled fish, green beans in the French manner, green salad, fruit compote . . .' England's New Health Society, founded by the famous surgeon Sir Arbuthnot Lane, presented him at a meeting for doctors only. They expected to hear yet another food faddist denouncing the modern diet. They found a delightfully deferential but highly knowledgeable young man insisting that all food is given for man's enjoyment: 'many highly restricted or "one-sided" regimes are neither normal nor healthful'. They were won over. The meeting was reported in the *Daily Mail* next day, and his lectures were gratifyingly well attended.

He moved on to Paris. And one afternoon, Lady Charles Cavendish took him out to Versailles to introduce him to Lady Mendl, now in her sixties.

A remarkable woman by any standards, Elsie de Wolfe Mendl had been presented as a girl at Queen Victoria's court, and grew up in the glittering social whirl of Edwardian London before embarking on three careers in rapid succession – in every one of which she made a name for herself. As actress, then as interior decorator, and finally as hostess – the wife by this time of a wealthy British diplomat, Sir Charles Mendl – she had been the darling of the gossip-columnists for years.

Hauser loved to tell the story of that first meeting.

'In the centre of a group in which everybody was "somebody", I was received by a tiny lady, soignée, with shining dark eyes and platinum-white hair. She showed me her copy of my book, *Eat and Grow Beautiful*. It was well marked and underscored. Across the front she had written, "I *like* that man!" '

She liked him even better when she met him. He became her protégé, launched by her into the most glittering circles of international social life, lionized at parties reported in all the glossies. At a party in 1937 she introduced him to the Duchess of Windsor, Lady Diana Cooper, Mrs Harrison Williams, the darling of social New York. The rich and famous became his friends.

Lady Mendl went further. She publicly proclaimed herself a convert to the Hauser regime. 'I have originated the modern style in clothes and decoration,' she told him. 'You have originated the modern manner of eating.'[12]

15

The Kitchen Front in Wartime

'**W**hy is potato like a lump of sugar?' asked the headline of a typical Ministry of Food advertisement in a 1942 British women's magazine. The advertisement also supplied the answer: they both give you energy. 'All the starchy and sugary foods are alike in this.' By 1942 most British housewives would have settled for the lump of sugar. But at least the potatoes never ran out.

The miracle of skilful planning and imaginative propaganda which was Britain's wartime food policy should rank among our most striking national achievements. 'The Kitchen Front was the only one where Great Britain never lost a battle,' observed Norman Longmate, truthfully, in his study of wartime Britain, *The Way We Lived Then*.

One of the Ministry's most memorable slogans – constantly repeated – was 'Food is a Munition of War – Don't Waste It!' For the first time in history, food became an important weapon of defence in 1939. The countries of Europe had learned grim lessons during the First World War. They had learned that wars or battles may be lost not just by lack of food, but by lack of the right kind of food. They now knew that the will to win, the energy to fight and the spirit to survive depended on quality as much as quantity: on Hopkins's accessory factors as much as Rubner's calories. 'The health line of the Home Front may become as important as the Maginot Line,' warned Orr in 1940.[1]

German planning had begun well in advance. In the mid-thirties Hitler called on his people to sacrifice butter for guns. Hopeful rumours spread that the Germans were short of food. What they were short of, as Orr found on a fact-finding visit in the summer of 1937, was meat, sugar and white bread, which were all scarce and expensive. But milk, vegetables, potatoes, black bread and other nourishing foods were plentiful, and astonishingly cheap into the bargain. There were no signs at all of the hope-for malnutrition on this diet, which Hindhede would have approved. On the contrary: the poorer people in Germany looked quite as healthy as anyone in Britain, Orr reported.

In planning its wartime food policy, the British government had to ask itself a painful question: can we win the war with the C3 nation revealed in so many recent surveys and studies? Since the answer was so obviously no, a first priority became equally obvious: to improve and maintain the health of this undernourished, devitalized third of the nation. On them would fall the brunt of the fighting, of munitions production, of working flat out on farms to double and treble the country's food supply.

Orr's studies had made it plain that ignorance and poor eating habits were quite as much to blame for their wretched state as poverty. The food must not only be rationed, so that everyone got a fair share, but priced so that everyone could afford it. Essentials must be subsidized, if necessary. And once the food had been made available at prices everyone could afford, they must be educated to eat properly. When the energetic Lord Woolton took over at the Ministry of Food in April 1940, a crash course in nutrition was immediately planned for the whole nation.

One difficulty, at least, had been solved in advance: the data were all there. The choice of essential foodstuffs could now be based on accurate information rather than guesswork. Over the years an immense amount of analytical data covering the nutritional needs of men, women and children, and the nutrient content of every imaginable foodstuff had accumulated, while the League of Nations, in its 1935 study, *The Physiological Bases of Nutrition*, had laid down the exact dietary requirements in terms of actual foods, of men, women and children. These were for optimum health – but nothing less was now good enough, and they were adopted. (Germany had already done so, for her own rationing scheme, some months earlier.)

The food situation was worrying, but not critical. 'With sufficient milk, vegetables and potatoes, there need be no malnutrition. With sufficient bread, fat (butter or margarine), potatoes and oatmeal, there will be no starvation,' predicted Orr. Glaring deficiencies in the national diet struck the Ministry's experts as they studied the pre-war surveys: the lack of calcium and vitamin A, due to a low intake of milk, and the shortage of vitamin B₁ caused by the national preference for white flour, were the most obvious. The Minister was advised that extra milk must be made available for children, pregnant women and nursing mothers, and as much as possible for everyone else; that to make up the vitamin A deficiency, margarine should be fortified with synthetic vitamins A and D; and that to supply adequate vitamin B₁, and the rest of the B complex, white flour should no longer be allowed for bread-making, and a higher-extraction flour should be used instead. The National loaf came into being.

Other suggestions were rejected. One of the Ministry's advisers, Hugh Sinclair, recommended that every dog in the country ought to be put down to save the tons of food they consumed. In the interests of national morale (and possibly of its own popularity too) the government turned down this idea. An earlier suggestion of Sinclair's – that (shades once more of Hindhede) the nation's beef-cattle herds should be destroyed, was also rejected by the Cabinet. Lord Halifax, at that time Foreign Secretary, was particularly eloquent on the subject: the Halifax herds of prize beef cattle were famous.

'Woolton's policy was simple,' noted Longmate; 'to ration nothing, however scarce, until there was enough to go round, and then to ensure that the ration, however small, was always honoured.'[2] Largely thanks to this decision, class differences melted away for the duration. A pound of butter was soon more highly prized than a Daimler, the Royal Family's tea ration was no bigger than any East End housewife's, and ranch minks swopped austerity jokes with shabby tweeds in the fishmonger's queue. Once the luxuries hoarded by the wealthy in the first months of war had vanished – the Fortnum's hampers, the cases of gin, the gleaming rows of tinned delicacies – the national cake was carved up with scrupulous fairness.

Under Woolton, the Ministry tackled another urgent task, that of telling the British what to eat and why. Jack Drummond was appointed to head a food-advice division, and from then till the end of war, the Ministry poured out a steady stream of information, advice, suggestion, encouragement. From advertisements in their newspapers and magazines, from vivid posters, from leaflets and booklets, from news flashes at the cinema, and in regular radio chats – 'Do you listen to the Kitchen Front on the wireless at 8.15 a.m.?' – the British learned how to cook and eat for health.

How to Keep the Vitamins in the Vegetables was revealed in one of the Ministry's Food Facts. 'Green vegetables must be cooked as quickly as possible, for slow cooking destroys their valuable vitamins . . . drain off any liquid from the pan and save it for soup . . .'

'Salads and vegetables every day!' advised a leaflet. 'Take at least one good helping of fresh salad every day as well as cooked vegetables. Plenty of salads, green vegetables, carrots, turnips and swedes will help you to resist infection.'

Because of its bulk, fruit had been among the first imported foodstuffs to be cut down; '. . . there's no denying we miss it,' soothed another summer advertisement, while the British longed for peaches, melons and grapes. 'But from the point of *health*, we can more than make up for the lack of fruit by eating extra vegetables . . . Vitamin C clears the skin, prevents fatigue and helps you to resist infection . . . Some vegetables . . . actually contain *more* of this health-giver than oranges do . . .'

As Orr had prophesied, potatoes, carrots and oatmeal remained plentiful at all but the darkest moments of the war: 'Three Winter Winners – Potatoes, Carrots and Oatmeal!' suggested a pamphlet issued by the Ministry of Food (winter 1941). 'Three foods to help you resist infection, to build up your strength and to give you energy to cope with wartime troubles! Supplies of each are plentiful, so eat some of each every day.'

Housewives who had once hardly known the meaning of the word 'vitamin' became nutrition experts. They learned that vegetables contained more vitamin C when they were eaten raw; that carrots were rich in vitamin A, which helped you see in the dark; that the dark outer leaves of vegetables were richer in minerals and vitamins than the pale hearts; that the pure white sugar they had once eaten at the rate of 2 lb (0·9 kg) weekly supplied energy but nothing else; that white rice and 'pearl' barley were little better; that the heavy National loaves that had replaced their white bread were richer in body-building, health-protecting nutrients; and that the 'roughage' in this bread and in vegetables helped prevent constipation.

Throughout the war, the vital importance of children's health – from conception onwards – was emphasized. Expectant mothers had extra milk and eggs; babies and small children had orange juice, cod-liver oil and vitamins as well.

One of the Ministry's most successful propagandists was 'the Radio Doctor', Charles Hill, whose fatherly reassuring voice was as well known as Tommy Handley's by the end of the war. 'Nations are born out of nurseries,' Dr Hill told British mothers. 'And children are like houses. If they are jerry-built, they never recover.'

He shamed the most reluctant into breast-feeding. 'The best food bar none. It's easier, it's cheaper, and it's better than anything else . . . For every breast-fed infant that does not live, five die that are fed other ways. Most women can do it if they try. A lot of them pretend they can't because they don't want to, or they think it isn't quite nice. That's folly, almost criminal folly . . .'[3]

He reminded his listeners how much healthier Norwegian schoolchildren had been on the famous Oslo Breakfast of raw milk, wholewheat roll, butter, cheese, raw carrot or lettuce or apple.* 'You've heard what happened to the children who were put on the Oslo meal for dinner, and afterwards compared with the good old English meat and two veg with a pudding as padding? The Oslo kids felt fitter and they looked fitter – clear-skinned, bright-eyed and full of vigour. They did better at play and at work.'[4]

With many exotic fruits and familiar standbys missing from their kitchen cupboards – pepper became like gold-dust – housewives were plied with hints for substitutes. One cookery writer, the French Vicomte de Mauduit, published *They Can't Ration These*, in which he pointed out many of the culinary treasures that were there for the asking in countryside or garden. Coffee could be made from dandelion roots or asparagus berries; mint or blackcurrant leaves and lime or camomile flowers all made agreeable teas (tisanes made from all of these had always been familiar on the continent); rose petals made beautiful jam; cauliflower leaves, leek tips, gillyflowers, violets and clary could all be added to salads. Why not try a purée of nettles – rich in iron – or a stew of starlings?

The Ministry later published its own *Hints for the Hedgerow Larder*. Elderberries were lovely with apples in a pie; tart crab-apples made a good substitute for the longed-for lemons; hips and haws were rich in vitamin C and could be made into

---

*The Oslo Breakfast was provided for school children in poor districts in Scandinavia. A similar meal given to poor children in London schools was shown to promote growth and weight increase more than conventional school meals.

delicious clear jelly; dried mushrooms made excellent flavourings for winter stews; and cobnuts, walnuts, chestnuts – even beech nuts – were all free as well as nutritious.

From 1940 on there was a rush of cookery books aimed at a brand-new market – thousands of middle-class housewives whose cooks and home-helps had deserted to make munitions. Many of them had never lifted a saucepan in their lives before, and were now compelled to practise a strange new art with depleted store-cupboards and half-empty shops. The new cookery books all stressed the importance of conserving food values, and were strenuously optimistic about the delicious dishes that could be concocted from the little still available. (I remember my mother scrawling in disgust across the flyleaf of one such offering – 'But the moral of all this is, you can't make a silk purse out of a sow's ear.')

In Jack Drummond's department, meanwhile, an army of dieticians and cookery experts toiled to evolve nutritious hints and recipes which could be passed on to desperate housewives over the radio, in the popular 'Food Facts' columns, or in demonstrations at the local Town Hall.

While the Ministry nutrition message came over loud and clear to housewives, under Drummond's direction, its own catering staff and dieticians often remained curiously ignorant of it. At the drab British Restaurants run by the Ministry to take the strain off housewives and supply an occasional hot cooked meal at a fixed price outside the limits of the ration-book, green vegetables were almost invariably boiled with soda to keep them bright green. When the Ministry was reminded that this practice was destructive of vitamin C, they blandly quoted in reply a Medical Research Council paper: 'You will note that the paper states that the addition of alkali hastens the destruction of the vitamins and does not necessarily destroy them all.' School catering habits were even more destructive: vegetables might be cooked as early as 7 a.m. and then kept hot all morning for the school dinners, which almost all schoolchildren were eating by the end of the war.

One nutrition expert who wrote pointing this out to the *British Medical Journal* suggested that as a result of such practices, vitamin C deficiency was widespread among members of the Services and those who ate in canteens. Such deficiency might well be causing the fatigue now so widespread – the people who were 'always tired' and 'feeling run down'. Recently, he added, 'several girls were sent home to have their teeth out "because of pyorrhoea"; they were canteen-fed. A few days of massive doses of ascorbic acid enabled them to return with their own teeth, some even without a dental clean-up. How many are sticking at their work but doing less than they could if they were well?'[5]

No nutrition issue, however, gave rise to such endless and acrimonious debate as the question of bread. Accusations of bad faith flew in all directions. As Lord Llewellin, who succeeded Woolton as Minister of Food, later said wearily, 'A number of the nutritionists think the millers are crooks, and a number of the millers think that the nutritionists are cranks.'[6]

By the beginning of the war, it had finally been conceded on all sides that white bread was inferior to wholemeal. 'A dead loss nutritionally' summed up one review of all the important vitamins and minerals lost in milling.

Even the millers were prepared to concede as much; by 1939 they were suggesting themselves that the vitamin B_1, now available in cheap synthetic form, should be added to white flour to make good the loss.

Shortly before the war, however, experimental work carried out by Mellanby (p. 79) gave the champions of white flour a new weapon. On diets high in bran but devoid of vitamin D, Mellanby's puppies got rickets, and the culprit was shown to be phytic acid, in which bran is rich – it is present in grains and seeds and pulses. On unbalanced diets, or diets in which excessive amounts of these foodstuffs are consumed – as in the case of Mellanby's puppies – the phytic acid may inhibit the body's uptake of calcium, though it has been shown that on a well-balanced diet it is no longer a problem. More work done by the food scientists R. A. McCance and E. M. Widdowson, published in 1942, appeared to confirm this. Against this limited amount of laboratory work might have been set dozens of studies of real people eating wholemeal bread over long periods of time, with excellent teeth and bones to show for it.

'Who that has seen the magnificent physique of the Sikh and the Pathan would dare to recommend them to change their staple diet of unleavened wholemeal bread for the white loaf of commerce?' wondered McCarrison.

Nearer home Norwegian children who had eaten their Oslo Breakfast for years showed not a trace of rickets. The Cheshire committee could point to the village of the 'Fertility Loaf', with its superb babies and children with perfect sets of teeth.

Much earlier, during the First World War, the inhabitants of the Channel Island of Jersey had been unwilling guinea-pigs for a mass trial of wholewheat bread – as Lord Hankey reminded the House of Lords during a debate in 1935. Under German occupation, potatoes, meat, sugar, fats and fish were all rationed, and supplies of some shrank almost to nothing during the last year of the war. But there were always plenty of vegetables, and there was plenty of wholewheat bread to which no calcium was added. What happened? Constipation became a thing of the past, and colds and digestive problems became rare. And when the children's teeth were examined at the war's end, they were startlingly good. Among 100 children, no more than twenty decayed teeth were found.

All this suggestive evidence was brushed aside, and on the basis of the McCance–Widdowson work – and at the urgent lobbying of the big milling interests – the government finally settled for an 85 per cent extraction National flour.

There was never any doubt where the interests of the millers lay. In the thirties, a number of firms had begun buying up the wheat germ stripped out of Britain's wheat supplies to be converted into patent foods and medicines; 99 per cent of the wheat germ extracted in this way was sold to a favoured half dozen of these companies, including Glaxo and Vitamins Ltd. The bakers sold their white flour for £13 10s. a ton – but wheat germ fetched £20.

The bran was another profitable byproduct of the roller mills, and hundreds of farmers relied on it to feed their cows and pigs. 'Why deprive the animals of their rightful feeding-stuffs?' queried *The Country Miller* piteously.[7]

To have settled for 100 per cent extraction would certainly have meant the slaughter of large numbers of livestock.

Yet another argument put forward revived the old balancing experiments to prove that, weight for weight, wholemeal bread provided fewer calories, less protein. These studies, carried out in the industry's own research station – taken over by the government for the duration – also showed that in the despised bran was concentrated most of wheat's nicotinic acid – another B vitamin. But as little work had been done on it, the fact was passed over.

As a compromise, 85 per cent was finally agreed – to be enriched with extra calcium – and announced to the House in April 1940. Those concerned about nutrition – among them Dr Lionel Picton, on behalf of the Cheshire committee – at

once asked if this 85 per cent would include the wheat germ –
amounting to about 2·5 per cent of the wheat berry. 'I am glad
to be able to assure the Committee,' replied Woolton, 'that millers have been instructed, when milling National wheatmeal [of
85 per cent extraction] to take all possible steps to include the
maximum amount of germ.'[8]

The eagle-eyed soon noticed, however, that when
National wheat flour was defined by statute in the autumn of
1940, no reference was made to the need to include all of the
germ; that millers in any case were allowed to include in their
National flour up to 5 per cent of other materials, including
imported white 70 per cent flour, rye, barley and oats; that
bakers were supplied with white flour as well as the National
flour – Picton observed that in his village, the baker received
three or four sacks of white for every seven of National; and
that the armed forces continued to eat white bread throughout
the war.

Critics of white bread certainly did not help their own
cause when they made invidious comparisons between German
and British troops in the early years of the war. The German
armies, like the Russians, ate wholemeal or rye bread throughout, and Americans who had seen them in Belgium were said
to have been deeply impressed: '. . . tall, broad-shouldered,
straight backs, clear skins, lustrous hair and bright eyes – they
looked like gods'.[9] This was not an argument calculated to win
friends for wholewheat bread in wartime Britain.

But whatever the shortcomings of their daily bread, many
of the British were actually eating better, in nutritional terms,
than they had ever done in their lives before. From 1942
onwards, the Ministry of Food kept careful records of the
amounts of various foods being eaten, and made regular dietary and nutritional surveys throughout the country to see how
the national health and morale were standing up to the strain
of wartime shortages. When the pre-war diets of a group of
Yorkshire working-class families were compared with the diet
of similar families in 1943 and 1944, it was found that they had
improved in every respect. The pre-war diets had supplied only
99 per cent of their estimated calories needs, 88 per cent of the
protein, 94 per cent of the iron, 41 per cent of the calcium. The
1944 diets supplied 105 per cent of the calories, 117 per cent
of the protein, 134 per cent of the iron, and 79 per cent of the
calcium.

By 1944 consumption of tomatoes, oranges, lemons and other imported fruit had fallen by up to 50 per cent; we ate 39 per cent less fish and poultry; 21 per cent less meat; 16 per cent less fat; and 31 per cent less sugar. But by 1944 the nation was eating 45 per cent more potatoes than between 1934 and 1938; 34 per cent more vegetables; 28 per cent more milk and milk products; and 17 per cent more grain.

Particularly gratifying to concerned observers like John Boyd Orr was the fact that war and rationing had abolished the dreadful class barriers to health of the pre-war years. On equal rations, the children of the poorest were now in as good shape as the wealthiest. At a Reading hospital, the milk of nursing mothers was monitored throughout the war, to check whether they were getting adequate diets. It had been assumed that the milk of the working-class mothers would be markedly inferior in quality. It was found very soon that there was no difference whatever.

The British themselves – spare tyres and middle-aged spread trimmed away by the lean years, more exercise and fewer creature comforts – were conscious of their extra fitness. Thanks to Drummond's solid work, they were also far more aware of the role diet had played in bringing it about. One popular women's magazine expressed the general desire to hang on to this bonus of better health:

> Food discoveries that ought to stay long after there's no stringent need for them are our new habits of eating raw vegetables in salads, raw cabbage and raw carrot; our new wisdom in cooking vegetables so that all the goodness and health-giving qualities stay in; our wartime substitute for a glass of fruit juice which is a glass of the water that the vegetables were cooked in . . .[10]

The improvement was already obvious half-way through the war: in both Scotland and England in 1942, the infant mortality rate was the lowest ever recorded, and children were growing faster.

'How can we afford this improvement in wartime, with so much money and effort being hourly blown to smithereens? And why could we not afford it when we were at peace and when there was nothing to divert our efforts from bettering the national welfare and standard of living?' asked Orr eloquently, in his book *Food and the People*, published in 1943.[11]

Orr at this time was one of a group of dedicated men –
it included his old League of Nations colleagues Bruce and
McDougall – who were trying to impress on the leaders of the
West the need for a coherent post-war food and agricultural
policy. In 1943 the problems that would arise when the war
was over already stared the world in the face. Hunger and
malnutrition worldwide. Millions of refugees – or displaced
persons, as bureaucracy now preferred to call them. Half of
Europe's industry in ruins. It would take years for the world to
stagger back to anything remotely approaching normal.

But if the war achieved nothing else, it produced in those
who suffered through it an overwhelming resolve that the
world to come afterwards should be a better and happier place,
in which all should lead what Churchill called 'a fuller life', not
just a lucky few.

These noble aspirations found voice in the Hot Springs
Conference, called by President Roosevelt in June 1943 to discuss ways of achieving the 'marriage of health and agriculture'
that would have to be brought about after the war if this ideal
were to have any chance of being realized.

A phoenix rising from the ashes of the old League of
Nations, this Conference gathered together many of the people
who had been responsible for the League's initiative on
nutrition in the mid-thirties, including Orr, Bruce and
McDougall. The outbreak of war had halted these activities, but
by contrast had made its discussions on nutrition increasingly
and urgently relevant. The League's views were aired by
McDougall in a US magazine article in 1942, and shortly afterwards, Eleanor Roosevelt invited him to the White House. Over
lunch, McDougall explained to the President the League's conviction of the need for a strong worldwide organization to tackle
the twin problems of nutrition and agricultural production.
Roosevelt listened noncommittally.

Months later, McDougall opened a newspaper to find the
Hot Springs Conference announced, to be held in May 1943.

The forty-three delegates who managed to get themselves
there, straggling in from all over the world, took away a vision
of Utopia.

'Given the will, we have the power to build in every nation
a people more fit, more vigorous, more competent, a people
with longer, more productive lives, and with more physical and
mental stamina than the world has ever known . . .'[12]

16
The Growth of 'Faddism'

T he recommendations of the Hot Springs Conference were music to the ears of big business. As one American captain of industry told Orr at the time, the new food policy would be 'a self-starter for a movement which will pull agriculture, industry and trade out of the slough of post-war depression and set them on the road to an expanding world economy with resulting prosperity to everybody'. The agro-chemical industry in particular could now look forward to the best years of its life, as it happily geared up for post-war expansion.

The future of the food industry had been seen in far more doubtful terms. Each country, the Conference had recommended, should set up its own national nutritional organization to guide food and nutrition policy. These organizations were to be composed of 'authorities in health, nutrition, economics and agriculture, together with administrators and consumers' representatives'. By implication, the representatives of the colossal food business were left standing outside the door. Decisions vitally affecting the health of their balance-sheets would be taken by academic bodies in which they had no say. Who knew what the consequences might be for them? The research done so far didn't exactly suggest that a diet of packaged and processed foods led to buoyant health. Maybe the food industry should try and get in on the act too.

Luckily for this billion-dollar business, some of its leaders had seen the writing on the wall years earlier.

One day in 1938 Clarence Francis, President of General Foods Corporation, was lunching with Charles Wesley Dunn, General Counsel of the Associated Grocery Manufacturers of America. Francis was a public-spirited man who felt that wealth conferred responsibility – he was later to chair the group of prominent New Yorkers who set up the multi-million-dollar Lincoln Center for the Performing Arts. The two men discussed the desirability of a grand public enterprise to be funded by the food industry with its vast wealth. What more appropriate than an intensive programme of nutrition research? The names Rockefeller, Ford and Carnegie were now synonymous in the public mind with the noble philanthropic achievements of the foundations they had endowed. Such an enterprise would be greatly to the credit of the American food industry. Both men felt strongly that the industry had 'an obligation to the public to cooperate with responsible leaders in agriculture, medicine, public health and education to develop and apply the young and growing science of nutrition for the betterment of mankind'.[1]

The more they discussed it, the more delighted with the idea the two men became. They sounded out other representatives of the industry, and were well received.

Not all of those who responded did so from such lofty motives, no doubt. Francis's suggestions made sound sense from other points of view. The proposed foundation would be a useful public-relations exercise for the industry, supplying some scientifically respectable clothing to cover its nutritional nakedness. It could serve as an early-warning system, alerting food-manufacturing companies to nutritional advances that might mean real trouble for them, so that they could plan adjustments and changes before these were forced on them by law or public opinion. (The millers had done just that, by themselves proposing the 'enrichment' of white flour with a few synthetic vitamins.)

Sooner or later, too, the foundation would be able to claim a voice in the decision-making process. And there was going to be a lot of decision-making, most of it crucially affecting the food industry, as the nation prepared for war and shortages and restrictions.

Well aware of the problems, Roosevelt had summoned a National Nutrition Conference in May 1941, out of which grew the Food and Nutrition Board, set up by the National Research Council – itself an offshoot of the National Institute of Health. The food industry was already well represented on this board, since its twenty-four members were chosen from three groups: industry itself, scientists from universities, and research foundations; but here was a tailor-made opportunity for industry to expand its influence in the decision-making process. The new foundation would launch a comprehensive programme of grants to fund specific nutritional research projects the following year. Thereafter it could legitimately claim to be itself a research foundation while, through its grants, it could extend its influence into universities as well.

One way and another, in fact, it struck everybody as a good idea. (So much so that when its first president, Cecil King, came to write its history later on, that was the title he chose for it.)

There was an obvious problem, however. Since nutrition research was bound to be bad for profits – an assumption, interestingly, that seems to have been made by everybody in the industry – who would believe in the stainless purity of their motives? The public would assume that any work financed by such a foundation would be bent to the needs of the industry.

Francis had an answer. The foundation must be Caesar's wife – it must be completely independent of the industry and seen to be so. Its chairman must be free of all industrial taint. It must have by-laws and controls to ensure its incorruptibility. Research must be carried out to benefit the public, not the industry.

This question settled, plans went ahead, generous contributions from the industry began pouring in, and the new Nutrition Foundation was unveiled to the press early in 1942.

Cecil King, the man chosen as first president, fitted the part to perfection. He had excellent contacts throughout the nutritional world. He was one of the original charter members of the American Institute of Nutrition, a member of the Institute of Food Technologists, of the American Public Health Association, and of the reputable British Nutrition Society set up in 1941. For two years King had been secretary of the prestigious American Society of Biological Chemists, in which role he had got to know leading figures in the academic and political worlds, as well as in industrial circles. And he had been one of the original members of the National Committee on Food and Nutrition.

As soon as it was a going concern, the Foundation began making grants for research. Not all of this turned out to be as disastrous for industry as it had been feared. One of the earliest projects to be funded by the young Foundation was a study of fat utilization by adult humans, carried out by Dr Daubert and Dr Baldwin, at King's old alma mater, the University of Pittsburgh, in association with Dr Herbert Longenecker. Most of the fats and vegetable oils being used by the food industry by this time were hydrogenated, which stopped them going rancid and thus extended the shelf-life of the foodstuffs in which they were used – a plus at any time, and particularly desirable now, since many of them would be used for army rations, and might spend months in transportation or storage. The essential fatty acids in these vegetable oils had been shown by research in the thirties to be just that – essential to human life and health. But the hydrogenation process selectively destroyed some of them (and, in some processes, all of the vitamin E), while completely altering the chemical structure of others. Questions had been raised about whether these newly formed fatty acids were as efficiently metabolized by the body – and whether they were safe.

The Pittsburgh study was reassuring. The altered fatty acids were efficiently utilized in the body, and no evidence of harm appeared. This was cheering news for the food industry, who were duly appreciative. 'It is a pleasure to note the subsequent leadership in the food industry of these two associates,' noted King in his history of the Foundation, 'Dr Daubert in the General Foods Company and Dr Baldwin with Cargill Inc.'[2] Dr Longenecker's distinguished career culminated in his appointment as Chairman of the Board of Trustees for the Nutrition Foundation.

Another study investigated the diet and health of large groups of mothers and babies in Nashville, Tennessee. They found that 'the results generally were in agreement that the detectable relationships between clinical indices of maternal and infant health and nutrition were not apparent above a level of nutrition widely attained by middle-income populations . . .'[3] In plain English, millions of American families were eating perfectly adequate diets. It was on the basis of findings like this that the American Medical Association and the food industry were able to assure the public that – contrary to what the scaremongers and 'food faddists' told them – they had never had it so good. One of the doctors responsible for this reassuring piece of research, Dr William J. Darby, later became President of the Nutrition Foundation.

Not all the research funded by the Foundation gave such unmixed pleasure. At the Alabama Institute of Technology two workers noticed that rats on a complete diet had a higher resistance to a cancer-causing agent than rats on a deficient diet. They noticed, too, that rats deficient in choline developed cancer-like changes in their livers. 'Unfortunately not enough information in this general field has been developed to clarify the potential significance of initial changes,' was King's comment. The two workers later reported their findings in the *Annals of the New York Academy of Sciences*: fourteen out of eighteen rats developed cancers on their choline-deficient diet, but when it was supplemented with 0·2 per cent of choline no cancers developed.

Since one of the richest sources of choline in the human diet is wheat germ – carefully removed from America's daily bread – and totally absent from 'enriched' white flour, the Foundation's lack of interest in this nutrient was hardly surprising. Only food faddists, at this time, worried about such missing nutrients. Only health-food stores, as a rule, still sold whole-wheat bread.

Both the food industry and the medical profession, at this time, were violently irritated by the activities of the tiny but shrill health-food industry. Denunciation of the American diet of 'denatured, devitalized foods' was a stock theme of their lecturers, Bragg and Hauser among them, and a new young writer, Adelle Davis, whose first book making the same points had been published in 1939. Many of the small companies supplying health-food stores had added vitamin supplements to their range by the early forties. Hain Pure Foods were producing Be-CompX Capsules, Hainol Capsules containing cod-liver oil, and Viodical Wafers with Viosterol and dicalcium phosphate. American Health Products advertised vitamin-fortified vegetable soup cubes, fruit bars, and chocolate and vanilla powder to add to milk, fortified with extra vitamins. Naturade Products recommended their A-Kare formula for tired eyes.

Vitamin A was invariably referred to as the 'anti-infection' or the 'anti-cold' vitamin; thiamine was 'the morale vitamin'; vitamin E, 'the fertility factor', often recommended to prevent heart attacks too. Huge doses of vitamin D were suggested as a treatment for arthritis. The first firm to make vitamin supplements for sale to the general public was that of W. T. Thompson, a pharmacist who had become fascinated by vitamins. He had begun marketing a natural B_1 based on rice polishings in the thirties, followed by a vitamin C based on green peppers. When war came, W. T. Thompson gave their publicity a patriotic twist: they plastered huge colourful posters proclaiming 'Vitamins for Defence' and 'Vitamins for Victory' around military bases and munitions factories, and their promotional literature quoted research work to back up claims that more vitamins meant higher production. Other companies followed suit.

Whatever the product, the companies promoting them all used the same argument: Americans eat badly and as a result they have a variety of health problems caused by numbers of nutritional deficiencies. So they need extra vitamins.

The evidence that the American nation might not be one of the best-fed in the world started accumulating the moment that the first team of nutritionists, led by Hazel Stiebeling, went out in the early thirties to look at just what Americans were eating. They found that among poorer families, perhaps 1 per cent were eating an adequate diet. On slightly higher incomes, this rose to 9 per cent. On incomes between $1,000 and $2,000 a year, Stiebeling and her team felt it should be possible to pay for adequately nourishing meals. Even at this level, they reckoned that under a quarter of their sample did so. And the Stiebeling estimates of dietary needs were later thought to be on the low side, if anything.

Dietary surveys turned into an exact science when the Recommended Daily Allowances (usually known as the RDAs) came into being in 1941, when the Food and Nutrition Board began making plans for rationing and troop supplies. To provide a rational basis for their calculations, three committee members sweated for over a year combing through all the available figures and cross-checking them with results from animal nutrition studies. The RDAs represented a consensus view of human nutrient needs.

With the RDAs as a yardstick, dozens more surveys were made. They were invariably discouraging.

They showed that people on low incomes almost always ate poor diets.

They also showed that when it was available, the good 'protective' food simply wasn't getting eaten. A 1942 study of over a thousand Maryland schoolchildren showed that almost every one of them ate enough meat, but only a fifth of them ate enough fruit and vegetables, and less than half drank as much as two cups of milk a day.

Researchers standing by the check-outs in industrial canteens watched men pile their trays with meat, pies, potatoes and puddings, while passing by the green vegetables and citrus fruit. Only 2 per cent of the diets were reckoned to include a reasonable proportion of all the nutrients in the RDAs.

Even these figures were probably optimistic. Two meals taken straight off the table in one big industrial canteen were assayed for thiamine and vitamin C content. One meal had lost 92 per cent of its nominal thiamine value and the other 52 per cent, while one of the meals had also lost 82 per cent of its theoretical vitamin C value. Since schools and hospitals have similar catering practices, it became clear that modern Americans were likely to be alarmingly low in essential nutrients, even when these were believed to be present in their diets.

If one private clinic was anything to go by, hospital diets weren't marvellous even in theoretical terms. In a survey of 225 patients it was found that more than 75 per cent were getting inadequate thiamine and riboflavin – two essential B vitamins – and a quarter of them were getting inadequate vitamin A.

Doctors, at least, knew how to plan a healthy diet – or did they? The indefatigable researchers quizzed another group of 225 individuals, with nice homes and comfortable incomes. A high proportion of the diets were inadequate – and the twenty-nine physicians in the group chose no more wisely than anyone else.

There were individual doctors with a genuine interest in nutrition. There were thousands more whose ignorance on the subject was profound. And the higher up the professional ladder they had climbed, the truer this was likely to be, since their medical training would have been finished before the great vitamin discoveries of the twenties. The average US doctor knew just about enough to identify flagrant cases of rickets or scurvy or pellagra, and that was as far as it went.

Few men were more aware of this than Dr James McLester, a former president of the American Medical Association, who since 1940 had chaired their Council on Foods and Nutrition. In an article published in the AMA *Journal*, McLester suggested that malnutrition was far more widespread than official figures suggested, simply because it was often unrecognized. How many cases were concealed in the medical statistics – in the 370,600 deaths recorded in 1938 as due to 'disease of the circulatory system', for instance? How many alcoholics or psychopathic patients were woefully deficient in thiamine? How many cases of 'neurasthenia' were undiagnosed pellagrins? McLester had examined a number of patients who had been admitted to an Alabama hospital with a diagnosis of neurasthenia, a catch-all term to cover such vague symptoms of ill health as fatigue, nerviness, irritability and depression. Some of the patients were children 'sluggish in their actions, poorly developed and retarded in school'. When they were given brewers' yeast, their condition improved dramatically.[4]

In his comprehensive work, *Nutrition and Diet*, first published in 1927 and reissued in 1943, McLester warned doctors: 'True deficiency disease occasionally appears in an outspoken form . . . but with vastly greater frequency it takes the form of vague borderline states of ill health, states which destroy the patient's happiness, and impair his usefulness . . . weakness, loss of initiative, lack of appetite, irritability and personality change.'[5]

As a striking example of how important dietary improvements might be, McLester quoted in his *Journal* article a study carried out in a Toronto maternity clinic. Two hundred and ten women whose diets had been shown as especially poor by analysis were divided into two groups at the fourth month of pregnancy. One group was given daily supplements of an egg, 1½ pt (0·9 l) milk, 1 oz (30 g) cheese, an orange, some canned tomatoes and ½ oz (15 g) wheat germ. The women on this vastly improved diet had shorter labours and fewer problems during labour, and were in much better shape afterwards. There were no miscarriages or stillbirths among them, and the babies, who all survived the first six months, were in good condition for the first fortnight of their lives. Among the women on poor diets, many more had complications in pregnancy, a difficult labour and poor health afterwards; ten had miscarriages or stillborn babies; three of the babies had died in the first six months of their life.

These results, concluded McLester, gave some idea of what might be achieved by improved nutrition.

A few months before this report appeared, McLester – as chairman of the AMA's Council on Foods and Nutrition – had been one of a small committee that met at the request of the Council on Industrial Health to consider the whole question of vitamin supplementation for industrial workers. It had turned into a highly public debate. Several small companies had sprung up for the sole purpose of satisfying this market. In the view of the AMA, however, vitamin deficiencies were disease conditions to be treated only by doctors. The vitamins they used were not manufactured by fly-by-night companies promoting their wares to the general public. They were 'ethical' formulations, produced by the big pharmaceutical companies – for whom vitamins were now a giant business – and thus no different from drugs. The medical profession had not shown any great interest in the therapeutic use of vitamin supplements; but it was adamantly opposed to their indiscriminate use by lay people. The issue was thus a key one for them.

There was no doubt whose side McLester was on.

Here, surely, was a golden chance to make public the disastrous findings of so many surveys, and publicize the damage that bad food was doing to the nation's health. Here was a chance to call for urgent reforms in factory canteens, in school and hospital kitchens; to urge on everybody the importance of good eating habits.

The committee didn't see it that way. The committee saw it as a first-class opportunity to flatten the popular vitamin industry. Their report – which appeared in the AMA *Journal* just one month before McLester's article – rushed to make the point in its very first paragraph. 'The mass indiscriminate administration of vitamins to industrial employees is . . . unwise . . . irrational . . . uneconomical . . . special vitamin preparations cannot take the place of valuable natural foods . . .' Surveys in one part of the country might not apply in others. Possibly workers ate better than their families. Broad generalizations about workers being ill-nourished were quite unjustified. No supplementation on this scale should be considered without elaborate and scientific examination of the situation. Maybe the food in some canteens could be improved. Between-meals snacks should supply 'both minerals and vitamins in addition to at least 30 g carbohydrate'. Local nutrition committees might assist with nutrition education programmes.

As for vitamins, it was easy to exaggerate their importance. 'Physicians are of course aware that many factors are required to prevent undernourishment, that vitamins are only a few of those needed . . . calories are particularly important . . . If wholesome natural foods are used as the source of the needed calories, the required vitamins and minerals will be secured automatically . . .'

On reading their recommendations over, it may have occurred to the committee that at least one 'wholesome, natural food' – wholewheat bread, an excellent source of vitamins and minerals – was no longer available to the majority of Americans. They added a note: 'Nothing in this report is intended to belittle the significance of vitamins in nutrition, or the value of the proper use of added vitamins in improving staple foods such as bread and flour.'[6]

When McLester finally retired from chairmanship of the AMA's Council on Foods and Nutrition in 1952, they awarded him the Joseph Goldberger Medal for outstanding contributions in the field of clinical nutrition. He was cited for 'translating the results of nutrition research into human values and . . . the integration of nutrition into the teaching of all phases of medicine'.[7] Perhaps one in ten of American medical schools at this time included courses of nutrition in their curriculum. In none of them was it considered of major importance.

When the Nutrition Foundation launched its own journal, *Nutrition Reviews*, at the end of 1942, another voice was added to the chorus denouncing supplementation of the American diet by vitamins – unless responsibly prescribed by doctors. In fact, the journal had come into being for this purpose amongst others: '. . . exciting claims and counterclaims, many of which were unfounded, frequently appeared in the literature . . . [and] created confusion among physicians, educators, food technologists, agriculturists and others who were responsible for public service and safety'.[8] It would be the task of *Nutrition Reviews* to sort the wheat from the chaff, to provide an expert and critical overview of reports scattered through dozens of different journals.

For the important role of editor, a young man called Dr Frederick Stare was chosen. A graduate of Wisconsin University, Stare had worked for his doctorate under Conrad Elvehjem co-discoverer of the anti-pellagra action of nicotinic acid. One of the country's most youthful senior academics, Stare was made Harvard's first Professor of Nutrition, in their School of Medicine and Public Health, when he was in his early thirties. With his horn-rimmed spectacles, loud tweeds and boyish grin, Stare was soon to become one of the best-known and most controversial figures on the American nutrition scene. For over forty years, Stare has cheerfully assured the American public that a varied diet supplies all the nutrients the average person needs; that vitamin and mineral supplementation are almost invariably a rip-off; that sugar plays a valuable part in any diet; that the additives 'faddists' worried about were perfectly safe; and that Americans are supremely lucky in their abundant, varied and nourishing food supply.

Stare was soon a trusted and staunch friend of the food industry. There were not many nutrition experts around that the American Sugar Research Foundation could have confidently asked along to address a room full of New York food writers over luncheon one day in 1951. They knew they could count on Stare. In fine form, Stare slated the 'faddists', ridiculed the notion that 'natural' foods were somehow superior to processed foods, and suggested that milk, ice-cream and yoghurt were all equally nourishing. Wholewheat bread? 'I personally would doubt that whole grains are superior nutritionally to enriched grains from the viewpoint of practical nutrition. I know of no experimental study that shows them to be.'[9]

He also went out of his way to slam the partisans of organically grown food. The soil in which a food is grown, he assured his audience, is incapable of influencing its content of vitamins, protein, carbohydrates and fat. If a soil was deficient in a specific mineral 'this is only important to a cow or sheep that is forced to live on one plot of land exclusively and eat the food grown there,' quipped Stare. 'Human beings now get their food from many places.'[10]

The organic agriculture thus dismissed in a couple of well-turned phrases was in fact being widely discussed in America at this time, far beyond a small circle of enthusiasts. One man was responsible. He was J. I. Rodale – blasted by Stare as 'one of the leading purveyors of nutritional nonsense'. An eccentric electrical manufacturer cum publisher cum author and playwright cum farmer, Rodale's was a self-made success story in the best American tradition; he rose from a childhood of drab poverty in New York's East Side Jewish immigrant colony (he was born Cohen but changed his name when he was twenty-three) to independence and wealth by the time he was in his thirties. With a family history of heart attacks and a heart murmur diagnosed in his twenties, he became deeply interested in health, a fan of Macfadden and an avid reader of health magazines.

Glancing through the British Nature Cure magazine, *Health for All*, one day in the late thirties, Rodale came across an article by Sir Albert Howard on organic farming and its relationship to health. It happened that among Rodale's own myriad interests was what others called 'old-fashioned' and he called 'scientific' farming. Immensely excited, he at once wrote off to Howard, a correspondence developed, and the two men became friends, while Rodale absorbed the revolutionary ideas put forward in Howard's *Agricultural Testament,* published in 1940. Completely persuaded, Rodale closed down one by one the assorted digest magazines he was publishing at the time, and in May 1942 – just as the agro-chemical revolution was getting into its stride – he launched a magazine called *Organic Farming and Gardening.* Interest was minimal at first, and for years it ran at a loss. Undaunted, he launched his own definitive broadside in the shape of a book published in 1945.

Pay Dirt was both warning and invitation. Rodale warned against the inevitable consequences of the agro-chemicals by which farmers were so mesmerized, and the neglect of sound farming practices that had followed in their train. Between 1914 and 1937, he pointed out, 61 per cent of America's cultivated land had lost much if not all of its fertility, to produce dustbowl conditions where there had once been fertile prairies. Chemical fertilizers, insecticides and fungicides were destroying the complex interrelationships between soil and plant, along with the myriad micro-organisms and earthworms essential to fertile soil, the healthy growth of plants – and the health of the human beings who ate them.

Instead of backing agro-chemicals all the way, Rodale believed the United States Department of Agriculture should devote a special section to examination of the connection between soil and human health: there was as yet little scientific proof of the strongly held beliefs of the organic 'cultists'.

The impact of *Pay Dirt* was slight at the time. The few critics who deigned to notice it jeered at what struck them as Rodale's rose-tinted *nostalgie de la boue*: 'I believe a whole new era of agricultural research is in the making . . . one that will more nearly help to create a healthy society and keep it in close touch with the land from which it gets its strength . . .'[11]

Few people took seriously his misgivings about the 953 different poisonous chemicals being used on fruit trees, or about the perils of DDT, launched in the early forties as a magic bullet against any and all pest problems – agricultural or domestic.

Those who read it with interest and appreciation, however, included most of the thoughtful writers on health and diet whom Stare castigated as faddists. Among them was Gayelord Hauser.

In books and on lecture platforms across the country, Hauser had been pushing his good-diet message for years. In 1951 he finally hit the jackpot. *Look Younger, Live Longer* took the health-food message up-market, to a wider, more sophisticated audience than it had ever reached before.

It sold half a million copies, was translated into nineteen languages, stayed high on the bestseller list for months on end, and de-mystified nutrition for millions of readers. He appealed unblushingly to the snob in his readers. Like all his books, it resounds with the sound of classy names being dropped . . . the Duchess of Windsor, Lady Mendl, 'my very good friend' Ann Astaire (mother of Fred Astaire and Lady Cavendish), 'the lovely Barbara Hutton', Paulette Goddard. Recipes came commended by the glitteringly beautiful people who had eaten them – 'I served these patties, and grilled grapefruit, to Greta Garbo the first time she ate at my house.' Throughout, there was a flattering assumption that his readers, too, moved in such rarefied social circles that they too could afford to spend money on good chiropodists, on reliable beauty experts. Take a day off to try the One-day Hollywood Liquid Diet, he suggested: '. . . be as elegant as the movie stars; rest all day. Have someone wait on you who will serve the juices absolutely fresh . . .'

Diplomatically, Hauser went out of his way to be nice about doctors, and was at pains to dissociate himself from many of his former supporters. 'We are not faddists or cultists in the *Look Younger, Live Longer* programme. With us, correct eating is not an obsession. It is fun . . .'

Health foods – from 'those dreary little *ill*-health-food places' – didn't belong in the Hauser scheme of things. Instead, there was healthy food – delicious, colourful, elegantly presented. ('There must be pleasure in eating: Americans eat with their eyes.') In his glowing prose, fresh salads and vegetable juices took on exotic appeal. 'Dark California carrots make the most delicious juice . . . Peel tender young rhubarb, wash fresh ripe strawberries and put through a vegetable juicer . . . sweeten this beautiful rose-coloured juice with honey.' For a Gayelord Hauser Cocktail – 'cut up equal amounts of dark-green celery, golden carrots and red apples'. Urged by Hauser, even the unfamiliar yoghurt, wheat germ, brewers' yeast and molasses sounded good enough to eat.

No nut cutlets and dandelion coffee for the new gourmet health-fiend. He enjoyed plenty of protein – lean hamburgers, roast chicken, grilled liver; enjoyed a glass of wine with his meal – 'festive and cheerful'; and a small cup of black coffee afterwards – 'made in the modern manner and taken in moderation it cannot be harmful to healthy people'; he was even allowed an occasional cigarette – 'in moderation, smoking is not harmful. It can be relaxing after meals.'[12]

For all its blatant snobbery, however, hundreds of thousands of ordinary Americans reading Hauser's book learned for the first time that there was more to nutrition than Stare's Five Food Groups and the Recommended Daily Allowances. Eating the right food, they read, could make them feel younger, fitter, sexier, more energetic; it could give them glorious hair, clear eyes, good skin, trim figures. Ideas that they had only heard denounced as faddism or medical heresies by Stare and his friends, they now learned, had been put forward by physicians or scientists of irreproachable professional standing. Foods grown with modern fertilizers were deficient in many nutrients; people who ate only organically grown foods were healthier and felt better for it. 'Enriched' bread was a con-trick: heart disease, high blood pressure, arteriosclerosis, diabetes and cancer had all increased enormously since refined flour had first become cheaply and widely available. American hospitals might not have heard of raw food – but perfectly respectable clinics in Europe were treating ulcers, colitis and liver problems with a diet of raw vegetable juices.

Like McLester, Hauser warned readers, 'Do not try to substitute vitamin pills for food vitamins.' Unlike McLester, he didn't think you could have too much of a good thing. As well as gulping down quantities of 'fortified milk' – heavily laced with brewers' yeast, skimmed milk powder and molasses – his followers were advised to take a daily halibut-liver oil capsule, a vitamin E capsule and extra calcium.

Shrewdly he pitched his appeal at the millions of women who felt they'd said goodbye to their youth. 'In this book . . . I shall teach you how to eat not merely to satisfy hunger, but to eat for health, good looks, youth, vitality, the joy of living. I will show you that you are not old at forty, fifty, sixty, seventy; that you need not be old at eighty, ninety . . .'[13]

With women all over America ordering his Body Slant board – as used on the Elizabeth Arden beauty farm – practising his Stomach Lift – 'recommended to me by Sir Arbuthnot Lane, physician to King George V' – and telling themselves firmly 'I am *only* forty-five!' as he suggested, Hauser became a celebrity nationwide, interviewed by *Newsweek*, quoted in the glossies, photographed in all his trim 6 ft 3 in elegance for the gossip columns.

The health-food industry readily forgave Hauser his disobliging remarks. His book set their cash-tills ringing and their profits rocketing for months on end, as customers flooded in wanting Hauser's Five Wonder Foods – brewer's yeast, powdered skim milk, yoghurt, wheat germ and molasses – that they couldn't seem to find anywhere else.

'The business boom from this book was tremendous, and it lasted for a long time,' recalled health-food retailer Stanley Phillips. 'But the biggest boom – and perhaps the most lasting – was the Adelle Davis books that brought people to the health-food stores in droves for natural vitamins and supplements.'[14]

Ironically, the uncrowned queen of the health-food industry had a background of impeccable medical orthodoxy. She was crisp about America's abounding health cranks – 'they usually have no scientific training, peddle tremendous amounts of misinformation, make unjustifiable claims, and are often out for commercial gain'. She was critical of their negative, 'should-not' philosophy: she had once sat on a platform listening to the chairman of a health organization make his introductory remarks. He ranted, she remembered, 'with astounding fury about "poison white sugar" killing people. Probably each person in the audience had eaten "poison white sugar"; yet some of them appeared to be alive . . .' She was appalled by their peculiar eating habits: '. . . a woman recently told me that her breakfast was wholegrain cereal, hand-ground immediately before it was cooked, on which she put powdered whey, bone meal, sunflower seeds, powdered milk, yeast, rice polish, cream and "raw" sugar. Her husband commented that it was like compiling a compost heap . . .'

Doctors to Adelle Davis were always 'wonderful people: I have met few finer' – and she meant every word of it. She defended them hotly against the charge of nutritional ignorance. 'Physicians are often overworked to the point of exhaustion; yet they must constantly keep up with recent developments in antibiotics, hormones, new survival techniques, treatments for new diseases, and new treatments in old diseases . . . You may find the time to study nutrition: probably [your doctor] . . . cannot . . .'[15]

When her bestseller *Let's Eat Right to Keep Fit* appeared in 1954, Adelle Davis was already fifty years old, with half a crowded, successful career behind her.

They had nicknamed her 'Vitamin Davis' when she was still at college because she was so fascinated by the strange new science of nutrition, reading everything she could lay her hands on about it. She went on to study nutrition and biochemistry at the University of South California Medical School, and became a dietician at New York's Bellevue Hospital because she wanted to work with people. She soon became restless with assembly-line diet-planning for anonymous patients – and horrified by hospital food. ('I tell you, in most hospitals, the food is so bad that if you weren't sick on admission, you'd get that way pretty quickly,' she later told a British journalist.)[16] After that she moved to the Judson Health Clinic, where she planned diets for poor Italian immigrant families, and became more and more convinced that eating the right food could help prevent most of the illnesses they suffered. Finally, she went west, started her own consultancy practice and began to build the huge dossier of patients successfully treated purely by diet on which she drew so freely and fascinatingly in her books. She worked for a time with the William E. Branch Clinic – a famous Hollywood establishment whose movie-star patients insisted on someone thoroughly knowledgeable about nutrition to advise them: Bieler, Bragg and Hauser had done their work well.

She wanted to help ordinary people, though, and few of those could afford the Branch Clinic – or her own – fees. So she began writing books; *Optimum Health*, the first, was privately printed. Dr Branch and his colleagues were full of admiration for the massive research she did before she put anything down on paper. In the late thirties came *You Can Get Well*, a story-book account of how to eat for good health – which instantly brought her a huge following at the health-store level. In 1947 she published her cookbook *Let's Cook It Right*, followed two years later by *Vitality through Planned Nutrition*.

It was *Let's Eat Right to Keep Fit* that made her famous overnight. Hauser had prepared the ground well. Millions of Americans now wondered what they should eat, why their doctors never seemed to mention the word nutrition, whether the American diet was really as wonderful as everyone said, whether there was any connection between this diet and the epidemic of killer diseases that had swept over their country – cancer, heart disease, arthritis, diabetes – whether an improved diet couldn't help them with health problems that baffled their doctors.

Where Hauser had taken his readers into society drawing-rooms and Hollywood parties, Adelle led hers into clinics, consulting-rooms, biochemistry laboratories. A crash course in nutrition from A to Z, her book was an eye-opener, distilling a huge volume of information and research in vivid, readable form that showed how closely diet and health – or sickness – were linked. Her style was racy, telling, persuasive. 'Strong well-nourished muscles automatically hold the body erect,' she told women. 'A mother who says to her child "stand up straight" is complaining of her own failure to provide nourishing food.'[17]

Her case-histories were more fascinating than any who-dunnit, a happy ending invariably supplied by sound nutrition. There was the twenty-eight-year-old woman – 'she was under-weight, pale, listless; her hair was stringy; tension lines cut her forehead; and fatigue was stamped on her face . . .' There was the eighteen-month-old boy whose father – an All-American football player – had set his heart on a strong athletic child. 'Instead this pathetic child was smaller than most one-year-old children and had been covered with severe eczema since he was three weeks old. The boy was lethargic and seemed dim-witted . . . thousands of dollars had been spent seeking correction . . .' There was 'the middle-aged woman whose brilliant mind worked sluggishly, and who had huge varicose veins . . . a history of repeated attacks of gout . . .'

Adelle introduced her readers to outstanding nutrition research that few doctors had heard of and no professional dietician was taught to read – particularly McCarrison, and an American dentist, Dr Weston Price, whose *Nutrition and Physical Degeneration*, published in 1938, is a searing indictment of the modern Western diet.

After years of studying the narrow, crowded dental arches and decaying teeth of his American patients, and wondering what defect in their diet was responsible, it occurred to Weston Price that it might be more instructive to study primitive people, isolated from 'civilization', who had sound teeth and excellent health, and find out what was *right* in their diets. He shut up his practice, packed his bags and took off. In the next years, he studied Swiss peasants, crofters in the Outer Hebrides, the Eskimos of Alaska, the Indians in the far north, west and central Canada, the Melanesians and Polynesians in the south Pacific, tribes in eastern and central Africa, the Aborigines of Australia, the Maori tribes of New Zealand, and remote people in Malaysia. Everywhere he found the same thing.

On a wide range of 'primitive' diets – the stoneground whole-rye bread, vegetables and cheese of the Swiss mountains, the milk, blood and meat of the African Masai, the caribou,

184 The Food Factor

fish, nuts and berries of the Alaskan Eskimos, the fish, oats and barley of the people of the Hebrides – all food whole and unprocessed – he found they enjoyed superb and robust health, the cheerfulness that McCarrison so much admired in the Hunzas, and marvellous teeth. In all his years of US practice, he had never seen the perfectly formed dental arches and the magnificent strong teeth that he studied with astonishment in tribe after primitive tribe.

And he found that within one generation of being introduced to Western 'civilization' in the shape of white flour, tinned foods, refined sugar, their superb health broke down, the dental arches became narrowed and crowded, the broad-cheeked smiling faces were replaced by narrowed and pinched facial structures, and tooth decay became rampant.

Sometimes this modern Fall of Mankind could be studied within half an hour's journey. On the island of Scalpay, the children were sturdy and healthy, with excellent teeth, on their diet of oatcakes, fish and barley. Examination showed only one tooth in a hundred attacked by decay. Ten miles away, at the little port of Tarbert, in Harris, he found that nearly one third of the children's teeth that he examined were decayed: the village store sold white bread, jams, white sugar, tinned food.

Western diet didn't simply mean decayed teeth, stressed Adelle. Among his primitive people, Price had found 'no physicians, surgeons, psychiatrists, no crime, no prisons; no mental illness and no institutions for the insane, feeble-minded, alcoholics, or drug addicts; no child delinquency, no homosexuality. Every mother nursed her babies, a non-functional breast was unheard of. Mental, moral and emotional health accompanied physical health.' Returning to populated areas Dr Price had found 'diseases of all kinds, crime, perversions, insanity and sexual immorality . . .'[18]

The diet of modern America made Adelle Davis despair: '. . . thousands of adults and millions of children in our country have never once had one mouthful of genuinely wholesome food; not one sip of delicious medically certified raw milk or one bite of delightful freshly stoneground, 100 per cent wholegrain bread or cereal or of unbelievably good organically grown fruits and vegetables'.[19]

Since this kind of wholesome food – 'grown on naturally mineralized, naturally composted soil' was no longer available, Adelle recommended vitamin supplements – reluctantly – as a necessary evil.

More even than Hauser, her book brought a boom in the health-food industry, as readers rushed to load up with more yoghurt, more yeast and wheat germ, more blackstrap molasses – and millions of dollars' worth of the vitamin and mineral supplements she mentioned.

Inevitably, Hauser, Davis and Rodale made powerful enemies, however careful they were to dissociate themselves from the health-food industry and its lunatic fringe.

They made enemies of the powerful and monopolistic American Medical Association, who saw dangerous subversion in their attempts to demonstrate the links between poor eating habits and ill health, and to teach people how to keep themselves healthy – and in no need of a doctor – through improved diet.

They made enemies of the pharmaceutical industry, for whom the future was more and better drugs, in an age of never-ending pharmaceutical miracles. Until antibiotics arrived in the war years, vitamins had been big business for drug companies who had poured millions into researching them. And then along came antibiotics. From being rarer than radium, more costly than gold-dust, penicillin and streptomycin became the mass-produced, low-profit staples of the entire industry. In 1948, according to the chairman of Chas. Pfizer, John McKeen, the New York Department of Hospitals spent nearly one half of its total budget on penicillin and streptomycin alone. In 1949 antibiotics accounted for 22 per cent of total value of all ethical drugs manufactured. By 1950 45 per cent of Pfizer's own sales were in antibiotics, and the sales potential seemed limitless, from these or other drugs just around the corner.

'It is roughly estimated that antibiotics can be used with fair to excellent results in 30 to 50 per cent of the cases requiring the attention of the physician,'[20] announced McKeen. The most level-headed became euphoric, and entertained visions of a future in which almost every disease that afflicted suffering humanity would be made to yield to some wonderful new product of the pharmaceutical industry.

Where antibiotics didn't work, doctors were soon turning to cortisone. In May 1949 a small medical audience at the Mayo Clinic watched a film showing the astonishing effect of cortisone on patients suffering intense pain from rheumatoid arthritis and hardly able to move their stiffened joints. Within two or three days of treatment, they were smiling, pain-free, mobile. Cortisone, a hormone secreted by the adrenal glands, appeared to 'switch off' symptoms of pain and inflammation throughout the body; ACTH, discovered soon afterwards, stimulated the adrenal glands into supplying extra cortisone to achieve the same effect.

Overnight, cortisone shot into the headlines, and stayed there for months while the list of diseases that responded to it, or to ACTH, steadily lengthened. Soon it included gout, arthritis and rheumatic conditions, skin problems, asthma and hayfever and other allergic conditions, ulcerative colitis, myasthenia gravis, shock, burns, even some rare forms of cancer such as Hodgkin's disease. More cautious observers – and doctors themselves – emphasized that cortisone's miraculous powers subsided as soon as treatment stopped, and that it could have deadly side-effects. But it was still invaluable for the relief of pain, in certain medical emergencies, and for intermittent conditions such as gout, asthma and hayfever.

Very soon, the public developed an insatiable appetite for miracles.

To companies making profits beyond their wildest dreams out of drugs like these, suggestions that the answer to modern ills was a good diet and prevention rather than the prescription pad were unwelcome, to put it mildly. And doctors who found for the first time in their harassed lives that they could now apparently halt disease in its tracks, and banish pain overnight with a course of injections or a bottle of pills, were in no mood to be told they should go back to school and learn all about vitamins.

But by far the bitterest enemy of Hauser, Rodale, Adelle Davis, and all those who advocated a healthy diet was the multi-billion-dollar processed-food industry. 'The smallest comment concerning the value of nutrition,' as Adelle Davis pointed out, 'is a criticism, direct or implied, of this industry, which allows nutrients to be lost during processing in order to increase profits.'[21]

When criticism and nutritional advice came from dreary little health-food publications and a handful of little-known lecturers, they could be dismissed as cranks and long-haired dreamers.

Now the advocates of healthy eating had moved from Greenwich Village to Fifth Avenue, and they were national figures. Instead of citing dubious nineteenth-century naturopaths, they quoted doctors and the latest biochemical research. Instead of addressing themselves to a chosen few, they found audience among the thoughtful, the intelligent, the influential and among doctors themselves. Instead of making their views known through pamphlets and small-time magazines, they were being broadcast in best-selling books, in national newspapers, in women's magazines, on TV chat shows.

With billions of dollars at stake, it was to be expected that the food and drug businesses, with the cooperation of the American Medical Association, should move to silence this opposition with every power at their disposal.

17
The National Health

A t the end of the war, the British were surprised to learn that they had never been healthier in their lives.

'The vital statistics during the war years,' reported the nation's Chief Medical Officer in 1946, 'have been phenomenally good.'

Particularly astonishing were the child mortality rates: they were lower than they had been for decades, even though the Blitz had claimed the lives of 7,000 children under fifteen, and there had been a sharp increase in accidental deaths due to the blackout. Fewer mothers had died in childbirth. Fewer babies had been stillborn.

The nation's children were sturdier and taller. Their teeth were better, too: in one Glasgow study, only 18 per cent of five-year-old children had had no decayed teeth in 1938; by 1944, nearly half the five-year-olds had perfect sets of teeth.

Tuberculosis was still a killer – but the deathrate had gone down steadily all through the war years, and this despite the fact that many patients had had to be sent home from sanatoria.

By the end of the war, too, there were fewer anaemic women and children, although the meat ration for years had been a few ounces a week at most.

Delivering the Milroy Lectures to the Royal College of Physicians in 1946, Dr H. E. Magee commented that these improvements had been achieved despite highly adverse conditions: '. . . no one could escape the general anxiety, the trials of the blackout, the harder work and the lack of amusements. In addition, housing and the general environmental conditions were worse than they had been for years, and there were fewer doctors, dentists, nurses and health visitors to attend to the needs of the people.'

It was therefore reasonable to conclude that the improved wartime diet had been almost entirely responsible for the nation's better health.

'If we are to retain what has been achieved during the war,' concluded Dr Magee, 'we must see that the quality and quantity of our agricultural products and imports are determined primarily by health requirements . . . that the public are made aware of the dietary requirements for health . . . and steps should also be taken . . . to make it possible for everyone to secure a diet sufficient for his needs.'[1]

The determination to maintain this steady improvement in the health of the British was universal: who could forget the horrifying pre-war revelations of want and widespread malnutrition?

Just how it was to be maintained was another question altogether, and one to which a number of different answers were being put forward in 1943, as the end of the war came in sight.

One of the most widely discussed was the Peckham approach.

The wartime evacuation of thousands of London children had forced the Pioneer Health Centre to close its doors. But a report on its work, *The Peckham Experiment*, was published in 1943; and this radical and imaginative approach to the question of health excited enormous public interest. The book went into six printings, sold 50,000 copies, and was widely quoted in journals and public debate both in Britain and the United States. Over the next two years, members of its staff gave a total of 300 lectures on the Peckham ideal, often at government expense, spelling out their message to British forces overseas, to physicians, to administrative and welfare personnel, to interested lay people. When the war was over, the two doctors were invited to the United States, where their audiences included the full assembly of the United Nations, the Community Service Society of New York and representatives of Harvard University, Johns Hopkins Medical School and the American Medical Association.

Essentially what the two doctors proposed was a double-decker health service. There would be, first, a nationwide network of health centres based on the Peckham model, with the same recreational facilities, the same untrammelled freedom for members to organize their own use of them, the access to good fresh organically grown food, the periodic health over-hauls. There would be the same dynamic approach to the health both of the individual and of the family as a biological unit. Advice on diet, antenatal care and infant welfare would be the natural concerns of these health centres.

There would also be a network of more conventional medical centres, staffed by groups of GPs – whom Williamson saw as the first line of defence against disease – and equipped with the most modern facilities for diagnosis and treatment, including simple surgical procedures. Where the GP wanted a second opinion, he might refer his case to the group for review. And it was to be he who controlled admissions to hospital for specialized treatment. So important was the role of the GP as Williamson conceived it that he suggested that all medical students should spend a full year at work in one of these medical centres.

A much earlier study of medical services, the Dawson Report of 1920, had also stressed the importance of the GP, since he had far better opportunities than any hospital specialist for careful observation of patients, and the detection of disease in its earliest stages. But the Dawson Report recommended involving the GP in preventive as well as curative medicine, whereas Williamson was adamant that services such as infant welfare and antenatal advice belonged in the health rather than the medical centre.

Even before the war, the Peckham experiment had attracted considerable attention – particularly its discovery that 'seven out of ten uncomplaining members of the public entering our doors had not even negative attributes of health – freedom from diagnosable disorder'. The people of Peckham certainly weren't particularly well off, but no more did they belong among the nation's poorest and most deprived. If a Peckham sample produced such a horrifyingly high incidence of conditions requiring medical attention, how much more must this be true of, say, Bethnal Green or the slums of Glasgow?

This consideration was certainly in the minds of the committee, chaired by Sir William Beveridge, which met early in the war to consider the national insurance scheme then in operation. This scheme dated back to Lloyd George's 1911 Act, under which all those in paid employment – although not their families – could call upon the services of a 'panel' doctor. Equally in the committee's minds, no doubt, were the shaming pre-war disclosures of poor health and serious illness due entirely to poverty. The rates of sickness, infant mortality and death all rose in proportion as the social ladder was descended; the lives of the very poor were still nastier, more brutish and shorter than those of the well-off. Thus a vast amount of ill health was preventable by the simple measure of improving social conditions.

The Beveridge Report was published in 1942 and made two revolutionary proposals: that social insurance should guarantee everyone the minimum income needed for subsistence; and that medical care of every kind should in future be available free to the poorest as to the richest.

The Report was hailed as a masterly solution to the problems of poverty and ill health – a giant step for mankind along the road to Utopia. There would be no more families living on bread and marge and tea, no more unnecessary suffering borne because a doctor's fees were too high. Malnutrition and deficiency disease would wither away as all became able to afford a decent diet. And though initially the cost of treating so many millions would be high, these costs would soon come down as they were all gradually dealt with, and a great explosion of health and well-being would result.

Yet another answer, as we have seen, was supplied by the Hot Springs Conference, with its emphasis on a massive increase in agricultural output.

To most of those taking part in the conference, or commenting on its recommendations, one conclusion seemed obvious. The post-war world would be heavily dependent on the agro-chemical industry if it was to feed all its hungry people.

A small and brave minority argued otherwise. Among these was Sir Albert Howard, who had written to *The Times* within weeks of the outbreak of war to suggest that by the nationwide adoption of his composting methods, a great increase in soil fertility, as well as an important benefit to the nation's health, might be achieved. In 1940 his *Agricultural Testament* was published, a detailed and scientific account of his life's work. His views were brushed aside as visionary and irrelevant. The agricultural policies being pursued in Britain at this time could hardly have been further removed from Howard's view of sound farming.

Long before the war broke out, British farmers had already learnt to rely on artificial fertilizers. The fertilizer industry itself – like the pharmaceutical business – was a child

of war. The new nitrogen-fixing process which had made possible the large-scale manufacture of explosives during the First
World War had proved wonderfully adaptable. No need for
explosives manufacturers to go out of business, they switched
to making fertilizers instead. A network of agricultural research
stations springing up across the country promoted these products as zealously as the industry's own salesmen: the Ministry
of Agriculture smiled on them.

In the Depression of the thirties, farm prices dropped
catastrophically, hundreds of farmers went bankrupt and all
over the country farms were left untenanted, with hedges uncut
and once-rich cultivated fields 'tumbling down' to grass. The
corn-growing areas were particularly hard-hit, and more and
more farmers were soon abandoning such traditional conservation practices as muck-spreading and crop rotation. Artificial
fertilizers were the relatively cheap new option. During the war,
as Howard later pointed out, farm purchases of fertilizers were
heavily subsidized by the government: '. . . the staff of these
vested interests were at the disposal of the Ministry . . . the local
War Agricultural Executive Committee soon became salesmen
of the contents of the manure bag; the frequent speeches of
the Minister of Agriculture invariably contained some exhor-
tation to use more fertilizers'.[2]

The enormous increases in crop yield which made it possible for Britain to survive without going hungry in the war years
were partly due to the huge amounts of fertilizer farmers were
now using, and which were generally seen as an indispensable
weapon of defence. To argue that reliance on fertilizers was a
dangerously short-sighted policy which in the long run would
have lethal consequences for the health of soil, crop, beast and
man was to court intense unpopularity and risk being branded
an unpatriotic crank.

Among this bold handful was Lady Eve Balfour, who,
after taking an agricultural course at Reading University, had
acquired New Bells Farm at Haughley in Suffolk at the end of
the First World War, which she had farmed ever since. In 1938
she became aware of the work of Howard, which she immediately began putting into practice at Haughley, where her neighbour, Alice Debenham, was also a convert. Gradually she was
drawn into the inner circle of the still-tiny organic movement:
she became familiar with the work of McCarrison, of Dr G. T.
Wrench, who had written glowingly of it in his 1938 book, *The
Wheel of Health*, of Dr Lionel Picton of the Cheshire Panel. A

robustly healthy countrywoman, she also noticed that her usual winter colds and bouts of rheumatism vanished when she began eating wholewheat bread made from her own compost-grown wheat.

In *The Living Soil*, published in 1943, Lady Eve translated the ideas of Howard and McCarrison into plain but eloquent language that any intelligent person could understand. She saw the work of these two men – one in the medical, the other in the agricultural field – as complementary, 'forming two parts of a connected whole'. This whole was her central thesis: 'that the health of man, beast, plant and soil is one indivisible whole; that the health of the soil depends on maintaining its biological balance, and that starting with a truly fertile soil, the crops grown on it, the livestock fed on those crops, and the humans fed on both, have a standard of health and a power of resisting disease, from whatever cause, greatly in advance of anything ordinarily found in this country'.[3]

At the heart of the organic argument is the law of return which the Hunzas obeyed so scrupulously: 'Only by faithfully returning to the soil in due course everything that has come from it can fertility be made permanent and the earth be made to yield a genuine increase.' Inattention to this law, she pointed out, had had dire consequences worldwide – spectacularly so in the United States, where 'the total loss of fertility has been estimated at 30 to 50 per cent of the total originally available', and where the biggest of the Midwest's horrendous dustbowls advanced as much as 40 miles (64 km) in one year. But there were examples much nearer home. In 1942, acres of the sugar-beet-producing fenland in East Anglia, which had been ploughed up, denuded of trees and hedgerows, and then heavily fertilized, had their topsoil blown away in high winds and the newly sown crops with it. 'An exhausted soil is an unstable soil: Nature has no further use for it and removes it bodily . . .'[4]

What exactly was the meaning of the word humus so enthusiastically bandied about by the organic movement? It was not, explained Lady Eve, some kind of muck or manure to be dumped into the soil. It was – and again she quoted – 'a product of decomposition of plant and animal residues through the agency of micro-organisms'. The living soil teemed with these benevolent micro-organisms. Some of these were fungi, forming the intriguingly named mycorrhizal association with plants, in which they wove their own myriad tiny thread-like substances through the roots of rubber tree or tea bush, vine or wheat plant, in what had once been thought to be a parasitic encroach-ment. Howard, Dr M. C. Rayner and others had shown that it was the very reverse, and that it was where this association was strongest that the healthiest and most vigorous plants flour-ished, though just how they were nourished by it remained for research to discover.

Some fungi were predators of crop pests, inflicting a grue-some death on their victims. They formed loops of sticky threads, and when a luckless eelworm crawled through, the loops tightened round his wildly thrashing body. Once his struggles abated, the fungus bored into his bodily cavity to fill it with more of the thread-like substances. Eventually these crowded out the eelworm's internal organs to cause paralysis and death.

The whole subject of the soil's micro-organisms and their role in promoting fertility had been, according to Lady Eve, astonishingly neglected – because, thanks to Liebig, it was soil chemists rather than soil biologists who were more and more in control of agricultural research stations.

Much the boldest claim made by the organic lobby was that better health resulted when people lived off the crops produced and the livestock reared on land which had been cultivated organically than when they had to depend – as almost all West-ern civilization now did – on the 'devitalized' products of 'chem-ical' farming. Lady Eve Balfour could point to no conclusive scientific evidence to prove this claim, but she could and did cite evidence of a very powerful association indeed – starting with the legendary Hunzas. Particularly striking was the tale told by Dr Scharff, who until the fall of Malaya had been the Chief Officer of Health at Singapore. At the outbreak of war, Dr Scharff had had 500 Tamil coolies in his charge, engaged on sanitary duties. He arranged for them to be given 40 acres of allotment for their use, on condition that these were composted according to Howard's Indore methods, and the vegetables grown on them used only for the Tamils and their families.

The results were startling. There was 'a surprising improvement in stamina and health acquired by those taking part in this cultivation. Debility and sickness had been swept away and my men were capable of, and gladly responded to, the heavier work demanded by the increasing stress of war.' The families of the coolies also improved dramatically, and by the time the Japanese invasion brought the experiment to an end, it was obvious that 'the health of men, women and children who had been served consistently with healthy food grown on fertile soil was outstandingly better than it was amongst those similarly placed but not enjoying the benefits of such health-yielding produce'.[5]

In developing her case, Lady Eve admitted that critical scientific proof was still lacking. But she argued that the circumstantial evidence in favour was so strong that the onus of proof rested on the government, which should put the question to trial without delay. Such tests had long been called for by the organic lobby. Among those doing so was Lord Teviot, a banker and chairman of the Liberal Party, who had baked his own wholewheat bread for years, and was known in the House of Lords as Uncle Wholemeal. In the *Farmer's Weekly* of September 1942 he had suggested that the government should run a comparison trial. On a given number of acres crops should be cultivated organically, and on the same number of acres and similar land the same crops should be grown with artificial fertilizers; the health of livestock reared on both kinds of land should be compared. He was confident what the outcome would be.

Perhaps the chemical-fertilizer industry was less confident. At all events, the government had failed to respond, and Lady Eve concluded her book by describing the major piece of research which she hoped would serve the same purpose. In 1939, several years before Lord Teviot's proposal, her neighbour Alice Debenham had set up the Haughley Research Trust, to which she had given her own eighty-acre Walnut Tree Farm, farmed jointly by Lady Eve with New Bells Farm. The two together would be leased or sold to the Trust, to form an experimental farm of some 236 acres on which it was proposed that a critical experiment should be carried out, comparing different farming methods and their effect on the health of soil, plant and animal. By the time war broke out, the experiment was already under way; it was to run for over thirty years, making an important contribution to the science of plant nutrition.

With farm labour at a premium and heavy yields a national necessity, Lady Eve's spirited defence of 'muck and magic' changed nothing in the wartime agricultural scene. But the case she had made out was a strong one, and the protagonists of agro-chemical farming were driven either to ignore her, or to make fun of the organic appeal to instinctive peasant wisdom. ' "If people ate more of what's grown with muck, there'd not be half the illness about . . . What's grown with chemicals may look all right, but it ain't got the stay in it . . ." '[6]

Thousands of intelligent readers, however, now encountering the ideas of Howard and McCarrison for the first time, were not inclined to dismiss them so cavalierly. To the author's astonishment, her book had to be reprinted within three months. Thereafter it went into a total of nine editions, was quoted and commented on all over the world, was translated into Swedish, Spanish and German, and before the end of the war had produced nearly 500 letters from people in countries as distant as Australia and South America as well as from British readers. Some of these letters were requests for advice or information. Many more were from people who had been thinking along the same lines, had carried out experiments for their own satisfaction with much the same results as Scharff's coolies and longed for news of similar work. Here was ample evidence for the organic case. What was obviously needed now was some kind of clearing-house for the exchange of information.

Thus was born the Soil Association, officially launched in November 1946 in a single London room made available by the directors of the Pioneer Health Centre in Peckham. Its stated objectives were: '(1) To bring together all those working for a fuller understanding of the vital relationships between soil, plant, animal and man. (2) To initiate, coordinate and assist research in this field. (3) To collect and distribute the knowledge so as to create a body of informed public opinion.'

In an important sense, the Soil Association was the first public expression of a new environmental awareness which had been quietly growing up alongside – and in opposition to – modern industrial civilization. Its opponents liked to stigmatize it as an exercise in woolly-headed nostalgia, an unrealistic hankering for some fancied bygone Arcadia, when the economy of England was still largely rural. But although the element of nostalgia was certainly not absent, the new movement had much stronger and deeper roots than this, while its leadership of deeply thoughtful doctors, farmers, biologists and agricultural scientists owed their inspiration to Howard and McCarrison, two of the most able and brilliant men of their day, whose scientific credentials were impeccable, however unacceptable their views might be in orthodox circles. What such people opposed was the industrial world-view of man using his sophisticated technological skills to triumph over his environment, and plunder its resources at will to gratify his needs or his desire for profit. Typical of this approach were the agro-chemist, forcing huge yields by the use of fertilizers while ignoring the complex biology of the soil – or the industrial food processor who threw out the heart and goodness of the wheat to feed the people on worthless white bread bleached with chemicals and 'enriched' with a few synthetic nutrients – or the medical specialist who was never taught to study the whole person, either in health or sickness, before settling down to a lifetime of concentrating on a single facet of ill health. The triumphs of such science, in the organic view, could never be complete because they failed to take into account the complex biological balance of nature, the 'wholeness' of which man was only a part.

The 'wholeness' of which Picton and Wrench, Scott Williamson and Lady Eve Balfour wrote was no mere sentimental notion, but the very cornerstone of their philosophy. Lady Eve Balfour summed up the attitude of those who formed the new Association as

> the ecological approach or the philosophy of Wholeness . . . the logical outcome of a positive approach, just as Fragmentation is the outcome of a negative approach. When the universe is seen as a whole, Nature is seen as being governed by the law of Order and Interdependence, and survival is seen to depend on biological balance, not cut-throat competition . . . Health (which means wholeness) depends on all the parts fulfilling their individual functions in cooperation with each other and with the organized whole. This does not apply only to the organs of the body . . . but to the whole man, who consists of body, mind and spirit, and these must also be in balance with each other, and in mutual synthesis with their environment . . .[7]

There could hardly be a better description of the objectives of the Peckham inquiry. And in fact from the outset, the new Association was seen as a bridge between the Haughley research into a positive concept of soil fertility, and the Peckham search for a positive concept of health. Scott Williamson was an active founder-member, and Peckham's energetic manager, C. Donald Wilson, became first honorary secretary to the Association, and later its full-time general secretary.

The Pioneer Health Club had opened its doors again after the war, in a war-scarred building and in difficult circumstances financially. Five hundred and fifty of its former member families had clamoured for its reopening, turning to with a will to make the building habitable again and restore their Centre to

life. Even in its straitened form, with all the problems of shortages and restrictions, the Centre exerted the old powerful spell.
There is an indescribable nostalgia in the comments of members who were allowed to enjoy its unique facilities for what
turned out to be a tragically brief spell.

> It was the atmosphere, it was like an extension of your
> home . . . It was like having a lot of brothers and sisters,
> being part of a huge family, but you grew from that, you
> expanded from that. Whereas you started off from two
> little rooms, just mum and dad and two kids, you were able
> to grow out of your own environment. I don't know how
> you explain that . . . When it closed there were lots of
> people not knowing what to do . . .[8]

Members knew that the Centre was unique. Outside
observers found it hard to resist the quite extraordinary spirit
that embued the place. 'Few who have close knowledge of Peckham ever do remain cold and detached about it,' wrote one
such observer, John Comerford, in 1947. One of the things that
struck him most was its positive promotion of health in people
whose lives before joining had been set unavoidably on a course
to ill health.[9]

To thousands of people, Peckham made the most obvious
kind of sense if only in terms of the vast sums that the state
would be saved in the long run, never mind the health and
happiness of those involved. The Beveridge Plan, however far-
sighted and admirable, catered only for those who were already
sick. Peckham would catch them a stage earlier.

> The healthy, if they are not given a proper outlet and
> environment for the cultivation of their health, can soon
> degenerate into the unhealthy . . . That is one tremendous
> achievement of the Health Centre, to keep the healthy
> healthy. The next achievement is to save the unhealthy
> from joining the ranks of the hopeless, and gradually to
> win them back to health.

In the first flush of post-war euphoria, other Peckhams
were planned, at least half a dozen of them, one of which was
to be at Coventry, where Dr Kenneth Barlow, who had been
associated with Peckham before the war, was now a general
practitioner. But new Peckhams needed money, premises,
staff, equipment. There were acute post-war shortages. As Dr
Barlow recalled, 'everything was controlled. This pushed
decisions into governmental departments. In particular it

pushed questions of national health into the Ministry of that name. The Minister, Aneurin Bevan, was challenged from several sides because the repute of Peckham still resounded. Bevan did what Ministers do. He took advice . . .'[10]

Among his advisers were the statistician Bradford Hill and the surgeon Rock Carling. Hill went down to Peckham and asked to see their statistical research. All around him was the living proof that Peckham worked, but how do you quantify on paper a new dimension of vitality, an improved ability to function in one's social environment, a consciousness of radiant health, an enhanced family life? The Peckham doctors could show him none of these things in figures and statistics: besides, some of their most valuable records had been destroyed in the Blitz. His verdict was negative. 'This is not science as I know it!' was his crushing comment. Rock Carling was no more sympathetic to Peckham's aims than Hill. It is likely that Bevan also took the advice of the medical profession in general – they were, after all, the nation's experts on 'health'.

But in the Peckham scheme of things, medical care was relegated to the background; its chief thrust was towards the promotion of positive health rather than the care of disease. And this responsibility was explicitly removed from the hands of the medical profession, to be placed in those of a new generation of carefully trained specialists in real health.

The British medical profession was to a certain extent in sympathy with the ideas of Peckham. In its own blueprint for post-war planning, A Charter for Health, it had echoed many of them, calling for 'the biological approach to physical and, more particularly, mental health . . . through the family' and suggesting that amenities for physical and mental recreation should be provided generously and at low cost. 'People,' they added, 'must not be made to feel in their leisure time that they are being "organized" or must "belong" to something. Unorganized leisure is a prime need at all stages of life . . .'[11]

Where the Charter, for all its imaginative call for a new approach, parted company with Peckham was in its vision of the role to be played by doctors in the brave new post-war world. The British medical profession had played an honourable and important role in the thirties move towards higher national standards of nutrition. It was not prepared to see its own importance undervalued now, or to take a back seat in any projects concerning the national health. The BMA's Medical Planning Commission, meeting in 1942, stressed that any reform of the medical services should ensure that GPs took responsibility not only for diagnosis and treatment, but also for the promotion of health. How, with their limited training, they were to do this, was not made clear. 'In the past,' stated the *Charter*, 'the doctor's primary role has been to heal the sick. Although this is still largely his duty, medicine in the future will become more and more concerned with the prevention of disease and the maintenance of health. The outlook of doctors is changing and broadening and they are less exclusively interested in the treatment of disease: the basis of their practice is health, not disease.'[12]

What had, of course, changed and broadened the outlook of thousands of doctors by this time was the very real – if remote – possibility, as it now seemed, of a future in which large numbers of them might become redundant. The National Health Service was actually planned on the assumption that a great deal of sickness only needed to be diagnosed and treated to disappear for good, while the equally enormous burden of sickness due to poverty and malnutrition would gradually be lightened, and in due course also disappear, as the incomes of the poorest were raised to the health standard.

Certainly, there would still be sickness due to poor hygiene and inadequate housing, but this would be tackled as a first priority of post-war planning.

Burdened as we now are with the monstrous and escalating costs of the National Health Service, it seems hard to believe that sane and responsible men can ever have entertained such optimism about the future role of medicine. But this is hindsight. The reality of the mid-forties was that a great deal of preventable disease was now actually being prevented – and, of course, the miracle of antibiotics.

Miracle seemed hardly too strong a word. The first miracle in the saga had been the epic and unprecedented effort of Anglo-American pharmaceutical cooperation which had produced the first antibiotic in the teeth of near-insuperable problems, in quantity and in the nick of time. The miracles penicillin could perform seemed limitless. 'Mothers in childbirth, men and women with meningitis, sufferers with pneumonia, it has healed them all . . . described as a magic bullet which goes right to the seat of the trouble, it is suitable for all ages and types of people. Unlike many other healing agents, it is nobody's poison, nor has anyone ever felt sickness due to it . . .' This was one view, published not in some sensational tabloid, but in the sober *Contemporary Review*. In thousands of years, the future of curative medicine had never looked so bright; and the pharmaceutical companies who produced this boon for suffering mankind were confident that many more miracles were in store. Today, the infectious diseases; tomorrow, perhaps, cures for the new killers, for cancer, for heart disease, for the racking miseries of rheumatism and arthritis?

This optimism seemed well-founded in statistical fact. People, pointed out the *Charter*, were actually living longer; according to statistics, the expectation of life had increased by nineteen years since 1871.

Looked at carefully, the statistics told a quite different story. One of the few who had troubled to examine them critically was Dr Hugh Sinclair. 'I became fascinated by human nutrition when I was doing my medical studies,' says Sinclair today.

> I learned that a fifty-year-old man had an expectation of life of twenty years in 1841 – and barely two years more a century later, in 1941. 1841 was before almost every great medical advance – anaesthetics, antisepsis, antibiotics, hormones – not to mention most of the major public health measures. What killed men in 1841 was TB or pneumonia. By 1941 these were relatively unimportant as causes of death. What was killing him now were the major degenerative diseases such as heart disease and cancer. I wanted to know why they had increased so enormously.[13]

A pupil, friend and great admirer of McCarrison – whose spiritual heir in some sense he has become – Sinclair was a Fellow of Magdalen College, Oxford, and had played a prominent role in the Ministry of Food's advisory team during the war. Now, after the war, he looked for a position of importance in the field of nutrition. He found that, for all the brave talk, public interest had withered away.

Among his colleagues at Oxford, Sinclair found there was a lack of interest, together with a complacent conviction that all was now well. There was also a general conviction that all was now known, too. In one sense, of course, this was true, as nutrition experts themselves often pointed out: '. . . the essentials of an optimal diet are so well known to us, so simple and so easy of access, that there is not the slightest justification for the existence of malnutrition or even of sub-optimal nutrition . . .' remarked Dr Bacharach in his *Science and Nutrition*, in

1945. The wartime figures appeared to bear out the view that all was now known. The rich had eaten rather less than usual, the poor had eaten a great deal better, and the health statistics had jumped for joy. All that was needed now, it was fondly supposed, was the equalization of income which would make possible continued improvement along these lines. 'For the vast majority of the world's workers, what is wanted is . . . simply more money. With that will inevitably come the purchase of more food by those who need it, and the rest will follow,' ran the concluding paragraph of Bacharach's book.[14]

The astonishing success of the wartime government's food policy was recognized in 1947 by an unprecedented tribute: the presentation of the Lasker Award of the American Public Health Association. 'Perhaps it was the magnitude of this success which led once again to the complacency which undoubtedly ensued,' has commented Dr Donald Acheson, the present Chief Medical Officer of the Department of Health. At the time of the Lasker Award, he was studying medicine at Oxford with Professor Florey – whose role in the penicillin saga had been so conspicuous and so dazzling – the Professor of Pathology. 'For most students in Oxford in those days,' recalls Acheson, 'there were no remaining unsolved problems in human nutrition. All the accessory food factors had been identified. All that was necessary was to eat a good mixed diet, preferably three square meals a day, avoid obesity and all would be well.'[15]

This view was widely accepted among scientists. Sinclair at Magdalen College was – in Acheson's words – 'a voice crying in the wilderness'. Florey had invited Sinclair to work with him on chemical pathology. Sinclair thanked him but declined: he preferred to concentrate on nutrition. Florey told him that he was a fool: 'Nutrition is totally uninteresting; we've solved the main problem and there's nothing left to study.' No doubt on the advice of men like Florey, Oxford University at this time turned down an offer from one of Britain's wealthiest private patrons, the Wellcome Trust, to fund an Institution of Human Nutrition. The university's scientific advisers had instructed the authorities that within ten years, nutrition would be a white elephant. 'Nutrition in rats is pure science and respectable; human nutrition is experimental science, and the university should not soil its hands with it,' was the view.[16]

Professor Cathcart at this time retired from being the first Professor of Physiology at Glasgow University. According to

Sinclair, it was made a condition of his successor's appointment that he should not work on human nutrition.

There was a general feeling among scientists that such scanty resources as might become available would be better employed in almost any other field. This feeling coincided with a shift of emphasis in the biomedical sciences. Investigations using whole animals, in the style of Hopkins, McCollum or McCarrison, seemed *vieux jeu*: the new thrust of research was in the field of molecular biology, its object the exploration of the life processes themselves right down at cellular level. If there is one science that has gained enormously from this new understanding of life at cellular level, it is of course nutrition. But at that time, it seemed to be a scientific backwater. And by the 1950s, almost the only serious research in nutrition still being carried out in Britain was that supported by the Agricultural Research Council, aimed at the better nourishment of farm animals. Farmers and stock-breeders at least were aware that not all was now known. What little research was still devoted to human nutrition addressed 'real' problems, such as the protein malnutrition common in underdeveloped countries and among refugees.

It is doubtful whether the Wellcome Trust themselves would have repeated their offer to Oxford University five years later. By 1950 major Western pharmaceutical companies had shifted interest massively from vitamins into antibiotics, with the promise of other miracle drugs to follow. Research funds were evaporating as steadily as scientific interest. The future for keen young biochemists was no longer what their rats ate for breakfast.

One man's interest remained undimmed: Lord Woolton's had been a personal passion as much as a ministerial duty. He was deeply disappointed when Oxford turned down the Wellcome offer: he would have been happy to see Sinclair, for whose abilities he had the highest admiration, installed as professor. He realized, however, that the subject was unlikely now to be studied properly in any university, or under government patronage. So he formed a group to set up a central Institute for Human Nutrition, with Sinclair as its director. He gave it a strong management council, so that no pressure could be brought to bear on it by either government, university or the interests of the food industry; as a politician, he was only too well aware of all three possibilities. This Institute, Woolton believed, would do more good for mankind than all of Nuffield's benefactions, soon to be liberally dotted around the Oxford city landscape. And when Woolton died tragically early, in 1964, he was still looking for a philanthropic millionaire to fund his Institute. It survives today, still directed by Hugh Sinclair, turning out work of brilliant originality, richly endowed with all McCarrison's papers – and still desperately in need of funds to carry out the important research tasks that Woolton and Sinclair planned for it.

Only a handful of doctors had ever been genuinely interested in nutrition, and at the end of the war their attention was distracted, first by prolonged political wrangles between the British Medical Association, with its predominantly GP membership, and the new Labour Minister of Health, Aneurin Bevan, over their exact terms of office and remuneration under the new National Health Service. By the time the dust finally settled, medicine found itself in the new post-war world of miracle drugs, with a public which was constitutionally entitled to have them prescribed at need, for nothing. In the first year, 187,000,000 prescriptions were written out. 'I shudder to think,' remarked Bevan, 'of the ceaseless cascade of medicine which is pouring down British throats at the present time.' Inundated with patients, hard-pressed to find ten minutes for a consultation, GPs had little time and less inclination for the subtleties of nutrition. There was anyway nothing in their training to suggest that they should. In 1950 Lord Horder, as chairman of the BMA's 1947 Committee on Nutrition, lamented 'the meagre place which the teaching of nutrition still occupies in the medical student's curriculum, that references to it are desultory and occasional, and that there is no systematic teaching of the subject, as there undoubtedly should be'.[17]

Neither the *Lancet* or the *British Medical Journal* quoted this comment in their reviews of the Committee's report, which finally appeared in 1950. These were lukewarm in tone, showing clearly the lowly status to which nutrition had once more sunk in medical eyes. Both journals, however, quoted the Committee's most surprising verdict: that the improved figures for wartime health were simply part of an upward trend already established well before the war. Apart from certain complications of pregnancy and childbirth, 'there is little evidence to suggest that the diminishing incidence of disease in general is due to improved nutrition'.

There may have been a strong psychological explanation for the general unwillingness at this time to discuss health in terms of nutrition. If their health was the product of the dreary wartime diet, the public were sick of it. After the stress of war, peace had been a monstrous anticlimax. Rationing, queues, power-cuts, restrictions, all the dreary shortages had simply gone on and on, without even the excuse of war to give them dignity and make them bearable. At the lowest point, in 1947–8, even bread and potatoes were rationed, as they never had been in the darkest hours of the war. Even the once-despised but now treasured dried egg disappeared from the shops for months at a time. By way of compensation, the Ministry of Food came up with thousands of tins of a mysterious fish called snoek, a pallid substance with an oddly resilient texture and a taste somewhere between fish and rubber. To add insult to injury, many of the luxury foods for which the British longed passionately were now being made again in this country, but for export only – and were occasionally returned to these shores inside food parcels sent by kindly transatlantic friends.

Since Britain, unlike other European countries, was not self-sufficient in food production, and had little money to spare for food imports, the shortages in this country continued long after other countries in Europe had romped back to pre-war plenty. In the autumn of 1947 I remember being sent to Tours to stay with a French family for three months. The city was flattened to the ground, half the shops had been replaced by wooden shacks, but the sturdy bourgeois family with whom I lived sat down twice daily to a three-course feast of creamy soups, meat and fish in plenty, vegetables cooked with real butter, and cheese or a fruit flan. We ate buttery croissants for breakfast, we covered our teatime *tartines* with jam, and between these, to me, extravagant banquets, I haunted every pâtisserie in town and gawped at windows displaying cream-stuffed éclairs, meringues, brioches and the wonderful French bread. Travellers returning with similar tales of plenty did little to help national morale.

Not only was there no war to make such shortages seem bearable, but there was no more Ministry of Food propaganda to help housewives make the best of them, no more helpful hints for the Kitchen Front. Bacharach in his book had spoken of the enormous change in public attitudes to food that the war years had produced, and he credited this to Drummond's brilliant work at the Ministry of Food: 'a public relations policy that has been as persistent and enthusiastic as it has, generally, been honest and intelligent', and which had helped make 'tens of thousands of people realize for the first time in their lives that eating and drinking may be . . . important in their effects on our physical health . . .'[18]

The need for this work of public education is obvious, and it had been stressed over and over again. In its landmark *Final Report* on the relation of nutrition to health, agriculture and economic policy, published in 1937, the League of Nations Committee had been emphatic: 'Surveys . . . have revealed that, in families spending the same amount of money per head on food, some secure adequate diets while others do not. A feature of nutritional policy should therefore invariably be the dissemination of nutritional information.' The *Report* quoted a study of ninety-three families in one New York state, whose diets had been surveyed at the beginning of a vigorous local nutrition-education campaign, and again three years later. No family had been approached individually, but there had been public lectures, talks by the district nurse, special classes at the local schools. As a result, the diets of almost all the families had improved out of recognition: they were eating more fruit and vegetables, more salads and more whole grains, and the local stores had had to change their stock to meet this new demand. (After a particularly rousing lecture on vegetables, one of them had sold a whole carload of cabbages!) The families themselves commented on how much better they felt.[19]

The British Medical Association's pre-war National Nutrition Conference had devoted an entire session to the subject, urging that nutrition be taught at schools, to housewives through the Women's Institutes, at domestic-science colleges and to the general public over the radio. Robert McCarrison, broadcasting his comments on the Conference, suggested that in future it would be an important function of any government to practise 'a food-education policy which would aim at teaching boys and girls in all classes of life how best to feed themselves and their children in future . . . No girl or boy should leave school without this knowledge.'[20]

But the Labour government, through its Minister of Food, had no interest in continuing this work of public education and information. And without Woolton's 'Food Facts' to remind them of their need for the 'protective' foods, of the value of vegetables eaten raw or lightly cooked, of the importance of fibre and roughage in their diet, housewives soon slipped drearily back into their pre-war ways, filling themselves and their families up with stodge. Two years after the war ended there was more fruit available and being eaten, but the consumption of vegetables had declined. In 1944 it was 34 per cent up on pre-war levels; by 1946–7 it was only 8 per cent above.

More and more people were eating out in cafés and industrial canteens, and here salads or fruits were scarcely to be seen; food lost half its nutritional value being kept hot for hours on end and vegetables were boiled to death in true British style. Britain's greatest cookery writer Elizabeth David had returned to this country in 1947 from the Middle East and was living in a Hereford hotel; she recalls the food with horror: 'There was flour and water soup seasoned solely with pepper; bread and gristle rissoles; dehydrated onions and carrots; corned beef; toad-in-the-hole . . .' That was 1947. To work out 'an agonized craving for the sun and a furious revolt against that terrible, cheerless, heartless food', she began writing descriptions of the Mediterranean and Middle Eastern dishes she remembered. 'Even to write words like apricot, olives and butter, rice and lemons, oil and almonds, produced assuagement.'[21] These words grew into *A Book of Mediterranean Food*, published in 1950, the start of a gastronomic revolution which shattered for ever the spell of meat and two veg.

This dreary and nutritionally poor tradition was meanwhile enshrined in statute by the 1944 Education Act, which obliged all state schools to provide dinners for those who needed them. The famous Oslo Breakfast had been tried with outstanding success in a number of LCC schools. It had produced 'brighter, fitter kids' and it saved labour and energy, and thus money. But it was abandoned in favour of the classic British meat or fish and two veg followed by a sweet and stodgy pudding. A doctor later making a study of such meals found that they were almost entirely lacking in B vitamins, vitamin C and fibre, while being high in saturated fat, sugar and white flour.

Interestingly, the BMA's 1950 *Report on Nutrition* found that the excellent wartime figures for the growth and physique of British children were not being maintained: by 1947 they were actually slipping back.

Increasingly, from the late forties, the emphasis of official thinking came to focus on cure rather than care; on the supply of medical services rather than the study of environmental factors; on the treatment of disease rather than the encouragement of positive health. An article in the *Lancet* in 1947 had smiled benevolently on the ideal of 'functional medicine' that Peckham represented, but concluded that it was 'an aspiration rather than an immediate probability'; something to be considered, perhaps, once doctors had coped with more pressing problems: 'as curative and preventive medicine grow more successful, doctors should have more chance to practise functional medicine – the promotion of positive health . . .'[22]

In such a climate, Peckham was clearly doomed. No funds were forthcoming from major charitable trusts, and since Williamson insisted that the payment of the weekly subscription was crucial to the whole ethos of Peckham, the Centre could not be assimilated into the National Health Service. In 1950 the near-bankrupt Centre was closed down, and the building sold to the LCC.

Perhaps nothing showed more clearly the growing indifference to nutrition of both the medical profession and the government than the fate of the National loaf. In the war years, the medical profession had come down heavily in favour of wholemeal bread. 'All the evidence goes to show that . . . in eating a quantity of refined foods people do indeed dig their graves with their teeth. It is a punishable offence to water milk . . . Why then should it be thought praiseworthy to remove from the wheat berry the valuable minerals and vitamins it contains?' wondered an editorial in the *British Medical Journal* in 1942.[23]

In 1944, however, the Ministry of Food, now under the direction of Lord Llewellin, quietly dropped the extraction to, first, 82 per cent and then 80 per cent. Lord Llewellin had visited the millers' research station at St Albans – where the staff had greatly impressed him with their 'keenness' – and had been convinced by them that since most of the thiamine in wheat was contained in the scutellum, or skin of the germ, the germ itself could be safely discarded. Thus the millers got back their precious and profitable wheat germ, together with 325,000 tons of 'offals' for pig food. Furious letters flooded in to *The Times*. In a House of Lords debate on the subject, hardly a single voice was raised in favour of white flour. One of the most ardent defenders of the higher extraction rate was Lord Horder, who had been Chief Medical Adviser to the Ministry of Food during the war, and was now Chairman of the Food

Education Society. He reminded the House that the 85 per cent loaf had made a great contribution to the health of the people. Anaemia and constipation had both decreased since it was introduced. 'Evidence accumulates that the more we tinker with natural foodstuffs, the less nutritious they become . . .' he said. 'I suggest that the people who are so anxious to give the germ of the wheat which we want in our bread to pigs and chickens should give the pigs and chickens the vitamins that they want to put back in our bread . . .'[24]

The *British Medical Journal* regretted that a great opportunity to re-educate the people of their country in a taste for better bread had been lost. The general feeling was that the nation's health had come a poor second to commercial interests.

Since the bread question was clearly a sensitive one politically, the Ministry of Food convened a Conference on the Post-war Loaf, at which the industry was represented as well as the various government departments and the Medical Research Council.

The millers made much of the fact that the public, supposedly, vastly preferred white bread. The truth was that millions of British people had never actually tasted wholemeal bread in their lives: the National loaf was the nearest they ever came to it. One Peckham member recalled her family's reaction to the Centre's wholemeal bread. 'To my children it looked horrible at first, they used to have it with honey. My son said it was the honey that got him to eat it. After that he would eat nothing but . . .'[25]

Thousands of housewives and their families may have tasted real wholemeal bread for the first time when they took it hot from their own ovens after reading *Your Daily Bread*, a small and charming book by Doris Grant published by Faber in 1944. This book had a runaway success, being reprinted half a dozen times over the next few years, and the easy-to-make no-kneading Grant loaf, baked in a flower-pot, became nationally famous. The enterprising manager of a large industrial works canteen in Cheshire flung out the National loaf and made only the wholemeal Grant loaf available. The works at once threatened to down tools in protest. But the manager stuck his ground – and eventually the bread became so popular that soon the workers were queueing up to buy leftover loaves for their families at the end of the day.

More recently a questionnaire circulated through twenty-one hospitals all over the British Isles asked patients – among other things – whether they liked brown or white bread best. As many said brown as white.

But to gratify the supposed public preference for white, the millers at the 1945 Conference urged the 'enrichment' policy which had been adopted in the USA, and which would restore to white flour – in synthetic form – most of the thiamine, nicotinic acid and iron lost in the drop from 85 to 70 per cent extraction.

The medical and scientific members, however, came out solidly in favour of the high extraction rate, as opposed to 'fortification' with the three token nutrients. 'It is impossible,' they argued, '. . . to be certain that artificially fortified flour will give results comparable to those from flour in which the known vitamins are retained together with the less perfectly known constituents of the wheat berry.'[26]

To settle this question, an experiment was proposed and carried out among stunted and undernourished children in two post-war German orphanages. The children were fed diets of vegetables, soups and potatoes, with supplements of calcium, and vitamins A, D and C – together with all the bread they wanted. Since the vegetables and soups were shown to contain all the B vitamins needed for their growth, the skinny little orphans all shot up and filled out gratifyingly whether they were eating wholemeal, 85 per cent, 80 per cent, fortified 70 per cent, or unfortified 70 per cent bread.

On the strength of this ill-conceived and short-term trial – which Sinclair has criticized as 'irrelevant' – the government felt able, in 1953, to end the ban on 70 per cent flour, though millers were required to add sufficient thiamine, nicotinic acid and iron to bring it up to the standard of 80 per cent flour. Another storm of protest followed, and a panel chaired by Lord Cohen was set up to consider the question. This time, nobody was looking at wholemeal bread at all: the panel simply compared the value of 80 per cent flour and 70 per cent fortified flour. The panel had before them charts showing the losses of nutrients – many of them barely studied as yet – entailed in the drop from 80 per cent to 70 per cent. Some of these – such as the B vitamins pyridoxine, pantothenic acid and folic acid – they considered. Others – such as vitamin E – were brushed aside as of no account.

Professor Sinclair, conducting the government case for retention, pointed out that among the nutrients so cavalierly discarded was vitamin B_6, pyridoxine, in which the national diet was marginal, and of which the human requirement was not as yet known. If we did not know, we should play safe, he suggested.

To the delight of the millers, the Cohen Report reached an exactly opposite conclusion.

> Human requirements of pyridoxine, pantothenic acid, biotin and folic acid are not known and information as to their distribution in foods and flours of various grades is far from complete. The Panel's view of the relevant literature leads them to believe that in spite of weighty opinions to the contrary, a lowering of the extraction rate from 80 to 70 per cent is very unlikely to lead to any nutritional disturbance from lack of these vitamins.[27]

In the three decades that have passed since the Cohen Panel made this feckless judgement, studies have demonstrated the importance of many of the nutrients so drastically reduced in the white bread the nation has been eating ever since.

18
The Deadly Environment

'What is the prime cause of cancer?' asked a British homoeopath, Cyril Scott, in 1940. 'After thirty-five years of reading and careful study of the subject I have come to the inescapable conclusion that its most frequent cause is nothing more spectacular than a faulty diet.'[1]

In this belief, Scott was in excellent company.

Advocates of Nature Cure had been saying for decades that cancer – like other degenerative diseases – was part of the price modern Western man paid for his abysmal eating habits. And some of the most distinguished physicians of the day agreed. Among them was Sir Arbuthnot Lane, who traced it to the ill-functioning colon that resulted from a diet of refined foods: 'in every case in which I have had the opportunity of verifying it, I have found that the cancer patient was suffering from intestinal stasis'.

Dr Bircher-Benner was personally convinced that 'cancer arises from the soil of disordered living, especially through disordered nutrition'.[2]

Robert McCarrison was one of several observers, as early as the twenties, already pointing out that cancer – like dental caries and diseases of the digestive tract – was rare, if not unknown, among primitive people making their diet from 'the unsophisticated foodstuffs of nature'. Dr Ernest Tipper, who spent twenty years as a medical officer in West Africa, made the same point in his book *The Cradle of the World and Cancer – A Disease of Civilisation*. In those twenty years, he had seen only six cases of cancer – not one of which was among the tribes living in the heart of the Niger delta, where food is 'perfectly natural and abundant . . . and there is no such thing as constipation, there is no such thing as cancer. At the first dawn of civilization amongst them this disease makes its appearance.'[3]

Among the dietary errors specially singled out by such writers was the refining of grains, in which valuable nutrients are lost: Bircher-Benner considered the loss of magnesium particularly significant in cancer. Magnesium is not one of the nutrients replaced in 'enrichment', and a slice of white bread may have only 15 per cent of the magnesium contained in a slice of wholemeal bread.

Excess tea and coffee, too much alcohol, the use of processed foods – canned, dehydrated, hydrogenated, condensed, pasteurized – nutrient losses in foods grown on impoverished, uncomposted soil: all these were viewed with suspicion. So was excess salt; Cyril Scott quoted a letter from a reader whose mother had died from an extensive and inoperable tumour: 'All her life my mother has eaten salt in ridiculous quantities, even to the extent of dusting it on thin bread-and-butter; she has always suffered from chronic constipation; she has always eaten the wrong kind of food . . .'[4]

All these writers and practitioners agreed that the consumption of fresh vegetables and salads was dangerously low in the Western diet, though consumption of fruit and vegetables had in fact almost doubled in Britain in the three decades up to the Second World War. From having been regarded as a luxury, fruit in winter was now considered a simple necessity of life by even the poorest classes. How much nutrition actually survived the British way with vegetables was another matter.

> Vegetables! The word conjures up a vision of a whole house stealthily pervaded by the stench of cabbage announcing that lunch, for which it has already banished appetite, will soon be ready, and that we must prepare to meet the cause of this nauseating odour face to face . . . We repair to the dining-room. The cover of the vegetable dish is removed and a veritable geyser of sewer gas, redolent of decomposing matter, mounts to the ceiling from a dingy wad of macerated leaves . . .[5]

The excess consumption of meat protein was, finally, an additional danger in the eyes of those advocating a natural diet. In Britain and the USA, meat-eating had risen sharply from the mid-nineteenth century, thanks to intensive cattle-breeding in the American Midwest, and supplies of cheap refrigerated meat from Australia, New Zealand and Argentina. By the late thirties Britain was eating an average of 50 lb (23 kg) a head each year – compared to 3 lb (1·4 kg) in the 1880s.

Forty years and countless careful clinical studies later, the US National Cancer Institute itself – which resisted for years the idea that the diet might have any connection with cancer – was publishing dietary guidelines remarkably similar to those being put forward by advocates of natural health in the twenties and thirties. Eat more wholegrain products, suggested the Institute's 1982 Report: avoid excess alcohol; reduce fat consumption (meat has high levels of saturated fat); minimize the use of salt-cured, pickled or smoked foods. Above all, eat plenty of fruits and vegetables – particularly those rich in vitamins A, C and beta-carotens. Since much of vitamins A and C are lost in cooking, the National Cancer Institute may be said to be echoing Dr Bircher-Benner. But even before he published his work on the 'organized sunlight energy' of fresh plants, the scientific evidence was already starting to accumulate.

Beta-carotene is a yellowish compound found in yellow, orange or dark green vegetables. Apricots, kale, sweet potatoes, carrots and spinach are all rich in it. In 1928 it was discovered to be a precursor of vitamin A, and it is now known to be a particularly active and protective form of this vitamin. As early as the twenties, studies were reported linking deficiency in vitamin A with increased risk of cancer, and the evidence now is strong. In 1981 Sir Richard Doll, President of the British Association for Cancer Research, was cautiously optimistic. 'I believe there is now a light at the end of the tunnel in our fight against this disease. All we can say at this stage is that current evidence suggests there is a 40 per cent lower risk of cancer occurring among men who maintain above-average consumption of vitamin A.' An American study may turn this strong suggestion into hard evidence. A Harvard research team monitored the health of some 26,000 male physicians between the ages of forty-five and seventy-five, who were taking aspirin, beta-carotene supplements or placebos; the four-year study was due to conclude in 1986.[5a]

Whatever the cause, cancer deaths were rising sharply by the thirties. The Swedish natural healer, Are Waerland, writing in 1934, quoted some thought-provoking statistics: '. . . the deathrate from cancer has, according to the report of the British Ministry of Health in 1923, increased *seven times* since 1838. In a single state, Massachusetts in the USA, the cancer deathrate increased more than fivefold between 1856 and 1913. In Boston alone the cancer deathrate has advanced from 65·4 in 1881 to 119·9 in 1914 per 100,000 of the population.'[6]

In the eyes of medical orthodoxy, however, the causes of cancer were virtually unknown, and the only reliable treatments were surgery – the earlier the better – and radium or X-rays. 'Alternative' treatments, of which there were already dozens, were specifically outlawed in Britain by Act of Parliament. And although this was no doubt a necessary measure to deal with a host of disreputable charlatans cashing in on a public scare, some of the therapies discredited in the same breath were dietary approaches which had been shown in practice to be of value.

Yet suggestions that diet might help prevent cancer, or be an important factor in its treatment, were already being brushed aside as rank medical heresy. Orthodox medicine had little to offer in the way of prevention, other than advice to eliminate 'irritation'. A book by J. Ellis Barker, *Cancer: How it is Caused, How it can be Prevented*, published at this time, reviewed the evidence strongly suggesting a link between diet and cancer. In it, he denounced the 'denaturalized, doped, embalmed and mummified processed foods' which were more and more crowding out fresh natural foodstuffs from the Western diet. His book was denounced as 'ill-informed' by the *Lancet*, and condemned in the strongest terms by the *Journal of the American Medical Association:* 'A book such as this of Mr Barker's will incline the lay reader to believe that his cancer may be prevented or its growth deterred by eating proper vitamins or practising good personal hygiene. There is not the slightest evidence to warrant such a belief at the present time. This book can be considered only as a pernicious and harmful piece of literature.'[7]

It was the fate of Dr Max Gerson to discover that orthodox opposition to any 'heretical' theories about the cause and treatment of cancer went much further than mere paper denunciations. Max Gerson was born in Germany in 1881. He entered medicine and became a specialist in internal and nervous diseases. But his career was threatened by appalling migraine headaches – for which, according to eminent German specialists that he consulted, nothing could be done. Desperate, he explored other avenues of hope: he may have come across the work of Bircher-Benner. At all events, he cured himself by a salt-free diet rich in raw vegetables and their juices, and fresh fruit. He tried the same diet on his migraine patients – and it worked for them too. One of his patients was a lupus victim, his cheeks and eyelids slowly being eaten away by this ravaging tuberculosis of the skin, for which there was at the time no cure. After staying on Gerson's diet for his migraine, his lupus cleared up too. Word got round, and other lupus patients came flocking to Gerson's surgery.

Soon Gerson was successfully treating patients suffering from a wide range of chronic diseases with his salt-free diet. Among them were cases of asthma, digestive problems, diseases of the liver and pancreas, arthritis, heart disease, sinusitis, ulcers, ulcerative colitis, high blood pressure, psoriasis and multiple sclerosis. Albert Schweitzer, who was cured by him of diabetes, called him 'one of the most eminent geniuses in medical history'. Gerson found that his diet gave particularly striking results in diseases affecting the liver and gall bladder, for which no other treatment then available was effective.

His work with lupus patients was violently attacked by specialists in this disease, who found it hard to believe that a simple diet could cure a condition that defeated their most complex theories and treatments. But one famous surgeon, Ferdinand Sauerbruch of Munich, had an openness of mind rare in his profession. After a chance encounter with a patient that Gerson had cured, he decided to see for himself if – and how – the odd dietary approach worked, although, as he said, 'I could see no apparent connection between treatment and cure.' Out of 450 lupus cases supervised in his Munich clinic by Gerson, and following the salt-free diet, only four were not cured.

Just when his work was on the eve of general acceptance by the German medical world, Hitler came to power, and the Jewish Gerson was obliged to flee the country. He settled first in Austria from which growing anti-Semitism soon uprooted him once more, so he then moved to Paris. In 1938 he left Europe and settled in New York.

Before he left Germany, Gerson had already begun treating cancer patients with his diet; of a dozen cases, he reckoned that he had cured seven. More successes came in Austria, then in Paris. In 1941 he began treating cancer patients regularly, and opened a residential clinic not far from New York.

Like Bircher-Benner, Gerson reflected deeply about the nature of the diseases he was treating so successfully. The very fact that a single therapy worked for such a startling range of sickness led him to the belief, which he stressed over and over again, that 'the entire sick organism must be attacked in its totality, especially in degenerative diseases'. All therapeutic action must be based on this idea of 'the body as an entity, which has to be supported and restored in its final silent perfection'. Cancer, arthritis, heart disease, ulcers, migraine, asthma: these were not distinct pathological conditions bearing no relation to each other. On the contrary, they were all manifestations of the same underlying cause: a disturbance or unbalancing of the entire metabolism of the body.

Cancer – the most terrifying and implacable form of this profound derangement – developed in a body 'which more or less has lost the normal function of the metabolism as a consequence of a chronic daily poisoning accumulated especially in the liver'. This poisoning was now almost inescapable in the Western world. It started with the soil 'denaturalized by artificial fertilizers and depletion, thus gradually reducing the topsoil. In addition, the soil is poisoned by sprays with DDT and other poisons. As a consequence, our nutrition is damaged by a decrease in the important K-group* content of fruit and vegetables grown on such poisoned soil.' Our bodies had adapted over millions of years to natural food produced from the soil, he said; when we disturbed its biological balance, dire consequences followed. And that was not all. The food grown on this now unbalanced soil was 'refined, bottled, bleached, powdered, frozen, smoked, salted, canned, and coloured with artificial colouring'. A body fed on this unnatural food 'loses the harmony and cooperation of the cells, finally its natural defences, immunity and healing power'.[8]

Long before it was fashionable, Gerson was an advocate of organic cultivation methods. During three years as consultant to the Prussian Ministry of Health, from 1930 to 1933, he pointed out how depleted the soils were around some of the biggest industrial cities – Düsseldorf, Essen and Dortmund – and suggested that instead of artificial fertilizers, animal and human wastes should be composted and returned to the soil. The State Secretary of Health observed that the vegetables grown in this way were both bigger and better.

As so often, however, it was the stock-breeders rather than the doctors who sat up and took notice. After reading an account of how the Gerson diet was curing cases of TB, the owner of a commercial fox ranch in the Harz Mountains wondered if it worked for animals too: some of his foxes were tuberculous. He procured vegetables grown organically and

*K is the chemical symbol for potassium.

fed them to the sick animals. Six out of seven responded to this unusual treatment. As a bonus, he noticed that the quality of their pelts had improved out of all recognition. He started growing his own fruit and vegetables organically. Soon he was running a highly profitable business, buying up sick foxes from other breeders at rock-bottom prices, and transforming them into healthy animals with thick and lustrous coats.

Gerson believed that cancer – along with other degenerative diseases – would never be wiped out until the West returned to organic farming. He insisted that all his patients ate organically grown foods as far as possible, and once they had recovered on his diet he suggested that they should adopt for life a regime in which three quarters of the food should consist of fruit and vegetables eaten raw, juiced, or stewed in their own juices; baked potatoes; plenty of salads; wholegrain breads, oatmeal, milk, butter, yoghurt, low-salt cheese, honey and brown sugar. Ice-cream was to be saved for special occasions – and he considered it rank poison for children. A quarter of the diet was left to individual taste: meat, fish, eggs, nuts, candies, cakes. But he advised all his patients to reduce their intake of tea, coffee and alcohol to the barest minimum; and to avoid altogether tobacco, salt, sharp spices such as pepper or ginger, and salted and smoked food.

For cancer patients the Gerson regime was draconian, aimed at complete detoxification of the entire system. One of his most famous patients was the seventeen-year-old son of the writer John Gunther, who has described the diet that this teen-age boy – used to the rich, high-fat, over-salted and sweetened American way of eating – found hard to bear. 'For breakfast, a pint of fruit juice, oatmeal, an apple-carrot mash, and a special soup made of fresh vegetables – parsley root, celery knob, leek, tomatoes.' He drank up to a quart and a half a day of this. 'For lunch, heaping portions of cooked vegetables, a salad, fresh fruit, the soup and mash, and a baked potato. For dinner the same . . . nothing canned. Nothing seasoned, smoked or frozen. Above all nothing salted. No meat, eggs or fish. No cream, butter, or other fats . . . No candy, sausages, ice-cream, pickles, spices, preserved foods, white flour, condiments, cakes, or any of the multitude of small things a child loves . . .' As well, there were countless enemas to assist the detoxification of the body and liver, injections of crude liver extract, dozens of vitamin and mineral pills, iodine. Johnny Gunther loathed the diet, which he described as a cure for tapeworm. 'Put the patient on the Gerson diet and the tapeworm will evacuate itself in despair.'[9]

Yet this boy with a massive brain tumour, whom his doctor had believed could not last the week out when he entered the Gerson nursing home, so low was his blood count, was feeling startlingly better within a week, his blood count rising, multiple bruises disappearing and the bump on his skull going down.

. Tragically, Gerson was not able to save Johnny Gunther, who had had weeks of X-ray treatment as well as two courses of the then experimental mustard-gas treatment, so toxic that it drove the white blood count right down, and had to be accompanied by huge doses of penicillin. But in his moving account of his son's illness, *Death be not Proud*, John Gunther paid generous tribute to the German physician who had cared so deeply for this patient. And in dozens of other cases, there were remarkable cures, like that of Mrs Anna Hanna. She had been operated on for suspected cancer of the colon, but the surgeons found it had grown and spread so extensively that they simply performed a colostomy and sent her home under sentence of death. On the Gerson diet she began to improve immediately, and five weeks later X-rays showed that the tumour had disappeared, and normal function was restored to her colon. In time the colostomy opening healed itself.

Anna Hanna was one of a number of his successes that Gerson presented to a subcommittee of the US Senate meeting to consider a Bill sponsored by Senator Pepper which would authorize the American President to allocate huge funds for cancer research. The astonished committee crossquestioned these walking tributes to the Gerson therapy during the three-day hearing, and heard an eloquent plea from a doctor that it should be fully researched.

'Fifty people have died of cancer while we have been here in this hearing,' Dr Markel reminded them. Millions and millions of dollars had been spent for fifty years on just three approaches – surgery, X-ray, radium – and out of it all had grown not even the faintest hope of a cure. One study had followed up a number of cancer patients over years; it actually showed that those who had no treatment at all survived longer than those undergoing the stress of surgery or radiation. If there was another avenue, it should be explored. 'In this case there have been outstanding scientists, I am told, who have been told of this and they do not even want to look at it.'[10] Gerson himself put it more bluntly: 'They do not like for me to cure cancer. They say it is not possible. I say it is possible, and I do it!'[11]

Among those present at this hearing was the popular ABC radio commentator Raymond Swing. Next day, 3 July 1946, millions of Americans listening to his show learned for the first time that there was now fresh hope in the century's most dreaded disease – and of a Senate Bill which would fund full examination of the exciting new approach. Gerson was rapidly becoming famous.

He was also generating dismay and anguish among thousands of doctors, scientists and businessmen who saw their livelihood threatened and their status imperilled. 'If this thing works,' commented one of Johnny Gunther's doctors, 'we can chuck millions of dollars' worth of equipment in the river, and get rid of cancer by cooking carrots in a pot.'[12]

Add to that equipment the armies of technicians servicing it, the specialists operating it, thousands of scientists employed in never-ending cancer research, the agro-chemical industry and the entire processed-food industry – estimated in 1963 to be worth around $100 billion a year – not to mention the vast ancillary commerce of advertising, promotion and packaging, and one has a glimmering of the huge vested interests which now moved swiftly and effectively to crush this insignificant little obstacle in their path.

In response to hundreds of inquiries, the American Cancer Society sent out a printed statement dismissing his work with the assurance that they had been unable to find acceptable evidence that it benefited patients; 'As you undoubtedly know,' they added for good measure, 'there is no evidence at the present time that any food or any combination of foods specifically affects the course of any cancer in man.'[13]

The Journal of the American Medical Association did an elegant hatchet job just four months after the Pepper hearings and Gerson's presentation of his patients. 'Fortunately for the American people this presentation received little if any newspaper publicity.'[14]

The Medical Society of the County of New York suspended him – on the grounds that he had received personal publicity in a radio show (on which many other doctors had from time to time appeared). Meanwhile, his staff appointment at New York's Gotham Hospital had been terminated. His malpractice insurance cover was withdrawn. And such was the cloud of medical disfavour overwhelming him in the last few years of his life that no young doctor dared risk his future by working for such an outcast.

He died in 1959, a disappointed man, aware that he left nobody trained to carry on his scientific work.

To this day, not one cent of the official US cancer research billions has been allocated to investigation of his therapy.

A dozen other doctors, in the United States and elsewhere, who successfully treated cancer patients using similar nutritional approaches, have found their path blocked by the same wall of hostile silence.

The Gerson clinic at present functions in exile, in Mexico, where 'terminal' patients continue to recover. And in 1985, a dozen of the fifty 'terminal' cases that Gerson presented to the US Senate subcommittee were still alive and well, up to forty-two years later.

It has been left to an Austrian hospital, the Landes-krankenhaus of Graz, to institute the first professional clinical trial of the Gerson method, under the direction of a young surgeon, Dr Peter Lechner: sixty patients with cancers metastasized to their livers are taking part. Other patients with metastasized breast cancers, who are receiving Gerson therapy as well as chemotherapy, do 'overwhelmingly better' than those on chemotherapy alone, states Dr Lechner flatly.

———

Gerson saw cancer as evidence of the damage that modern man had inflicted on himself with his artificial fertilizers and his devitalized processed food.

The work of Dr Theron Randolph, a Chicago allergist, runs in curious parallel to that of Gerson. Four years after *A Cancer Therapy* was published, Randolph broke entirely fresh medical ground in 1962 with his book *Human Ecology and Susceptibility to the Chemical Environment*. Increasing chemical pollution of the world we live in, he suggested, was responsible for a devastating toll of human sickness. Domestic cleaning materials, oil- or gas-burning appliances, exhaust fumes, chemical additives or pesticide and insecticide residues turning up in food and water, chemical pollution of the air we breathe – all these could evoke an allergic response in just the same way as pollens might give a man hayfever or asthma. In Randolph's experience, they were an even commoner trigger of allergic

problems than the house dust or grass pollen on which orthodox allergists chose to concentrate their attention. And the sickness such chemicals could cause affected 'man in his totality':
not merely physical symptoms such as colitis, migraine,
arthritis, and the classic asthma and rhinitis, vague joint pains,
and general malaise, but many of the mental problems then
considered the exclusive province of the psychiatrist –
depression, panic attacks, nervous irritability.

The word allergy – meaning altered reactivity – was coined
by a Viennese paediatrician, Clemans von Pirquet, in 1906 to
describe a phenomenon already familiar to doctors – and actually mentioned as an established medical observation by Hippocrates – that one person might react with pain or discomfort to
a substance which had no effect on another person. In 1905
an Australian psychiatrist, Francis Hare, published a weighty
study of dozens of case-histories, called *The Food Factor in
Disease*; both mental and physical symptoms, he showed, might
occur in people after they ate perfectly ordinary everyday
foods – an observation confirmed by a number of American
doctors in the twenties. The root cause, suggested Hare, was
their inability to metabolize sugars and starches. Hare's work
was confirmed in the twenties by Albert Rowe in California,
who found that he could cure patients of all kinds of intractable
diseases – including ulcerative colitis, eczema and digestive
problems – by identifying the mischief-maker in their diet and
instructing them to avoid it. Around the same time another
allergist, Dr Warren T. Vaughan, suggested that migraine
headache might be a common allergic reaction.

Spotting the villain among dozens of different items in
your daily menu, though, could be difficult – until, in the early
thirties, Dr Herbert Rinkel stumbled across something very odd
about allergies. As a medical student, married and with one
child, Rinkel had been so hard up that he and his family virtually lived on the quantities of eggs sent to him by his Kansas
farming father. After a year or two of this high-egg diet, his
health began to deteriorate. He had heavy catarrh, a nose that
ran nonstop, headaches, fatigue, sore throats, bouts of earache.
A strapping ex-army man and keen footballer, Rinkel was puzzled and irritated by this. After graduation he set up a practice
in Chicago, came across Rowe's work, and wondered if he might
be sensitive to eggs. He downed six at one go, found he had
absolutely no reaction at all and dismissed the idea. Four years
later, by this time an allergy specialist and still plagued by poor

health, he wondered again about eggs and decided to try eliminating them from his diet. After two or three days, he felt distinctly better. Then on the fifth day of his eggless diet he ate a piece of angel cake and collapsed in a faint. There had been egg in the cake, he learned. Had he, perhaps, suffered a delayed reaction? He avoided eggs for another five days, then tried again: another collapse.

He tried the same approach on a number of particularly baffling cases in his allergy clinic, and found the same thing happening. Here, he realized at once, was a facet of the allergy problem that nobody before him had identified. He described it thus: 'If one uses a food every day or so, one may be allergic to it but never suspect it as a cause of symptoms. It is common to feel better after the meal at which the food is used than before mealtime. This is called masked food allergy.'[15]

Chance favoured the prepared mind in another case, that of Dr and Mrs Arthur Coca. In 1935 he was Medical Director of the giant pharmaceutical company Lederle and his wife was active in medical research. A sudden attack of angina hospitalized her, and the specialists were pessimistic. A similar attack was touched off by a dose of a morphine derivative which sent her pulse-rate soaring to 180 (80 is high in a normal healthy person). Visiting her the same day, Dr Coca was horrified by this high pulse-rate, and commented on it. Mrs Coca added casually that her heart raced in just the same way when she ate certain foods. Maybe she should keep a note of which ones they were, suggested her husband. Together, they noted that eating beef or potatoes brought a sharp rise, and she began avoiding them. Eventually, she was left with a list of foods that didn't affect her pulse-rate; on this limited diet of chicken, fish, cheese, rice, tea and coffee, and one or two fruits and vegetables, she remained attack-free. They were elated. A few weeks later, Mrs Coca noticed that a number of other afflictions she had learned to live with over the years – migraine headaches, colitis, dizzy spells, fatigue, indigestion – had quietly made their exit from her life. She waited some time to be absolutely sure this was no temporary remission and then told her husband. 'Van Leeuwenhoek, centuries ago, could not have been more deeply thrilled – and awed – at his first view of the strange new world of the micro-organisms through his famous microscope than I was at this vision of the new medicine, which leapt to my mind with my wife's assured statement.'[16]

The 'palpitations' experienced by many people, and usually credited to digestive problems, are often caused by Coca's racing pulse, a reaction to a food to which the sufferer is allergic. And the Coca pulse test is still being used by allergists today, as well as by thousands of patients who have learned that with its help they can identify their own food allergies.

In 1944 Randolph and Rinkel met for the first time, just as Randolph opened his own private allergy practice in Chicago and joined the staff of Northwestern University Medical School. Students became fascinated by his demonstrations of allergy to foods as common as corn, wheat and milk, and his explanation of how these allergies could be 'masked'.

Working together, comparing notes, the two men pushed out the frontiers of this new science – particularly after Randolph discovered the explanation of masked food allergy. He realized that he had in fact learned it years earlier, listening to Professor Hans Selye of Montreal presenting his explanation of stress and the human adaptation syndrome.

Most people think of stress as a purely psychological reaction – the twitching nerves of the overworked executive. Walter Cannon, Harvard's brilliant Professor of Physiology in the twenties, explored it as a physiological phenomenon. Studying the autonomic nervous system, he did early work on the function of the adrenal glands, and the 'fight or flight' syndrome by which man reacts to threat or danger in his environment. Cannon showed that the mastermind of this defence system was the adrenal gland, which at the first signalling of danger, pours adrenalin into the bloodstream to raise the heartbeat, rush emergency supplies of blood to brain and muscle, fill the lungs with air. It is this rapid and effective mobilization of our physical resources, which happens without any conscious decision-making on our part, which allows people to achieve at moments of crisis a remarkable speed of reaction and an extraordinarily heightened physical strength – the father bodily lifting a car which has run over his child, for example.

Selye took Cannon's work further to examine the way the adrenal gland functions. He found that as well as the adrenalin (now usually called epinephrine) produced by its medulla, the adrenal cortex produced other hormones, including cortisone, which acts as it were to damp down the intensity of the defence reaction – by calming inflammation, for instance. In a historic study, exposing rats to severe cold, Selye showed that the adaptation syndrome had three stages. First came the severe reaction seen in acute shock, when blood pressure and temperature fall, and the adrenal glands shrink. In the second stage, some forty-eight hours later, the adrenal glands are enlarged* and, as the body adapts to stress, it apparently returns to normal, even if exposure to small doses of the stress factor continues. But when Selye then re-exposed his rats to severe cold, he found that they went through the same stages of shock followed by apparent adaptation, but that they collapsed and died sooner than normal, their adaptive powers exhausted.

Randolph realized that masked food allergy was a classic instance of this three-stage adaptation syndrome. Initially, an allergic reaction may develop when a person is repeatedly exposed to a particular substance over a period of time. At first this reaction takes an unpleasant form – rash, headache, digestive malaise, feeling 'low'. At this initial stage, the allergy is rarely recognized. In the second stage, the sufferer learns to live with it. The reaction is a delayed one, and taking his allergen gives him, at first, a pleasant feeling of stimulation and well-being which may last several hours – the bliss of that first cup of coffee in the morning. Now his allergy takes on the pattern of true addiction he needs a regular fix of his allergen to give him that pleasant feeling; thus he will crave chocolate, or a piece of cheese, another cup of coffee or a cigarette. If he doesn't have it, he experiences a disagreeable withdrawal syndrome: the hangover relieved by the 'hair of the dog', the aching morning head lightened by the first coffee – or by an analgesic containing small amounts of caffeine, as many do – are both instances of this stage two.

By stage three, the adaptation response is exhausted. The cigarette, the cup of coffee, the drink are no longer a pleasure but a necessity; the junkie cannot live without his fix. It is now that the victim becomes genuinely, if sporadically, ill, with endless headaches, joint pains, depression or draining fatigue.

Applying this knowledge, Rinkel and Randolph were bringing hope to patients for whom there had previously been no hope: patients who had bankrupted themselves trying out one form of treatment after another – drugs, surgery, psychotherapy – for their inexplicable woes and sickness, without

---

*At post-mortems on rats fed acutely deficient diets, McCarrison had also noticed that their adrenal glands were invariably enlarged, a fact which he was unable to explain, but felt must be significant.

relief; patients who had been dismissed as 'hysterical' or, if they were middle-aged women, menopausal; patients who had been told that nothing could be done for their raging migraines, their baffling aches and pains, their nervous symptoms. Randolph's work in particular was attracting plenty of notice. He had an enthusiastic following among his Chicago medical students, many of whom were stimulated by this bold new approach, and by the late forties he was publishing paper after paper in various medical journals.

'In my experience,' wrote Randolph, 'food allergy is one of the greatest health problems in our country. Combined with the chemical-susceptibility problem . . . it is a growing source of ill health and particularly of those chronic, vaguely defined problems which almost never respond to conventional medical treatment.'[17] Marshall Mandell, another pioneer in this field, has estimated that allergies may form 50–80 per cent of the daily medical practice of any GP.

As Gerson had found, however, Randolph was making himself powerful enemies, particularly in his own specialized field of allergy. After its exciting beginnings, allergy had got itself into a rut by the twenties, and by the forties, most allergists were content to stay there. This conventional approach limited the definition of allergy to those cases where the condition could be demonstrated by the existence of antibodies to the particular antigen, or offending substance, in the patient's blood. Most allergists confined their practice to conditions like asthma, hayfever and urticaria – of which in all conscience there was a plentiful supply – which could be identified by means of skin tests and treated with courses of desensitizing injections.

When Randolph and Rinkel revealed that the field of allergy was incomparably wider, more important and more complex than this, they made themselves highly unpopular. The profession closed ranks, and the two men encountered bitter hostility and opposition. Randolph was forbidden to mention his medical school affiliation and stripped of his staff position at Northwestern; his visiting facilities at another hospital were cancelled. He lost most of his income, many of his private patients. Doggedly, he soldiered on.

He had already made himself enemies in the powerful food industry when he demanded at FDA hearings in 1949 that such ingredients as corn, cane and beet sugar should be detailed on food packages. Soon after, a major food company cancelled a research grant it had earlier made him. Then in

1951 he made another set of enemies when he realized – and began publicizing the fact – that many of his patients reacted not only to common foods, but to the chemical additives in them, and to chemicals widespread in the human environment.

Over millions of years, mankind has had time to adapt to changes occurring very slowly in his surroundings and his diet. But with the development of organic chemistry in the nineteenth century, his environment was suddenly bombarded with a host of unfamiliar chemical compounds, which polluted his food, his water, the very air he breathed, and put to ever-mounting stress his powers of adaptation. His body metabolism cannot cope with these unfamiliar compounds; his resistance is lowered, and the stage is set for allergic disease, either physical or mental, which another clinical ecologist, Marshall Mandell, has described as 'an inability to cope with the *natural* as well as the unnatural things that surround him because of an out-of-kilter body metabolism, enzyme dysfunctions, nutritional deficiencies, and hormonal imbalances'.[18]

The general public does not read immensely technical medical journals. And although by the early sixties a whole chorus of voices had been raised in protest against the increasing chemical contamination of man's diet and environment, they were largely those of a minority who could be dismissed as cranks or faddists of one kind or another.

Rachel Carson was certainly no health-food crank, and she was at pains to dissociate herself from the organic lobby. Yet her book *Silent Spring*, published in 1962, gave such passionate and eloquent voice to the fears of this minority that its impact on public opinion was dramatic. A sharp new concern for the environment – particularly in the young – dates from its publication, together with the first questionings of the philosophy that had made possible the mindless chemical contamination of our world which Carson revealed to her appalled readers.

Rachel Carson was both a gifted writer and a specialist in natural history. From 1937 to 1952 she had been genetic biologist for the US Fish and Wildlife Service. In those years she had seen the introduction of synthetic pesticides and insecticides, and the explosive growth of their use, to the point where they were now widespread throughout the physical world and stored in the tissues of almost all living creatures. For wild life the consequences had often been lethal: the robins which had always nested in the tall elms on Michigan University campus were wiped out over four years when the trees were sprayed with DDT to control Dutch elm disease. Yet, even in the short-term, this chemical warfare was not always triumphant, as insects rapidly developed resistance to one spray after another: blackfly in Ontario became seventeen times more abundant after spraying. Nature's own checks were often destroyed, too, with disastrous consequences: the spider mite flourished when DDT killed off its natural predators. In 1956 the US Forest Service sprayed some 885,000 acres of forest with DDT to control budworm. When the forests were surveyed by air the following summer, 'vast blighted areas could be seen where the magnificent Douglas firs were turning brown and dropping their needles'; this summer had brought the worst infestation of spider mites ever seen.

The soil from which man draws his nourishment teemed with myriad organisms whose role in the intricate web of life has hardly been studied. 'What happens,' asked Carson, 'to these incredibly numerous and vitally necessary inhabitants of the soil when poisonous chemicals are carried down into their world? . . . Is it reasonable to suppose that we can apply a broad-spectrum insecticide to kill the burrowing larval stage of a crop-destroying insect, for instance, without also killing the 'good' insects whose function may be the essential one of breaking down organic matter?'

And what of man himself, who now sat down daily to a chemical feast in which traces of all these toxic substances lingered? 'As matters stand now, we are in little better position than the guests of the Borgias.' Who could tell whether daily exposure to even the smallest dose was without risk? 'It is impossible to predict the effects of lifetime exposure to chemical and physical agents that are not part of the biological experience of man.'

The rising toll of cancer was surely one grim consequence. 'In the year 1960, leukaemia alone claimed 12,290 victims. Deaths from all types of malignancies of blood and lymph totalled 25,400, increasing sharply from the 16,690 figure of 1950 . . .' Cancers accounted for 15 per cent of all deaths in 1958 compared with only 4 per cent in 1900. On current figures, the American Cancer Society had estimated that 45,000,000 Americans then alive would develop cancer. Even children were now its victims. 'A quarter century ago, cancer in children was considered a medical rarity. *Today, more American children die of cancer than from any other disease.*'

Silent Spring was a grim warning that we disturb the delicate balance of nature at our peril:

> The 'control of nature' is a phrase conceived in arrogance, born of the Neanderthal age of biology and philosophy, when it was supposed that nature exists for the convenience of man . . . It is our alarming misfortune that so primitive a science has armed itself with the most modern and terrible weapons, and that in turning them against the insects, it has also turned them against the earth.[19]

She might have added 'and against man himself'.

19
All in the Mind?

With respect to mental disease our attribution of cause
is chiefly determined by fashion. At one time . . .
the only causes attributed were sexual excess and
syphilis. These were followed by heredity; heredity
was followed by toxins; toxins were followed by ⤶
repressed complexes . . . now we know that the
mental diseases that we used fondly to ascribe to sexual
excess and syphilis are, in fact, due to repressed
complexes and infantile incestuous longings. How
foolish were our predecessors! How enlightened
are we![1]

Dr Charles Mercier (1916)

Mercier was for some time Physician for Mental Diseases
at London's Charing Cross Hospital and his merciless ribbing
of Freud's disciples among his colleagues must have made him
many enemies.

He was, however, an observant doctor with a keenly logical
mind, who took the trouble to read widely in other fields of
medicine beyond his own specialized subject. And in a lifetime
of studying mental illness, he was drawn irresistibly to the conclusion that Freud was barking up the wrong tree. We were
looking in the wrong places for the causes of mental disease,
he suggested: 'instead of searching for them in the privy and
groping in the night-stool, on the principle of Freud, we may
possibly find them on the dinner table and in the butter dish.'[2]

Mercier was led to this avenue of research by considerations so obvious it is surprising that psychiatrists can continue
to ignore them: among them, the fact that mental disease can
be produced by substances in the diet – such as alcohol. Moreover, he had followed with fascination the nutritional studies
of pellagra and beriberi, and the researches of Hopkins and
Funk on 'vitamines'. 'Whatever the nature and whatever the

mode of action of these puzzling substances, it is beyond question', he asserted, 'that their absence from the food does profoundly affect not only the physical health, but the mental
health also.'

Over the years, Mercier had been looking at the diets of
the out-patients he saw at Charing Cross Hospital. He found
that they were often appalling. There was the married woman
whose depression had already lasted for years and was now 'so
severe that she contemplates suicide . . . Cries for hours every
day, and can take no interest in her work nor in her child.'
Mercier found that she 'lived chiefly on bread and butter . . .
is very fond of butter, and eats a great deal of it. Drinks much
tea, and likes it sweet.'

There was the forty-four-year-old married woman,
obviously schizophrenic, who suffered from severe headaches
and hallucinations, and heard voices talking around her all day
and all night; 'the voices abuse her, and their language is cruel,
dreadful'. Mercier found that she ate little meat and then only
the fat, was 'very fond of fat and butter' and ate little besides
'bread and butter, the butter spread thick, and puddings'.

There was the sixty-six-year-old man who looked much
older and complained of near-total loss of memory, even to
the names of his children. 'Is very fond of sweets, jams and
puddings,' noted Mercier. 'Spreads sugar on his bread and butter. Eats meat only once or twice a week, and then very little.'

He was surprised to find, too, that many of his cases
seemed to live very largely on milky puddings.

As is the way with out-patients, many of them never
appeared in Mercier's consulting-room again. But all of them
were given suggestions about their diet – usually to eat more
meat and less fat. And of those that Mercier was able to follow
up, he noted, 'all but one recovered or very greatly improved
when their diet was rectified.'

In Mercier's day, a good diet meant one with plenty of
protein, preferably meat in it. 'In case after case in which the
diet was subsequently found to be deficient in meat, the mental
state is described in almost or quite the same terms: "I feel
muddled or dazed"; "a wave of confusion comes over me"; "I
feel half-dazed and don't know what I am doing".' These
patients were firmly told to cut down on sugar and fat, and eat
more meat. Those who did so usually recovered with startling
speed.

Mercier also noticed a link between high fat intake and severe headache – or, as we should say today, migraine. He had read Hare's *The Food Factor in Disease*, where this association had been pointed out, and had found it confirmed among his own patients. Rinkel would have been fascinated by another obvious case of masked food allergy among the doctor's London patients: a man suffering from insomnia, headaches and depression, who ate two raw eggs beaten up in milk for breakfast every day of his life – and the same again at teatime.

Mercier stressed that he had only detected faults in the diet in a small number of cases: half a century ahead of their investigation, he could not know of the imbalances or deficiencies in amino acids, trace elements and vitamins, or of heavy metal toxicity, today being studied as possible factors in mental illness. He drew no sweeping conclusions. 'Let me assert once more that I do not hold that there is only one cause of mental disease. If I did so hold, I should be little better than a psychoanalyst.'[2]

He still felt that the success of dietary reform in many of his cases was too striking to ignore. Gowland Hopkins himself had remarked that 'many forms of mental disorder would seem to depend on disturbances of metabolism which are revealed by chemical studies, and there is increasing hope that methods of treatment may be found to correct the errors so discovered'.[3]

But the spell of Freud was too potent, the charms of playing God the Father too alluring to resist. Psychiatry marched firmly down the route signposted by the Viennese prophet. And for half a century, very little research was carried out into the possibility that a poor diet might be literally mind-boggling. So slight was the interest that even forty years after Mercier's article appeared in the *Lancet*, one of the few workers in this field, Professor Josef Brozek, was able to give a concise overview of it in one paper read to the Third International Congress on Nutrition in Amsterdam in 1955.

In his paper, Brozek pointed out some of the difficulties facing researchers in this field. Chief of these was the fact that 'psychodietetics' – the name had been coined in the thirties – was a science cutting across a number of specialized fields, including nutrition, biochemistry, psychology, biology and anthropology. In the increasingly specialized world of twentieth-century medicine, it thus became a Cinderella subject, attracting little attention. Mental illness does not lend itself, either, to the single-nutrient approach which had been so rewarding in diseases like rickets, beriberi and scurvy. Lack of the B vitamin thiamine had certainly been shown to produce a wide range of mental symptoms, but as Brozek pointed out, 'the overwhelming majority of behavioural manifestations of nutritional deficiencies are non-specific'.[4]

There were other reasons for the lack of interest. Little was known at this time of the complex chemistry of the human brain, work on which only began in earnest in the late fifties. Thus the basic data for controlled studies was lacking. And unlike physical disorders such as liver disease or problems of circulation, disorders of the brain are remarkably difficult to diagnose with any accuracy,* let alone quantify; so even the best-designed trials lack the precision and objectivity so dear to the researcher. But such trials, yielding rows of neatly tabulated results, were by this time coming to be regarded as the *sine qua non* of medical truth. Careful clinical observations, such as those of Dr Mercier, were increasingly being brushed aside as mere 'anecdotal evidence'.

Hardly surprisingly, few doctors – and even fewer psychiatrists – were tempted to explore a biochemical approach to mental illness. One of the few was a blunt, down-to-earth and compassionate Canadian physician, Dr Abram Hoffer, who had begun his career in the early forties working on the 'enrichment' of the white flours then being shipped to Britain. Work with vitamins lured him first into nutrition, and soon into medicine. But his first year's work in hospital after graduation switched his attention to psychiatry. 'There were an enormous number of patients in our wards who did not have an illness you could pin down, just vague mental or physical symptoms.' Were these perhaps instances of psychosomatic disease?

Boldly, he suggested to the Saskatchewan Department of Public Health that he set up a psychiatric research unit to study

---

*The difficulty of diagnosing insanity was neatly if worryingly demonstrated in the early seventies by a California psychologist, Dr Rosenhan, in a study worthy of April Fools' Day. Rosenhan and six colleagues managed to get themselves admitted to a total of twelve mental hospitals by claiming that they had 'heard voices'. Once inside, they behaved perfectly normally, gave truthful answers to all questions, and did their utmost to get themselves released. The only people who spotted that they were normal were other patients; the specialists unhesitatingly labelled them 'schizophrenia in remission'. Next, Rosenhan announced that he would be repeating the study at one of the hospitals already tested . . . and then sat back and watched. The harassed staff were so anxious to retrieve their reputations that of the next 193 genuine patients admitted, 41 were judged fakes by at least one of the staff.[5]

the question. 'Since I didn't know any psychiatry,' drily recalls Hoffer, 'I was at a tremendous advantage: I hadn't been told what I couldn't do.'[6]

Eventually, with the help of a massive grant from the Rockefeller Foundation, and with four years' training in psychiatry behind him, Hoffer was able to launch his research programme. Among the staff recruited was a British ex-naval surgeon, Dr Humphrey Osmond, who together with another British psychiatrist, Dr John Smythies, had been working on a biochemical hypothesis about the origins of schizophrenia since the early fifties.

Of all mental diseases, schizophrenia is the most disabling – and the most dreaded. It affects millions throughout the world. In Britain's mental hospitals, some 70,000 patients are schizophrenic, and there are ten to fifteen new cases in every 100,000 of the population annually. Like the poor, schizophrenia has always been with us. Marilyn Monroe and Judy Garland may have been among its victims; Van Gogh, Franz Kafka, and the great Russian ballet dancer Nijinsky almost certainly were; the mad destructive rages of Hitler's later years may have been due to the progress of this disease – paranoia is a common schizoid symptom.

The victims of schizophrenia suffer hallucinations and curious distortion of perception which scramble time, size and distance for them. Like Mercier's middle-aged woman patient, they hear voices and imagine themselves surrounded by enemies in an implacably hostile world. Confused and frightened, patients are often physically unwell too, suffering from overwhelming fatigue, insomnia and lethargy, as well as digestive disorders.

By the 1950s, the accepted psychiatric mythology of the disease pronounced it a personality disorder caused by bad mothering or fathering, or some form of psychological trauma in childhood. The families of schizophrenics were crushed by guilt – 'Where did we go wrong?' – as they still are today. Treatment was either by electroconvulsive therapy (ECT) or deep insulin shock. ECT sometimes worked: insulin was occasionally fatal. Psychoanalysis, it was generally agreed, was a waste of time. Suggestions that it could actually be a physical disorder – like infective hepatitis or diabetes – which happens to affect the brain rather than the liver or the pancreas, are greeted with derision and disbelief even today by the overwhelming majority of Western psychiatrists.

So complete has been their preoccupation with the patient's mind, indeed, that any physical problems he may have tend to be brushed aside as irrelevant if they're noticed at all. Mental hospitals often lack facilities for carrying out even the most elementary physical diagnostic tests. In one American study, forty-six out of 100 psychiatric patients were found to have medical illnesses that either caused or exacerbated their symptoms, while another thirty-four had ordinary illnesses that needed treatment. Gwynneth Hemmings, founder of the Schizophrenia Association of Great Britain, tells a horror story of one patient whose complaints of agonizing stomach pains fell on deaf ears – until he collapsed and died from acute appendicitis.

No research has ever been carried out to substantiate the 'poor mothering' myth so beloved of psychiatrists, as Hoffer and Osmond point out. Their own inquiries led them in a very different direction.

Smythies and Osmond had noted that LSD and other mind-blowing drugs being experimented with in the early fifties could touch off psychotic episodes very like those of true schizophrenia. They speculated that perhaps schizophrenics might be manufacturing compounds like LSD as an aberration of their body chemistry. In Canada, Hoffer and Osmond now followed up this hypothesis together.

By a million-to-one chance, Professor Duncan Hutcheon, one of the Saskatchewan research team, had done his doctoral thesis at Oxford University on just such a compound, adrenochrome, manufactured in the body as a breakdown product of the hormone adrenalin. When this had been synthesized in their laboratory, the two men bravely tried it out on themselves . . . and ran a terrifying gamut of schizophrenic experience. Dr Osmond watched the ceiling of his laboratory change colour, and saw bright dots which formed fish-like shapes. He believed that he was a sea-anemone in an aquarium, with a shoal of brilliant fishes. He looked at a portrait by Van Gogh and felt that it was alive: 'Van Gogh stared at me from the paper, cropheaded, with hurt, mad eyes . . .' Later, noted this most courteous and warm-hearted of men, 'I felt indifferent towards humans and had to curb myself from making unpleasant remarks about them.'[7]

Since adrenochrome could clearly cause symptoms indistinguishable from schizophrenia, Hoffer and Osmond looked for a way to stop the body synthesizing the perilous stuff. The treatment must be non-toxic, so that it could be administered for months or years if necessary. With his background in vitamins, Hoffer was able to suggest the perfect candidate: niacin of vitamin B_3, which – converted inside the body to nicotinic acid – could mop up the chemicals needed to convert noradrenaline into adrenalin. Since adrenochrome was produced by an oxidizing reaction, they added an antioxidant, vitamin C. The pharmaceutical company Marck generously presented them with vast drums of these vitamins, which were still at this time very expensive.

Neither vitamin had any known toxicity; in February 1952, Hoffer and Osmond chose as their first guinea-pig a seventeen-year-old boy who had been admitted to Saskatchewan Hospital with acute schizophrenia. He was responding only occasionally to ECT, deep insulin therapy had had to be stopped when he developed palsy on one side of his face, and he was going downhill fast. They started him on 5 g niacin and 5 g ascorbic acid – vitamin C – daily.

Within twenty-four hours he was better; ten days later he was near-normal; after another month the vitamins were stopped; and three weeks later he was discharged. Three years after, there had been no recurrence of the problem. Seven other patients recovered, some just as dramatically. Greatly encouraged, the two psychiatrists embarked on the first double-blind* studies ever carried out in North America.

It was generally accepted that about 40 per cent of schizophrenia patients eventually recovered with or without treatment. At the end of the first year, when the results of the double-blind were in, Hoffer and Osmond found that they had nearly doubled this recovery rate, to 75 per cent. In 1955 they began another double-blind, this time involving 120 patients. In 1959 they published a five-year follow-up, and in 1962, a nine-year follow-up. No other psychiatric treatment had ever been subjected to such relentless trials.

In each of these trials, using their safe, pain-free and low-cost treatment, Hoffer and Osmond had achieved the same 75 per cent recovery rate. These astonishing results, published in reputable medical journals, might have been expected to send

*In double-blind studies of a new drug, patients are randomly assigned to one of two or more groups, one of which will receive the drug under study, and the other a dummy pill, or placebo. None of those participating – patients, nurses or doctors – are aware which group is which until the study has been completed.

shock-waves through the whole world of psychiatry. They stirred scarcely a ripple. For in the meantime, tranquillizers had appeared and taken over.

The first major tranquillizer, chlorpromazine, appeared in 1952. Overnight, the treatment of mental illness was revolutionized. Governments and state finance departments hailed the new drugs with delight: from now on, patients could quietly disappear. Thousands of them were discharged back into the community, clutching their little bottles of pills, and whole mental hospitals in Britain and the USA were closed down. 'Many patients were considerably benefited,' reported Osmond, 'but a lot of them didn't get well. They simply stayed tranquillized and though this condition is a great deal better than being frenetic, it's not very comfortable. As time went on, too, certain things became clear about the tranquillizers. They tended to knock out the white blood cells, and affect the liver.'[8]

Soon psychiatrists began to see their patients returning. The benefits which had been so striking in the early days of treatment seemed to diminish as time went by. One psychiatrist joked: 'First we had the closed-door policy; then we had the open door; now we have the revolving door.' There were dismaying side-effects: one of the worst was tardive dyskinesia, which could occur after no more than two years of treatment, and often only appeared months after the drugs had been stopped. Its symptoms were involuntary muscle movements, particularly around the face; it completed the social isolation of its luckless victims because of the grotesque facial contortions – twitching, blinking, even sticking out the tongue – which they could not control.

Whatever their disadvantages, however, tranquillizers were incomparably more effective in the treatment of mental illness than ECT or insulin. And with major drug houses racing for a stake in this pharmaceutical gold-rush, intensive study now developed of the 3 lb or so of mysterious matter that we carry around protectively packaged inside our skulls. Over the last three decades, neuroscience has enormously increased our understanding of that most astonishing and complex of all creations, the human brain. It contains, we now know, billions of cells or neurons: estimates range between 10 and 100 billion. (A bee's brain has 950, an ant's 250). A myriad of messages continually flash around this network of neurons, carried by chemical messengers known as neurotransmitters. These chemicals have been found to orchestrate a wide range of brain functions, including movement, pain, sleep, emotion, behaviour, mood. Fluctuations in the level of their activity have been shown to be directly related to such mental disorders as schizophrenia. Two neurotransmitters particularly crucial to our mental stability are serotonin and dopamine. Too much dopamine has been linked with schizophrenia, and some major tranquillizers act by blocking dopamine receptors in the brain. Serotonin levels affect mood, emotion and sleep.

The brain has been described by US biochemist Jeffrey Bland as a 'voraciously hungry glycolitic tissue', consuming 22 per cent of total blood sugar and 25 per cent of resting oxygen. 'It's one of the most nutrient-dense regions of the body,' he points out. 'It requires very high levels of trace elements and vitamin-derived co-factors for function, and therefore one of the first things that happen in a state of under-nutrition is, brain chemistry is affected.'[9]

Since tranquillizers obviously worked by tinkering with brain chemistry, it might have been supposed that their success would have focused attention on the Hoffer–Osmond biochemical approach. The two men had published a number of papers, and Hoffer had described their work in technical detail in a book, *Niacin Therapy and Psychiatry*. 'If the treatment is so damned good,' queried a sceptical psychiatrist, 'why isn't everybody using it?' 'It's so damned good that nobody believes it!' retorted Hoffer. Since both men felt strongly that patients and their families should not be denied the benefits of this safe new treatment, they finally addressed themselves directly to the public in 1966, with a book called *How to Live with Schizophrenia*.

It came to the attention of Dr Linus Pauling, the double Nobel Prizewinner, at this time nearing what was expected to be the end of a long and brilliant career. Intrigued and fascinated, he shelved his retirement plans to confer the prestige of his great authority on the new therapy. He coined a concept – which he christened 'orthomolecular psychiatry' – to explain it: 'that a change in behaviour and mental health can result from changing the concentrations of various substances that are normally present in the brain'. These substances include vitamins, minerals, trace elements and the amino acids present in all proteins, which are attracting more and more exciting research today. As Roger Williams had pointed out in *Biochemical Individuality*, individual needs of any one nutrient can vary enormously; and schizophrenics, alcoholics and children with learning disabilities may have startlingly high requirements for such nutrients as thiamine, niacin or vitamin C.

How to Live with Schizophrenia was no more than a modest bestseller, but it attracted public attention out of all proportion to its sales, and the handful of psychiatrists offering orthomolecular treatment were swamped with patients.

The suggestion that mental problems which kept thousands of analysts and psychiatrists busy might have a biochemical origin, rather than stemming from personal relationships out of whack, appeared very threatening to the psychiatric establishment, and in turn the American Psychiatric Association sat up and took notice. The major drug houses, clocking up soaring sales of a dozen different tranquillizers, were no happier with the idea. The United States Institutes of Mental Health had earlier turned down a request for an $8,000 research grant to study the orthomolecular approach; they now found themselves able to provide a total of $208,000 for the definitive study intended to demolish this dangerous heresy. Dr Wittenburn in New Jersey found in an initial trial that he got no results with the treatment. But in a second study, when he went back and studied his results more closely, he found that he had got the same good results with his acute patients as Hoffer and Osmond, although his chronic patients – like theirs – had remained unimproved. His second report was studiedly ignored: the APA Task Force, set up to evaluate these trials and pronounce on the controversial treatment, was a kangaroo court with a flagrant bias against it. The chairman, Dr Morris Lipton, had earlier expressed his hostility; one of the committee members was a subordinate of his, and unlikely to vote against him; two other members later revealed that most of their research grants came from drug companies marketing tranquillizers. The Task Force completed its task and found, to nobody's surprise, that orthomolecular psychiatry was not worth the paper it was printed on. This report was printed in full in the *Journal of the American Psychiatric Association*, and mailed to every psychiatrist in the USA, to deadly effect. Hoffer, Osmond, and a small brave handful of doctors – including Alan Cott and David Hawkins – became the pariahs of the psychiatric community. Hoffer and Osmond published a dignified and cogent rebuttal of the Task Force findings, pointing out its bias: their reply was ignored by the APA. 'If you can't stand the heat – get out of the kitchen,' cracked Hoffer unabashed.

Dr Carl Pfeiffer is also used to being treated like a leper by fellow-psychiatrists. As an undergraduate in 1927 at the University of Wisconsin, he saw a patient go into catatonic trance after absorbing too much carbon dioxide: 'I realized then that mother-love wasn't the only factor in mental states . . .' Today, he points out that no less than seven diseases once assumed to be madness pure and simple have turned out to be physical in origin. Pellagra is one. Another is porphyria – identified in 1969 by two British psychiatrists as the disease which afflicted England's tragic King George III. Thyroid deficiency may be the cause of their symptoms in 1 in 200 schizophrenic patients; syphilis of the brain is now a recognized syndrome.

A thorn in the side of conventional psychiatry, Pfeiffer cheerfully maintains that as of now, the cluster of mental symptoms loosely labelled schizophrenia – which he describes as a waste-basket diagnosis – can be successfully treated once the underlying metabolic abnormality has been identified.

In 1952, Pfeiffer asked the US Army Medical Center for their most powerful sneeze-inducing agent. He wanted to test the observation that schizophrenics were low in histamine, the neurotransmitter responsible for the sneezes, the runny noses and the streaming eyes of the hayfever victim, or the wheezing of the asthmatic. Pfeiffer and his students were convulsed with sneezes as they held the bottles – at arm's length – under the noses of their schizoid patients, many of whom didn't bat an eyelid, let alone sneeze. It's a matter of record that schizophrenic patients are often magically immune to such histamine-related problems as hayfever or asthma – until they get better, when their immunity disappears too. Pfeiffer points out that histamine levels are particularly high in those areas of the brain that regulate behaviour, and that histamine works in tandem with zinc. Schizophrenic patients at his Brain Bio Center in Princeton, New Jersey, have their histamine levels monitored as a matter of routine, and he estimates that some 50 per cent of schizophrenics have abnormally low levels of histamine, together with high levels of the trace element copper, which, he has shown, can be toxic to the brain and nervous system in excess. Depression, paranoia, and autism or hyperactivity in children may all be caused by too much copper. Pfeiffer has successfully treated hundreds of such patients with high doses of niacin, together with zinc and manganese, to lower copper. Histamine levels, he is convinced, are an important and highly neglected factor in schizophrenia.

By contrast, he reckons, some 20 per cent of all schizophrenics may be what he terms histadelics: they have too much histamine. Particularly hard to treat successfully, this group includes the suicidally depressed, and junkies, since alcohol, coffee and hard drugs all release histamine. Marilyn Monroe, surmises Pfeiffer, may have belonged in this lost legion: Histadelics cry easily, have a low pain threshold, complain of terrible insomnia, may be highly sexed, and often have wonderful figures because of their high metabolic rate.

The Mauve Factor sounds like the name of a thriller. Its actually a substance first pinpointed in a Saskatchewan laboratory, under the direction of Hoffer, as the clue to a biochemical abnormality: in lab tests, the urine of many schizophrenic patients produces a fetching lavender-hued spot, caused by a chemical christened kryptopyrrole. In one study, the Mauve Factor was found in no normal subject; in 10 per cent of those physically ill, in 40 per cent of alcoholics, in 50 per cent of the mentally retarded – and in 75 per cent of schizophrenics. Pfeiffer's researches showed that it could induce severe deficiency of vitamin B_6 or pyridoxine, since kryptopyrrole complexes with B_6 to carry it out of the body, together with much of the body's vital hoard of zinc. Pfeiffer has treated many of these patients, too, with high doses of B_6, zinc and manganese; their schizophrenic symptoms often disappeared within days. The symptoms of B_6 and zinc deficiency are now well-known, thanks to Pfeiffer: zinc-deficient people have white-spotted fingernails, often paper thin, and you're probably B_6-deficient if you can't recall your dreams.

Studies made by Pfeiffer and his team of trace-elements such as zinc, chromium and manganese have made a massive contribution to the advancement not just of psychiatry but of nutrition in general. Ironically, animal and poultry feeds had been lavishly enriched with these vital nutrients for years before the earliest studies were made in human beings. Eating a typical Western diet, we may be getting little more than 8–10 mg of zinc a day. Since the mid-fifties, pigs and chickens in the West have had their feeds spiked with extra zinc at anything up to twenty times this level: the extra feed efficiency produced is one reason why pork and chickens are still such cheap foods.

Zinc is one of several vital trace elements – others are chromium and manganese – scoured out of refined flour or destroyed by chemical sequestrants used in freezing. Only now, in the eighties, are food companies like Kellogg's beginning to 'enrich' their breakfast cereals with some of the missing zinc, as well as iron and the B vitamins. Among other consequences of zinc deficiency, Pfeiffer points out, may be dwarfism – since it is needed for normal growth and sexual development; morning sickness in pregnancy; stretch marks after childbirth; retarded wound healing; acne; and the aching joints in teenagers often dismissed as fanciful 'growing pains'. Where zinc – and manganese – are deficient, copper levels will rocket; among the resulting problems, says Pfeiffer, is postnatal depression, which can often be cured by doses of zinc together with B_6, with which it acts synergistically. Shortage of zinc also exposes us to overloading with toxic metals like lead and cadmium, both of which are zinc antagonists.

Professor Derek Bryce-Smith, the British expert on lead and its horrific impact on twentieth-century health, has recently suggested in the *Lancet* that yet another disorder claimed as their domain by psychiatrists may in many cases be a zinc deficiency in disguise: anorexia nervosa. Loss of appetite and the sense of taste are among early warning signs of zinc deficiency. When anorectic girls were given a zinc solution to taste, it had no taste to them – though ordinary people found it quite metallic and objectionable. Anorectics, it has often been noticed, are inclined to deluge their food with salt, pepper, mustard, strong sauces – presumably for this reason. A hormone connection – together with the young girl's urge to look like a fashion model – accounts for the vastly greater number of female anorectics. The active sports – running, swimming, jogging – to which many anorectics are addicted, compound their problems by using up still more zinc. And as they eat less and less, their zinc stores dwindle to zero, in a vicious downward spiral. The handful of doctors who have acted on Bryce-Smith's suggestion have found that in about 80 per cent of cases, giving anorectics supplements of zinc can bring about a dramatic change in appetite and psychological outlook almost overnight, but at the time of writing this, he has not been able to persuade a single psychiatrist to run a controlled trial of zinc therapy among their many anorectic patients.

As early as the seventeenth century, milk-drinking has been linked with 'melancholy'; a pioneering observation, perhaps, of mental symptoms produced by a common allergen. Theron Randolph reported that of the 20,000 patients he had treated over the years for food or chemical sensitivities, over a third – around 7,000 – were suffering mental symptoms such as acute depression or anxiety. And the Chicago allergist Dr Marshall Mandell has focused his work specially on this field of cerebral allergy. In 1971, Dr William Philpott, Research Director of the Fuller Memorial Sanitarium at South Attleboro in Massachusetts, heard about Mandell's work, and invited him to lecture on it at Fuller. For four hours doctors and nurses listened fascinated while Mandell told them of case after case in which depression, anxiety, neuroses of every kind, severe psychosis and mental confusion had been shown to result from eating foods or from exposure to chemicals to which patients were allergic. He showed them dramatic film shot in his consulting room of mental symptoms appearing almost immediately after challenges with suspect foods or chemicals. And he played tapes which showed how even their voices changed – they stuttered, stammered, hesitated – as their thinking became cloudy and confused.

So impressed was his audience that Mandell was offered a staff post, and over the next five years, he and Dr Philpott treated hundreds of patients for what they called B E M I – bio-ecologic mental illness. They found that 90 per cent of the patients at Fuller were suffering from allergies that seriously affected their minds. One of the worst cases in the hospital was Jennifer, a young schizophrenic who had been in and out of mental hospitals for eleven years, had had endless sessions of talk therapy, treatment with every type of major tranquillizer, a series of shock treatments. She was weak, suicidal, deeply depressed; at intervals she went into rigid catatonic trances. In just four days of fasting she became completely normal. In careful tests, Mandell and Philpott found that she was extremely allergic to tobacco smoke – as 75 per cent of schizophrenic patients are, in their experience; to the chlorine routinely used to treat drinking water; to lamb, house dust, several kinds of mould and saccharin. Bio-ecologic treatment gave her life back to this tortured young woman. After completing her studies at a small religious college where smoking was prohibited, she sent the two doctors an invitation to her wedding – and a few years later, the announcement that she had had a baby boy.

'Perhaps many thousands of schizophrenic patients and patients with other disorders now in mental hospitals would be helped in the same way,' wrote Marshall Mandell in 1979, 'if there were a way for bio-ecologically oriented physicians to reach them. At the present time, the doors to these psychiatric institutions are closed – along with the minds behind those doors.'[10]

After five years, the closed minds in the Massachusetts State Department banned the use of allergy testing and therapeutic fasting in mental hospitals within its boundaries. Philpott and Mandell protested in vain, sending in details of thousands of patients successfully treated by such methods. The Department was adamant: such tests could only be carried out in a general hospital. A sick mind was a sick mind was a sick mind.

Despite this depressing display of small-mindedness, the work of the two doctors had enormous impact: out of it grew the US Society for Clinical Ecology, which has brought hope to hundreds of thousands of patients. Thousands more, reading Mandell's best-selling *5-Day Allergy Relief System*, have learned how to test themselves for the allergies which most doctors – and almost all psychiatrists – still refuse to admit can be the cause of their devastating mental symptoms.

Abram Hoffer, with his usual open-minded generosity, was one of the first to acknowledge the importance of Mandell's work. The niacin therapy had never been successful for chronic schizophrenic patients, and Hoffer had a number of intractable cases for whom nothing seemed to be working – nutrition, vitamins, ECT, psychotherapy. Then Hoffer saw a film Mandell had made, and his interest was aroused.

One of Hoffer's patients was a sixteen-year-old girl, hopelessly schizophrenic. Hoffer felt she was doomed – and acted.

> I persuaded her to fast for four days. On the fourth day she was normal. This I had never seen in over twenty years of practice. She was allergic to milk and a number of other foods. A glass of milk reactivated her psychosis in an hour. Over the next two years I made about 160 patients fast. About 100 responded in the same way. There is no further doubt in my mind that certain people's brains react adversely to a variety of substances by becoming schizophrenic.[11]

Milk and grains seem to be the chief culprits. One US psychiatrist found that 50 per cent of his patients were allergic to milk. Dr F. Curtis Dohan of Pennsylvania has fed gluten-free diets to numbers of psychiatric patients, and found that they often recovered with startling speed. Dohan points out that when the wheat consumption of Norway, Finland and Sweden was reduced by about 50 per cent during the war, schizophrenia

admission rates fell by around half. Coeliac disease and schizophrenia tend to run hand in hand in some families, and schizophrenics have been shown to have a high incidence of gut
disease. At a conference organized by the Schizophrenia
Association of Great Britain, Professor Buscaino described the
results of screening schizophrenics for digestive problems: 50
per cent suffered from gastritis, 88 per cent from enteritis, 92
per cent from colitis.

More suggestive still, treatment by fasting under medical
supervision – for up to a month – has been practised both in the
USSR, where it was pioneered by Dr Nicolaev of the Moscow
Psychiatric Institute in 1945, and by Dr Allan Cott in the USA.
Cott found, too, that the manic phase of manic depression
could be controlled in the first week of such fasts. After the fast,
patients return to a diet of fruit, vegetables and some form of
acidulated milk, before going on to a 'normal' but carefully
controlled diet. About 65 per cent of Dr Nicolaev's 'hopeless'
cases improved enough to be discharged from hospital and six
years later half of these were still well, with the relapses occurring among those who had broken their diet.

The pioneer of clinical ecology in Britain has been Dr
Richard Mackarness, who spent months in the States learning
all about it at first hand from Randolph, Rinkel and Rowe. He
battled for twenty years to establish the validity of the concept,
in the teeth of orthodox suspicion, incredulity and blatant hostility. In Britain as in the States, the public has reacted far more
swiftly than their doctors, and while he was grappling with professional antagonism on one hand, on the other he has helped
introduce the concept of allergy to a wide British public,
through his two lucid and fascinating books, *Not All in the Mind*
(1976), which has sold over a quarter of a million copies to date,
and *Chemical Victims* (1980).

The most startling case he described was that of Joanna,
a young woman happily married with two small children. The
birth of a third baby left her with a deepening postnatal
depression, which was treated with drugs and shock therapy.
Over the next seven years, she was in and out of mental hospital,
after violent episodes in which she attacked her children and
viciously slashed at her own arms. By the time Mackarness saw
her, she was in a chemical straitjacket of heavy drugs, and
psychiatrists had decided that surgery of the brain – pre-frontal
leucotomy – which would reduce her to a passive vegetable
condition, was the last option left. Since there was nothing to

be lost, it was felt, by letting Mackarness try out his bizarre ideas on this desperate case, she was handed over to him. He found that the psychiatrists had pinned any number of labels on her: pre-senile dementia, schizo-affective psychosis, neurotic depression with anxiety/hysteria. Overweight, chronically depressed, sitting hunched and silent, her skin dulled and her eyes glazed except in her violent fits, she was the most pitiful of sights. Mackarness questioned her gently about her diet, and learned that she seldom ate fresh fruit or vegetables, and lived on snacks, canned food, sausages and chips, cheese and biscuits, washed down with daily gallons of sweet milky coffee. She smoked forty to sixty cigarettes a day.

A five-day fast turned this abject creature into a normal, lucid woman who could talk and even smile. They found together that she was allergic to pork in any form – ham, sausages, bacon – to eggs, to porridge, to coffee and chocolate and many other foods. For years she had suffered from a spectrum of symptoms that would have alerted any clinical ecologist – itchy, running nose, wheezing, palpitations, heavy sweats. On a diet made of 'safe' foods, Joanna was discharged drug-free from hospital, and three months later her GP reported that she was 'happy, gay, euphoric, sometimes almost hypo-manic in her enjoyment of life' – though she had learned that if she needed attention, she could eat some forbidden fruit and evoke her old symptoms.

Depression, anxiety, panic attacks, fatigue were being blamed as early as the forties on low blood sugar – hypoglycaemia , a 'disease' which has had an oddly chequered career. Its discovery grew out of the research that produced insulin as a treatment for diabetes. Insulin is a hormone produced by the poetically named islets of Langerhans in the pancreas. When you eat carbohydrates, your digestive processes convert them into glucose – blood sugar. This triggers the release by the pancreas of the hormone insulin, the function of which is to regulate blood levels of glucose: the excess is carried to the liver where it is converted into glycogen for storage. A drop in blood sugar – the energy fuel of the brain, the nervous system and every single cell in the body – is an emergency which prompts the adrenal glands to action: they release cortical hormones which signal the liver to convert some of its stored glycogen back into glucose, and release it into the blood to get levels back to normal. In health, blood sugar is kept at a steady level by the interplay of these hormones.

The diabetic's problem is a malfunction of the insulin process, and all diabetics were doomed to an early death until the discovery of insulin in the twenties. But sometimes, the dose they were given was too high – and their blood sugar levels nosedived, resulting in insulin shock. An observant physician, Dr Seale Harris, noted that he had seen other patients, not diabetic or on insulin, with identical symptoms of dizziness, weakness, blurred vision, palpitations and so on; he christened the condition hyper-insulinism, and described it in a paper published in the *Journal of the American Medical Association* in 1924. It could be produced in anyone, he said – not just diabetics taking extra insulin – by doses of refined sugar: glucose in such a concentrated form that the alarmed pancreas overreacted by pouring out a mega-dose of insulin, to send blood sugar levels crashing. The remedy was simple: stay away from refined sugar or refined flour.

Other doctors followed Harris's lead, and found that low blood sugar was a factor in a huge spectrum of conditions they found hard to treat successfully, especially vague disorders such as chronic fatigue and lack of concentration.

The brain and nervous system are heavily dependent on a steady supply of glucose, so mental and nervous symptoms are among the earliest signs of hypoglycaemia – that shaky, light-headed feeling when you haven't eaten for a long time, for instance. And gradually, over the years, chronic low blood sugar was suspected of being a factor in a growing list of disorders, among them alcoholism, antisocial behaviour, slow learning in schoolchildren, depression and addiction. A standard Glucose Tolerance Test – which involved hourly checks on blood sugar levels after the patient had broken an overnight fast with a dose of sugar – was set up, and the diet proposed by Seale Harris generally adopted. Sugar was barred in any form – as were tea, coffee and alcohol; other carbohydrates were severely limited; and patients were urged to have small frequent meals or snacks high in protein. This diet brought relief – often almost overnight – to hundreds of patients. In 1949, the AMA awarded Seale Harris their Distinguished Service Medal to honour his pioneering work on low blood sugar.

But professional interest had already declined. Doctors were reluctant to tell their patients that tea and toast was out for breakfast, doughnuts and coffee a no-no for elevenses, and the pre-prandial martini absolutely barred. As Theron Randolph points out, too, the medical profession is unhappy with unifying concepts in disease: 'Specialization has turned out to be a convenient and, of course, lucrative way of dividing the labours of medicine.'[12] Specialists in the mind – psychiatrists – are the unhappiest of all; hypoglycaemia can be diagnosed by any GP and treated on a do-it-yourself basis by any layman.

By the fifties, a Los Angeles psychiatrist had already christened hypoglycaemia 'the stepchild of medicine', and ignorance of it was so widespread that a young Florida doctor, Stephen Gyland, spent three years vainly trying to get treatment for his disabling anxiety, tremors, memory and concentration problems and general washed-out feeling. He saw fourteen different specialists, was examined at three nationally known clinics, was told he was suffering from anxiety neurosis, brain tumour, diabetes, and cerebral arteriosclerosis and a constellation of other diseases before a physician finally gave him the Glucose Tolerance Test, at his own request, after he had chanced upon Seale Harris's original paper. Cured by the Harris diet, he began examining a number of cases: he found hypoglycaemia in 94 per cent of those with 'nerves', 89 per cent of 'irritable' patients; 77 per cent of those suffering from depression; 62 per cent of his insomniacs – the whole range of problems for which today's GP is most frequently consulted, and for which his answer is likely to be a prescription for tranquillizers. When Gyland had gathered a splendid harvest of 600 detailed case-histories, he presented a paper on them at an AMA meeting. To his dismay, the AMA refused to publish this paper – as did every other reputable American medical journal. (It finally appeared in a Brazilian journal, in Portuguese.) According to the AMA revisionists, hypoglycaemia was now a non-disease.

What prompted this change of mind is uncertain. In all probability, though, it was the publication some years earlier of a book that had turned hypoglycaemia into a well-known disorder which hundreds of thousands of Americans were now diagnosing and treating themselves. *Body, Mind and Sugar*, by Dr E. M. Abrahamson and A. W. Pezet, published in 1951, was a runaway bestseller which sold a staggering quarter of a million copies in hardback before going into paperback. In a 1966 nationwide health survey, nearly half the 134,000 people interviewed volunteered the unprompted information that they suffered from hypoglycaemia. Two years later, popular nutrition lecturer Carlton Fredericks collaborated with a physician to publish *Low Blood Sugar and You* – another bestseller, proclaiming 'the startling facts of how millions of Americans suffer from hypoglycaemia . . . *without knowing it!* Often disguised as neurosis, alcoholism, lack of sexual energy, and obesity . . .'

Highly irritated, the AMA now disowned this too-popular stepchild altogether. In 1973, their *Journal* pronounced that while the symptoms of low blood sugar might include shakiness, anxiety, headaches and weakness, 'the majority of people with these kinds of symptoms do not have hypoglycaemia'.

A small number of open-minded psychiatrists continued to bear it in mind as a possibility when examining their patients. Hoffer found that 100 per cent of his alcoholics were hypoglycaemic. A California psychiatrist, Michael Lesser, counted 189 among 283 cases – nearly two thirds. 'Not only are the common symptoms of neurosis identical with those of hypoglycaemia,' he wrote, 'but the blood sugar pattern in the two appears to be the same. I do not say that hypoglycaemia causes neurosis, just as I would not say neurosis causes low blood sugar. I *do* say that one accompanies the other. Each is an expression of the other, occurring at a different level.'[13]

But while many of these patients improved on the Seale Harris diet of lots of small, high-protein meals, others did not, or even got worse. And the hypoglycaemia saga took another twist when Marshall Mandell pointed out that every single one of the supposedly hypoglycaemic patients he had tested were actually suffering from food or chemical allergies, and that their low blood sugar symptoms were simply the withdrawal stage of their allergy – likely to be most acute when they were still fasting in the morning. Hypoglycaemia was 'a currently popular misinterpretation of food withdrawal symptoms' – and when the diet worked, it was because it withdrew specific allergens – corn, wheat, sugar, tea, coffee, alcohol – from the diet. But in the long run it could only be a disaster for many, he argued, since it exposed them to frequent meals of eggs, milk, pork and chicken, all common allergens, to which they were likely to become sensitive in turn, if they were not so already. And in point of fact, numbers of patients on the Seale Harris diet complained that although their hypoglycaemia symptoms were controlled, they began to feel sluggish, low in energy, and to suffer from constipation, arthritis, gout, headaches and skin disorders.

The high-protein diet came under fire from another quarter in 1977, when America's best-known naturopath and nutritionist, Paavo Airola, denounced the stark folly of consuming massive daily amounts of animal protein. Long-term, it could only cause worse problems, he suggested, among them B vitamin deficiencies, over-acidity, and degenerative disease. Help the body heal itself, he suggested, with a diet based on man's natural foods: complex carbohydrates, seeds, nuts, grains and vegetables, together with supplements of vitamins and minerals. The Airola diet has been adopted by numbers of psychiatrists and doctors, who report that not only does it successfully cure the majority of cases of hypoglycaemia, but that people following it often begin to enjoy better health than they have ever known before.

Airola pointed out that allergies, to caffeine and sugar, for example, were not the only causes of low blood sugar: emotional stress or nutritional deficiencies could also trigger it – even the dreary, monotonous lives of those whose days are filled by 'dull, repetitive chores without a sense of achievement'.[14]

And nutritionally oriented physicians today see hypoglycaemia as not so much a disease entity to be treated by a specific diet, as a clear physical indication of stress produced by a number of factors – of which sugar or food allergies are the most likely.

The condition is now in process of gradual official rehabilitation, but it is still unpopular with psychiatrists as a marker for possible biochemical causes in mental conditions, which they prefer to blame on father-fixation, disturbed interpersonal relationships, poor self-image, role ambiguity or some other currently fashionable label.

They should remember that Freud himself suggested that a chemical basis might one day be found for mental illnesses, which would revolutionize their treatment. 'I am firmly convinced,' he said in 1927, 'that one day all these disturbances we are trying to understand will be treated by means of hormones or similar substances.'[15]

Many of these substances are now being looked at.

One of the most important is the role in brain chemistry of amino acids – the chemicals into which proteins are broken down in our bodies during digestion. The amino acids and their importance have been studied since the late twenties, and it is now known that specific amino acids are the precursors of neurotransmitters in the brain. A number of diseases caused by the defects in the body's handling of these amino acids have now been identified – among them homocystineuria and phenylketonuria – and mental retardation is a common symptom. But it was long believed that the brain – unlike any other part of our bodies – was able magically to synthesize its transmitters without more than token help from the diet, and that it carried on its mysterious activities in regal independence of such lowly considerations as the boiled egg eaten for breakfast, or dinnertime's fish and chips.

One of the first psychiatrists to question this assumption was the British Dr John Smythies, who had originally developed the adrenochrome hypothesis with Hoffer and Osmond, and published a paper on it in 1954. Now running his own clinic and research centre in Birmingham, Alabama, Smythies began studying these amino acid precursors, and was particularly interested by tryptophan, the dietary precursor of serotonin, which helps regulate mood and emotion. Low levels of this neurotransmitter may be responsible for irritability, insecurity, feelings of acute pessimism, even of suicidal depression. Since niacin or niacinamide – the B vitamin needed by pellagra victims – is actually converted into tryptophan inside the body, the mental symptoms of pellagra can be said to be due to tryptophan deficiency.

The work of Hoffer, Smythies and Osmond has now been supplied with impeccable scientific credentials in the form of research carried out by Richard and Judith Wurtman in the very shrine of orthodoxy, the Massachusetts Institute of Technology. In studies with rats, they showed that fluctuating levels in the blood of the two amino acids tryptophan and tyrosine, following meals supplying them, had very marked effects on the brain levels of, respectively, serotonin and another neurotransmitter, dopamine, excess of which has been demonstrated as a factor in schizophrenia. Dr Mercier would have been charmed by this work demonstrating the importance of protein in the diet.

As one spin-off of the Wurtmans' research, tryptophan is now being used in both depression and insomnia; that traditional Christmas afternoon snooze after the feast is fostered by the high amounts of tryptophan in turkey.

The Wurtmans' work also showed that upping brain supplies of B_3 can also help raise serotonin levels. Major pharmaceutical companies are now investing massive sums in research into this new breed of natural tranquillizers, which in megadoses behave like pharmaceuticals rather than vitamins.

Researchers for Roche – who first launched Valium on the market – have discovered that niacinamide, one of the two forms of vitamin B_3 – binds to the same receptor sites in the brain as Valium or Librium; it is a natural tranquillizer, in other words. Work on vitamin C, meanwhile, has shown that mega-doses can block the output of too much dopamine, just as the major tranquillizers do, but without their appalling side-effects.

The amino acids are seen today as highly promising 'natural' pharmaceuticals that can be used to treat a wide range of conditions, many of them mental. Tyrosine is effective for some forms of depression; glutamine, as Roger Williams showed, protects the alcoholic not only against the ravages of drink but even against the desire to reach for the next one. Methionine brings down high levels of histamine – responsible for one form of schizophrenia – and together with the amino acids cysteine and cystine is used today to detoxify the system of those whose minds are addled by toxic metals such as lead and cadmium.

Mental illness is today a growing and terrible threat to the happiness of millions. When I asked Roche if they could supply any statistics on depression, they came up with the staggering estimate that perhaps 100 million people in the world today are suffering from depression so acute that it is a clinically identifiable condition – not just the grief or despondency that life inflicts on us all from time to time. Cases of depression have multiplied so rapidly over the past decade that it is now officially considered epidemic. And like heart disease or cancer, its victims are getting younger all the time: among American teenagers, suicide is now the third commonest form of death, while alcoholism and other forms of addiction – modern plagues as terrifying and as little understood as the Black Death – claim victims barely out of the nursery.

Four or five hospitals in the USA now offer their handful of lucky patients a humane and effective treatment based on the biochemical concepts discussed in this chapter. They are screened for low blood sugar and allergy problems; their hair is analysed for trace mineral imbalances, such as the copper or zinc abnormalities which can be so crucial. They are put on a healthy wholefood diet in which fresh fruit, vegetables and whole grains are emphasized, and from which white sugar, white flour, caffeine and chemical additives are eliminated. Vitamin and mineral supplements – often including mega-doses of niacin and vitamin C – are routine; regular exercise and plenty of sleep are mandatory. Just as importantly, the patients are treated with love and respect, their cases are discussed openly with them, and their families are involved at every stage of therapy.

No hospital in Britain offers anything remotely approaching such humane and rational treatment. And both here and in the USA, the overwhelming majority of patients and their desperate families who get to know about such therapies have little hope of finding a psychiatrist who will supervise their administration. Huge sums of money are spent investigating drug treatment; tiny sums on the far more promising – and vastly cheaper – biochemical approach.

And millions of patients and their families continue to suffer all the traumas of mental illness, with its agonies and its painful social stigma, as well as the perils of drug treatment. Those 'lucky' enough still to obtain hospital treatment can usually count on a diet almost calculated to exacerbate their condition – high in refined carbohydrates, low in fresh fruit and vegetables, washed down with unlimited cups of tea and coffee. In many mental hospitals, the treatment of patients – like the gloomy Gothic buildings in which they pass their comfortless lives – has hardly improved in a hundred years, relegating them to subhuman status: '. . . the treatment of the symptoms of mental disease, and the avoidance of nature's weapons to prevent mental trouble, promises to be one of the blackest pages in medical history,' wrote Roger Williams angrily in 1970.[16]

The psychiatrists who have pioneered the use of 'nature's weapons' are not quacks or charlatans, but responsible practitioners deeply concerned about their patients. They have described their work in solidly professional journals, delivered papers, been ready – indeed anxious – to submit their work to competent clinical trial. With depressing predictability, the reward of their work has been ostracism by their colleagues.

In the long run this studied professional boycott of biochemical approaches may be counterproductive: mental illness is fast turning into a do-it-yourself proposition, like allergy and hypoglycaemia. Hoffer and Osmond, Pfeiffer, Marshall Mandell, Alan Cott and Michael Lesser have all in turn come to the conclusion that while it may be unprofessional to address the public directly, they cannot morally withhold from millions of sick people the knowledge that is their only chance of treatment. As with physical disease, the American psychiatric scene today offers the extraordinary spectacle of numbers of eminent practitioners writing for public consumption what are in effect manuals of self-treatment. After reading Pfeiffer's *The Schizo-phrenias, Yours and Mine*, published in 1970, thousands of patients went ahead and treated themselves, often with considerable success, and then went on to treat other sufferers. Pfeiffer's more recent *Golden Pamphlet* offers minutely detailed prescriptions for carefully described metabolic ailments, including the various types of schizophrenia, depression and insomnia.

Responsible physicians can hardly be happy with such a situation. But what other choice do they – and the public – have?

20
Whole Food and Health Foods

Can food that is so conveniently processed, refined,
frozen, canned, pre-cooked, ready-packed, ready-
to-serve be *all* that is needed for a really good diet? . . .
it is a sign of the times that more and more people
are using more and more of what used to be called
'health foods'. In most large towns there are new
and prosperous shops specializing in them, and more
grocers and chemists are stocking them because of
the demand. These foods are no longer synonymous
with raw carrots, sandals and an earnest attitude to
life . . .

British *Vogue* (February 1956)

The ubiquitous Gayelord Hauser could take much of the
credit for this switch in sophisticated public opinion. In 1955
his bestseller *Look Younger, Live Longer* took off in Britain too,
on the heels of its much-trumpeted success in the United States.
And in Britain, as in the States, its appeal was decidedly up-
market. It was the *Daily Herald* that sneered: 'The style is
straight out of *Tiny Tots*. . . Beverley Nichols and Godfrey Winn
have not lived in vain . . .'[1] The world of the glossies was
inclined to take him much more seriously.

So were the health-food stores. In the mid-fifties there
were perhaps 200 of these, most of them banded together in
the National Association of Health Stores which had been
founded in 1937. In its twenty years of life, the number of
shops had trebled, and their owners were already grumbling
about the way that grocers and chemists were cashing in on
markets the health shops had pioneered for them. Hauser's
book brought them a welcome boost, together with the beginnings of a new buying public.

It was in response to this widening interest that Wholefood
opened its doors in 1960. Its directors were at pains to point
out that it was most emphatically NOT just another health-food

store. It existed to sell, quite literally, whole food, McCarrison's 'unsophisticated foodstuffs of nature': raw milk, free-range eggs and poultry, fruit and vegetables, whole grains, sun-dried fruit, pulses, nuts, seeds – all grown or produced without artificial chemicals. Wholefood was the child of the Soil Association, and among the believers who generously gave money to start it were the violinist Yehudi Menuhin, an ardent advocate of natural foods, Lord Kitchener, a leading organic farmer, Sam Mayall and Mrs Elizabeth Murray. Among its directors, as she still is today, was Mary Langman, who had been secretary of the Pioneer Health Centre down in Peckham till it closed its doors. And soon it was being run by Lilian Schofield who, after years of working in the pharmacy department of Boots, encountered Nature Cure in the authoritative person of James Thomson in Edinburgh, when she faced surgery for crippling ulcerative colitis. Cured and revivified, she looked for a new challenge, and found it in Wholefood.

For health foods or whole foods, though, the market was still tiny. The backbone of their trade was still the dedicated vegetarian and the disciple of Nature Cure. Almost the only health magazine then was Stanley Lief's *Health for All*, with its articles on fasting, food reform and the drugless way to health, and the books sold in health-food shops were strictly for the converted: *The Diet Reform Cook Book, Building Physical Efficiency* and *Nature Cure in a Nutshell* were hardly titles you would expect to see on the bestseller list. The new and prosperous shops *Vogue* mentioned certainly existed, among them branches of the London Health Centre, run by Ernest Cooper, in Swiss Cottage and Notting Hill Gate, and in Oxford, but these were exceptional; the far more typical health-food store of the time was a sedate, back-street establishment with a middle-aged clientele, an array of vegetarian rissole mixes and soy-milks in among the wholemeal bread and herbal remedies, and an indefinable air of purpose which checked the inquiring layman uneasily at the door. The great British public stayed away *en masse*. Cosseted by their wonderful new National Health Service, assured by experts and the government that their diet provided all the vitamins and minerals they needed, dazzled by the unending stream of new miracle drugs ('a pill for every ill'), and instructed by their doctors that nutrition had nothing to do with diseases, and that nobody was undernourished, the British had put rationing and austerity behind them at last in 1953. Now, just like Americans, they were eating their way solidly to soaring rates of heart disease, diabetes, cancer, arthritis, digestive disorders, to the whole host of wretched ailments which McCarrison had produced among his ill-fed mice decades earlier.

In 1954 the British spent £242m on sweets and chocolates; the national consumption of ice-cream doubled between 1956 and 1965, and during the same period the consumption of biscuits, soft drinks, cakes, pastries, packet pies and instant desserts (in which the only real food might be the milk added by the housewife in making it up) soared. More and more women went out to work, and relied on canned and frozen foods for weekday meals, though they might still make an effort to produce the classic meat and two (fresh) veg. for Sunday. And from the beginning of the sixties on, in increasingly affluent Britain, teenagers became a spending force to be reckoned with, and sales of snacks, confectionery and soft drinks aimed directly at this market began climbing steadily. Whiter than white, softer and springier than ever before, meanwhile, most bread was now being baked by the revolutionary Chorleywood Process, a triumph of technology evolved by the British Baking Industries Research Association. In this process mechanical beating replaced yeast as a raising agent – although yeast was still used; a softer and cheaper wheat could be used; 7 per cent more bread could be produced from the same amount of flour as pre-Chorleywood bread; and less time was needed for the preparation of the dough. Up to twenty-six additives might go into the making of this flabby 70 per cent loaf – flour improvers, bleaches, yeast stimulators, emulsifiers, preservatives and antioxidants. 'Tests are run on these additives before they appear on the approved list,' Hannah Wright wrote in a devastating 1981 study of the food industry, 'but neither the history of these tests nor the way in which government food committees are organized make that mouthful of white sliced lie very easy in the stomach.'[2] The government watchdogs are part-time committees, she pointed out, much of the testing is done by the industry itself and some of the additives have been banned for years in other countries. The handful of independent bakers still producing old-fashioned crusty bread or real wholemeal bread declined throughout the sixties, as Garfield-Weston's Associated British Foods and Rank Hovis McDougall bought out small bakery businesses and squeezed competition off supermarket shelves with a policy of massive discounts. And soon wholemeal bread was not only several pence dearer than

Mother's Pride, but almost unobtainable too; in 1973 only two
out of thirty-five Manchester shops visited in one survey were
selling real wholemeal bread. The myth that the British housewife 'preferred' white bread was thus established.

On this deteriorating diet, the national health deteriorated too, despite the abolition of gross poverty and the rise in
the general standard of living, despite all the wonderful new
drugs being trumpeted in the press from time to time, and
the vast sums now being spent on free medical care for all.
Cardiovascular disease had been a medical rarity at the beginning of the century. By the sixties, it was the West's biggest
killer, claiming 100,000 victims every year, many of them
middle-aged or in their twenties, and a million new cases were
being diagnosed annually. Between 1941 and 1962 the diagnosed cases of diabetes jumped ten-fold. Arthritis, digestive
problems, cancer, multiple sclerosis – for all of these the rates
climbed.

Any connection between her family's ill health and the
over-refined and processed food they ate much of the time,
however, was unlikely to be made by the British housewife, who
was now once more as nutritionally illiterate as her mother
had been in 1939, before Drummond began his great wartime
campaign of nutritional education at the Ministry of Food.
Lambert Mount records a 1966 survey which found that only
one woman in five knew why vitamins were essential in the
diet – and, almost invariably, it was the older women at that;
most young housewives were abysmally ignorant.

An equally dense cloud of unknowing enveloped the
medical profession, with rare and honourable exceptions. One
of these was Surgeon-Captain Cleave of the Royal Navy, who
first put forward in 1956 his theory that the hideous proliferation of degenerative diseases as varied as diabetes, coronary
conditions, *Escherichia coli* infections, constipation, piles, varicose veins and obesity could all be blamed on the enormous
rise in consumption, since the end of the nineteenth century,
of the refined carbohydrates white sugar and white flour. This
rise had had dire consequences, according to Cleave. It
removed fibre in the form of the bran in wholemeal flour as
well as the cell walls of fruit and vegetables, which led to the
constipation now rampant in the West with its attendant woes,
varicose veins, piles and diverticular disease, as well as dental
caries. And it led to huge over-consumption. The British ate a
daily average of 5 oz (140 g) sugar per person. To get the same

amount of sugar unrefined, they would have to eat a score of apples, or chomp their way through a 2½ lb (1·1 kg) sugarbeet. This over-consumption, particularly the sugar, led to diabetes, obesity, coronary thrombosis, *E. coli* infections and gallstones.

Cleave knew what he was talking about. He had wiped out constipation in the ships he sailed with by regularly dosing their crew with bran, and he was a careful and thorough observer. But his interesting speculations were brushed aside – did not every nutritional pundit of the day assure the British nation that there was absolutely no difference worth worrying about between brown and white bread?

Those who suggested, like Cleave, that diet and ill health might be intimately related, were ignored by most doctors and dismissed as 'cranks' by the general public. (The name Cranks was picked, as a stylish gesture of defiance, by David and Kay Canter when they opened their beautiful vegetarian-plus restaurant in London's Carnaby Street in 1961.)

But help was at hand for the health-store business, in the person of a near-millionaire who was equally fascinated by nutrition and big business. James Lee-Richardson had had the natural-health gospel instilled into him by his mother, and grew up with stoneground wholemeal bread, herbal remedies and a fervent belief in the importance of nutrition. He began his career in journalism writing endless articles on these and other equally fringe subjects, such as yoga and astrology. He soon realized, however, that there were no fortunes to be made in pen-pushing, and, turning to publishing, produced the first popular book on yoga.

Publishing books didn't seem to be the golden road to fortune either, he soon found. 'One had to publish magazines. They would attract advertisements. Advertising would yield real profits.' In 1959 he not only started a magazine devoted to his favourite subject, nutrition – it was called *Here's Health* – but also launched his own company, Healthcrafts, marketing a number of vitamin supplements; he realized that, in Britain as in the United States, it was the supplement industry which must largely fill the advertising pages of such a magazine, and help float it financially. All he needed now was a market, and the health-food stores were the most logical outlet. But there was a snag. 'The trouble with the health-food stores,' he later recalled, 'what that they were all then owned by vegetarian and Nature Cure disciples. The idea of a pill containing nutrients was anathema to them . . . However, we edged our way in . . .'3

The readers of *Here's Health* began demanding the vitamin pills so excitingly described in the pages of their magazine. Slowly, the trade's resistance crumbled, and vitamin pills were soon selling merrily up and down the country. Some stores held out, though, including the biggest chain: Lee-Richardson simply bought them.

He bought up suppliers too – Alfonal, who produced vegetable oils and margarines. Next he added a wholesale company, Brewhurst, which had been started by the old-fashioned milling company, Prewett's. As business grew, he encouraged newcomers with the carrot of four months' credit. By 1966 the Economist Intelligence Unit reckoned there were around 100,000 health-food consumers, in a market worth some £12 million a year. It was hardly competition for Associated British Foods. But it was no fleabite either.

The *éminence rose* of this baby empire was Barbara Cartland, till then more famous for her romantic novels than for her command of biochemistry. Now every issue of *Here's Health* carried her glowing tributes to the magic of bee pollen – of honey – of B complex vitamins to revitalize your sex life; and no gathering of the faithful was complete without her radiant pink presence flashing smiles and diamonds as she toured the stands at the first London health-food fair in 1966, presided at luncheons and lectures, or demolished her opponents on television with a few crisp, pithy comments about men who didn't have enough vitality to do *anything* . . .

Throughout the sixties, the British health-food movement became more and more the Lee-Richardson empire. And as he had edged in, others were edged out, among them Stanley Lief's *Health for All* which couldn't compete with the bright, snappy *Here's Health* and its get-well-quick vitamin advertisements.

'The flowing tide was with us,' Lee-Richardson says of his early days. In retrospect, one factor may have been the appalling story of thalidomide, which burst on the British press in 1962. Thousands of women in Germany, Britain and Sweden had given birth to grotesquely deformed babies after taking a new sedative in the early weeks of their pregnancy. Developed by a German pharmaceutical company, Chemie Grunenthal, the drug was marketed as completely safe even for pregnant women and small children. It was later learned that in fact it affected babies in the womb at the critical moment when their limbs were being formed: they were born without arms or legs, or with vestigial limbs that were hardly more than flippers, as well as other crippling abnormalities. Over the next few years, in one of the most energetic press campaigns ever seen, the *Sunday Times* battled for the rights of these victims, and relentlessly exposed not only the carelessness which had made the disaster possible, but the cynical commercialism which put profits before the health of its customers even after the drug's sinister potential was known.

There had been publicity about adverse reactions before, but it was still optimistically assumed by most people that these reactions were on the whole few and slight, and part of the price that had to be paid for miracle drugs. The pharmaceutical industry, meanwhile, had come up with a couple of other blessings for Western civilization, the contraceptive pill and the tranquillizer. But an undercurrent of doubt persisted. Slowly the number of those turning away from orthodox medicine to naturopaths, osteopaths, herbalists, acupuncturists and so on grew.

Then came the mid-sixties and the hippy movement, with its joyous reverence for all things natural, earthy and untarnished by big business; the health-food movement took off.

By 1970, riding the crest of the new wave, the Lee-Richardson health-food empire had a turnover of around £7m – about half the total health-food market. It was snapped up by the giant Booker-McConnell conglomerate, whose commercial interests ranged from pharmaceuticals and sugar to marine engineering. Here was a business, as they saw it, with vast growth potential, still largely in the hands of amateurs. They launched a chain of bright new health-food stores called Holland & Barrett, and set about repackaging the product with brisk professionalism. The new commercialism jumping on to the health-food bandwagon horrified old-timers, but gave the industry – and with it the whole concept of eating-for-health – a new public visibility. Newspapers and magazines began investigating this odd phenomenon.

Their reports made merry fun of the merchandise, and sneered at what they saw as pure escapism – 'a strong and non-rational longing for the simple and the rural'.[4] They were obliged to concede, though, that 'most of the people who go to the health shops, at whatever level, are people who care about what they eat and about their health, and as such tend to be healthier than the average citizen'.[5]

Even the 90 per cent plus of the population who never set foot inside such shops were being progressively influenced by what Lee-Richardson had called 'a protestant crusade against the chemicalization of modern foods'. Government legislation which made the listing of ingredients mandatory on packaged foods was pushed through in 1973 largely thanks to the health-food lobby. Housewives keen-sighted enough to read the small print could now see for themselves just how chemicalized were the processed foods they bought so unthinkingly. An educated consumer movement was now growing steadily in Britain.

'A decade ago . . . the health-food market was static and insignificant,' commented a 1970 article in *New Society*, 'its image one of . . . faddists genuflecting before compost heaps and miscellaneous weirdies warning about poisonous chemicals on farm and in food factory. Now all has altered. The Pollution Thing of a sudden has the support of a wide and unweird public, the blessings of the most impeccable of scientists, and it looks like those many warnings, so crankish they once seemed, were right after all.'[6]

Women's magazines, always a sensitive barometer of public mood, reflect this change interestingly. Throughout the sixties, if they wrote about diet at all, they wrote about dieting, and preached the conventional high-protein wisdom that lumped all carbohydrates together and condemned them out of hand for the figure-conscious. 'Eat plenty of proteins – lean meat, fish, eggs, cheese. Eat plenty of green vegetables and have your share of fruit. Cut down drastically on carbohydrates . . . cakes, chocolates, puds and bread . . .' *Woman* instructed its readers in 1963.[7] Sound nutrition and good looks were seldom seen as related. In a special Beauty Supplement to *Vogue* in June 1965 the word diet is nowhere mentioned.

By the seventies, light was dawning. The very last issue of *Queen* magazine – for a decade the high-priest of the consumer society – hailed the new ecology. 'A modern woman is aware that beauty is based on health and on the correct use of her body, while her predecessor believed that beauty could literally be painted on . . . a new awareness of the necessity to preserve our natural environment if we are to survive is mirrored in a new concern for total beauty, in care of the whole person.'[8]

Britain's nutrition pundits continued to flog the tired old official line: 'The plain truth is that people who eat a variety of foods, in moderation, have no need to fear deficiencies of any kind. However food faddists may argue, it is as simple as that,' said the nutritionist, Magnus Pyke.[9] It was Ministry wisdom that nobody could possibly be short of vitamin C because we ate potato crisps and chips, didn't we? The textbooks used by home economists and dieticians stoutly maintained that white bread was just as good for you as wholemeal. An advisory panel on bread and flour reported in 1972 that there was absolutely no need to consider adding any vitamins and minerals other than the four (calcium, iron, thiamine and nicotinic acid) established a couple of decades back: the British diet ran over with all these good things.

Lay people increasingly questioned such ill-informed complacency.

———

'Americans are the "most fed" nation in the world, but not necessarily the best,' warned one of the founders of the US frozen-food industry in 1956. Speaking at the National Frozen Foods Conference, Edwin I. Gibson went on to suggest that hardly a quarter of American families were eating proper food. Their dogs were often better nourished than they were. American housewives, urged Gibson, should read up on the carefully balanced nutritious food they fed their pets – and then compare it with what they dished up for family meals.[10] Gibson was for years executive vice-president of the General Foods Corporation, so presumably he knew what he was talking about.

But such rumbles of criticism were drowned by the vociferous chorus of experts telling Americans how wonderfully well fed they were. 'Americans have to go out of their way, nutritionally speaking, to avoid being well fed,' declared the FDA.[11] This statement enchanted the food industry, and was quoted by a former President of the American Medical Association, Dr E. V. Askey, in the *Journal of the American Medical Association* in 1960.

Nobody touted the good news more assiduously than Dr Frederick Stare of Harvard, the nation's best-known and most widely quoted nutrition expert. When an Ohio physician asked the *Journal* in 1962 whether the average American needed vitamin and mineral supplements, Stare was at hand to pooh-pooh the idea. 'In my opinion, the average American in reasonably good health, regardless of age, does not need, nor will his health be improved by, vitamin and mineral supplements. A varied diet of cereals, fruits, vegetables, milk and its products, eggs, meat, fish and poultry, will supply good nutrition which includes an abundance of vitamins and minerals.'[12]

Americans looking for official guidance on a healthy diet could turn to the US Department of Agriculture's *Essentials of an Adequate Diet*, published in 1957. Eat from each of the four basic food groups and you can't go wrong, they were told: milk and dairy products; meat; fruit and vegetables; bread cereals. Nobody could quarrel with this concept, or with the advice to eat at least four servings a day of fruit and vegetables. But the guidelines were elastic enough to embrace a wide spectrum of junk food. Dairy products? An adult's daily needs might be met by half a cup of evaporated milk, an ounce of Cheddar cheese and half a cup of ice-cream. Protein? How about a couple of eggs, a frankfurter and half a cup of baked beans? Cereals? Wholegrain, enriched or restored bread and breakfast cereals, of course. Or maybe . . . crackers, macaroni, muffins, cakes and cookies.

The average American housewife, brainwashed by a daily battering of TV ads, pushing her trolley round the colourful aisles of her supermarket, tended to go for the soft option in each of these groups. Cereals could be heavily sweetened breakfast treats – Kellogg's Apple Jacks were 52 per cent sugar – 'enriched' with a few token nutrients, or one of a staggering variety of cookies, pies, processed desserts and Betty Crocker Cake Mixes. As for the protein, it could be luncheon meat or bologna sausage, handy for the day-long snacking that was more and more crowding out old-style family meals – or else the omnipresent hamburger which together with Coke was by now part of America's cultural heritage.

To those who worried that such a diet might not be exactly ideal, Stare was reassuring. 'Contrary to opinions held by some people, frankfurters and luncheon meats are good food and furnish high-quality protein,' he stated in his book *Eating for Health*, published in 1964.[13] 'Nutritious snacks', according to this book, might mean nuts, cheese and crackers and a glass of milk – or ice-cream, corn chips and cookies, washed down with a soft drink. Coke was a fine after-school snack.

Sugar consumption in the USA had risen to record levels by the sixties, and health writers like Adelle Davis, Lelord Kordel and Gayelord Hauser warned repeatedly of the threat to health that this huge intake of a refined and valueless carbohydrate represented. Time and again, Stare sprang gallantly to the defence. 'Those who speak with disdain of the empty calories of sugar and fat or of processed foods as though they were a blight are also doing a fair share of exaggeration. The empty calories of sugar and fat have always been important to any normal, well-balanced, nutritious diet and add taste, zest and pleasure to a meal.'[14]

When the Swedish Nutrition Foundation – carefully patterned after the US industry-funded Nutrition Foundation – held a Symposium on Nutrition and Caries Prevention, Stare was there to make sure that sugar did not get too rough a ride. With breathtaking insouciance, he brushed aside suggestions that the stuff might rot teeth. 'I don't know of any evidence that it makes much difference with regard to caries in the child . . . as to whether the child receives as between-meal snacks, milk, crackers, fruit juice, candies, ice-cream or apple . . . particularly when these in-between snacks are valuable, as they are in practice.' Natives who ate unrefined foods had little or no caries? Stare bit back authoritatively: 'I disagree with those who say that frequent eating of sweet food favours tooth decay and that unrefined foodstuffs are less cariogenic than refined foods. There is no confirmed evidence for such statements . . .'[15]

American doctors thumbing through their bible – and the world's most influential medical publication – the *Journal of the American Medical Association*, were unlikely to spot the flaws in Stare's evangelism for the food industry. The *Journal* hardly breathed a word about nutrition from one year's end to the other. In this it accurately reflected the views of most of its readers. As one doctor, who trained in the late fifties, recalled:

> During my years in medical school and formal post-graduate work, there was no nutritional training in the required course work except for routine topics such as infant feeding, electrolyte balance, etc. The science of nutrition simply did not seem to be relevant to medical training, whether in the outlook of my professors or in the curriculum or philosophy of the excellent medical school which I was privileged to attend.[16]

Whatever America's huge and swelling army of dieticians and home economists learned in their basic training courses, it didn't seem to be nutrition. Adelle Davis was once asked to help a hospital dietician plan more nourishing meals for the hospital patients. In the kitchen she found mountains of frozen French-fried potatoes and French-fried shrimps thawing out for lunch;

the fruit and vegetables served were almost all frozen or canned; greasy hot breads and chiffon pies also figured on the menu. Refined foods were recommended throughout the American Dieticians' Association manual. At the high school in Adelle's town the girls in the home-economics class learned how to make pastry, cakes, cookies, biscuits, muffins and rolls using white flour and hydrogenated fat. The 'enriched' doughnut had official blessing in New York state schools. A group of fourth-graders, asked to name the four food groups, replied 'Burger King, Pizza Hut, McDonalds and Arby's'.[17]

It was left to popular health writers like Carlton Fredericks, Lelord Kordel, Adelle Davis and Gayelord Hauser to tell Americans just how badly they were eating and why they were so often ill. In doing so, they called down on their heads a host of furies. 'I have been involved for forty years in a continuous and virulent battle with government agencies,' commented the health writer and broadcaster Carlton Fredericks drily in 1980, 'with medical, dental and psychiatric societies, with the nutrition departments of giant universities, with the food-processing industry and its trade associations, and with the establishment in dietetics, nutrition, cancer, arthritis, cerebral palsy, multiple sclerosis, and myasthenia gravis . . .'[18]

American medicine is private medicine, and fewer patients means less income. Those who taught patients to take their health into their own hands, maintain it by sound diet and treat their ailments with nutrition and doses of vitamins and minerals were understandably construed as dangerous by the medical profession, quite as much as by the processed-food industry and the pharmaceutical business.

By the sixties such writers were a force to be reckoned with. Instead of reaching small audiences in lecture halls, they were getting their subversive message across to millions of Americans through the mass media; their books were featured on bestseller lists and serialized in newspapers and magazines, their voices were heard at peak times on popular radio, their faces were becoming familiar coast to coast on TV shows and their views circulated through columns syndicated in dozens of newspapers.

Attempts to silence them were fronted by the Food and Drug Administration – 'protecting' the public from quackery, with the tacit support of the AMA. These attempts took a variety of ingenious forms: smear campaigns, lawsuits, confiscation of their books – on the pretext that they were 'misbranding' since they mentioned vitamins being sold in the same shops as the books – an 'official' hint dropped in the ear of their sponsor or editor, and endless public blasting of them as quacks, food faddists and dispensers of nutritional nonsense.

As a counterblast to the threatening amounts of nutrition information such writers conveyed to the American public, the Nutrition Foundation discreetly helped finance the Dial-A-Dietician programme started in Detroit in 1958. In this scheme, anyone could call a telephone number supplied and be given 'official' information, blandly reassuring, about the quality of their food. If they wanted to know more, the service could fire off a list of recommended books about nutrition – as well as a blacklist of books described as dangerously unsound, unbalanced and unreliable, by authors like Adelle Davis, Carlton Fredericks, *et al.*

Two years later, the Nutrition Foundation launched its own public information service, and soon articles on the subject began appearing in newspapers and magazines acknowledging the assistance of the Foundation; editors and TV programme directors learned that the Foundation would be happy to vet articles and scripts for them. And it was the Nutrition Foundation which put together a Fact Kit on Rachel Carson's *Silent Spring*, which was sent out to scientists, academics, public bodies, librarians, health-care professionals and women's organizations throughout the country. The Fact Kit contained damning reviews of the book by Frederick Stare and others, a printed letter from the Foundation's president denouncing the book as 'unscientific' and a defence of chemical pesticides drafted by the New York State College of Agriculture.

Some of the writers jumping on the health bandwagon were no doubt ill-informed amateurs with only the most superficial background in nutrition. And in his book *Nutrition in a Nutshell*, published in 1962, Roger Williams was severe about them, advising his readers to disregard these 'eloquent' people with wild ideas, particularly if they had no background in biochemistry. Members of the American Institute of Nutrition and the American Society of Biological Chemists were far more trustworthy, he advised, listing them; among them was Dr Frederick Stare, whose works Williams described as 'solid and dependable', and whose help and encouragement, among many others, he acknowledged in a foreword.

Williams was one of America's most distinguished bio-chemists. He had personally discovered one B vitamin – panto-thenic acid – and had done pioneer work on another, folic acid, which he named. He had been heaped with academic honours. And in 1956 he had published one of the most outstanding contributions to the science of nutrition in this century, his *Biochemical Individuality*. In it, Williams showed with a wealth of biological and anatomical evidence that any man's biochemical make-up is as individual as a fingerprint and hence his personal nutritional needs are too; assessment of his needs based on some mythical 'average man' might be disastrously misleading. Williams went on to suggest that alcoholism, mental problems such as schizophrenia, arthritis and diabetes were just a few of the diseases which might arise from the special vulnerability of a patient whose specific nutritional needs were not being met. 'In a population in which the diet is very much alike for all, only certain individuals show pellagra symptoms . . . These presum-ably are the individuals who have higher than average require-ments [of niacin].'

The dogma that the Recommended Daily Allowances sup-plied all the vitamins and minerals any honest American might possibly need was by this time enshrined at the heart of Amer-ican medical orthodoxy. Official complacency about the appal-ling American diet was based on this belief. To question it was deadly heresy. So Williams's bombshell became a scientific non-event. It was unchallengeable. And it was ignored.

So was his highly interesting and important work on alcoholism, which disrupts the lives of an estimated 10 million people in the USA today. Conventional psychiatry assumed that the alcoholic was a weak-willed character with a personality disorder. Williams pointed out that in any group of people, only one or two would become compulsive drinkers, so it made sense to look for a nutritional deficiency unique to them. Sev-eral studies supported this; in one, Williams had kept rats on a nutritionally wretched diet and then offered them alcohol: some of them turned into staggering drunks before his eyes. But when he fed them supplements of an amino acid, gluta-mine, many of them became reformed characters, and left the alcohol untouched. Other promising nutrients were mag-nesium and niacin.

Williams's chief heresy, of course, was his recom-mendation to the public of vitamin supplements as a sort of all-purpose health insurance. Critical of the dozens of formulae on the market, he even put forward his own Insurance Formula, which several companies leapt to make up. His recommendations were far more cautious than the reckless amounts being recommended or advertised in health magazines. But the mere fact that he approved of them at all was enough to damn him. He soon found his works ranked with those of the popular health writers as unsound, unreliable and misleading: 'not to be recommended'.

Even qualified doctors who ventured to suggest that all was not well with the American diet found themselves on the medical Index. In 1962, a Pennsylvania physician, Dr Curtis Wood, published a book called *Overfed but Undernourished*, in which he speculated how much healthier Americans could be if they improved their diet. His book was seized in an FDA raid. Dr Wood wrote angrily demanding an explanation. 'I am writing to you for a statement as to whether free American citizens, supposedly enjoying freedom of speech and freedom of the press, may or may not recommend my book . . . to friends of theirs; may or may not own copies and give or lend them as they see fit and, lastly, if they are allowed to have copies of this book in their possession?' Dr Wood's book mentioned no product by name, but the FDA wrote back to say that if the book were considered to be promoting 'any article subject to the Federal Food, Drug and Cosmetic Act in such a way as to be labelling and it misbrands the article, the books, as well as the article, is subject to seizure and condemnation'.

'In our opinion,' added the FDA letter, for good measure, 'the contents of your book are not in agreement with informed medical and scientific consensus concerning the state of nutrition in this country and the value or necessity of the addition of vitamins and minerals to the ordinary diet.'[18]

21

Eating Hearty

When Martha Weinman Lear sat down to write *Heart-sounds*, a harrowing account of her husband's fatal case of coronary heart disease, she produced a bestseller that gripped its millions of readers from the very first sentence: 'He awoke at 7 a.m. with pain in his chest . . . His breath was coming hard. He felt faint. He was sweating, though the August morning was still cool. He put fingers to his pulse. It was rapid and weak. A powerful burning sensation was beginning to spread through his chest . . .'[1]

Dr Harold Lear suffered this first heart attack on 10 August 1973. A physician himself, a distinguished urologist, he could call on the 'best' medical attention that New York could offer. He was treated with the most up-to-date drug therapy. He underwent the then comparatively new bypass surgery. He died surrounded by the glittering gadgetry of the intensive-care unit. Nutritional advice? Cut down on salt, his doctors told him. Of his own accord, he had been on the conventional low-cholesterol diet for years. His cholesterol levels, though, had remained 'sky-high'.

In the muddled modern mythology of heart disease, cholesterol is seen by the public as the Number One risk factor, with stress a close second. Cholesterol means bacon and eggs for breakfast, and too much lovely butter with the toast and marmalade. Stress, in the popular view, is the executive going home late from the office with a bulging briefcase. Switch to muesli for breakfast and learn to delegate at the office: you may add a couple of decades to your allotted span.

Cholesterol, the yellowish fatty stuff, fear of which has switched Western gourmets to *nouvelle cuisine*, is an essential component of bodily tissues, especially the nerves and the brain. Since animals, birds and fish need cholesterol just as badly as we do, it turns up in our diets too, unless we're strict vegans, with eggs – at 274 mg a time – notoriously high in the stuff, and beef liver loaded at 372 mg for a modest helping. It was first identified in the early nineteenth century, and as early as 1843 it was noticed in atheromas, the greasy deposits sometimes found at post-mortem examination on artery walls. Since atheromas appeared to be made up of cholesterol and other fats, a Russian scientist fed rabbits on a high-cholesterol diet – and they obligingly developed atheromas. Rabbits are vegetarians whose bodies can't cope with animal cholesterol, and they were being fed the equivalent of about fifty-four eggs a day for a human being. So it's hardly surprising that their arteries became clogged with fat. But other researchers followed this lead, and soon atheromas had been produced by cholesterol-rich diets in chickens, guinea-pigs, dogs and monkeys. Gradually, dietary cholesterol settled into the role it's been playing ever since: Suspect No. 1 in heart disease.

'When I graduated from medical school in 1911,' wrote Dr Paul Dudley White, one of America's leading heart specialists, 'I had never heard of coronary thrombosis – which is one of the chief threats to life in the United States today – an astounding development in one's own lifetime.'[2]

He was writing in 1943, by which time cardiovascular disease had become epidemic. Its slow rise began in 1900, when it caused something like 20 per cent of all deaths. By the mid-thirties, according to the calculations of the American Heart Association, the figure had doubled to around 40 per cent and the upward trend was relentless. By 1950 the figure was over 50 per cent, and by 1960 it was climbing on towards 55 per cent. By 1965, one third of those dying in what should have been the prime of their lives – between thirty-five and forty-four – were victims of heart attacks or strokes. Similar figures can be quoted for almost every country in the Western world, though today Britain has the unenviable distinction of topping the charts.

What exactly is cardiovascular disease? Public understanding of what it's all about isn't helped by the medical profession's tendency to switch to a new name from time to time, to describe the various conditions lumped together in this catch-all name. Roughly speaking, the term means any condition affecting the heart or the major blood vessels of the body, including strokes, heart attacks, high blood pressure, hardening of the arteries and phlebitis (when a clot of blood settles down in a vein and blocks local circulation).

At the beginning of this century, the chief cause of heart disease was rheumatic fever, which inflamed and damaged the lining and valves of the heart. By the twenties, atherosclerosis had overtaken it as a more common cause of problems. In this condition, the arteries gradually become clogged and narrowed by atheromas or deposits on their lining – alternatively called plaque – the artery walls lose their elasticity and become hardened, and the flow of blood is slowed. Blood pressure rises as the heart struggles to maintain level supplies, and blood clots easily form.

A stroke – the apoplexy of our ancestors – occurs when a clot blocks circulation in the brain area. Coronary thrombosis is a result of a blood clot blocking one of the arteries which feed oxygenated blood into the heart, depriving this mighty little muscle of blood, and causing serious damage to the heart wall, or even death. This event, popularly known as a heart attack, is also called a coronary, and is now technically described as a myocardial infarction, or infarct for short. Its unmistakable symptom is angina pectoris, the severe chest pain which Dr Lear experienced that August morning; and the pain itself can be life-saving, since it immobilizes the victim and so dramatically reduces the amount of oxygen needed by his beleaguered heart.

High blood pressure, or hypertension, is often thought of as a disease in itself, and treated as such with one of dozens of drugs. It is in fact a symptom of an underlying disorder – such as atherosclerosis – and, if not treated, it can eventually cause death through serious damage to the overtaxed heart and kidneys.

It was for long believed that heart attacks were a 'natural' way to go, and that our ancestors were only immune because they died younger, from other diseases. Then in the twenties and thirties medical researchers began looking much more closely at the health and habits of other races, or primitive peoples whose way of life and daily menu were still close to those of Western man's ancestors. And it became clear that, far from being either natural or inevitable, heart disease was a latter-day scourge particularly visited on the affluent Western world, a disease of the twentieth century.

One of the first to look closely at the possibility of a dietary factor was the American Dr Lester Morrison. He had been much struck by statistics from post-war Europe which showed that in countries which had their food supplies severely rationed, heart attacks had shown a dramatic wartime drop. Were lower levels of fat and cholesterol responsible? He put fifty of his patients on to low-fat, egg-restricted diets just as in wartime Europe – while another fifty patients, who acted as controls, went on eating ordinary rich American food. On the low-fat diet, the cholesterol levels of his patients dropped from an average of around 300 mg per cent, to just over 200. Levels in his controls remained high. By 1960, all of the control group had died, but nineteen of the low-fat dieters were still alive.

Other researchers by this time had established that circulating fats in the bloodstream were intimately connected with the build-up of atherosclerosis, and by the sixties the scenario most widely favoured was high blood cholesterol resulting from high fat and cholesterol consumption leading to clogged arteries and high blood pressure. Two impressive studies supported this.

One was Dr Ancel Keys's landmark study of seven nations and their diets. Keys was an epidemiologist, and in the early fifties he combined business with pleasure to take his wife on a trip to Naples where – according to some reports – coronary disease was rare. In the intervals of basking in the golden February sunshine, he studied the cholesterol levels of ordinary Neapolitans, and found that they averaged 165, against the 230 level normal in his home town of Minnesota. Coronary disease was almost unknown, doctors told him, in the big general hospitals. If he wanted to study it, he should take himself off to the private clinics of the wealthy.

Rich and poor alike shared the same climate; the poor in their startlingly overcrowded and noisy slums were obviously exposed to stress unknown to the rich in their villas. It must be diet that made the difference. So what did poor Neapolitans eat? Ancel and his wife ate in humble sea-front trattorias, backstreet pizzerias where the dough was freshly made before their eyes. Their description of the daily Neapolitan diet is mouthwatering:

> home-made minestrone [vegetable soup]; pasta in endless variety, always freshly cooked . . .; a hearty dish of beans and short lengths of macaroni; lots of bread, never more than a few hours from the oven and never served with any kind of spread; great quantities of fresh vegetables; a modest portion of meat or fish perhaps twice a week; [and] always fresh fruit for dessert.[3]

It would be hard to imagine a diet more unlike the diet being eaten by millions of Americans at the time, with its processed cereals, steaks and chips, hamburgers, ice-cream, doughnuts, Cokes, and processed foods loaded with sugar and chemical additives. But the factor instantly singled out by Keys was its lower fat content. Neapolitans were getting only about 20 per cent of their calories in fat; while back in Minnesota, the fat content of the diet was as high as 40 per cent. Furthermore, the fat in the Neapolitan diet came largely from vegetable oils, whereas Minnesotans ate plenty of cream, butter, bacon and good red meat – all high in saturated fats.

With the saturated-fat connection in mind, Keys went on to look at diet and heart disease rates in a total of 12,000 middle-aged people in seven countries, including Finland, Japan and the USA. He found direct correlations between the incidence of cardiovascular disease, the cholesterol levels and the consumption of animal fat. Over the years since, a number of other ambitious research projects have attempted to nail animal fats and cholesterol as the arch-villains of the piece. Among them was the famous Framingham study, launched in 1948, when over 5,000 people in one small Massachusetts town undertook to supply details of their diet, exercise, smoking and other possibly relevant factors. High blood pressure, high animal fat, high cholesterol levels and heavy smoking all emerged as key factors.

Another study, carried out at a Los Angeles home for war veterans, followed 846 subjects over eight years, half of them on a 'good' diet, high in vegetable oils, half on a 'bad' diet, eating mainly animal fats. On the vegetable oils, there were slightly fewer heart attacks – and cholesterol levels were lower.

These and other studies convinced the American Heart Association – a powerful and influential body – and from 1961 onwards it has been plugging a diet of lower animal fat and less cholesterol as the spearhead of its attack on heart disease. Only 30 per cent of the diet should be fat, says their 1984 statement for public consumption; no more than a third of that 30 per cent, should be saturated fat; and cholesterol intake should be no more than 300 mg a day: eat an egg, drink a cup of milk for breakfast and that's it for the day.

With the authority of the American Heart Association behind it, the cholesterol theory has become firmly embedded in the public consciousness. Since 1965, the American consumption of butter has plunged 30 per cent, of eggs 14 per cent, of animal fats a whopping 60 per cent. It takes a certain courage these days to eat bacon and eggs for breakfast or make a three-egg omelette, and hostesses apologize nervously for putting temptation before their guests in the shape of cream with the pudding. Some British supermarkets have already started indicating fat content on their food packaging, well ahead of any legal requirement to do so. And in 1985 Boots the Chemists took full colour advertisements to tell us about their new low-fat sausage, among other healthy goodies: '. . . they contain half the fat of your standard banger, which means less saturated fat going round your system. Saturated fats, you see, can eventually clog up your arteries . . .'[4]

Coincidentally with the decline in intake of animal fat, deaths from heart disease have fallen dramatically in the USA: by almost 30 per cent since 1968. So the American Heart Association can claim with some reason that their advice has been followed, and that it works. Certainly, stuffing ourselves with steak and chips, hamburgers, butter, cream and rich fried foods is far from healthy. Equally certainly, cholesterol-consciousness has been a powerful factor in the healthier diets that most of us eat today. So whether justified or not, you could say that it has been a Good Thing.

But the promotion of animal fats plus dietary cholesterol as Public Enemy No. 1 has allowed the American Heart Association, together with massive vested interest in the manufactured-food industry, to push under the rug a great deal of evidence to show that other factors could be at least as important. The Los Angeles veterans on the 'bad', high-animal-fat diet, for instance, had more heavy smokers and octogenarians in their group than the 'good' dieters: when these factors were taken into account, their death rate was actually lower.

The American Heart Association doesn't talk much, either, about the fate of the 'Prudent Diet' experiment, started by Dr Norman Jolliffe of the New York Nutrition Bureau in 1957; 814 apparently healthy middle-aged men were put on a diet low in cholesterol and animal fats, but high in vegetable oils – they consumed at least an ounce each daily. A control group of 463 went on eating their usual diet, with much more saturated fat. Five years later, there had been eight coronary deaths among the Prudent Dieters – even though they had been watching their weight, eating less salt and even taking more exercise in some cases. There had been *no* coronary deaths among the control group. Dr Jolliffe himself was not around to see his diet so sadly discredited: he had died from 'vascular complications of diabetes'.

A far higher success rate has been achieved by the 'Pritikin Diet', evolved in the fifties by an engineer named Nathan Pritikin, and widely promoted by a bestseller, *The Pritikin Programme*. At the age of forty-three, Pritikin was told by a specialist that his arteries were in rotten shape, his cholesterol sky-high, and that he must stop all unnecessary exercise and take cholesterol-lowering drugs for the rest of his life. A badly frightened man, Pritikin began to wonder if drugs were really the only answer. Three years later, he was doing without. From a red-meat-eating American who often downed a pint of ice-cream after dinner, he had turned into a lean dedicated vegetarian who renounced animal fats; from a man scared to walk a block, he had worked himself up into a fit athlete who ran a daily eight miles. At the Pritikin Centre today, overweight cardiac cases cheerfully stump up thousands of dollars for a crash course in a new way of life, in which regular exercise is a must, tea, coffee, alcohol and eggs are barred, and animal fat and sugar are drastically reduced in a monk's diet, stressing vegetables, whole-grains and pulses. The regime works well for a high percentage of cases, but the diet, although healthy, is certainly heavily restricted by normal standards: 'If you don't hear the Grim Reaper sharpening his scythe, you may not be able to hear Pritikin telling you to put down that slice of Swiss cheese.'[5] Pritikin himself committed suicide after learning that he was suffering from leukaemia; his arteries at autopsy were as beautifully clear as those of a seven-year-old.

But we may reasonably ask whether this degree of restriction is really necessary for the average person – or even desirable? Do we really have to be quite so mean with eggs – that cheap and excellent source of protein and so many other essential nutrients, for instance?

The animal-fat theory, noted Roger Williams, 'may not be entirely in error, but it is misleading in its emphasis . . . Most of our good foods contain substantial amounts of cholesterol, and if we try to eliminate cholesterol consumption, we sacrifice good nutrition . . . Anyone who deliberately avoids cholesterol in his diet may be courting disaster.'[6]

Plenty of studies show that those with high serum cholesterol have a higher risk of cardiovascular disease. But when these studies are looked at critically, none of them proves conclusively that high fat or cholesterol intake is alone responsible for high cholesterol levels in the blood.

And how was it that returning prisoners-of-war were often found to have advanced atherosclerosis after years of appalling diets in which animal fats and eggs hardly featured at all?

Critics of the hypothesis point, too, to the Masai or the Eskimo races. The Masai tribe in Africa live largely on milk, meat and blood – hardly a low animal-fat diet – yet their serum cholesterol levels are around 120 mg. And the Eskimo people, eating little but fish and whale blubber, have wonderful hearts and superb arteries; only when they take to trading-station luxuries such as refined flour, white sugar and jam does the arterial rot set in.

So maybe refined sugar is the culprit? John Yudkin, Emeritus Professor of Nutrition at London University, pointed out that a far better case could actually be made out against this product of Western civilization than against fat, if international statistics were to be relied on – as Keys had done. In the decades that saw heart disease rocket, sugar consumption rose in parallel, increasing sevenfold since 1900.

Moreover, cholesterol was only one of the fats to be found in the bloodstream. Another type of fat, triglycerides, might be just as important. Yudkin found that when he fed pure white sugar to rats and human beings, cholesterol levels did not always rise – but triglycerides invariably did. A trial in Sweden, reported by Dr Andrew Stanway, followed over 3,000 men for nine years, relating cholesterol and triglyceride levels to their heart health. It was found that 'triglyceride levels were a much better risk indicator than were cholesterol levels'.[7]

Yudkin speculated, too, that about a third of the population might be abnormally sensitive to sugar. On a high-sugar diet, some of the people he studied put on weight much faster, and had higher levels of insulin in their blood. And it was precisely in these sugar-sensitive people, he found, that blood platelets were liable to stick together forming clots.

Yudkin's suggestion has been confirmed by recent work. Studies at the United States Department of Agriculture Carbohydrate Research Group have shown that in around 15 per cent of the population, there seems to be a genetic sensitivity to sugar: and when it's eaten in excess of 20 per cent of a day's calorie intake, both insulin and blood lipids rise. More interesting still is work that suggests both Yudkin and Keys are right – up to a point: neither fat nor sugar by themselves can lead to atherosclerosis. But combine them in a doughnut and you're heading for disaster: it's the combination that's deadly. Since two thirds of the calories in the average Western diet come packaged as sweet fat – cakes, biscuits, puddings, pies, sweets, chocolates – the implications of this suggestion are mind-blowing.

But the refining of flour, in Yudkin's view, was a red herring. We had been eating the same old refined white stuff for years before the present epidemic of heart disease began, he pointed out. The only difference is that we eat less of it now than then – and that at least some of the nutrients have been restored. 'Don't kid yourself that brown is beautiful,' he quipped.*[8]

As may be imagined, Yudkin made himself highly unpopular both with the powerful international sugar lobby, and with the partisans of the fat-equals-cholesterol theory. Ancel Keys thundered into print to denounce him with shrill fury. Sugar consumption was already rising, he argued, long before the present epidemic of heart disease, and Cuba – where the natives chewed sugarcane the way GIs chewed gum – had very low heart deathrates.

It was Surgeon-Captain T. L. Cleave, a one-time naval doctor who came to Yudkin's defence, arguing that Keys had failed to allow for the necessary incubation period for heart problems – some twenty to thirty years – and that it was the refinement of sugarcane which had caused the mischief. Like Yudkin, Cleave had remained unconvinced that foods such as butter, cream and roast lamb, all 'extolled in the Bible' and eaten with pleasure by man for thousands of years, should suddenly have become fatal around the year 1920. But in Cleave's opinion, the mystery of the heart-death toll – like that of so many other 'Western' diseases, could never be solved by singling out this or that dietary factor.

In his masterpiece *The Saccharine Disease*, Cleave invited his readers to take a much broader view, to begin thinking in terms of underlying disease patterns rather than separate disease entities, and to look at man's nutrition as a whole. Of the heart, he wrote that it is 'a machine unparalleled, a machine whose action-cycle is repeated 100,000 times a day for seventy years without a single refit or a single servicing'. There was only one safe way to preserve the structural integrity of this marvellous little machine: 'the meticulous maintenance of its natural environment – the environment achieved by trial and error over many millions of years. And since the environment of the heart consists

*Following up work by Professor I. I. Brekhman, Yudkin found that rats on standard laboratory chow with muscovado sugar substituted for its starch lived longer, and had more and healthier baby rats than those on ordinary chow, or chow plus white sugar.

essentially of the bloodstream, and since the constitution of the bloodstream is basically dependent on the type of food eaten, it is above all on the *naturalness of the food* that the structural integrity of the heart must ultimately depend.'[9]

There were two 'anti-evolutionary' foods *par excellence* in the Western diet: refined flour and refined sugar. Statistically, the two together could be implicated in the whole spectrum of 'Western' diseases – from constipation to coronary disease, from diabetes to varicose veins. It was relatively easy to show that the lack of fibre in our diet had made a mighty contribution to profits from laxative sales – or that a sweet tooth plus low willpower could lead to diabetes in middle age. The connection between refined foods and coronary heart disease was much less clear, and when Cleave first made it, in the fifties, well ahead of Yudkin, he was guided by general principle – a true gut conviction – rather than elegant laboratory work.

What convinced him that he was on the right track was the way diabetes and coronary heart disease turned up side by side in all the figures: as though they were twin facets of the same basic disorder. In tribal Africans living on unrefined carbohydrates heart disease was rare and so was diabetes. When negroes living in the United States were studied, though – eating white flour and sugar just like everybody else – they had almost the same rates of both diseases. A. M. Cohen showed in 1960 that the 'Black Jews' of the Yemen who ate largely fat and protein foods, with minimal sugar, were almost free of both heart-disease and diabetes – until they moved to Israel and began bingeing on the perilous white stuff, as the Israelis themselves did. Twenty-five years later, they too had rocketing figures of heart disease and diabetes.

Revising his work for 1974 publication, Cleave could point to more recent work which showed that sucrose could trigger rises in blood triglycerides. And he speculated that unnaturally high levels of blood sugar in diabetics might eventually damage the walls of the arteries and trigger the fatal clotting of the blood. But he could not see – and he admitted this quite candidly – how the absence of fibre in refined flour could have any direct association with either diabetes or coronary disease: '. . . if the cause lay directly in loss of fibre, the treatment would consist in the giving of bran, instead of, as it should, mainly in the replacement of sugar consumption'.[10]

While Cleave studied the refined carbohydrates now so prominent in Western diet, other researchers by the seventies were already looking at the complex carbohydrates that Western man had left behind: the legumes and the whole grains, the fruits and vegetables which still make up the diet of most primitive people. These diets are very rich in fibre.

Just what exactly *is* fibre? Found only in plants, fibre is the stuff that holds them together, the assorted substances from which their cell walls are made, whether they're a soft and squashy strawberry or a big strong oak tree. We think of fibre as tough, chewy, stringy, and some plant fibre is like this: brown rice is distinctly chewier than mushy white rice, a stick of celery can be so chewy it's hardly worth eating. When I was a child, my enlightened mother encouraged us all to eat not only the skins of our locally grown, unsprayed apples, but the pips and core too. 'Roughage,' she told us; 'very good for you.' Roughage is another name for fibre, and in the nineteenth century doctors already knew all about roughage and how important it was for their constipated patients.

Then carbohydrates, fats and proteins were discovered. Since fibre was none of these things, it was clearly worthless: indigestible rubbish. The forties work on bread which suggested that the phytic acid in wheat bran might be absconding with all the minerals in wheat gave fibre a bad name. Wholewheat bread might actually be bad for you.

Given this professional bias, it took both courage and vision for Cleave to make his stand. But by the early seventies a number of British doctors were working towards the conclusion that lack of fibre was one of the most disastrous features of the Western diet, and partially responsible for a whole spectrum of diseases – among them gallstones, cancer of the colon, diverticular disease, rotten teeth, diabetes and heart disease. After Cleave, the two men most responsible for putting fibre back on the medical map were Denis Burkitt, a surgeon, and Dr Hugh Trowell. Both men spent years working in Africa, where both were struck by the almost complete absence of 'Western' disease among primitive tribes eating fibre-rich diets based on whole grains, legumes, fruits and vegetables. On these diets, they had very low levels of cholesterol too. When they moved to cities, and switched to Western-style low-fibre diets, up went their cholesterol levels, and up went their deathrates from heart diseases.

Our fibre intake in the West has declined as our sugar consumption has risen: between 1910 and 1960 it declined by at least 30 per cent. The average hospital patient in the USA, it has been calculated, may eat as little as 4 g fibre a day. Average consumption in Britain is around 18 g daily. But on junk-food diets of refined food, with little or no fresh fruit and vegetables (and many of our schoolchildren are eating just such diets today) fibre intake could be negligible.

One of the most obvious consequences of lack of fibre, as Cleave and Burkitt pointed out, was constipation. On their fibre-rich diets, tribal Africans passed stools twice a day, long and soft like ribbons of toothpaste. Hard small stools like rabbit droppings are the product of constipated civilized man. Over years of practical experience, Cleave – like Horace Fletcher – learned to recognize another key difference: stools from a healthy, properly working colon were odour-free. Rank, smelly stools were a sure sign of trouble brewing in the colon – that intestinal stasis which to Arbuthnot Lane was the precursor of so much disease. On fibre-rich diets, transit times are speeded up, too, with a meal taking no more than twenty-four hours to make its long journey down the gastro-intestinal tract. This is because fibre swells when it meets liquid to make much larger, bulkier stools, the size our colons are programmed to handle. On low-fibre diets, stools are smaller and harder, and may take two days or even longer to make their journey.

But although the wheat bran Cleave fed to his constipated sailors did wonders for their bowel transit times, it would not have had much effect on their blood cholesterol levels; nor would rice or corn bran. Of the cereals commonly eaten in the West, it's oats that have turned out to be our hearts' delight. As long ago as 1963, some researchers noticed that whole oats could lower the cholesterol levels in rats with experimentally induced high cholesterol. Intrigued, they fed rolled oats to a group of healthy young men at the rate of about 6 oz (170 g) a day for three weeks.[11] Their cholesterol levels dropped by an average of 11 per cent; 6 oz a day is a lot of oats, even if you're gone on muesli, so later researchers like Dr James Anderson at the University of Kentucky switched to oat bran instead, and found that it gave even better results. Pectin – found in apples and citrus fruits (the stuff they use to 'gel' jams) – and guar gum (found in beans) did better still. Alfalfa has been promoted as a dietary wonder-worker by health-food stores for years: Dr Malinow of the Oregon Regional Primate Center found that it certainly worked wonders for his atherosclerotic monkeys. Not only did their cholesterol levels drop sharply – but atheromas in their arteries began to melt away. Alfalfa, it appears, contains materials called saponins, which complex with cholesterol in the digestive tract to help carry it out of the body. Dr Malinow actually bought his alfalfa seeds from a health-food store, roast and ground them, and then began taking them at the rate of 10 teaspoons a day. After three weeks of this seed therapy, his own blood cholesterol had dropped by 20 per cent.[12] One of his patients, however, developed anaemia on the same regime; Cleave himself – or any naturopath – would have exclaimed at the unnaturalness of such huge amounts of a seed.

In the last few years, research into fibre has continued at an accelerating pace, with highly exciting information coming to light. More fibre in our diets has been shown not only to lower cholesterol levels, but to alter favourably blood-fat composition in general, raising the proportion of high-density lipoproteins (H Ds), which are good guys in the blood, and lowering the low-density lipoproteins (L D Ls), which are undesirable.

For diabetics, too – as Cleave insisted – fibre is now seen as a crucial component of the diet. For years they were officially urged to limit their intake of carbohydrates in general and fruit in particular. It turns out that they were robbed; it is refined carbohydrates like white sugar or white flour that play havoc with blood-sugar levels, by triggering a too-rapid insulin response. Fibre-rich foods prevent this by slowing the rate at which their sugar is released through the intestinal walls into the bloodstream. Dr James Anderson picked twenty diabetics, all on regular doses of insulin, and fed them a diet conforming to the guideline of the American Diabetic Association for a week. Then for a fortnight he fed them a diet high in fibre and complex carbohydrates. On the high-fibre diet, eleven of the twenty patients were able to give up their insulin shots, and their cholesterol levels dropped by an average of more than 25 per cent. Anderson and his fellow-workers speculate that the high-fibre diet seems to boost the activity of the patient's own insulin supplies, thus lowering the blood glucose level without extra insulin.[13]

Just how does fibre achieve this? Researchers are still groping for the answers. It's known that one kind of fibre, the pectin found in apples and citrus fruits, helps clear cholesterol by carrying out of the body the bile salts into which cholesterol is converted by the liver. It's known, too, that fibre affects gastric emptying time, the rate of absorption of nutrients from the intestine, faecal bulk and the frequency of bowel movements.

So one thing is clear, as Dr Anderson puts it: 'from mouth to anus, fibre profoundly influences the handling of food.' Two ways in which it does so should particularly recommend fibre to us. First of all, it encourages the proliferation of benevolent micro-organisms in our gut, to keep it functioning sweetly and cleanly. Second, it seems to cushion our gut against noxious chemicals in our food – or even carcinogens – by buffering or absorbing them. It was shown in one trial that rats eating refined food diets became ill or died when fed toxic chemicals – which included some food colourings. On high-fibre diets, they ate the same chemicals without turning a hair. If this is true for human beings too – which seems possible – it would mean that those already eating poor diets high in white sugar and refined flour are much more at risk from the chemical contaminants that nobody today can escape in their diets.

Research into fibre, incidentally, has also laid to rest the phytic acid bogey, which still has people suggesting today that wholemeal bread is a perilous food. Anderson increased the fibre intake of his diabetic patients from 20 to 50 g a day, and over periods as long as five years, he found no signs of mineral deficiency.

Capitol Concern

'**V**itamins and minerals are supplied in abundant amounts by commonly available foods. Except for persons with special medical needs there is no scientific basis for recommending routine use of dietary supplements.'[1]

If the Dietary Food Regulations proposed by the FDA in June 1966 had taken effect, all supplements thereafter would have had to carry this label. The same regulations also prohibited the general sale of vitamin supplements containing more than 150 per cent of the recommended daily allowances. Above this level, they would be deemed a drug, and available only on a physician's prescription.

Vitamins and mineral supplements were by this time big business, much of it in the hands of companies like W. T. Thompson and Dietaids, which had sprung up in the thirties and forties to supply the earliest health stores. These supplements were the economic bedrock of the entire health-food industry. Without revenue from the advertisements for them that filled page after page in every issue, magazines like *Prevention* and *Let's Live* could not have stayed afloat, and without the income from their sales, health-food stores by the score would be driven out of business. With them would disappear the chief market for dozens of books branded as 'nutritional nonsense' by the establishment.

There is nothing like persecution for closing ranks and raising morale, and the health-food industry had been living on a stimulating diet of anathemas for years. When the FDA had proposed similar regulations in 1962, the industry had sprung nimbly into action, pressure groups like the National Health Federation had orchestrated a public chorus of protest, and the FDA had withdrawn their regulations and retired to think matters over. Now they were ready to try again.

The regulations proposed in 1966 were even more draconian than the earlier ones. Among other things, they would have banned statements implying or suggesting 'that a dietary deficiency or threatened dietary deficiency of vitamins and/or minerals is or may be due to the loss of nutritive value of food by reason of the soil on which the food is grown, or the storage, transportation, processing and cooking of food'. If its conduct in the past was anything to go by, this meant that the FDA would be free to seize practically any book likely to be sold in a health-food store, on the grounds that it either advocated organic agriculture or criticized processed food as nutritionally deficient.

Another proposed regulation limited the nutrients which could be mentioned in advertising, or listed on the label, to those considered essential according to the RDAs. The banned list included nutrients which were beginning to excite particular attention at that time, including amino acids, minerals and trace elements such as zinc, selenium, chromium and manganese, the B vitamins choline, inositol, biotin and para-aminobenzoic acid, the bioflavonoids, lecithin and linoleic acid. Study of the amino acids was only just beginning to reveal their huge potential in the treatment of illness. Adelle Davis considered methionine – found in garlic, eggs and onions – as one of the body's most powerful detoxifying agents; and one of its uses today is to bring down high lead levels in children. The glutamine that Roger Williams found so useful for alcoholics is another amino acid.

Acting for the entire health-food industry – as well as for millions of consumers – the National Nutritional Foods Association immediately filed its objections and demanded a public hearing.

Even before the hearings started, however, it was clear that the regulations were unlikely to have a smooth passage. Scores of objections were entered, one of the strongest coming from Dr William Sebrell, Chairman of the Committee on Recommended Dietary Allowances: '. . . there must be many thousands of people in this country,' he told the FDA, 'who are on restricted diets for the purpose of losing weight . . . or special diets of other kinds for various reasons medical and non-medical, for whom there would be scientific basis for dietary supplementation'.[2] The US Department of Agriculture, meanwhile, reminded the FDA that its recent nationwide survey had shown that nearly half of all American families were eating diets that didn't meet the RDAs for at least one vitamin or mineral.

Undeterred, the FDA went ahead. The Vitamin Hearings ran for two solid years, filled over 32,000 pages of testimony,

and turned into a grandstand vindication of vitamin supplementation, to the discomfiture of the FDA. Speaker after
speaker, called by them as an expert witness to buttress their
case, either failed dismally to substantiate it or gave testimony
that shot it to pieces.

Many of the FDA witnesses, for instance, testified that
teenagers, children, alcoholics, the elderly, the poor, pregnant
women and those on special diets – about half America, in other
words – might all be suffering from nutritional deficiencies.

Dr Arnold Schaefer, Chief of the Nutrition Programme
at the Department of Health, Education and Welfare, put it
more bluntly: most American pets eat better than their owners.

Another FDA witness, Dr William Allaway, was a soil
scientist with the United States Department of Agriculture, and
the FDA were counting on him to shore up their contention
that the nutrients in food crops were unaffected by fertilizers
or soil composition. Dr Allaway showed that, on the contrary,
soils poor in minerals and trace elements such as potassium and
molybdenum will produce plants equally poor in them, and that
even levels of vitamins such as beta-carotene can be affected.

Other witnesses showed that significant nutritional losses
occurred in processed foods.

Under oath, and in the teeth of so much evidence, even
Dr Stare for once felt unable to defend the average American
diet with his usual verve. 'We simply don't know how well or
how ill nourished the nation is,' he told the hearing. 'I don't
see how anyone at this time can intelligently recommend new
regulations of special diet foods, vitamin and mineral fortified
foods, and supplements.'[3]

The hearings were a media event which millions of Americans watched with growing interest and concern. As the FDA's
case crumbled in ruins, and uncomfortable truths about the
American diet emerged into the full glare of publicity, it
became clear that they were proving an embarrassment for the
FDA rather than a pushover. And Stare was one of several
men in prominent positions who wrote to the FDA urging
them to call a halt, at least for the time being. They persevered –
and examiner Harris, handpicked by them as one who saw eye
to eye with them throughout, found in favour of the FDA.
It was now up to the FDA to review the massive amount of
testimony, and draft their final regulations.

But the public debate that the FDA attempt to regulate
vitamins had provoked, and the much-publicized hearings that

followed, had raised public consciousness of the issues at stake to an unprecedentedly high level. Millions of Americans who had never given a thought to nutrition before now realized that there were grounds for real concern about the quality of the American diet and what it was doing to the national health. The statistics were horrifying.

Heart disease was wiping out over 700,000 Americans every year. Public health service statistics for 1961–2 indicated that 80·3 million – 44·1 per cent of the civilian population – were suffering from such chronic problems as arthritis, heart disease, hypertension, diabetes and mental sickness. By 1965 this figure had risen to 87·3 million, or 46·3 per cent of the population. Ten million suffered from arthritis and rheumatoid conditions and heart disease, 9 million from mental illness. Millions more were being treated for sinusitis and hayfever. The number of brain-damaged, mentally retarded and hyperactive children began rising steeply from 1960 onwards; the US census of 1970 showed 2,800,000 mentally retarded children, and 740,000 more whose learning ability was significantly impaired.[4]

It was a cliché of official medical thinking that the degenerative diseases were increasing simply because – thanks to the marvels of modern medicine – people were living long enough to develop them. The tragic truth concealed behind these glib assurances was that diseases once seen as striking down only the elderly or middle-aged were now claiming younger and younger victims. Autopsies on eighteen-to-twenty-one-year-old men in the First World War showed almost no cases of atherosclerotic disease. In the Second World War the condition was found quite often. An article in the *Journal of the American Medical Association*, in May 1959, reported that half of the American soldiers killed in Korea – their average age was twenty-two – had atherosclerotic plaques in their coronary arteries. In striking contrast the Korean soldiers who fought them were vigorous young men with healthy, well-muscled hearts, although 'they had survived two decades of war and revolution, and been under stress far longer than the Americans . . .'[5] In the Vietnam war, it was rare to find a US soldier who did not have atherosclerotic disease.

Most frightening of all were the American draft figures, which clocked a relentless decline over fifty years. In the First World War, 31·2 per cent of the young men examined for military service were rejected; in the Second World War, when the standards were lowered, 41 per cent were rejected. Some

51·9 per cent of the Americans tested for the Korean war –
when physical and mental standards were lowered once more –
were rejected. And for Vietnam the standards were lower still –
and the rejection rates still higher. 'These are not sickness figures,' as Adelle Davis pointed out; 'merely statistics of our finest
young men at the height of their physical development.'[6]

In the late sixties public concern about the national health
was becoming so vocal that the Department of Health, Education and Welfare was moved to action: the first National
Nutrition Survey was launched. By 1969, when it was ready to
make its first report, the Nixon administration had responded
to a vociferous 'Hunger Lobby', nagging the nation's conscience
about its malnourished millions of poor and deprived people.
The Senate Committee on Nutrition and Human Needs,
chaired by Senator McGovern, was set up to study the question
in depth, and it was to this committee that the directors of the
survey made their report. It was widely reported in the press.

A horrified America learned that diseases of malnutrition
which it was thought belonged back in the dark ages of the
Depression, or were to be found only in deprived Third World
countries, were once more becoming rampant in the wealthy
United States. Shaken members of the survey team reported
cases of goitre, of rickets, even the severest deficiency diseases,
kwashiorkor and marasmus. They reported hundreds of children under five who were inches below the average height for
their age. Forty per cent of those surveyed were deficient in
vitamin A, 12–16 per cent low in vitamin C, 19 per cent in
vitamin B_2, 9 per cent in B_1. Iron deficiency was widespread:
one third of the under-six-year-olds were so low in iron as to
be clinically anaemic. Dental conditions were a disaster: 90 per
cent had decayed teeth needing treatment; in many cases the
teeth were decayed to the gum margin, nearly half had
periodontal disease, and in 20 per cent it was so severe that it
hurt to chew or bite.

Dr Arnold Schaefer and Dr Ogden Johnson, who presented the survey findings, emphasized an acute concern that
malnutrition was affecting not only physical but mental development. 'If this proves true, we have a practical, urgent, compelling reason to eradicate malnutrition in America.' If infants,
children and pregnant women all received adequate nutrition,
they pointed out, 'we could . . . interrupt this morbid cycle and
remodel the future . . . With this there would come to our children improved growth and development, certainly of body and

probably of intellect. Educational accomplishments and achievements would improve and, with this, economic status would rise . . .'[7]

Every member of the survey team, finally, agreed that one fact stood out clearly from their findings: the desperate need for nutritional education. Many of the families they looked at simply did not know the right things to eat, although a healthy diet was possible even on their low incomes. It was a knowledge gap as often as a poverty problem.

The immediate result of Nixon's crusade to 'put an end to hunger in America itself for all time' was the allocation of huge new sums for food stamps and school lunches for millions more children.

But in the longer term, politicians now knew they could no longer afford to ignore the existence of an increasingly well-informed, aware and highly critical public. Nutrition, as one journal put it, was 'an idea whose time has come'.[8] And in the seventies, the initiative passed to the consumer.

It was to this public that Roger Williams chose to address himself when he published another landmark work, *Nutrition against Disease*, in 1971. For more than a decade he had seen potentially life-saving advances in nutritional knowledge ignored by the medical establishment, which responded with mockery and abuse to those attempting to put them forward. There were no more bouquets for Dr Stare, whose own words are quoted to deplore the numbers of physicians 'not well trained enough to identify malnutrition except for gross under- and overweight, and this anyone can do'.[9] If doctors and dieticians deplored the rise of nutritional charlatanism, they had only themselves to thank: 'The very people who should have been able to give expert guidance to the layman's institutions about nutrition have, in fact, virtually abandoned the field.'[10]

The only hope of action, as he now saw it, lay in a strong and informed public opinion.

The public themselves by this time had come to much the same conclusion. Rachel Carson and Ralph Nader had made Americans aware of the increasing pollution of their environment, and consumers had their own one-woman crusader in the person of Beatrice Trum Hunter, whose *Consumer Beware!*, published in 1971, made stomach-churning reading. One of Nader's team, James Turner, opened American eyes to what was going into their food in *The Chemical Feast*, published in 1970. Few readers of these and other works can have had any illusions left about the concern of the food industry for the health of its consumers, or the effectiveness of the FDA as a public watchdog. By this time Americans were consuming an estimated 4 lb (1·8 kg) annually of chemical additives – today the amount is around the 5 lb (2·3 kg) mark – along with their food. Over 3,000 different chemicals were being used, as colouring, flavouring, flavour enhancers, humectants, bleaches, stabilizers, anti-caking, anti-staling and anti-foaming agents, acidulants, plasticizers, retardants, mould inhibitors, emulsifiers, and all the other dubious tricks by which nutritionally poor or even worthless raw material could be transformed into something calculated to please a public of whom it was said that 'eating is just something done in response to advertising'.[11]

Thousands of these additives, the public now learned, had never been tested for their cancer-causing potential, or their possible effect upon the unborn child in the womb. And when additives were tested, it was done 'scientifically'; in other words, one at a time, on healthy animals fed a nutritious diet, whereas in the real world people were more likely to be consuming numbers of different additives simultaneously, of which the chemical composition might be altered by baking, boiling, mixing in acidic media or reacting with other chemicals.

In many cases, the industry conducted its own toxicity tests, and committees set up to evaluate safety procedures were often composed largely of food-industry representatives, if not actually chaired by them, and of academics whose university departments were funded by the food industry.

While Americans learned just what was happening to their food supply, they were rapidly learning, too, what they might be missing in improved health care through nutrition, thanks to the prejudices of the medical profession. There are no figures for the numbers of Americans who were turning away from their doctors in the 1970s to treat their own illnesses by altering their diets and taking supplements. But a vast literature was springing up to meet this need. Some of it was ill-informed rubbish. Much more was written expressly for the public by research scientists and disillusioned doctors who had found out the hard way that if the answer was nutrition, their colleagues and the AMA didn't want to know.

Self-reliance had been an old pioneer necessity; modern America was attempting to regain its health in the pioneer way again. People were learning how to treat their arthritis by the Dong diet, or by avoiding foods of the nightshade family –

potatoes, tomatoes, aubergines, peppers – to which, as a Professor of Horticulture, Dr Gordon Childers, had discovered, thousands of arthritics are allergic. They wrote by the thousand to Roger Williams asking him for exact details of his nutritional approach to alcoholism. They learned from popular lecturers like Carlton Fredericks how to treat the hypoglycaemia that was making them depressed or fatigued or neurotic, after their own doctors had dismissed them with a prescription for tranquillizers. They were becoming experts at diagnosing their own and their family's allergy problems. From Roger Williams they had learned to take vitamin and mineral supplements routinely by way of 'health insurance'. And when they read Linus Pauling's *Vitamin C and the Common Cold*, published in 1970, they began taking regular 1–2 g daily doses of vitamin C – although according to the recommended daily allowances, 45 mg daily was more than enough for most people.

The Nobel Prizewinner, Linus Pauling, first became interested in vitamin C in 1966. One evening he found himself sitting next to the biochemist and novelist Irwin Stone, and told him what he wanted to live at least another ten to fifteen years, because there were so many things he wanted to do. Irwin Stone, who had been researching vitamin C for years, later sent Pauling suggestions for a regimen, based on his own research, that included high doses of vitamin C. Pauling and his wife, a nutritionist, began taking 2 g of vitamin C daily, and soon noticed that not only did they feel much better, but that they caught far fewer colds. Intrigued, Pauling began following up earlier work on vitamin C. In 1949 G. H. Bourne had shown that the free-ranging gorilla may take in around 4·5 g daily of vitamin C on his diet of greenstuffs. Stone calculated that if human beings synthesized the vitamin at the same rate per kilo of body weight as rats, they'd be producing between 1·8 and 4·1 g a day. Pauling speculated that since man, along with fruit-eating bats and guinea-pigs, had lost the ability to synthesize his bodily supplies of vitamin C – presumably as the result of a genetic mutation millions of years ago – he had probably developed, by another mutation, some compensatory biological mechanism. But since 'these mechanisms require energy and are a burden to the organism' Pauling recommended daily doses of 1–2 g.[12]

Vitamin C turned into another health-food-store bestseller – and the stores themselves were doing very healthy business indeed by the early seventies, with much of the growth coming at the young end of the market. The number of stores in America had swelled from around 500 in 1965 to around 1,200 in 1968, and nearly 3,000 by 1972. The total market was reckoned for health foods in 1971 to be worth some $300m, with a projected growth to $500m by 1975. Uneasily doing its sums, the food industry calculated that the market could be worth $1bn by 1975 – and quite possibly as much as $3bn by 1980.

The US pharmaceutical industry clocked up domestic sales in 1985 of $16·2bn, a rise of $2·1bn on its 1983 figures. Total 1985 sales of the US food industry are virtually impossible to compare; informed guesses are all in billions of dollars. Compared to either of these, the health-food business was a drop in the ocean. But its very existence – and the persuasive power of its 'misinformation' – constituted a massive threat to these twin gigantic concerns. Billions of dollars, hundreds of thousands of jobs were at stake. Equally at risk was the professional reputation of the American Medical Association which through its public pronouncements and its *Journal* had done so much to promote costly drug therapy and so pitifully little to encourage research into the food factor in disease.

A national survey carried out for the FDA in 1972 brought dismaying news for all three.

Twenty per cent of the population believed that both arthritis and cancer might be caused by vitamin and mineral deficiencies; 42 per cent of all Americans wouldn't accept that an 'alternative' cancer cure was 'worthless' simply on the say-so of the prejudiced AMA – and a majority of 55 per cent thought it was wrong to make such treatments illegal; 75 per cent of those questioned said they believed that extra vitamins gave them more pep and energy.

Most Americans – unlike their doctors – now believed that a faulty diet was the cause of most of their health problems. And millions of Americans were treating themselves for a huge range of illnesses without bothering to go to the doctor. This was heresy on a grand scale.

Rushing propaganda supplies to the front line, *Nutrition Reviews* in the summer of 1974 brought out a whole supplement devoted to *Food Faddism*. There were merciless attacks on all the familiar targets: Adelle Davis ('glaring . . . misquotations and inaccuracies'), Vitamin E ('no value in heart disease or in any other condition with the exception of vitamin E deficiency'),

Carlton Fredericks ('a charlatan . . . brilliant and aggressive'), Rodale ('fuzzy thinking . . . hogwash').[13]

Another article – reprinted from the *Dairy Council Digest* – repeated a familiar charge: 'the false promises of superior health and freedom from disease which are believed to accrue from the use of "health" foods delay individuals from obtaining necessary competent medical attention'.

Additives and pesticide residues were a threat to American health? Rubbish. The FDA was doing a magnificent job of policing pesticide residues and checking additives for safety. Additives themselves were carefully vetted, and no less a person than Harvard's own Dr Stare was reassuring on the subject: 'As a physician and student of nutrition . . . I am convinced that food additives in use are safe.'[14]

Much more difficult to counter was the revelation of widespread nutritional deficiencies in millions of Americans eating the supposedly adequate 'average' diet. Ronald Deutsch had an answer to this one too: '. . . these are *dietary* deficiencies . . . It does *not* mean their bodies show signs of lacking the vitamin.'[15]

The actual deficiency states revealed in the survey – the scurvy, the anaemia, the rotting gums – could not be dismissed so easily. But here too Deutsch was ready with an answer which he brought out at the 1974 White House Conference on Food, Nutrition and Health. Millions, he charged, couldn't afford to eat properly *because they were bankrupting themselves buying overpriced health foods and vitamins.* 'Those who cannot afford poor food choices are especially exploited. The poor, in particular the old, the ill, and the least educated are cruelly victimized . . .'[16]

An even more ingenious explanation for the national ill health had already been suggested: in *Food Facts, Foibles and Fables*, A. T. W. Simeons admitted that 'modern man has become alarmingly subject to a number of fatal diseases the true causes of which are still utterly baffling . . . diabetes, obesity, peptic ulcers, strokes, rheumatism and coronary thrombosis . . .' Might not the explanation lie at least partially in modern man's 'fear of what he eats' fed by the food faddists and triggering 'just the emotional conditions favourable to the insurgence of those many disorders in which the working of the brain may well play by far the most important role'.[17]

If it's all in the mind, you can hardly blame it on the doughnuts and the Kool-Aid. This is an argument that appeals to the champions of the US food industry. One of the most fervent of these is Dr Victor Herbert, Professor of Medicine at the State

University of New York, a self-declared foe of the health-food industry. Claims of a connection between diet and disease are an irresponsible myth put about by 'health hustlers', he claims. 'This is not so. Inspect any medical school textbook or ask your doctor. They will tell you that most diseases have nothing to do with diet. Malaise (feeling poorly), tiredness, lack of pep, aches (including headaches) or pains, insomnia and similar complaints are usually the body's reaction to emotional stress, overwork, etc.'[18]

In referring his readers to received medical opinion, Herbert was of course on safe ground. As the public were fast beginning to realize, one reason why their doctor was likely to be so down on nutrition was that he didn't actually know much about it. In 1976 the *Journal of the American Medical Association* carried a report about the teaching of nutrition in medical schools. The author had sent a questionnaire to sixty of them, inquiring whether they offered instruction in nutrition and if so, how much. Of the forty-four schools who replied, only one had a complete department of nutrition, with thirteen faculty members; seven had none at all; twenty-five offered *some* instruction ranging from just an hour up to a total of forty hours; and the rest said that the subject was 'touched upon in other courses'.

By way of contrast, the same author wrote to thirty agricultural colleges to ask if they taught animal nutrition. They all replied. Every single one of them offered numbers of courses, both graduate and postgraduate.[19]

It wasn't that nutritional 'experts' were exactly lacking. Commenting on a statement that Americans were nutritionally illiterate, made at the White House Conference, *Nutrition Today* indignantly pointed out that there were 'more American women trained in dietetics; more home economists teaching more students, domestic and foreign; more educational materials and more research on nutrition education . . . more enlightened well-directed efforts by the Council on Foods and Nutrition of the American Medical Association; more money spent by industry to educate the public and professions about nutrition . . . than in any other land . . .'[20] So wasn't it a little surprising that, according to findings revealed to an AMA Symposium in 1974, the diet of numbers of Americans consisted of 'Oreos, peanut butter, Crisco, TV dinners, cake mix, macaroni and cheese, Pepsi and Coke, pizzas, Jell-O, hamburgers, Rice-a-roni, Spaghetti-Os, pork and beans, Heinz ketchup and instant coffee'?[21] Patients in US hospitals, meanwhile, under the direct care of those expert dieticians, were so badly fed that half of them suffered from some degree of malnutrition, according to a jolting survey published in 1974, and between 5 and 10 per cent of them actually died of starvation.[22]

Stare's often-repeated assertions that American food was wonderful were beginning to ring a little hollow in public ears, too, as the extent of his cosy relationship with the US food industry became more widely known. Stare's department at Harvard, it was pointed out, had had massive grants from such companies as Coca-Cola, Kellogg, the Sugar Association and the Carnation Company, while Stare himself had been on the board of directors of the Continental Can Company for years. He had testified at Congressional and FDA hearings on behalf of Kellogg, Carnation Milk, the Sugar Association and Nabisco.[23]

Since Stare was the nation's premier nutrition 'expert', such revelations were an embarrassment all round, and a feature in *Nutrition Today* – not noted for its sympathy with the health-food industry – charged that Stare and other academics who moonlighted for industry were rapidly becoming a liability to the profession. 'Such scientists are often summoned from academia to defend their funding resource when the need arises. Few disappoint and then only once. It is a system which demeans everyone associated with it and destroys reputations. A better way must be found.'

The writer suggested an alternative: industrial funding sources might appoint consumer advocates and unconventional nutritionists to their boards of directors, so they might have a voice in funding research. 'At the present time, we expect research funded by the International Sugar Research Association, Inc., to find that sugar has only a minimal role in the development of caries, that it does not cause diabetes mellitus, and that it has no role in the development of heart disease.'[24]

Since Stare has lost much of his credibility, and the Nutrition Foundation is closely identified today by many Americans with the interests of the food industry, big business has now invested heavily in another public-relations ploy: the American Council on Science and Health, or ACSH. Set up jointly by Stare and his colleague and co-author Elizabeth Whelan, ACSH was billed as 'a new scientific organization whose purpose is to investigate chemicals in our society', with a full-time staff of researchers, and a forty-five-person scientific advisory committee. Whelan was hurt by suggestions that ACSH was not Simon Pure and impartial: '. . . we do not accept

contributions from any sources which have a commercial interest in the issues we are investigating,' she claimed piously.[25]

It was soon noticed, however, that the findings of ACSH
seemed to be coming up oddly favourable to industry: for
instance, that caffeine as generally consumed presented little
threat to the health of Americans, and that no scientific reports
presented to date had shown any convincing relationship
between use of the herbicide 2,4,5-T (agent orange, used in
Vietnam) and adverse health effects in humans.

A Nader consumer group, the Center for Science in the
Public Interest, began digging – and found that far from sternly
refusing help from industry, ACSH was in fact handsomely
funded by Coca-Cola, Hershey Foods Corporation, the
National Soft Drinks Association, and International Flavors
and Fragrances Inc., makers of artificial flavourings and
colourings, to name some.[26]

As early as 1973, though, in a David and Goliath situation,
it was David who won against all the odds; the FDA was massively defeated when it attempted to issue its final Vitamin
Regulations Order. Fifteen lawsuits were at once filed, which
were ultimately consolidated into a single lawsuit, brilliantly
contested on behalf of the health-food industry by their
attorney Milton Bass. The regulations were thrown out by the
US Circuit Court of Appeals, and when the FDA attempted to
appeal this decision before the Supreme Court, it refused to
intervene.

Since the FDA was obviously determined to press ahead,
another massive campaign to rouse public opinion was mounted
to steamroller the regulations out of existence. 'You're going to
have to get a prescription to buy two carrots,' quipped a health
magazine.[27] The FDA gave up counting when their protest mail
passed the 100,000 mark. Congress stopped counting after a
million letters – more even than Watergate had prompted. And
vitamins found a doughty champion in the person of Senator
Proxmire. By an overwhelming majority, in April 1976, the Senate passed the Proxmire Amendment. In future, the FDA would
be able to regulate vitamins only on the basis of known toxicity.
(By the same token, it should logically put aspirin and hundreds
of other over-the-counter drugs on prescription only, which it
has given no indication of wishing to do.)

'What the FDA wants to do,' thundered Senator Proxmire, 'is strike the views of its stable of orthodox nutritionists
into "tablets" and bring them down from Mount Sinai where

they will be used to regulate the right of millions of Americans who believe they are getting a lousy diet to take vitamins and minerals. The real issue is whether the FDA is going to play "god".'[28]

The FDA has certainly not lost its determination to regulate vitamins. Immediately after Proxmire, they reshaped their nutrition research programmes, and turned over at least half their resources to exploring nutrient toxicity. Currently, there are moves under way in the US to pass legislation forbidding any but recognized dieticians from giving nutritional advice. This could make it illegal for health-food store owners even to discuss what constitutes a healthy balanced diet when talking to their customers.

But by this time the McGovern Committee had developed a momentum of its own. Not just hunger but nutrition problems in general were now the focus of its attention. And in 1977, its investigations concluded with the publication of the famous Dietary Goals: Americans were urged to eat more fruits, more vegetables, more whole grains; less sugar, refined flour and fat; fewer egg yolks and other high-cholesterol foods; less salt and salty foods. Choose fish instead of meat, they were advised, white meat rather than red meat, lean instead of fat. And cut back on junk foods, they were admonished. Anticipating the roar of protest from the food industry, the livestock breeders, the farmers and the dairying industry, Dr Mark Hegsted observed in the preface: 'The question to be asked, therefore, is not why we should change our diet, but why not?'[29]

Thoughtful Americans noted that this elementary advice had come, not from the Department of Health, Education and Welfare, nor yet from the US Department of Agriculture, and certainly not from the American Medical Association – who had indeed dismissed these dietary goals as unproven, unnecessary and premature – but from a group of unbiased lay people, listening to overwhelming evidence that America was digging its grave with its teeth.

––––

The supplements question has dominated the nutrition scene for half a century now, but the debate has become polarized into two extreme and opposed views, neither of which is based on calm, rational and independent scientific consideration. The AMA and FDA opposition to the supplement question is based as much on hostility to the health-food industry as on a genuine appreciation of the nutritional issues involved. And in the health-food industry itself no real discussion, let alone serious study, is possible, because without the supplement business and the income it generates, there would be no health-food industry at all. And without a health-food industry, there would have been no health lectures, no lively magazines to take the nutrition message to the public, no market for writers like Gayelord Hauser and Adelle Davis; nowhere for people to buy unrefined natural foods, and no rallying-point for critics of a drug-oriented medicine and the mammoth processed-food industry.

In the circumstances, any criticism of the supplement concept from inside the ranks of the faithful is seen as a dangerous rocking of the boat, while when it comes from outside, it's assumed to be hostile or aggressive in intent. But any such words of caution are unlikely to reach the public that spends most on vitamin pills, because health magazines can't afford to upset their most important advertisers by publishing such heretical views. Instead, the assumption that supplements are good for you is implicit in the pages of almost every health magazine, although American publications tend to plug the message with rather more enthusiasm than their opposite numbers in Britain. (Picking up issues of three at random, I find the following headlines: 'Vitamin E against Cancer'; 'Manganese: A Key to Mental Wellbeing'; and 'Magnesium – The Little Mineral with the Big Heart'.) There are many, however, both inside the health movement and outside it, who feel that preoccupation with vitamins and minerals has distracted attention away from more important and urgent questions, such as the quality of our food supply. There are those, too, who feel that there is no essential difference between administering supplements to patients and giving them drugs, and that naturopaths who do so are wolves in sheep's clothing.

'Stanley Lief and James C. Thomson would turn in their graves,' says Keki Sidhwa, 'to see modern naturopathy turn into a second-hand imitation of doctors' prescription, with emphasis on the modification of patients' symptoms.' The role of the 'Nature Cure' practitioner, he insists, is to 'educate not medicate'. Health, he tells his patients, is not something you get out of a bottle: your health is something you create yourself.[30]

Sidhwa argues that there are probably many vitamin-like substances present in food which will be discovered to be essential as the years go by, which are not yet available in supplements; that the body does a much better job of balancing its own chemistry than the most skilled biochemist; and that we can never know exactly how much of any one vitamin or mineral our bodies need. An excess may be toxic in ways of which we are not aware: iron, he points out, is present in food in a colloidal state, so that the body can easily avoid absorption when it requires no iron. But when iron is consumed, as in supplements, in the crystalline sulphate form, unwanted iron may be absorbed with dire results.

'Food supplements are not and cannot ever be part of a health-giving regime.' Keki Sidhwa speaks with conviction. The child of a wealthy Bombay family, he fell seriously ill at the age of fourteen with typhoid: legions of doctors and specialists were summoned and watched him helplessly through seven relapses. 'I still remember the agony,' says Sidhwa. 'Five thousand injections in eleven months – my hands stretched out night and day with the drips in them.' At the end they pronounced him dead. But his mother refused to give up his body. 'My son is not dead!' she told them through locked doors. After three hours she finally allowed them to re-examine him – and at this moment he fluttered an eyelid. For the next six days he lay in a coma while his mother allowed no drugs, no food to be given him. Night and day she sat beside him, wetting his lips from time to time with a little fresh coconut milk. Finally he recovered consciousness and his temperature dropped to normal.

'That six-day fast saved my life,' says Sidhwa. 'Why did my mother do it? Because her bosom friend at college had been the daughter of Macfadden's disciple – Behramji Madon.' Seven years later, studying to be a surgeon at Bombay University, Sidhwa collapsed with typhoid again. This time something clicked in his mind. 'What is this Nature Cure you are always talking about?' he asked his mother. She gave him Tilden on *Toxaemia* to read. He devoured it, threw away his medicines, fasted himself better in ten days – and then took himself off to Britain to study with Thomson at Edinburgh.[31]

Today, Keki Sidhwa – a vigorous slightly built, gentle but forceful sixty-year-old – is president of the British Natural Hygiene Society and vice-president of an Inernational Association of Professional Natural Hygienists that still transmits the message of Graham and Trall: health by healthful living.

23

EFAs, EPAs
and All That

In country villages around the Mediterranean you can still find the cloudy, greenish olive oils with a pronounced fruity taste produced by primitive cold-pressing methods. The olive or sunflower oil you pick up from the supermarket shelf, though, is clear, pale and free-running, often smelling and tasting of absolutely nothing at all. It has been refined, which sounds pleasing: in other words, it has been extracted by chemical solvents, treated with caustic soda to remove fatty acids, bleached, and deodorized by heating at high temperatures for up to twelve hours. A wide range of vegetable oils are further submitted to the process of hydrogenation, complete or partial, which hardens them enough to make margarine.

In the processing of oils, not only can the natural anti-oxidant vitamin E be destroyed; hydrogenation also partially or completely destroys the family of vital nutrients known as essential fatty acids, or EFAs. In any degree of hydrogenation, some of these fatty acids are altered from a benign and necessary *cis* form, in which the body readily takes them up and makes use of them, into a malign *trans* form, which acts much like saturated fatty acids.

Hydrogenation was first devised in the late nineteenth century, and has been hailed as a boon and a blessing by food manufacturers ever since. We have no cause to share their delight. In the view of a growing number of experts in this field, the refining and hydrogenation of vegetable oils has been an unmitigated dietary disaster, comparable to the refining of grains and sugar – and perhaps in the long run even more lethal.

The first grim warning on this subject was sounded decades ago: by coincidence, in the same year, 1956, as Cleave first put forward his saccharin theory. In an immensely long letter to the *Lancet* – which, to their everlasting credit, they published in full – Hugh Sinclair pointed out that 'the dietaries of the more highly civilized countries are becoming increasingly deficient in the essential . . . fatty acids . . . and increasingly rich in saturated fatty acids and unnatural fatty acids which may act as anti-vitamins'.[1] If animal studies were any guidance, we could expect EFA deficiency to be far commoner in men than in women,* and to give rise to an epidemic of such diverse diseases as coronary thrombosis, lung cancer, atherosclerosis, leukaemia, duodenal ulcers, eczema, and disorders of the nervous system, such as disseminated sclerosis (as MS was then called). If he was right, then the low-extraction flour which had just been given the blessing of the Cohen panel would be a triple disaster, since it would have lost not only some of these EFAs, but most of the vitamin B_6, which was needed before the body could make use of them, and the vitamin E, which protected them.

'With no sympathy for long-haired naturalism,' concluded Sinclair, 'I humbly plead that we should give more thought and perform more research before extracting and 'improving' wheat, manufacturing unnatural fats that then appear in margarine (which could otherwise be an excellent food), and before foisting upon the public sophisticated fodder which it unsuspectingly accepts.'[2]

Sinclair's views on EFAs were shared by few nutritionists of his day. Ancel Keys, who worked at Oxford with Sinclair in the early fifties, held that all fats were equally harmful, and EFAs devoid of interest. John Yudkin, then Professor of Nutrition at London University, had already assured the *Lancet*'s readers that EFA deficiency was rarely if ever seen in man. But then, as Sinclair tartly remarked, he had the disadvantage of not having worked upon EFAs.

Sinclair's own interest in EFAs – in which field he has giant authority today – dates back to his undergraduate years in the early thirties. Why, he wondered, had the degenerative diseases begun their dramatic rise at the beginning of the twentieth century? If there was a dietary factor involved, what was it? The refining of flour was an obvious suspect. But few before Sinclair had suggested that the EFAs present in the wheat germ, and obliterated in refined and bleached flour, together with those destroyed or distorted in refined and hydrogenated vegetable oils, might be so crucial for our health.

*In the USA at this time it was noted that men under fifty-one were twelve times more likely than women to have heart attacks: but in the years 1967–71, men were only four times more likely.[2] It has been suggested that the contraceptive pill may be responsible for this change. Lung cancer was for years more common in men than in women.

The study of E F As was in its infancy at this time. It had begun in 1927, when Herbert Evans and George Burr at the University of Minnesota found that rats on fat-free diets stopped growing. Two years later, George and Mildred Burr reported that as well as arrested growth, skin problems and roughened scaly tails appeared in their fat-free rats. Unsaturated fatty acids reversed this condition: saturated fats did not. Unsaturated fatty acids were therefore said to be – essential.

What exactly are these essential fatty acids? They are the basic chemical building blocks from which fats and oils – otherwise known as lipids – are constructed. They are composed of carbon atoms linked together like beads on a chain. As well as joining up with its carbon neighbour to make the chain, each carbon atom also joins up with two atoms of hydrogen; and in saturated fats, there are no empty links. The chain is 'saturated'. There may be as few as two carbon atoms in the fatty acid chain – or as many as twenty-six. But 18-carbon chains are the commonest, among them the saturated fatty acid, stearic acid, found in tallow.

There are also monounsaturated acids, in which two neighbouring carbon atoms have a double link or bond between them, leaving room for two more hydrogen atoms. Oleic acid, found in olive oil, is an 18-carbon-chain monounsaturated fatty acid. When there is more than one of these double bonds, then the fatty acid becomes known as polyunsaturated – or P U F As for short. And two of these P U F As are also E F As.

One is the 18-carbon chain with two double bonds, called linoleic acid, found in corn, safflower and soybean oils among other common sources. The other is an 18-carbon chain with three double bonds, called linolenic acid, found in hardy northern plants such as flax (giving us linseed oil), wheat, walnuts, chestnuts, barley, oats and rye. Cold-water fish such as herring, salmon and mackerel contain other long-chain polyunsaturated oils.

Both linoleic and linolenic acid must be supplied in the diet, and from them the body manufactures other fatty acids. Linoleic acid and its derivatives are known, rather poetically, as the Omega-6 family, because the first double bond is the sixth from one end; the linolenic family are known as Omega-3 because their first double bond is third from the end.

Most of the early research was done on the Omega-6 family: Sinclair was almost alone in insisting that the Omega-3 fatty acids were just as important, based on the fact that one of them –

docosahexaenoic acid, or DHA for short, is found in large amounts in man's brain. He was also intrigued from the outset by the fact that Eskimos – with the world's highest fat intake – have almost no heart disease on their traditional diets. Others pointed out that the Faroe Islanders, eating plenty of fish, had no multiple sclerosis, while the Shetland and Orkney Islanders, who ate little fish, had plenty.

By the late fifties, these marine oils too were being carefully researched, and research into EFAs generally was enormously stimulated by the discovery in 1962 that EFAs were the precursors of lively little substances called prostaglandins.

Essential fatty acids are today generating the same kind of excitement as vitamins aroused in the twenties and thirties, and with very good reason: the more we learn of the range of functions they perform, the more we realize how literally essential they are to every single cell and almost every biochemical process in our bodies. Hardly surprisingly, deficiencies of them have been linked with an astonishing spectrum of diseases: multiple sclerosis, cardiovascular problems, eczema, schizophrenia, hyperactivity in children, alcoholism, diabetic retinopathy and rheumatic disease are among those in which they are already being tried out clinically, with highly promising results.

When researchers began devoting meticulous study to animals that had been totally deprived of EFAs, they catalogued devastating damage: wounds that failed to heal, hair fall-out, stunted growth, failure to reproduce, hypertrophy of the kidneys, eczema, liver degeneration, atrophy of many glands, and collapses of the immune system – as well as leaky permeability of cell walls throughout bodies which were, almost literally, falling apart.

Both linoleic and linolenic acid are only of limited use to the body in their original form: they have to be 'processed' first. Linoleic acid is converted into gammalinolenic acid – GLA – with the help of a useful little enzyme called delta-6-desaturase; and GLA in turn is converted into a substance with an even longer name, dihomogammalinolenic acid – DGLA. This is precursor to a series of benevolent prostaglandins called 1-series PGs, or PGE1, which, amongst other things, shut off the inflammatory process which gives us headaches or the swollen painful joints of arthritis, help lower blood pressure by dilating blood vessels and inhibit the production of excess cholesterol and blood clotting. But DGLA is also precursor to arachidonic acid, which gives rise to two series, prostaglandins and a group

of leukotrienes – potent regulators of different bodily processes. Both groups, when derived from a rachidonic acid, tend
to be too aggressive for our good – especially when it comes to
inflammation – and they are found in plenty at the site of any
inflammation. More than a century and a half after aspirin first
made its triumphant entrance on to the medical stage, we at
last know how it works: it blocks the enzyme activity which
produces these nasties from arachidonic acid.

It doesn't sound like a very sensible arrangement to have
one substance provoking inflammation and another damping
it down, so it has been suggested that – as so often in the marvellous biochemistry of our bodies – a balancing or feedback mechanism normally operates between DGLA and arachidonic acid.
A high dietary intake of arichadonic acid (from meat) might
overwhelm this feedback mechanism: which perhaps explains
why Are Waerland's blinding headaches left him for good when
he turned vegetarian.

Cows' milk contains no GLA, but human breast-milk
does – which may explain why poor bottle-fed babies so often
get eczema. And for some time it was thought that human breast-milk was the only source of GLA. So one of the most exciting medical discoveries of recent times has been a reliable plant
source of GLA: the pretty evening primrose or *Oenothera bien-
nis*, for long a despised weed of railway embankments. Evening
primrose oil is now being tried out with considerable success in
a huge range of illnesses, including multiple sclerosis, premenstrual syndrome, eczema and schizophrenia. Nowadays other,
even richer, sources of GLA are becoming available, so its price
is coming down to more realistic levels. Borage oil (23 per cent
GLA) and blackcurrant-seed oil (16 per cent GLA) are both
now available commercially, and are usually cheaper than
evening-primrose oil (9 per cent GLA).

EFAs generally are vital in the prevention of cardiovascular disease, since they keep cholesterol levels under control. But
in the affairs of the heart, it is one of the Omega-3 family in
particular which is now making headlines in the medical and
scientific journals: eicosapentaenoic acid, or EPA for short. It
can be produced inside the body from its dietary precursor,
alpha-linolenic acid, but our bodies aren't very good at this, and
a much more reliable supply of the stuff is found in the bodies
of cold-water fish who have feasted on alpha-linolenic-acid-rich
plankton.

The major role of E P A is to reduce the tendency of blood platelets to clump together and form clots, which is why coronary thrombosis is unknown among Eskimos still living on a primitive diet. Trials of a commercial form of this E P A, called Max E P A, as well as the cod-liver oil produced by Seven Seas, have both given highly promising results in heart disease. Doctors and researchers are also studying the effects of linseed-oil supplements, as Sinclair had done in the early sixties. And in other studies, subjects have been plied with mackerel, salmon and salmon oil: blood fat levels invariably fall, and so does blood-clotting time, reducing the likelihood of coronary thrombosis. Sinclair himself had studied the Eskimo diet in 1940, and since it is known that Eskimos bleed very easily, had put himself on to a diet of nothing but seal meat, fish and water for a hundred days – with true researcher's dedication – in order to establish just how and why fish oils should prevent blood clotting. At the end of the time he felt fit and well, his high-density lipoprotein count had shot up, his cholesterol levels and platelet counts had dropped – but he bled abnormally easily.

The E FA story – as much perhaps as the refining of our carbohydrates – makes clear how deadly has been the industrialization of our food supply. For E FAs are not lone wolves. Without a host of other key nutrients – B_6, zinc, vitamin E, selenium – we cannot manufacture or make use of them. Other threats to their production are ageing, diabetes, too much alcohol, too much sugar in our diets and radiation.

But while other researchers have pinpointed this or that dietary deficiency – of B vitamins, of fibre, of vitamin C – resulting from industrialization, a Pennsylvania physician, Donald Rudin, argues forcefully that what he calls the Modernization Diseases are caused by the lethal interactions of a large number of adulterations of our food and drink. We are suffering, he says, from Synergistic Malnutrition.

It is generally assumed that Americans were eating more animal fats by the seventies than in the early years of the century. In fact Americans were eating 76 per cent *less* butter in 1975 than in 1910: it's the consumption of vegetable oil, much of it in the form of margarine, that has zoomed – by a whole 68 per cent. Most of these oils are partially hydrogenated. In the process, points out Rudin, the vital Omega-3 E FAs are selectively destroyed, while hydrogenation produces, in their place, a number of chemically altered *trans* fatty acids. (The US diet contained a daily 4·4 g a head in 1910; in 1972 it had risen to

12·1 g – and may have climbed higher since, as more and more people switched to 'healthy' margarine.) The deformed *trans* fats, Rudin suggests, block the body's uptake of normal EFAs to act as anti-nutrients. Margarine, in other words, is 'a nutritional time-bomb – and yet no one has even bothered to test it for its safety through the life cycle of primates'.

The Omega-3 family of essential fatty acids are, according to what has become known as the Rudin hypothesis, 'a newly discovered, universal, tissue-level hormonal system . . . which controls every function in our body – physical, mental and behavioural'. Through hydrogenation, refining of our grains and other adulterations, 'we have been ravaging our lipid chemistry *in every way it is chemically possible to do*'. As a result, 80 per cent of the Omega-3 EFAs in our diet are destroyed, along with their essential co-factors. And adulteration has also introduced anti-nutrients such as vast quantities of *trans* and saturated fats, cholesterol, and refined sugar.

Man today, suggests Rudin grimly, should view himself as 'a member of an animal colony which is fed by a multitude of unschooled keepers who . . . unchecked by responsible experts, introduce endless food and dietary novelties with little concern for the collective result and no attempt to conduct elementary tests of safety'.

The Rudin hypothesis underscores what current research makes more and more obvious: that it is the synergistic action of nutrients that is crucial to our health. Deficiency of any one may be the weak or missing link that snaps the chain.

Even fifteen years ago, Roger Williams could already point to massive research showing up one nutrient after another as crucial to the protection of our vulnerable hearts. More studies carried out since have stressed and re-stressed the importance of every single nutrient he discussed, among them vitamin C.

In 1983, a scientific study was picked up and published by newspapers throughout the USA under the banner headline: 'Vitamin C does not Lower Cholesterol'. In this study, a group of volunteers taking high daily doses of ascorbic acid had done no better than the control group taking no extra: their serum cholesterol levels had remained almost unchanged. What the authors of the study failed to point out, however, was that *all* the participants had starting levels of cholesterol which were already in the lowest 25 per cent of recorded ranges. The researchers made no mention, either, of the work done by Dr Emil Ginter, of Bratislava in Czechoslovakia, who has been studying vitamin C with his team since 1959. To study the effects of vitamin C deprivation on the arteries, Ginter took guinea-pigs, who – like man – cannot synthesize their own vitamin C. Pre-study photographs of their aortas, using an electron-scan microscope, showed beautifully regular rows of endothelial cells lining healthy aortas. After just a fortnight on diets deprived of vitamin C, the aortas now looked like bare lunar landscapes, with eroded cells, and debris beginning to accumulate. Two months later, they suggested scrapyards, choked with a jetsam of cell debris, fibrin and cholesterol. Ginter and his team went on to show that in the absence of vitamin C, the liver continues to produce cholesterol, but can no longer convert it into bile acids for excretion, and it begins to pile up in those arteries.

Other studies suggest that vitamin C may actually help wash out existing plaque from aortas. But it would be surprising if vitamin C were not vital to the health of the heart, since the arterial walls depend on this vitamin for their health and general resistance.

In the mid-seventies, a cardiac specialist carrying out open-heart surgery was able to coin a new name for a heart attack: coronary vasospasm. In mid-operation he actually saw his patient's heart go into spasm: when he touched it, it was locked rigid, shutting off the blood supply to the heart. The quick-thinking surgeon instantly ordered an intravenous surge of magnesium, the heart relaxed and the patient survived. Here was the explanation of the 'silent' heart attacks which had baffled heart specialists for years, and which may account for as much as 20 per cent of coronary deaths, where there is little or no atherosclerosis to explain them. The heart muscle needs calcium to contract, and magnesium to relax; and a series of complex chemical interactions keeps the calcium–magnesium balance carefully tuned in the cells of the heart muscle. A deficiency of magnesium wrecks this balance: the cells take up too much calcium, or are unable to pump it out, and vasospasm may be the fatal result.

In 1976, at a conference on heart disease, Dr Charles Shamberger and Dr Charles Willis displayed a map of the United States on which heavily shaded areas showed where heart disease struck most often, and most fatally. Then they superimposed on it another map, on which were shaded the areas where a trace element, selenium, was most deficient. The shaded areas on both maps corresponded with eerie exactitude:

they included Connecticut, New York, Massachusetts and Ohio . . . and the district of Columbia, where the heart-disease deathrate was 22 per cent above the national average. The light, selenium-rich areas included Texas, Oklahoma, Alabama, Kansas . . . and the city of Colorado Springs, which can proudly claim a heart deathrate 67 per cent below the national average. It's barely thirty years since the trace element selenium was first recognized as an essential nutrient, but from a lowly position at the end of the chorus line, it has already advanced to star billing.

Its most important function may be as a component of the antioxidant enzyme, glutathione peroxidase. Free radicals sound like a bunch of left-wing activists.* In fact they are potentially lethal molecular fragments formed when polyunsaturated fats in the blood react with oxygen to turn rancid, liberating these semi-stable peroxides in the process. Free radicals survive only for microseconds – but that's long enough for them to do plenty of damage to cell walls throughout the body, as they touch off chain reactions that leave a trail of havoc in their wake. Glutathione peroxidase stops the whole production line in its tracks. If Washington pathologist Dr Earl Benditt is right – and his theory is widely accepted today – free radicals may be the villain of the piece in atherosclerosis. He first theorized nearly twenty years ago that the trigger for plaque formation isn't excess cholesterol, but damage to the arterial cell wall by free radicals. The damaged cell mutates and begins to multiply – as in cancer – producing a bump in the smooth arterial wall, and turbulence as the smooth, laminar flow of blood eddies round it.

The body's defence system rushes white blood corpuscles to the spot and these then die, depositing their debris, and the disaster area is cordoned off by bandages of cholesterol and calcium.

Like selenium, vitamin E or tocopherol is a powerful antioxidant. But for years, merely mentioning this controversial nutrient to a heart specialist was enough to put him at grave risk of high blood pressure. The case for vitamin E was first argued by two Canadian doctors, the brothers William and

*New York-based Argentinian Professor Bazan likes to tell the story of a colleague who flew to Argentina during the regime of the Generals to deliver an important research paper at a medical conference on cardiovascular disease. He was held up for three days at the frontier by intelligence agents alarmed by the paper's title: 'The Movement of Free Radicals out of Red Cells'.

Evan Shute, who claimed to have successfully treated 40,000 cardiac patients, wrote paper after paper, and finally published a popular book. Thanks to the Shutes, vitamin E became a health-food-store bestseller, and hundreds of thousands of Americans began taking regular supplements. It did their hearts a world of good, they agreed. Their accounts, together with the work of the Shutes, were dismissed by orthodox cardiac specialists as anecdotal, and worse, and the Shutes were severely criticized for not having carried out double-blind studies. Biochemist Richard Passwater points out that neither aspirin nor digitalis have ever been subjected to double-blind trial, though millions of doctors have relied on them. Nor for that matter has the bypass operation – which doesn't seem to deter heart surgeons from performing thousands annually.

Passwater himself collected records from thousands of people who had been taking vitamin E for up to ten years, with the help of the magazine *Prevention*. More than 80 per cent of those who already had heart disease reported improvement, among them angina patients who had been able to throw away their nitroglycerin pills. And vitamin E emerged as a doughty champion for the heart: in one group of 2,508 people between fifty and ninety-eight years old who had been taking vitamin E daily for ten years, there were only four cases of heart disease – less than half of 1 per cent of the national average.

Vitamin E appears to work for hearts in several ways: it helps stop blood platelets sticking together to form clots and helps dissolve them if they do form; it increases the blood supply of oxygen; and it helps keep cholesterol levels down.

Applying all this knowledge, doctors are beginning to find that there is an alternative to bypass surgery, even in advanced cases of atherosclerosis; that cholesterol levels and high blood pressure can be lowered by diet more safely than – and just as effectively as – by drugs; and that the threat of thrombosis can be warded off by nutritional means. At his Environmental Clinic in Tacoma, Washington, biochemist Jeffrey Bland has records on more than 10,000 coronary patients. On an aggressive programme that combines exercise, diet, stress reduction, weight management and therapeutic nutrition, more than two thirds of these patients have an 80 per cent improvement within a year, without either drugs or surgery.

Millions of diabetics have learned, too, that insulin shots don't have to be part of the daily ritual.

The public, as usual, got there long before most of its medical advisers. Since 1968, not only have saturated fat and cholesterol consumption nosedived, but literally millions of people have started taking regular supplements of vitamin C and vitamin E, the twin stars today of the supplement business.

Sales of wholemeal bread are rising, just as those of white bread are slowly declining. And fibre-rich muesli, an excellent source of Omega-3 fatty acids, is slowly nudging high-sugar cereals off the supermarket shelves.

24
Diet and
Delinquency

They found him with the girl when they burst into the empty house waving their flashlights and shouting. The six-year-old girl was naked. The twenty-one-year-old boy seemed dazed. They dragged him away and threw him into jail while the little girl was driven weeping home to her parents. At the preliminary hearing next day he was charged with kidnapping and child molestation: ugly, too-common crimes in our big cities. He would get twenty years, if the judge went by the book. And to safeguard him from the violent disapproval of other prisoners, he would spend those twenty years in isolation: he had already been badly beaten up in the bus on the way back to jail.

His family and friends couldn't believe it. Such a quiet, kindly boy, they said, he'd never hurt a fly. By a brutal irony, he was a teacher's aid and a child-abuse counsellor. He must have been out of his mind, they said. Then somebody suggested to the boy's weeping, frantic mother that she should contact Alexander Schauss. If anyone can help, they told her, that guy can.

She finally got to him late on Sunday night; he was already in bed, with the beginnings of flu, a sore throat. Listening to her pleas, her explanations, though, he agreed to take on the case. At 4.30 next morning he was on his way. By noon, with a splitting head and a soaring temperature, he was reading through the thick police files, and questioning the boy's family. This is my kind of case, he thought.

He learned that the weedy, 5 ft 5 in boy had a background of deprivation and disability. As a baby he had not been breast-fed: instead, at his grandmother's suggestion, he was fed Karo syrup mixed with concentrated evaporated milk. As a child he was hyperactive, emotionally disturbed, and underdeveloped. He had every allergy going. Later on, he got meningitis, and then hepatitis. And at the age of nine they found out he was diabetic. But the family lived on junk food anyway, and he never learned to take his insulin well. When his parents took him out to a restaurant to celebrate his twenty-first birthday, he had had no insulin for two days. During that birthday celebration he drank seven highballs and four tequilas in four and a half hours and left the restaurant at 2.30 a.m. That night he still didn't take any insulin. Next morning he got up at his usual time, 8.30 a.m., in a daze. A friend came by: how about a celebration drink? They drank four highballs and then sat in the car smoking a little pot. At 2 p.m., after 3 cups of black coffee, a candy bar and some potato chips, the friend dropped him off at school. Half an hour later, he drove to the City Park. Three children were playing there, eating popcorn. 'Share it with me!' he cried, holding on to the little girl. He took her to his car and they drove around for half an hour. The rest was a blank – till the shouting and the flashlights.

Children who knew him were in tears, because they were so sure the police had the wrong person. His behaviour was bizarre, totally out of character. 'What he did was situational – unique,' says Schauss.

Such walking metabolic disasters are common in our society today. They are conceived by mothers who drink, smoke, down endless cups of coffee and live on junk food during the pregnancy; they are fed from birth on artificial sweetened formulas; they are weaned on to refined and processed food out of tins; as they grow older, they are accustomed to a diet of junk food and snacks, with a Coke and a Big Mac to mark a festive occasion. How can we expect such people to think straight, reason clearly, perceive the consequences of their actions, asks Schauss, when their brains are starved of the nutrients that they need for normal function?

'We're just beginning to learn about the effect of these nutrient deficiencies on human beings,' says Schauss. 'We can't just go on locking people up. If there's something wrong we've got to find out what it is and start treating it. Society is not well served by our refusal to face these facts.'[1]

Can the wrong diet actually cloud our minds and affect our behaviour as well as injuring our health? Does junk food breed delinquency? Can violence be triggered by what we eat – drink – inhale?

Most people are still outraged by such suggestions, which they see as part of a disastrously 'soft' approach to crime. It took Schauss years to arrive at such questions himself. But he was familiar with crimes of violence from an early age. He grew up in one of the most deprived parts of New York, an area ravaged by the gang wars of the fifties and early sixties.

> Rape, muggings, robbery, it got so bad that an old person couldn't go to the bank for fear of having her purse snatched. I once saw a father cover his child with liquor and set light to her. There were heroin junkies shooting up on the stoop in every street. That's how bad it was. That's partly why I was drawn to the correctional system.[2]

At the University of New Mexico, on a four-year scholarship, Schauss studied sociology and history, as well as taking an advanced course in criminology. 'I was kind of probing through these questions of diet at the same time as being brainwashed into accepting all the theories and the premonitions and the assumptions and the conjectures of those disciplines I was studying – history – sociology – chemistry – biology – psychology. But the notion of nutrition was never there.'

Students in the senior year of the criminology course were required to put in twenty hours weekly in some correctional facility: Schauss was taken on at the state's largest state probation and parole department in Albuquerque, gradually became addicted to the work, and stayed on at the end of the university year: at twenty-one, he became America's youngest probation–parole officer.

'Conditions were horrendous,' he recalls.

> We had 14,500 cases a year and there were nine of us. My introduction to the real world of work was something like the seventy-to-eighty-hour week young doctors put in. We never heard of the forty-hour week. I didn't know it was going to be like that. I didn't know that I would still be talking to a child in the detention centre at 2 a.m., and that I would have to be in court ready with my reports at 8.30 a.m., and that that meant maybe two hours of sleep. I had to learn to type, too, because we had a very small secretarial staff who came in at 8.30 a.m. and left at 5 p.m. You were so busy you didn't realize how much you hurt, and the deep depression of what you were doing. I quickly found out, too, that I simply didn't know what I was doing; I didn't feel that my colleagues knew either, and they had the sense to admit it. And all the time I felt, there's something else.

Then in his first year, Schauss was landed with one of the worst cases the probation department had ever dealt with: a boy of fourteen who had been in and out of detention for almost every crime in the book, including arson, burglary and drug offences: a nonstop one-man criminal justice show, they called him.

This master criminal, to Schauss's amazement, turned out to be a weedy, slight boy. Schauss put him through a battery of psychological evaluation tests, concluded that there was no real psychological problem, engaged a lawyer for the boy and turned up in court on the day of the hearing ready to recommend that for the protection of society, he should be sent to a detention centre for at least four years.

Just as the judge was about to pass sentence, the lawyer interrupted him. 'Wait a minute,' he said, 'you can't just sentence this kid, we don't know why he's doing all this. His probation officer hasn't really evaluated him for anything. Maybe there's something physically wrong with the child.'

Schauss felt insulted: hadn't he spent hours testing the child and writing up his reports? 'Oh come on,' he protested, 'you're not going to tell me that physiology is the cause of deviant behaviour.' The judge paused. 'Mr Schauss, why don't you get a doctor to take a look at this child?' 'You mean, a psychiatrist?' queried Schauss. 'No,' said the judge. 'A paediatrician.'

Two days later, Schauss was called by the paediatrics department of the hospital to which the boy had been sent. He was suffering, they had found, from a chromosomal abnormality known as Klinefelter's syndrome: he had a small penis, no pubic hair and the breasts of a fourteen-year-old girl, and he was quite weak.

Schauss was devastated. 'Here I was, about to send him off to a reformatory for four years. That child would have been abused and raped continually from the first moment that they forced him into a shower. How would *I* deal with a condition like that myself, in macho New Mexico? Who am I to be working with these kinds of children? What am I doing here?'

It became his constant preoccupation to find out whether other physiological factors might contribute to this type of deviant behaviour. Immediately, he was confronted by the whole issue of nutrition. But he soon discovered that if he even mentioned the possibility of a connection between diet and crime, his colleagues would look at him as if he were half-mad. 'Alex, don't jeopardize your career and your reputation,' they would beg him. The more resistance Schauss encountered, the more curious he became. It struck him, too, that the whole field of correction was little more than conjecture, intuition, hunches and guesswork, with a great deal of rational and interesting theory put forward to account for deviant behaviour, but absolutely no scientific proof of its efficacy. And he made a decision: he had to stop being just a 'sociologist-criminologist', and develop the scientific basis for a much more multi-disciplinary approach.

Schauss's drive and energy have always been phenomenal, fuelled by one hundred per cent commitment to the task in hand and a formidable capacity for sustained hard work. Over the next nine years he put himself back to school in every hour of spare time, mastering the basic sciences of this physiological approach, reading through thousands of papers, combing through the scientific literature for any evidence of a connection between what people eat and the way they behave.

One day he picked up a copy of the British magazine *Ecology*. 'Does Lead Create Criminals?' queried the cover. Inside, he devoured a long article in which Derek Bryce-Smith reviewed the dozens of clues to a connection between lead toxicity and disturbed or antisocial behaviour. Among them was a US National Academy of Sciences Report that concluded: 'many children with documented prior attacks of symptomatic lead poisoning develop hostile, aggressive and destructive behaviour . . .' Maybe, suggested Bryce-Smith, we should treat vandals and football hooligans by administering penicillamine to lower lead levels, rather than giving them jail sentences.[3]

Schauss also studied gastroenterology, enzymology and nutrition. He devoured the latest research on vitamins, minerals, amino acids and heavy metal intoxication. He learned of Randolph's and Mandell's work on allergies and the way they could affect mood and mind. Shrewdly, too – in this minefield of scientific controversy – he learned statistics and methodology. Throughout his work in this field, he has been at pains to deal in terms of exact science as far as possible.

Meanwhile, his career was going ahead by leaps and bounds. The governor and legislature of South Dakota had just launched a radical programme to deinstitutionalize their juvenile justice system. They wanted new men, fresh ideas. A juvenile court judge, who had been impressed by Schauss when the two men met on a training course, suggested he apply for the vacant post of Assistant State Administrator. At twenty-six, Schauss was startlingly young for the job. But they hired him.

One of the group home facilities he was responsible for evaluating was Our Home, in Huron, South Dakota. When he visited it, Schauss was impressed by the positive attitude of its house-parents. 'We try to keep our children here for as short a time as possible,' they told him; 'we don't want them to become institutionalized and forget the importance of family life and school friends.' He stayed to join the children for lunch, and learn more about the way it was run. Rather apologetically, its directors explained that they had some ideas about diet, which he might consider a little odd. They liked the children to have completely natural food, so they grew their own vegetables and froze the surplus for winter; sweet sodas, tea and coffee were all banned, there were no sugar-bowls on the tables, and the bread and cereals served were all whole grain.

Schauss checked their record as soon as he got back to his office. He found that although they were getting some of the worst cases in the whole state, the time the children spent there was between three and six months – never longer. The same child might be sent to any one of several much more impressive facilities, where the staff had received long and sophisticated training – and be there for two years. Our Home was saving the state of South Dakota significant sums of money. Perhaps it was the evident care and humanity of its directors that was working such magic? Other homes – in Minnesota and Michigan – had the same positive approach, the same concern for the children, Schauss found. But their children still stayed for eighteen months to two years. There *was* a variable; and perhaps it was what he had always suspected: diet.

'I was now so convinced I was on to something that I could hardly sleep nights,' he relates. 'But I knew I had to be ultra-cautious, ultra-scientific.' He had no controlled studies to quote, and he knew he would need hard scientific evidence to convince people. 'I couldn't accuse criminology of theory, intuition and guesswork if that was all *I* had to offer – and that *was* all I had, at this time. But I knew I had to get out of Corrections to do it.'

South Dakota were a step away from closing down their correctional institutes when elections brought the Republican party back to power. Schauss knew a Republican governor would be totally unsympathetic to their programme, decided the time was ripe for another move – and became the nation's youngest judicially appointed chief probation officer in the state of Washington, on the west coast. At once he began instructing the staff in the 'new' science. His first lecture was on Derek Bryce-Smith's research into lead and its effect on behaviour.

Soon afterwards, one of Schauss's younger probation officers came up to him in great excitement to say that he had come across a bad case of lead poisoning among his clients. The man had had a criminal record since the age of twelve and was considered highly dangerous. He was also an incoherent psychotic; psychologists had rated him schizophrenic. Schauss was inclined to be sceptical – it's a medical school truism that the day after you lecture on nephritis, students start spotting cases among the patients – but finally agreed that perhaps the man should have medical tests done on him. The probation officer managed to find a doctor who ran not only the standard blood and urine tests on him, but also a hair-trace mineral analysis, a technique new to Schauss and then in its infancy. Hair is a cellular product excreted by the body, and analysis of the hair closest to a subject's head – in other words, the most recent growth – provides a useful and fairly reliable record of the way the body uses, stores and disposes of elements such as zinc and copper, as well as recording dangerous levels of such toxic metals as lead and cadmium.

Two weeks later the doctor called to say that he could now account for the man's behaviour: he had the highest levels ever seen of lead, cadmium and mercury. 'I can straighten him out for you,' went on the doctor. For three weeks the man was escorted daily to his doctor's surgery for detoxification treatment: he had vitamin C fed into him by intravenous drip, he swallowed a daily total of eighty-four mineral and vitamin tablets, he was given supplements of the detoxifying amino acids methionine, cysteine and cystine, as well as quantities of the onions and garlic in which they are heavily concentrated. And in the third week – as it happened, when Schauss was present – he woke up from his psychosis. Now he was almost a normal human being again.

That year Schauss's department was hosting the state Correctional Association meeting. Attendance was high. Word had spread rapidly of Schauss's radical new approach to the problem of juvenile delinquency, he had discussed it at high-level committee meetings, he had presented his theories on the radio and television, and with his impressive track record, his colleagues in the correction system were eager to hear more.

He decided to present this exceptional case as confirmation of what he had been saying, and he put the man's mother on stage to do it.

She spoke for an hour and a half to an electrified audience. She told of an educated family, of well-behaved children, of a boy who had done well in school and never incurred so much as a traffic fine – until by degrees he turned into a monster. She spoke of all the family had been through – the anguish, the special education classes, and finally the verdict from a psychiatrist that the boy should have a lobotomy. If he did, they had been told, he would probably be a vegetable by the time he was thirty. Without it, he would always need psychotropic drugs to calm him down. Tears running down her cheeks, she ended: 'But because a probation officer knew what he was doing, and tested him for something that fitted in with his signs and symptoms, my son is today entering junior college.'

The boy's sister later solved the riddle of where so much lead came from. Just before his problems began, the family had moved to an island in Puget Sound, not far from one of the largest copper smelters in the world, which was emitting quantities not only of copper, but of lead, arsenic and cadmium too. The boy had an unusual liking for shellfish, and ate oysters and clams by the dozen. But, as every marine biologist knows, shellfish are toxic metal scavengers, accumulating high levels of these dangerous metals.

Schauss gave the story to the local press – and woke up suddenly to the fact that his theories might come into collision with powerful vested interests. The smelting business employed 3,200 people – and Schauss found himself the victim of a press smear campaign.

A year later he changed jobs yet again – this time to become official instructor for the State Training Commission. Instead of supervising a staff of fifty probation officers, he would be planning training courses for some 6,500 people, from guards all the way up to chief probation officers and judges, in the state correction system. By this time he had tested his theory on dozens of the probation cases he had always continued to handle personally, and a randomized trial he had set up had produced strong confirmatory evidence. Now in 1978 it snowballed. His ideas were having an impact nationwide. From states as far afield as Michigan, Texas, Nebraska, even British Columbia, the calls came flooding in for Schauss to tell them about his revolutionary new approach to crime.

He was also meeting people who, he now learned, had been quietly working away in the same field for years already, among them psychiatrists and probation officers who had given evidence to the evergreen McGovern Committee when, in 1977, it began a new set of hearings on the links between diet and mental illness. Psychiatrist Michael Lesser had been treating cases of depression, anxiety and psychotic behaviour with diet and vitamin therapy since 1970. Ohio probation officer Barbara Reed had watched her failures turn up over and over again in court, until – inspired by a Gayelord Hauser book – she began wondering if diet might have anything to do with their cases. On questioning, she found that very few of her clients were eating anything remotely resembling a balanced diet. One man lived on potato chips, baked beans and sweetened soda pop. By 1973, she was taking them through a written questionnaire to test them for hypoglycaemia, and getting them to change their diet. Lean meat, fresh or frozen fruit and vegetables, fruit juices, herb teas and milk, nuts, seeds, some health foods and cold-pressed oils were allowed; strictly forbidden were white sugar, white flour and anything made from them, pastries, cola and soda drinks, processed foods, and alcohol. By 1975, she was getting the worst cases to deal with – and at least one judge was telling them: 'Mrs Reed is going to put you on a diet and you will stay on it or go to jail.' Out of 252 prisoners she had put on her diet, and on vitamin supplements, she told the McGovern Committee, none who had stayed on it had been back in court. The physical as well as the mental improvement in some of her clients had been dramatic.[4]

In 1979 Schauss and Barbara Reed were invited together on to the Phil Donahue show – a TV programme that reaches an audience of some 20 million nationwide. In the hour-long programme, ex-probationers told in moving, simple words how they had been able to think straight and go straight after Schauss or Reed had taken them off their terrible fast-food junk-food diets, and got them eating plain healthy food for the first time in their lives. The programme shook a nation. Suddenly millions of Americans woke up to the idea that maybe soaring crime rates weren't as inevitable as death and taxes, that there was something that could be done.

The widening impact his ideas were having brought its own problems. Calls were coming in from all over the States, and they wanted to hear him on nutrition and criminal behaviour. But the job he had been hired to do was strictly for the

State of Washington, and he was supposed to be coordinating instruction in the whole range of correctional activity, not just on the role of diet in delinquent behaviour. He was finding it harder and harder to organize classes on riot control and cell search when his mind was gripped by the study that had become an obsession with him.

Destiny once more intervened, in the person of Dr Clifford Simonson, a criminologist from Ohio and an ex-US-army general with years of experience and wide-ranging contacts at the highest level. He listened with interest to Schauss's theories, grasped his consuming need to work full-time in this one field, and supplied the answer: the Institute of Biosocial Research, set up by private funding, with himself as director and Schauss as staff associate. When Simonson left to take up a new university appointment, Schauss moved up to become director, a post he has held ever since.

Now Schauss could respond to invitations from all over the States, from Maine to Los Angeles, from Miami to Anchorage. He was still very reserved in his approach. These are possibilities worth looking at, he would say; here's what we know from isolated experiences; this is what Barbara Reed found, this was my experience. But the response was already enthusiastic – not so much because of Schauss's impressive credentials as instructor but because he spoke from experience and with insight: he was an ex-chief probation officer, and chief POs and wardens were the lynchpin of the entire correctional system.

'The Californians were marvellous,' recalls Schauss. 'They started trying it out at once – San Luis Obispo, Los Angeles County, San Diego – then two months later I'd get a call: "It works! Schauss, you're right!" And little by little, I built up a huge support.' Chief probation officers were listening to him now, and telling judges what they had heard. He was invited to address the national juvenile-court judges' meeting, the national district attorney meeting. He was interviewed by the press, invited to speak on radio and TV.

Over the years, his classes have grown into highly structured seven- and eight-day intensive training courses for professionals within the correctional system. He has conducted more than a hundred such programmes, not only in the United States but in Canada, New Zealand, Australia and South Africa, too. The state in the forefront of research is Alabama, where Schauss and his team spent ten days over four months training the entire youth services staff, from the top man down. Schauss

emphasizes that his approach is useless unless the staff themselves are prepared to become models for their delinquents and
criminals: smoking, drinking and endless cups of coffee are
habits out of place in the brave new world of Schauss. (He
himself is super-fit, lean, clear-skinned, doesn't drink, doesn't
smoke, goes for a regular morning run.)

In the book that he wrote for his classes in 1980 – *Diet,
Crime and Delinquency* – in the *International Journal of Biosocial
Research* that his institute publishes, and in his lectures and writings today, Schauss can point to a volume of hard scientific
facts, as well as impressive anecdotal evidence, from highly
reliable and trained observers, in favour of his approach.

Preliminary findings from current studies suggest that the
incidence of food and chemical sensitivities may be as high as
90 per cent among juvenile offenders. As well as physical symptoms, these can provoke disturbances of the brain chemistry in
which the normal balance between inhibitory and excitatory
function is deranged: literally, the victim can no longer 'think
straight', his judgement is warped, his perception of the possible consequences of his actions is clouded. Challenging their
patients with minute doses of foods or chemicals to which they
are sensitive, after a five-day abstention, clinical ecologists have
been able to induce every kind of abnormal mental state, from
raging psychosis to silent, withdrawn depression, and including
hyper-aggressive behaviour. Schauss shows his audiences a
video of a real-life Dennis the Menace, in which a charming,
lively five-year-old turns into a monster five minutes after nib-
bling a banana – scratching, biting and kicking his mother,
wrecking his toys, hurling books to the ground and weeping
with misery at the confusion of his small mind.

One of the commonest allergens, Schauss has found, has
been ordinary milk. Researchers have often been puzzled by
the inordinate quantities of milk some delinquents were drinking – as much as 120 US fl oz (3·5 l) a day in some cases – and in
one group of offenders tested, 88 per cent were found to be
sensitive to milk.

Nutritional deficiencies may also contribute to deviant
behaviour. Deficiency of vitamin B_1 is common in those eating
an unbalanced diet high in refined carbohydrates. In a Cleve-
land study, adolescents who were found low in this vitamin were
described as 'impulsive, highly irritable, aggressive, angered
easily, and sensitive to criticism'. When they were supplemented with vitamin B_1, their behaviour improved.

Iron deficiency may be another powerful contributory factor. Iron is highly concentrated, it has been shown, in critical neurotransmitter pathways in the brain; it is vital to left hemisphere functioning – that side of the brain which controls logical, analytical thought; and its deficiency may lead to impairments of judgement and reasoning as well as lowered ability to learn. In a highly intriguing study carried out in Fairfax County, Virginia, 242 offenders were offered freshly squeezed orange juice for breakfast, lunch and dinner, and compared to 239 'controls'. In the juice drinkers, antisocial behaviour declined by 47 per cent. Orange juice contains vitamins B_1 and C, and folic acid: vitamin C promotes non-heme iron absorption by as much as six times. And iron deficiencies have been shown by nationwide nutrition surveys to be more common across the social board than those of any other nutrient.[5]

Chemical pollution of the environment is indicted by Schauss as a key factor in rising crime and delinquency rates today. Using hair analysis and blood serum testing, researchers have found a correlation far too common to be coincidental between high levels of lead, cadmium, aluminium and copper, and aggressive or deviant behaviour. When these are treated by supplements of such nutrients as zinc and vitamin C, carefully tailored to each individual's need, the resulting improvements in behaviour have to be seen to be believed. Violent criminals often have significantly higher levels of lead, together with low levels of a vital trace element, cobalt. Copper is another essential nutrient, but when zinc is low, copper levels can rise and become toxic to the brain; often leading to irrational and aggressive behaviour in adolescents; zinc and copper need to be kept in balance. Supplementation with measured doses of zinc has been successfully used to calm aggressive behaviour.

High levels of lead and cadmium have been shown in careful studies to be particularly common in slow and backward children. As child psychiatrist Alan Cott has pointed out, it is typically the backward child of today who becomes, first, the social drop-out and finally the delinquent or the criminal of tomorrow. And the glue-sniffing, the smoking and the drinking which give him a passing 'high', or make him feel that he belongs somewhere, if only in the school's underworld, will be hard to resist. In 1967 the US Public Health Service reported that 75 per cent of delinquent children in New York were illiterate. And a Bureau of Prisons Report revealed that 90 per cent of those in federal prisons had reading problems.

The whole field of heavy metal intoxication and its consequences has huge implications for education. Schauss suggests that it may be possible to identify potential trouble-makers by the biochemical markers shown up in various clinical assessment techniques, and help them before a behavioural problem actually develops. In future, he has suggested, schools might routinely order a biochemical evaluation of their unruly children. The cost of hair or blood analysis, blood tests, dietary changes and – if needed – nutritional supplements is trifling, he points out, compared with the cost of psychological evaluation and counselling; and microscopic compared with the cost to the individual, and ultimately the state, of delinquency and crime.

Schauss's great strength has been his insistence on developing a strong scientific underpinning for his approach. Much of what he has been saying today has been the common currency of health writers criticizing poor diet and modern processed foods for decades now. But Schauss asks his audiences to accept only those findings which have been backed up by a solid body of experimental evidence, or by studies carried out according to the most rigorous scientific criteria. He is not interested in speculation: he criticizes sloppy work or woolly-minded conjecture just as harshly when it supports him as when it is put forward by his antagonists. And he stresses over and over again that diet is *not* a panacea: that nobody is saying that poor diet *causes* crime. 'Behaviour,' he says, 'is far too complex to be reduced to "You are what you eat".' What he is saying is that diet is evidently a highly important factor in many cases which we have no right to ignore, and that the more severe a person's psychological problems, the more likely he is to have physiological problems too. 'What we have begun to realize,' he says, 'is that when a person is placed on a good diet, at least it gives him or her the chemistry to respond to direction, information, to education. There have been a lot of programmes, a lot of studies – and not one of them has failed to show substantial positive results.'

Among studies which have convinced even sceptics have been those carried out by a California criminologist, Stephen Schoenthaler, who was no believer himself, initially. In April 1981 he was commissioned to carry out a large-scale controlled study for the Los Angeles County Board of Supervisors. After reviewing the evidence in Schauss's *Diet, Crime and Delinquency*, the Los Angeles County probation department had already banned candies, soda, chocolate, sugar and refined-flour products from its juvenile centres. The Schoenthaler study was designed to see what results this controversial move had produced . . . and when the results came out, two years later, they were startling justification for the ban on junk foods. Among 1,382 inmates in three separate juvenile halls, the incidence of antisocial behaviour dropped by a measurable 44 per cent.[6]

Hard-pressed state administrators and prison authorities have a compelling reason today to take notice of Schauss. The economic cost of rocketing crime rates in the West is becoming year by year a more intolerable burden. In 1983 there were around a million Americans in custody – in jails, detention centres, juvenile homes. Looking after them, or otherwise involved in the criminal justice system were a further 1,163,000 people The total cost to the community of those criminals and delinquents amounts to billions of dollars annually. By 1983 it had already risen to an estimated $32bn annually. In that year, the Governor of California asked his Department of Corrections for a breakdown of the prison figures. He learned with horror that the prison capacity of the state lagged far behind the growth of the prisoner population, which was rising by a hundred weekly. The huge new 550-bed jail just completed at a cost of $90 million would house barely six weeks' intake. And the projected cost per prisoner, it was estimated, could rocket to as much as $85,000 per head annually by 1988.

In Britain, interest in Schauss's, ideas is only just beginning to awaken, but the financial realities of crime make just as grim reading. There are over 47,000 British people behind bars, at an estimated annual cost for 1986–7 of around £639m. With an aggressive new programme of prison-building in the pipeline, these costs are likely to rise sharply in the coming years.

When public-spending budgets the world over are being trimmed back ruthlessly, not even the richest country can afford such massive increases in spending on just one sector. And the public that clamours for harsher jail sentences for crime will clamour even more loudly when the budget for schools, hospitals and social security has to be cut back to pay for it.

The governor of Britain's Maidstone Prison was among those who listened attentively to Schauss when he visited Britain in 1984. His comment was pertiment. 'We shouldn't be doing this in the prisons,' he said. 'The change has got to happen with the parents – and in the schools.'

That, too, is beginning to happen in the United States. Los Angeles city and New York City have led the national move to provide more nourishing junk-free food for the children in their schools.

Given the highly controversial nature of Schauss's work, it would be surprising if it had not come in for bitter criticism. Most of it has come, though, not from within the correctional system, where he has met both respect and open-minded readiness to listen, but from the ever-conservative medical establishment and – inevitably – from the processed-food industry.

> What I'm affecting is companies like Cargill, worth $28 billion and privately owned by one family; I'm affecting General Foods, Kellogg's, Nestlés, Beatrice, General Mills, Coca-Cola. When you see New York City schools – the state's fourth largest food buyers – going for all-junk-free food, what do you think that means in dollars and cents of profit? When you see a million inmates eating less sugar and no packaged or processed food, what do you think that's costing the industry?

One of the bitterest attacks on the Schauss line came from Dr Gregory Gray and his dietician wife Lorraine, who dismissed numbers of careful, well-observed studies as misleading, cast doubts on researchers' accuracy or integrity, misquoted papers, suppressed relevant comments, suggested that if anything did happen, it was probably due to some kind of placebo effect, and concluded that the nutritional approach was inordinately expensive, ineffective, and potentially risky both physically and psychologically. This paper, quoting some sixty references, appeared in the May 1983 issue of the *Journal of Nutrition Education*. Schauss slammed in a concise reply citing fourteen references. So did Schoenthaler and many others. None of these letters were published. Finally, the December issue carried Schauss's comments – now abbreviated to a few lines. Gray's paper was sent – anonymously – to every schools district in the States.

The privately funded California Council against Health Fraud set up a special committee to rubbish Schauss's views, chaired by a woman with no background in social and behavioural sciences. Their report, in a nutshell, carried the same message as the Gray piece: This stuff doesn't work, it's dangerous, and it costs several thousand dollars per child. The report was carried almost word for word in a newsletter published by the American Council on Science and Health.

This council also set up, jointly with the American Medical Association, a three-day forum on nutrition and behaviour, which took place in Washington DC in November 1984. Conspicuous among those not invited to address the two-and-a-half-hour session on nutrition and criminal behaviour were Schauss and Schoenthaler, or any other university-based researcher who had actually done fieldwork on this question. And this crowded evening session was chaired by Dr Gray. But his line-up of speakers failed to impress at least one man present. He rose at the end to comment. He had listened with great interest, he stated, as one speaker after another poured cold water on the suggestion that diet and behaviour might be closely linked. He had not heard any hard evidence that the theory was without validity. In the circumstances he felt strongly that national funding should be forthcoming to investigate the matter fully.

The man was the distinguished psychiatrist, Dr Morris Lipton. Thirteen years earlier, he had headed the American Psychiatric Association Task Force that condemned orthomolecular psychiatry out of hand.

Today, Schauss allows himself to be guardedly optimistic. 'It's beginning,' he says. 'State authorities are starting to fund studies of specific biochemical problems in offenders compared with non-offenders. There's a lot of research going on, a lot of papers being published.'

In Britain, Schauss has now lectured at length on his work. In 1983 the McCarrison Society invited him to address their three-day conference on Nutrition and Mental Health. The following year he was back by special invitation to address a small audience of prison officers and probationers.

And in 1985 he was the star speaker at another conference on nutrition and behaviour, organized at Oxford's John Radcliffe Hospital. Among other speakers were Dr Ian Menzies, a psychiatrist from Dundee who has successfully treated dozens of children with appalling behavioural problems by eliminating allergens from their diet – usually in the form of brightly coloured junk foods and drinks – and Munich neurologist Jo

Egger, who in a full-scale clinical trial at London's Great Ormonde Street Hospital (reported in the *Lancet*) found that behavioural problems and hyperactivity, as well as severe migraine and even epilepsy often abated in children on a diet free of foods to which they were allergic.[7] Troubled Liverpool, with its appalling inner-city problems and its financial plight, may see the first British trial of Schauss's approach: Liverpool social worker John Connor told of a dietary study at a residential assessment centre where the inmates are now eating a healthy wholefood diet.

Paediatrician Dr John Richer, whose idea the conference was, had hoped to stir a little mild interest. In fact it was a sell-out, packing in some 450 family doctors, paediatricians, nurses, psychologists, remedial teachers and health visitors, as well as just plain parents with a problem child.

'Three years ago, I'd have said all you lot were cranks,' was one man's terse comment. 'But not after what I've heard here today.'

25
Self-help – and Self-interest

'**R**ight from the moment Daniel was born, he cried,' recalls his mother. 'He screamed nonstop for eight weeks. He wouldn't breast-feed, could never lie still a minute. He never slept a night through, it was half an hour here and there, I forgot what it was like to have a proper night's sleep.

'The doctors didn't know what to do: they just kept on giving him more and more medicine to try and quiet him down: Vallergan and Triominic and Phenergan, and eventually they even suggested trying Mogadon on him. When he was a little bigger, he'd bang his head all the time, on anything noisy: the more noise he made, the harder he banged – his favourite place was inside the drum of the washing machine. He didn't seem to hurt himself, didn't seem to care; one day he fell right down the staircase from top to bottom, and he just smacked the staircase.'

Daniel was the second child of a young Kent policeman and his wife. Their oldest was a delightful, bright, perfectly normal little girl. Nothing had prepared them for the horrors that lay in store – apart from a mother's fearful conviction that something was terribly wrong. 'I felt dreadful all the time I was pregnant, from the third month he was thrashing around inside me; I felt black and blue by the time he arrived. He was born in just an hour and a half, he lifted his head up straight away, and he began to cry.'

None of the doctors who saw her and Daniel were helpful: none of them showed any interest or wanted to be involved. The desperate couple fell out with their own GP because of the total detachment he projected. 'There's no such thing as hyperactivity,' he told them. He gave them the impression that he blamed them for the child's condition.[1]

Horror stories like this have been routine reading for Sally Bunday and her mother Irene Colquhoun ever since they founded the Hyperactive Children's Support Group in 1977.

Sally knows exactly how the mothers of these manic babies feel. Her own son – now a healthy, normal teenager – was born hyperactive. Within days of his birth, he was struggling out of his Moses basket; he smashed up three cots; he never wanted to be cuddled, seldom slept more than fifteen minutes at a stretch. Then she learned of the work of US doctor Ben Feingold, the paediatrician whose diet emphasizing additive-free food has been successfully used by thousands of American parents to turn their hyperactive monsters into normal children. Sally was so desperate she was ready to try anything. The results were near-miraculous. 'Within five days he was happy and cheerful, he went off to bed like a lamb, and slept right through the night.'

In her astonished relief, Sally told all her friends and relations. Word got round, letters and phone queries began trickling in, and soon the trickle turned into a flood. Responding to an obvious need, Sally and her mother launched the Hyperactive Children's Support Group, which instantly took over their lives. On an average day they receive around sixty letters: any press mention can send the total well over the hundred mark. To date, they reckon they have received and responded to over 150,000 letters from desperate mothers.

> They all say the same thing. 'The doctor can't help or doesn't want to know – please write back by return post, please don't let me down, please.' Reading between the lines, we know that some of the babies are being battered, that some of the parents are suicidal, that there is enormous depression and other major problems. It's whole families that are disturbed, not just one child.[2]

Research has established that the hyperactive baby of today is highly likely to grow up into tomorrow's problem child, delinquent, drop-out, junkie – or even criminal. The problem is bad enough in this country. It is far worse in the USA, where an estimated 10 million children are either hyperactive or else locked into the silent world of autism. Conventional medicine hands them over to the psychiatrist, who treats them with a parade of drugs or with counselling therapy, and usually fails dismally. Treatment by nutrition, correcting vitamin and mineral deficiencies, coping with the effects of toxic doses of lead and other metals, and sorting out allergies is often brilliantly effective. Sally and her mother take fresh heart for their grinding burden of self-imposed toil when they read letters which tell them: 'We can live like a normal family now, instead of a front-line fighting force.'

In the years since they began work, they have seen a considerable change in official medical attitudes – in the last year or so particularly. They find now that many parents are being referred to them by GPs and psychologists; they have letters asking for their help from health visitors, hospitals, residential homes or special schools for disturbed and problem children. They're greatly heartened, too, by the ready response they have had from the food industry, and some supermarkets.

But in all these years they have not received one penny of official financial support, though they have several times applied to the Department of Health. The response is always the same: 'Studies are not conclusive – a lot more work needs to be done.' But of course the work is not being done.

The problems of the hyperactive baby usually start soon after he is conceived, since the cells of the baby's brain and nervous system are laid down in the very first weeks of pregnancy. Significantly, many mothers of hyperactive youngsters report that even in the womb their babies thrashed around restlessly from an early age. Poor diet, alcohol, tobacco, high caffeine intake, intoxication with lead and other heavy metals such as cadmium, now widespread in our environment – all these can play havoc with the fragile developing nervous system of the baby in the womb. Allergy is another possible culprit: such problems are especially common in what are medically termed 'atopic' families – with a history of asthma, migraine, hayfever or eczema.

A jazzed-up nervous system is not the only problem afflicting many babies born today.

> One in four children comes into the world with brain damage leading to learning disabilities; one in twenty-five has eczema, thousands of babies are stillborn or premature, thousands more have congenital abnormalities such as club foot or cleft palate; children today are getting arthritis and cancer. And almost all of it is preventable on the basis of what we already know about nutrition: there has been a huge amount of research done in this field.

This is Belinda Barnes speaking – who often finds it hard to subdue the anger and frustration at so much preventable tragedy. Six years ago she set up Foresight, the Association for the Promotion of Preconceptual Care. She shouldered this appalling burden because, quite simply, she was horrified by what was happening to Britain's babies. 'One way and another, I've been dealing with babies since I was about seventeen. I've had three children of my own, I've bred labradors – and cats – and horses – and the appalling thing is that it's all done so much better for animals in this country. No herd of dairy cattle, no prize mare, no champion bitch would be allowed to breed on anything but a completely adequate diet.'

In the six or seven years since she founded Foresight, she has launched over forty clinics up and down the country, some of them NHS, where both parents – not just the wife – are encouraged to go along for a full medical check-up, screening for heavy-metal problems or allergies, and comprehensive advice about their diet and lifestyle. The Foresight medical advisory committee includes three university professors – among them lead expert Derek Bryce-Smith of Reading – and around forty doctors. But medical disinterest or hostility, together with bureaucratic obtuseness, sometimes wear down even Belinda Barnes's resilient spirits. What sustains her are the marvellous letters that come through her letterbox: 'We keep hearing about exceptionally bright and happy babies; they seldom weigh under 7 lb (3·2 kg), we're endlessly told that they smiled for the first time at three or four days, that they breastfeed well, that there are no problems, that they're happy, contented babies who sleep right through the night.'³ Of encouragement, even of recognition by official medicine, there has so far been no sign.

The mushrooming of such self-help groups has become a phenomenon of the eighties. They have grown up alongside, often in opposition to, the stately quasi-official bodies representing sufferers from specific diseases, who can offer practical help and advice to their members – how to apply for disablement grants, coping with life in a wheelchair and so on – but who tend to parrot the stereotyped view of their distinguished medical advisers: that such afflictions are totally unrelated to diet.

The new-style self-help groups – both here and in the United States – are usually launched by desperate, practical women with first-hand knowledge of the problem from their own or family experience, who have come to realize that nutrition may have answers where drugs do not. As the years go by, they attract a growing handful of enlightened and sympathetic doctors, while their own scientific expertise becomes formidable. Among these countless heroines are Amelia Nathan Hill who founded the battling Action Against Allergy, at a time when official medicine still denied the very existence of most food or chemical sensitivities; Gwynneth Hemmings of the Schizophrenia Association of Great Britain and Margery Hall of Sanity, who campaign for research into the biochemical factors in mental illness; and Shirley Trickett, a trained nurse who was helping desperate women through the agonies of withdrawal from the benzodiazepine tranquillizers long before psychiatrists and doctors acknowledged that the problem existed.

There are countless others, springing up daily, often run from a kitchen on a shoestring, surviving on unpaid conscript labour in the form of husbands or children licking stamps and sealing envelopes on messages of hope that professional medicine could not deliver.

Their very existence is a profound criticism of Western medicine, which for decades has been perfectly happy to ignore the subject of nutrition, to the point where it hardly even features in the seven or eight long years of a doctor's training. From time to time, it is true, there have been sporadic breast-beatings and suggestions that the matter be looked into. In 1960 the American Medical Association called a conference to debate the question. Strong recommendations were made, but little if any action resulted. A second major conference on nutrition education in medical schools, in 1972, reiterated the recommendations, which were once more brushed aside. 'There are all kinds of worthwhile interests like nutrition that well-intentioned people want to include in medical education,' commented Dr John Benson, President of the American Board of Internal Medicine. 'It is just simply impossible to fit everything in.'[4]

A mere 15 out of 143 US and Canadian medical schools listed courses in nutrition as a graduation requirement at this time. British medical students were equally unenlightened. In 1965 a Royal Commission was set up to consider just what our young doctors-to-be should be taught. It sat for three years and received representations from – among other concerned parties – the Nutrition Society. But when its findings were published, as the Todd Report, three years later, this Cinderella subject was not even mentioned. And there was at this time just one solitary Professor of Nutrition in all the nation's medical schools.

'Nutrition is taught to medical students as fag-ends of physiology, biochemistry, clinical medicine and paediatrics,' lamented the *British Medical Journal*.[5]

In 1976 the General Medical Council returned to the subject and set up a special working party to consider it. When it failed to propose that nutrition should be a required subject in the curriculum, Dr Kenneth Barlow, chairman of the McCarrison Society, wrote to protest. He received a courteous reply from the working party's chairman, Professor John Walton: '. . . the Education Committee is satisfied that nutrition is covered extensively in the teaching of other courses in the undergraduate curriculum, such as paediatrics.'

The result of this astonishing neglect has been generations of doctors who are often almost totally illiterate in matters of nutrition, however formidably well-informed in other fields. Presumed experts on health, they have assured us for years – in defiance of a staggering volume of research – that nobody need worry about being badly nourished, since the 'average' diet provides all the nutrients anyone could possibly require.

As an extreme example of such illiteracy, here is the view of an American doctor, author of a book for the lay reader on arthritis. 'Almost all arthritis,' he pronounces, 'is the natural result of the way our bones and joints are made and keep themselves going.' So what is to be done about this natural process of degeneration? '. . . the first thing to forget about is most diets for arthritis. None of them have anything that can help you.' Vitamins and minerals, perhaps? Forget them: '. . . the average diet is all that's needed'. Vitamins 'aren't burned up or used up in their job. A tiny amount, less than a speck of dust, is lost each day by washout and that's all that needs to be replaced each day in adults.'[6]

Dr Bieler quotes an American physician's bland advice to his patients: 'In general, what you want to eat will be good for you.'[7]

I recently interviewed a young ex-anorectic woman who had been hospitalized in the psychiatric ward of a big London hospital when her weight fell to a dangerously low level. This desperately malnourished patient was force-fed like a Strasbourg goose for twelve weeks, under the eagle eye of her doctors, on a stodgy, high-calorie high-sugar diet of which the single professed objective was weight gain. The menu featured white bread, sugary cereals, heavily sweetened tea or coffee several times a day, butter, cream, eggs, pasta, potatoes, over-stewed vegetables. But she never saw a single piece of fresh fruit. And salad was a taboo word because it was 'empty of calories'. Only calories counted.

And when did your GP last question you about your diet? 'Many of the chronic problems which fill a modern GP's surgery are nutritionally related,' points out Dr Stephen Davies, 'and they are exactly the areas where modern medicine most patently fails. Arthritis – angina – hypertension – psoriasis – chronic fungal infections – recurrent mouth ulcers – psychiatric presentations such as anxiety, anorexia, depression, migraine, urticaria. And what I call GUY – General Undiagnosed Yuckiness: "Do you have that Monday morning feeling every day?" That's one of the classic allergy symptoms – fatigue unrelieved by rest.'

Davies himself first became intrigued by nutrition when in the early seventies, in his very first medical posting in Newfoundland, he realized that for all the lengthy and prestigious training he had received, he simply did not know enough to help patients with this kind of problem. Returning to Britain, he took time off to plunge into the study of nutrition, and was staggered by the extent of his ignorance. 'I realized, in fact, that I knew nothing whatsoever about nutrition other than iron, folate, B_{12} and the classic deficiency diseases we'd learned in medical school.'[8]

His response has been to found, together with a small group of like-minded British doctors, the British Society for Nutritional Medicine, to promote the use of nutrition rather than drugs in clinical medicine, and to help doctors plug the gaps in their own nutritional education.

There are, happily, growing numbers of doctors today who have voluntarily put themselves through a crash course in nutrition, and the weight of medical evidence has now convinced the British Medical Association itself that the cautious pronouncements of COMA – the Committee on Medical Aspects of Food Policy – are not nearly strong enough. (The members of COMA are hand-picked by civil servants from the Department of Health.) And in March 1986 the BMA came out with their toughest statement yet on the traditional diet. Their report, *Diet, Nutrition and Health*, slammed the high-fat, high-sugar, low-fibre diet eaten by millions in Britain today, pointed out that a third of the nation was overweight, and called on the government to switch to an agricultural policy that would promote healthier eating for us all.

As well as doctors, governments can also call on real experts in nutrition, actual professors, or at least those who have taken degree courses in the subject and made it their life's work. By these surely they will be better advised? But here, too, we are up against a hard fact of life. Just as much of modern medical education simply trains customers for the pharmaceutical industry, so too much of nutrition training today is equally industry-orientated. The plushest and most highly rewarded jobs for the graduates of our rare nutrition courses will be in the food industry, with its glittering technology. In both the USA and Britain, an enormous amount of nutrition research is either financed or carried out by the food industry. Such research is unlikely to discover that our 'average' diet is anything but an unmixed blessing for us all. And in fact that is precisely the message conveyed to us by our established food pundits.

Arnold Bender, retired Professor of Nutrition at London's Queen Elizabeth College, recently took time out to castigate the health-food industry in a diverting book called *Health or Hoax?* He makes perfectly valid criticisms of over-selling and scare tactics, and utters some well-founded warnings against the dangers of over-supplementation. But his concern about the perils of too many vitamins – 'we do not know the consequences of moderate overdoses for a lifetime for most of the essential nutrients'[9] – is only matched by his complacency on the subject of additives. For those who might worry that here, too, we do not know the consequences of moderate daily doses over a lifetime, Bender pronounces firmly that 'no one in Great Britain has ever suffered harm from an intentional additive . . . processed foods can be safer than raw, natural unprocessed foods'.[10]

And it's hardly reassuring to find a professor of nutrition – even a retired one – asserting that 'with the wide choice of food available in industrialized countries, not even those living on snack foods and making a poor choice of diet could be so short of any vitamin that real signs of deficiency would appear';[11] or that 'Any shortfall in general health standards due to a shortfall in vitamin intake would be too small to measure . . .'[12]

This same complacent assumption – that vitamins are only deficient in our diets when they produce the classic deficiency diseases – is echoed in John Yudkin's latest publication. Vitamin inadequacy, he tells us, may indeed produce 'specific symptoms and signs of deficiency', but 'an intake greater than the amount needed to prevent these effects does not improve normal bodily function to superior levels'.[13]

The dangerous fallacy of these assumptions was already being exposed more than fifty years ago, while individual vitamins were still being identified. Writing in 1931, from the Rowett Research Institute in Aberdeen, John Boyd Orr noted that while the identification of the deficiency diseases had been a great achievement, 'the practical importance of this work is much greater than the mere cure or prevention of these pathological conditions. In experimental studies with animals it has been observed that there are all stages of malnutrition ranging from what we regard as normal health to that in which the gross and terminal symptoms appear.' The earliest symptoms, he pointed out, were signs of lowered vitality: 'young animals have a lower-than-normal rate of growth, the reproductive powers of adults are defective, the coat is dull and lustreless, appetite is decreased, and the animals show, instead of the *joie de vivre* of the perfectly healthy animal, lethargy and other signs of premature senility'.[14]

These signs of lowered vitality – the dull skin, and the lank hair, the lethargic posture and dispirited looks – were perfectly familiar to McCarrison, and can be studied today in any busy GP's surgery.

Orr went on to make another key observation: that 'susceptibility to certain infectious diseases is definitely greater in groups of animals on deficient diets than in animals on complete well-balanced diets'.[15] This point – the heightened resistance which a healthy diet confers – was constantly rammed home in Ministry of Food propaganda during the war.

And when the Medical Research Council published its authoritative state-of-the-art monograph *Vitamins: A Survey of Present Knowledge*, in 1932, they were careful to stress the importance of these fundamental concepts.

> A deficient vitamin intake may not immediately result in actual disease, but may bring about abnormal development of specific structures which makes disease of these parts ultimately almost inevitable . . . it is no doubt true that the rareness of . . . scurvy, xerophthalmia and beriberi indicates that an absolute deficiency of vitamins scarcely ever exists. On the other hand, it is now becoming generally recognized that much subnormal health and

development, and even incidence of disease, are associated with a partial deficiency of one or more of these accessory substances. The influence of such partial deficiencies, even when relatively slight, may be extremely serious when they occur in very early life . . .'[16]

Such ideas are dismissed as fanciful today by our modern nutrition experts, although the ease with which hospital patients on their appalling diets succumb to any passing infection – one thinks of the lethal Wakefield outbreak in 1984 – should underline their importance.*

Since its marriage of convenience with the food industry, however, official nutrition has become – in the words of Canadian biochemist Ross Hume Hall – 'a stagnating science' with 'a bias towards defining nutritional problems in nineteenth-century terms'. This approach has produced what he calls the 'single-cause-single-effect adding-machine concept of nutrition',[17] in which certain nutrients are seen as more essential than others, because they can be linked with specific deficiency diseases such as scurvy or rickets. It thus allows nutritionists to brush aside as 'unimportant' deficiencies in a whole host of other nutrients which, they assure us, are all lavishly supplied in our food.

On the subject of nutrition the British government usually consults the British Nutrition Foundation as well as doctors and nutritionists. And since it was set up in 1967 with the cash and blessings of the food industry, we can hardly be surprised by the poor quality of the advice the government receives, and which it in turn passes on to the general public. In a Granada TV 'World in Action' programme, 'The Great Food Scandal', screened on 7 October 1985, a former director-general of the British Nutrition Foundation, Derek Shrimpton, spoke of his surprise on finding, when he took up his post, that the Foundation was not the independent research organization he had supposed it to be, but acted 'as a front for the food industry . . . and as a tool for Whitehall'.[19]

Typical of this narrow view is the conclusion of the distinguished Panel on Bread, Flour and other Cereal Products,

*When a group of American researchers studied the diets of 152 elderly patients admitted to hospital, they found that 41 per cent of them were actually malnourished; 64 per cent of these suffered an infection during their stay, compared to only 26 per cent of those reckoned adequately nourished; and 28 per cent of the malnourished patients over sixty-five actually died, compared to only 4 per cent of the others.[18]

set up in 1978 by the Committee on Medical Aspects of Food Policy, which – while agreeing that wholemeal bread was nutritionally superior to white – supposed that no harm would result if white bread were no longer to have extra thiamine, nicotinic acid, iron and calcium added to make up some of its deficiencies, and that 'in the absence of a public-health problem of deficiency, there was no need to worry about any other vitamins, trace elements or organic salts removed in refining'.[20]

The differences between wholemeal and white bread, it was concluded, were anyway less striking 'when considered in the context of the mixed diet usually eaten in Britain'.[21]

This argument is enormously popular with the food industry for obvious reasons, since it allows official blessings to be rained on even quite poor foodstuffs, on the cosy assumption that nutritional deficiencies in one area can easily be made up elsewhere in the diet.

As Sir Alan Marre, chairman of the British Nutrition Foundation, puts it: 'There are, broadly speaking, no "good foods" and "bad foods" – there are "good diets" and "bad diets",' which is one more way of saying that a varied Western diet, including animal and vegetable foods, is unlikely to lack anything important.[22]

What one might call the varied-diet hypothesis has been shown up as the misleading rubbish it is by every single national nutritional survey undertaken in the West. As just one example, the Nutrition Canada Survey, which studied a population cross-section of 27,000 people, and finally reported in 1975, found widespread deficiencies in iron, thiamine, folic acid and calcium. Iron, thiamine and calcium, as a matter of interest, are all added to 'enriched' Canadian white bread. Had the researchers studied zinc, magnesium, manganese and B6, no doubt they would have found equally serious deficiencies in these too. Our own Ministry of Agriculture has recently warned us that the British diet is quite seriously deficient in zinc.

At rather less expense of time and effort, an enterprising researcher recently took a pocket calculator and the Food Composition Tables to the varied-diet hypothesis. First, he calculated the nutritional value of a typical British diet, supplying 2,320 calories, and based on the British National Food Survey: containing milk, cheese, beef, fish, eggs, margarine, white bread, cornflakes, Brussels sprouts, carrots, peas, salt, tea, apples, sugar and potatoes, it would certainly be styled a good well-varied diet by most middle-of-the-road dieticians. He substituted wholemeal bread for the white, Weetabix for the cornflakes, and added extra peanuts, beans, and a little more apple and potato to make up the calorie difference, so that this diet too gave 2,320 calories. Then he totted up the nutritional differences.

They were startling. The white-bread-and-cornflakes diet provided 50 per cent less fibre, 61 per cent less selenium, 54 per cent less folic acid, 45 per cent less vitamin E, 38 per cent less B6, 30 per cent less choline, 15 per cent less chromium, 65 per cent less magnesium, 31 per cent less zinc, 72 per cent less manganese, 48 per cent less copper and 31 per cent less potassium than the unrefined diet.[23]

A huge body of perfectly respectable research now suggests that fibre deficiency makes us more susceptible to heart disease, diabetes and cancer of the bowel or colon; that we need selenium to protect us from heart disease, cancer and premature ageing; that folic acid deficiency in pregnant women may be a key factor in cases of spina bifida in babies; that vitamin E, like selenium, may keep cancer, heart disease and premature ageing at bay while safeguarding our circulatory system; that B6 deficiency may be a factor in premenstrual tension, post-natal depression and other mental problems; that chromium deficiency can result in the abnormal sugar metabolism which can produce diabetes; that magnesium is vital not only for the health of our hearts, but for the functioning of every single cell in our bodies; that zinc deficiency can lead to anorexia nervosa, stunted growth, acne and poor healing; that manganese is important in the formation of bone structures and the central nervous system; that potassium deficiency can threaten the health of our hearts and induce drowsiness, mental confusion and nervous irritability. Carl Pfeiffer considers that copper is one nutrient we may be getting in excess today, thanks to new-style copper plumbing, and none of us needs more sodium.

The sheer financial clout of the lobbies pressurizing Western governments to stand aside from intervention in nutritional matters is daunting. As Caroline Walker and Geoffrey Cannon showed in *The Food Scandal*, the meat and dairying interests in Britain, the Common Agricultural Policy with its butter mountains and grain surpluses, the sugar empire, and the sweet-fat industry manufacturing baked goods, soft drinks, confectionery and other forms of processed foods, all combine to bring pressure on Whitehall decision-making, through the Department of Trade and Industry or the Ministry of Agriculture, Fisheries and Food. It doesn't help matters that food and health are so far from being connected in the bureaucratic mind that decisions about our foodstuffs which can vitally affect our health – additives, the 'enrichment' or otherwise of bread, nutritional labelling and so on – are made, not by the Department of Health and Social Security, but by the Ministry of Agriculture, Fisheries and Food, thus making it even more likely that in any conflict of interests, it will be the health of the consumer that goes to the wall. It has to be borne in mind, too, that the difference between an official government recommendation that we should all eat less sugar, or a strong suggestion that we should cut it out altogether, may be a quarter of a million jobs in the confectionery industry. At a time of high unemployment, this is not a consideration that governments can ignore. And whatever they may do to improve the health of their voters through nutrition is unlikely to be very healthy, in the short term at least, for those massive commercial interests which employ millions of people, and can put forward their own pressing claims for consideration.

So nobody should be surprised that when the National Advisory Committee on Nutrition Education was set up in 1979 to look at our British diet and ponder what advice we should all be given about our food, its recommendations were considerably watered down and publication of its Report was stalled for over two years by massive pressure from an alarmed food industry. Only after this nutritional Watergate was exposed by Geoffrey Cannon in the *Sunday Times* was the NACNE Report finally published. It was promptly disowned by the Department of Health who – like another participant, the British Nutrition Foundation – had criticized and stalled progress throughout. But it has now been accepted on all sides as the best quasi-official nutritional guidance we're likely to get: Britain's belated answer to the United States' *Dietary Goals* of 1977.

Nor should we be astonished that after months of pondering the labelling question, the Ministry of Agriculture, Fisheries and Food should have come up initially with proposals that food labels should simply indicate protein, fat and saturated fat, and carbohydrate: such labelling would give a Mars Bar the same carbohydrate content as Puffed Wheat, at 67 per cent, instead of telling the public what it really needs to know, which is that there is 66 per cent added sugar in the Mars bar and only

1·5 per cent in the Puffed Wheat. According to these proposals, fibre content need not be shown either, although Audrey Eyton's bestseller, *The F-Plan*, if not N A C N E, has at least made sure that we all know what fibre is.

It was predictable, too, that confronted with irrefutable evidence that Western man is busily digging his grave with what few teeth he has left, the 'classic' nutritionists employed by the food industry are now urging on governments the need for caution, as though eating a healthier diet were a particularly reckless form of experimentation; the evidence, we are told, is still not 'conclusive'.

But although it is tempting to look for villains, to see the whole issue of diet and health in black and white terms as a struggle between gallant little health-conscious David and the big, bad, profit-hungry Goliath of the food industry, such a view is both unrealistic and unfair. 'Conspiracy,' Geoffrey Cannon has remarked, 'is the wrong word. Let's just say that all the interests line up on one side.'

All but one, that is – the public itself.

26
Food for
the Future

T he public – or at least a vocal minority of it – is today well
enough informed to be deeply cynical about the sincerity
of government intervention in nutrition matters and the advice
of some of its experts. They will no longer buy glib assurances
that all is well with those eating what has been dubbed SAD –
the Standard American Diet. They are often more conscious
than their doctors of the importance of diet for health, and far
better informed. And since the government both in this country
and the USA seems to be dragging its feet, many of them have
now taken matters into their own hands.

We are today witnessing a true grassroots movement
towards a sense of personal responsibility for our health, which
can – if the Department of Health has the sense and sanity to
encourage it – lead to a huge improvement in our health,
together with a jumbo-sized drop in our horrendous health
bill – £17½bn in 1985. It is slowly dawning on us as a nation that
doctors exist to treat us when we get sick – but that whether or
not we get sick is largely up to us; that what we eat and drink,
as well as how we work, live and play are all crucial factors in
our health; that we can, if we so choose, stay healthy.

When *Woman* magazine set out to discover the 'Woman of
1984' with an elaborate questionnaire, analysis of the many
thousands of replies showed that 67 per cent of those responding had become aware of what they ate and the difference it
could make to their health.[1] It is rare to pick up any women's
magazine these days without at least some passing reference to
the subject.

The same health-consciousness has swelled the ranks of
vegetarians to an estimated 3 million – a matter of acute concern
for our livestock industry. When the BBC nervously ran a
series on vegetarian cooking, it turned out to be one of their
biggest-ever successes, to their astonishment; the cookery book
of the series by Sarah Brown had sold nearly half a million

copies by the end of 1985. 'Brushed clean of ideological cob-
webs, the new veggie image, sophisticated, sensuous and fit,
is mopping up foodie voters,' commented Jocasta Innes in a
Christmas review of 1984 cookery books.[2]

People who switch to a healthier diet find out for themselves that – contrary to what 'classic' nutritionists preach – they
can actually enjoy a superior level of health and fitness, often
for the first time in their lives. When *Woman* magazine asked
for twenty volunteers for a three-month healthy eating experiment, they were snowed under with eager offers. Almost all of
those who took part – including three large families – said at
the end of the three months how much better they felt: 'We just
feel we have so much more energy . . . I just feel so much better
in myself . . . I'm getting up earlier, I'm busier, and I have a
lot more stamina . . . we feel so much better now than we *ever*
did before.'[3]

Newspapers and magazines, TV and radio all reflect
growing public interest and concern in a spate of articles and
programmes, with the BBC's Food and Health Campaign,
launched in the autumn of 1985, making a particularly forceful
contribution through such major programme series as 'A Taste
of Health' and 'You Are What You Eat'.

Healthy eating, in fact, has become the Flavour of the
Month – a matter of bewilderment as well as gratification to
all those who only yesterday, it seems, were being scornfully
denounced as cranks, and who now find themselves in the
height of fashion.

Far from battling against these trends, some sections of
the food industry are showing an eager readiness to respond
to them. In January 1985 – well ahead of government legislation – the Tesco supermarket chain launched a commendable
scheme to tell its customers just what they were getting in their
trolleys. They were acting on a specially commissioned Gallup
poll, which showed that 72 per cent of those interviewed were
concerned about eating healthily, while only 29 per cent
thought that food labelling was informative enough. Over a
year, Tesco undertook to supply this information on over a
thousand items in its own-label range, although – perhaps
understandably – they have ducked the complexities of trans,
saturated and polyunsaturated fats. As well as indicating total
fat, protein, carbohydrate and calorie content, the label on a
Tesco can of baked beans now tells the housewife buying it that
an average 5 oz serving will supply 10·2 g fibre, 4 g added salt,

and 6 g added sugar. Other labels will indicate vitamin and mineral content; special package symbols indicate products high in vitamin C, low in salt or without added sugar; and through a series of 'Healthy Eating' leaflets, Tesco aims to hasten on the nutritional education of its customers. Safeway have gone one better: in the summer of 1985, they announced that no artificial food colourings would in future be permitted in any of their own-label products, only 'nature-identical' ones – a move that has delighted the Hyperactive Children's Support Group.

Other supermarket chains have shown similar awareness of customer anxieties. Marks and Spencer have produced dozens of items in their gourmet chilled-cabinet range of made-up dishes which are totally free of additives apart from modified starch for bulk: their lead is now being followed by most of the major supermarket chains. And on any supermarket shelves, the high-sugar breakfast cereals like Coco-Pops are being displaced to the remoter top shelves by new ranges of nutty, crunchy fibre-filled cereals for the health-conscious. The foods that health cranks were once mercilessly ribbed for eating – the yoghurt and muesli, the lentil rissoles and nut cutlets, the brown rice and bean dishes – are run of the mill today on supermarket shelves or women's magazine cookery features.

It's often assumed that supermarkets and food manufacturers have a vested interest in selling us junk food. This is not so. They have a vested interest in selling what we want; now that that is turning out more and more to be healthy food, it will be fascinating to watch a major industry struggling to adapt. The Soviet biochemist I. I. Brekhman writes that since this is an age of huge population concentrations, there can be no return to the simple on-the-spot harvesting techniques of our ancestors. Instead, he calls for what he calls 'neo-gathering' – a scientifically based approach to mass food-supplying which will have as its first object 'the preservation of all the complex of biologically active substances present in natural sources of food . . .' Thus instead of using dubious chemicals, 'neo-gathering' would employ these same biologically active substances as additives. Other advances in food technology – surely not beyond the wit of our dazzlingly inventive food industry – would make it possible to preserve the whole complex of nutrients in vegetable oils instead of refining them away. Brekhman also calls for a wider range of traditional foods to be made available to city-dwellers. Instead of the extremely limited range of foodstuffs – beef, pork, wheat, milk, oranges, sugar – from which so many people eat today, he would like to see the choice of products extended to include game, new types of fish, marine products such as seaweed, wild plants, berries, nuts, grasses and seeds, together with a greater range of fruit and vegetables to be grown in our market gardens. Such a diversity would ensure to us, he points out, a supply even of nutrients which are at present unknown to us, but which future research may show to be important.[4]

Will food manufacturers and supermarkets rise to this splendid late-twentieth-century challenge? I believe that they can and will, because pressure from informed consumers will leave them no other option. This is already happening in agriculture.

For years the agro-chemical lobby has insisted that without continuous massive doses of fertilizers and pesticides, the world would starve to death, and that minute traces of pesticide or insecticide in the foods we eat is a small price to pay for the cheap, abundant food we enjoy thanks to the skills of modern scientific farming. Many of the public no longer agree.

In 1974 the US National Cancer Institute issued an official warning against a pesticide widely used for fumigating stored grain, called ethylene dibromide, or EDB for short. Further tests by the US Environment Protection Agency showed that it was one of the most potent carcinogens ever tested. Not until 1983, however, did the EPA finally get around to banning its use and setting standards that forced the removal of over 200 grain products from supermarket shelves. An alarmed America woke up to the fact that despite these measures, corn treated with EDB would be on the market for a year longer, wheat for another three years until 1986. Stories like this have not enhanced public confidence in the government agencies that are supposed to be safeguarding our health. Nor has the recent revelation in the USA that federal approval of over 200 agro-chemicals made by such leading companies as Monsanto, Dow and DuPont was based on studies carried out at the largest testing centre in the USA – four of whose directors last year faced trial for fraud. American consumers have been appalled to learn that 94 per cent of their food now has residues of either pesticides or herbicides in it, that US water sources are heavily contaminated (all the wells in Iowa are now unsafe), and that there are now 50,000 major chemical dumps in the USA, many of them leaking quietly and lethally into underground water tables from which the nation draws its drinking water.

Understandably, a poll conducted for one US magazine in 1983 showed that 71 per cent of all those questioned worry about pesticides, and half of all those polled voted for a complete ban on them – even if it meant paying more for fruit and vegetables.

In Britain, public anxiety has not been allayed by the faint-heartedness of proposed government measures intended to crack down on pesticide abuse, previously monitored by voluntary action inside the industry itself. In 1984 a coalition of environmental groups, including the now revivified Soil Association, the Friends of the Earth and Oxfam, launched PAN–UK – the Pesticide Action Network. The million-word report they published, which received plenty of publicity, unearthed 'evidence of a major environmental scandal, with an industry essentially out of control'. The five main crops grown in Britain, it revealed, received an average of 2·3 sprayings in 1979; by 1982 this had risen to 3·3, and many crops are sprayed far more often than this, the record being held by one crop of lettuce which in 1982 received no less than 46 different sprayings. Potatoes may be treated with as many as eight different pesticides, onions up to fifteen.[5] Food cranks have always eaten fruit and vegetables complete with their skins because so much of the nutritional goodness is concentrated there; they were particularly affronted by official Ministry warnings that fruit and vegetables should be peeled before eating because of pesticide residues in the skins.

In *Pall of Poison*, a specially commissioned report, the Soil Association publicized another problem, that of the spray drift occurring when fine droplets of chemical sprays were carried by currents of air away from their target areas to inflict damage on neighbouring fields, crops, gardens, wildlife, animals – and even people.

'The belief that organically grown foods are the only reliable foods is characteristic of the nutritional neurotic,' scoffed the American Medical Association in 1971.[6]

If this is so, there are millions of neurotics today, deeply concerned about the growing contamination of our environment, our food and ourselves. The question so hotly debated by the Soil Association in its earliest years – whether organically grown foods are actually biologically superior – has been overtaken by another consideration: that organically grown foods are at least free of the man-made chemicals which have so often been shown to be perilous for our health.

And here too the giant supermarket chains are responding as fast as they can to what they sense is a major consumer concern. Ten years ago, an inquiry about organically grown food would have received short shrift from any of them. Last year my inquiry as an interested consumer to two, Sainsbury and Waitrose, brought long and considered replies. Both regretted that they could not sell organically grown fruit and vegetables because of supply problems, both assured me that they encouraged rigid control over the use of agro-chemicals by their suppliers – Sainsbury actually employs a staff of fulltime inspectors for this purpose.

The Safeway chain has managed to corner supplies of organically grown food for some of their bigger supermarkets, and wish they could lay their hands on ten times the amount. Even at higher prices it vanishes off the shelves almost as soon as it is put out. The energetic farmer, Peter Segger, is determined to make supplies of fresh, attractive produce a commercial proposition. In 1984 he launched Organic Farm Foods, a nationwide distribution system, and sales through their London warehouse were already running at £1m by 1985.

The Soil Association itself – which nearly foundered in the doldrums of the sixties – is now revivified, active and influential, with its membership rising by leaps and bounds. Even 'The Archers' knows all about going organic these days.

The pioneers of organic farming in the thirties and forties were fond of quoting Theophrastus: 'If you drive out nature with a pitchfork, she will ever come sneaking back on you . . .' It is hard for their successors to suppress a grim satisfaction as they consider the problems facing agro-chemical farming today. The most frightening of these is the progressive soil erosion which writers like Lady Eve Balfour and Jacks and Whyte were already describing half a century ago.

A report published by the World Watch Institution, an environmental organization partly funded by the United Nations, has recently described the worldwide erosion of topsoil as a 'global crisis', and blamed it on intensive farming with large amounts of chemical fertilizer, together with monoculture and the ploughing up of marginal land typical of modern farming practice. Figures from the US Soil Conservation Service showed that between 1977 and 1982 1·7 billion tons of soil were lost. Nearly half of American farm land is losing soil faster than it is being replaced. 'Indeed the crop surpluses of the early eighties, which are sometimes cited as the sign of a healthy agriculture, are partly the product of mining soils,' they conclude. 'What is at stake is not merely the degradation of soil, but the degradation of life itself.'[7]

Farmers may be oblivious to topsoil losses invisibly eating into their agricultural capital, but they can hardly fail to notice the size of their fertilizer bill. And the financial cost of agrochemistry has already reached the point of no return for many farmers. Britain now spends £270m on agro-chemicals annually. 'All of us in farming are in hock to the chemical companies,' as one rueful farmer put it. An official American study of corn pest management showed in 1984 that corn farmers' returns on a dollar's worth of herbicides and insecticides were $1.05 and $1.03 respectively – and that didn't include the cost of applying them.

In a world of non-renewable resources, too, modern chemical farming makes less and less sense.

One USDA study showed that while farm income between 1910 and 1980 rose from $2bn to $11·5bn, farm expenses in the same period had risen from $3·5 bn to a mind-boggling $128bn.

Not surprisingly, hundreds of farmers large and small are beginning to see organic farming as an attractive alternative, and the USDA as well as our own MAFF are now for the first time funding long-term studies on the subject, while important pioneer studies have been going on for years now at the University of Kassel in Germany.

Robert Rodale, son of J. I. Rodale, spends $1m annually on exploring the future of agriculture at the Rodale Research Centre, working towards what he calls Regenerative Agriculture – a concept that goes even further than the organic farming of Howard and Balfour, to combine ideas of energy efficiency, conservation and biological innovation with their ethical commitment to the land. Regenerative Agriculture would actually work towards increasing topsoil, and would make farming more energy-efficient. Rodale also points out the absurdity of a farming system that uses more and more energy, at a time when its costs are rocketing, and fewer and fewer people, at a time when unemployment is a national headache. The Rodale magazine *New Farm* has a healthy circulation and a steadily rising readership, in a farming community that's increasingly receptive to the organic gospel.

The same public that wants additive-free food, and fruit and vegetables untainted by pesticide or insecticide residues, is beginning to demand a revolution in its health care. Addressing the British Medical Association on the occasion of its 150th anniversary, HRH the Prince of Wales put his finger on a jumping pulse when he criticized modern medicine for its 'objective, statistical, computerized approach to the healing of the sick', which relies on more and more powerful drugs, and reminded his distinguished audience that 'the health of human beings is so often determined by their behaviour, their food and drink, and the nature of their environment'.[8]

Millions of people today are turning to gentler, 'natural' therapies because they sense the growing irrelevance of conventional medicine, with its mechanistic high-tech approach, and its inability to take a broad ecological view, to the major health problems of today.

'It's what we think we know already that often prevents us from learning,' shrewdly remarked Claude Bernard, the great nineteenth-century French physiologist.[9] Doctors find it hard to shed the habit they acquired in medical school, of sticking labels that say arthritis or eczema or multiple sclerosis on a specific set of signs and symptoms, and congratulating themselves on the accuracy of their diagnosis before passing the patient over to a specialist in the field. These labels obscure understanding of the common underlying disease processes at work in such chronic conditions. The pioneers of Nature Cure, and Bircher-Benner, Gerson, McCarrison and others, together with more recent researchers, grasped instinctively what the modern study of subcellular physiology is more and more making plain: that almost all of the chronic diseases that plague Western man arise from a profound disturbance of body chemistry, which may be caused by nutritional imbalances and deficiencies, or by psychological stresses, or by the assault of toxins in our environment, causing toxic overload which overwhelms even our marvellous built-in defence mechanisms.

Even doctors who have become aware that there is more to nutrition than the deficiency diseases and their appropriate vitamins, find it hard to shed the professional mental conditioning that equates a nutrient with a drug, and expects it to act accordingly. Nutrients are not drugs, and the double-blind clinical trial, which is of doubtful value even for assessing drugs, is not merely useless but potentially misleading as well when it is applied to nutrients such as essential fatty acids: highly complex substances with a host of potent metabolites of which the activity in our bodies depends on a wide range of nutritional co-factors.

With the newer knowledge of nutrition – as it was then hopefully styled – the Western medical profession already had in its hands more than half a century ago the tools to an understanding and mastery of many of these diseases which plague us. It chose to ignore them, and to go off at the therapeutic tangent so invitingly signposted by the pharmaceutical companies. For decades medicine has stood still in one important sense. A frightening amount of time has been lost, huge resources tragically squandered, while an incalculable burden of suffering went unrelieved.

But we have not only failed to make headway. There is evidence that as a species we may even have degenerated in that time. As a nation we were more healthy in 1945, at the end of an appalling six-year-ordeal by war, than we are today. Britain tops the world league of heart disease today. Our infant mortality figures may have improved in half a century, but are still higher than those of several countries who are poorer than we are. The number of babies born congenitally malformed, or who grow up educationally subnormal has been rising steadily since the late forties. The figures for degenerative diseases such as arthritis, cancer, diabetes, show no sign of decline. And a comparison of 5,000 people born in 1946 and their firstborn children a generation later, had bad news as well as good to record. Cases of asthma increased from 6·2 per 1,000 to 18·9; cases of juvenile diabetes rose very nearly sixfold; and there was a sixfold increase in cases of eczema.

In the thirties and forties a US dentist called Francis Pottenger made a number of nutritional experiments with cats. Two sets of cats were both given raw milk and cod-liver oil, but one group were fed on raw meat, the other on cooked meat. Pottenger observed them closely over several generations. He found that while cats on the raw-meat diet flourished, with sleek, glossy fur and excellent bone structure, those eating the unnatural cooked-meat diet developed poor dentofacial structures with crowded jaws and small skulls; their bones were poorly developed, their bodily tissue soft and inelastic. Most of the second generation male cats became sterile, while the females often miscarried or produced sickly underweight kittens. Allergic problems were common – wheezing, asthma, nervous irritability, itchy skins.

What makes Pottenger's studies so alarming, however, is the strong suggestive evidence that the damage done by poor diet does not affect simply the generation that eats it, or even their offspring: it causes genetic havoc too. The first generation of Pottenger's allergic cats produced kittens who were even more allergic than they were: by the third generation, the incidence was almost a hundred per cent.

There are many thoughtful and observant doctors today who feel that we are now witnessing evidence of exactly this kind of genetic damage in our own populations. 'I'm seeing the children of malnutrition now,' Dr Abram Hoffer told me, 'and soon we'll be seeing a third generation. We're seeing a horrible impact on our whole genetic structure.'

Perhaps it will be generally accepted one day that the rise in chronic disease at all ages, the frightening vulnerability of our young to addictive habits like smoking, drinking and drug-taking, the learning disorders which are now so common, the behavioural problems and hooliganism which turn classrooms into battlegrounds, and the escalating violence in our Western society which baffles sociologists and politicians alike, are at least in part the result of this genetic damage.

As it has always been, too, disease is socially selective. 'The lower down the social scale you are, the less likely you are to be healthy and the sooner you can expect to die,' was a bald summary of the findings of a report, *Inequalities in Health*, issued by the DHSS in 1980. 'Your children too will be at greater risk of injury, sickness and death.' Moreover, matters have not improved over all the decades of the wonderful Welfare State: 'the gap in health standards between the upper and lower classes has increased steadily since 1949'.[10]

This difference is partly due to worse housing, worse environments generally, worse health care and less money. But also, overwhelmingly, it's a problem of education. Today's awareness of nutrition remains almost wholly an upper- and middle-class preserve: it has hardly penetrated the working classes. Few of them today are so grindingly poor that they're forced to fill their aching bellies – as their parents and grandparents did – with oversweetened tea, white bread and marge. They eat filling junk food not only because it's cheap but because nobody has told them that it's killing them. They may actually spend more on junk food treats for their children than the nutrition-conscious middle-class mother; in a 1984 study of 15,000 teenagers, it was found that the highest amounts of chocolate, sweets and cola drinks were given to children in families where income was less than £50 a week. (National consumption of chocolates and sweets, incidentally, was 4 per cent higher in 1984 than in 1983.)[11] These same children grow up in homes where dinner may be fish-fingers washed down with brightly coloured orange squash; they will go to schools operating cafeterias where they can fill themselves up with chips and pudding for lunch; and on family outings they'll enjoy treats of bars of chocolate, packets of crisps, a Coke. When they grow up they'll believe that a white cheese roll, a doughnut, and a cup of oversweetened tea is an adequate lunch for a working man.

They need to be told, eloquently and persuasively, that these eating habits not only lay the foundations of ill health in later life, and may lead to an early death, but they also stunt their mental abilities, sap their energy and enterprise, and help confine them forever in the ranks of the disadvantaged and the underprivileged.

Nobody is claiming that attention to nutrition alone will solve all these problems, bestow bounding health on us all, or wave some kind of magic wand over society. There are no easy answers. But until we do attend to the food factor, much of the effort, goodwill, hard work, time and money devoted to our social ills and our health problems will be thrown away.

'Nutrition,' said Dr Bircher-Benner, 'is not the highest thing in life. But it is the soil on which the highest things can either perish or flourish.'[12]

Bibliography

The complete list of books, journals, papers, pamphlets and other sources that I have read, skimmed or dipped into would be tediously long. I have listed here the more important, and those to which my debt is greatest. Others are acknowledged in the Notes. The editions given are those quoted in the Notes.

Abrahamson, E. M., and **Pezet**, A. W., *Body, Mind and Sugar*, New York, Avon Books, 1977.

Alcott, W. A., *Tea and Coffee*, New York, Fowlers & Wells, 1850.
The Young Housekeeper, Boston, G. W. Light, 1842.

Allinson, T. R., *Medical Essays*, 6 vols., London, Dr T. R. Allinson, 1915.
A System of Hygienic Medicine, London, F. Pitman, 1886.

Aykroyd, W. R., *Vitamins and Other Dietary Essentials*, London, Heinemann, 1936.

Bacharach, A. L., *Science and Nutrition*, 2nd ed., Watts, 1944.

Balfour, Lady Eve, *The Living Soil*, Faber & Faber, 1943.

Beasley, Joseph D., and **Swift**, Jerry J., *The Impact of Nutrition on the Health of Americans*, Report no. *1*, July 1981, funded by the Ford Foundation, New York.

Beeuwkes, A. M., ed., *Essays on The History of Nutrition and Dietetics*, Illinois, The American Dietetic Association, 1967.

Bieler, Henry G., *Food is Your Best Medicine*, New York, Ballantine Books, 1983.

Bircher, Ruth, *Eating Your Way to Health*, London, Faber & Faber, 1961.

Bircher, Ruth Kunz, *The Bircher-Benner Health Guide*, London, Unwin Paperbacks, 1983.

Bircher-Benner, M., *The Essential Nature and Organisation of Food Energy*, London, John Bale, Sons, & Curnow, 1939.
Fruit Dishes and Raw Vegetables, London, C. W. Daniel, 1951.
The Prevention of Incurable Disease, New Canaan, Conn., Keats Publishing Inc., 1978.

Bland, Jeffrey, *Your Health Under Siege*, Brattleboro, Vt., The Stephen Greene Press, 1981.

Brekhman, I. I., *Man and Biologically Active Substances*, Oxford, Pergamon Press, 1980.

and **Nesterenko**, I. F., *Brown Sugar and Health*, Oxford, Pergamon Press, 1983.

British Medical Association, *A Charter for Health*, London, Allen & Unwin, 1946.

Carpenter, Kenneth J., ed., *Pellagra*, Stroudsbury, Penn., Hutchinson Ross Pub. Co., 1981.

Carque, Otto, *Vital Facts About Food: A Guide to Health and Longevity*, Los Angeles, 1933.

Carson, Rachel, *Silent Spring*, Boston, Ma., Houghton Mifflin, 1962; Harmondsworth, Penguin Books, 1965.

Cheraskin, E., **Ringsdorf**, W. M., Jr, and **Clark**, J. W., *Diet and Disease*, New Canaan, Conn., Keats Publishing Inc., 1977.

Cleave, T. L., *The Saccharine Diseases*, Bristol, John Wright & Sons, 1974.

Coca, Arthur F., *The Pulse Test*, New York, Arco Publishing Inc., 1982.

Crawford, Michael and Sheilagh, *What We Eat Today*, London, Neville Spearman, 1972.

David, Elizabeth, *An Omelette and a Glass of Wine*, London, Robert Hale, 1984; Penguin Books, 1986.

Davis, Adelle, *Let's Eat Right to Keep Fit*, London, Allen & Unwin, 1976.

Let's Get Well, London, Allen & Unwin, 1979.

Deutsch, Ronald, *The New Nuts among the Berries*, Palo Alto, Ca., Bull Publishing Co., 1977.

Dr. Bircher-Benner's Way to Positive Health and Vitality, Zürich, Bircher-Benner Verlag, 1967.

Drummond, J. C., and **Wilbraham**, A., *The Englishman's Food*, London, Jonathan Cape, 1957.

Dufty, William, *Sugar Blues*, New York, Warner Books, 1975.

Fenelon, K. G., *Britain's Food Supplies*, London, Methuen, 1952.

Garrison, Omar V., *The Dictocrats' Attack on Health Foods and Vitamins*, New York, Arc Books, 1971.

Gerson, Max, *A Cancer Therapy*, New York, Dura Books, 1958.

Graham, Sylvester, *Lectures on the Science of Human Life*, London, 1854.

Graham, Thomas J., *Modern Domestic Medicine*, London, 1835.

Guggenhiem, K. Y., *Nutrition and Nutritional Diseases*, Lexington, Mass., Collamore Press, 1981.

Gunther, John, *Death Be Not Proud*, New York, Perennial Library, 1965.

Harnik, Peter, *Voodoo Science, Twisted Consumerism*, Washington, Center for Science in the Public Interest, 1982.

Haught, S. J., *Has Dr. Max Gerson a True Cancer Cure?*, Canoga Park, Cal., Major Books, 1978.

Hauser, Gayelord, *The Gaylord Hauser Cook Book*, London, Faber & Faber, 1971.

    Look Younger, Live Longer, London, Faber & Faber, 1979.

    The New Diet Does It, London, Faber & Faber, 1974.

    Gayelord Hausers's New Treasury of Secrets, London, Faber & Faber, 1974.

Hay, Dr W. H., *A New Health Era*, London, Harrap, 1935.

Health Education Council, *A Discussion Paper on Proposals for Nutritional Guidelines for Health Education in Britain*, London, NACNE, 1983.

Herbert, Victor, and **Barrett**, Stephen, eds., *Vitamins and 'Health' Foods: The Great American Hustle*, Philadelphia, George F. Stickley Company, 1982.

Hess, John L. and Karen, *The Taste of America*, Harmondsworth, Penguin Books, 1977.

Hill, Fredric W., *The American Institute of Nutrition*, Bethesda, Md, The American Institute of Nutrition, 1978.

Hindhede, Mikkel, *Protein and Nutrition*, London, Ewart Seymour, 1915.

Hippocratic Writings, ed. G. E. R. Lloyd, Harmondsworth, Penguin Books, 1978.

Hoffer, Abram, and **Osmond**, Humphry, *How to Live with Schizophrenia*, Segaucus, NJ, Citadel Press, 1974.

Hofmann, Liselotte, ed., *The Great American Nutrition Hassle*, Ca, The Mayfield Publishing Co., 1978.

Hunter, Beatrice Trum, *Consumer Beware!*, New York, Simon & Schuster, 1971.

    The Mirage of Safety, New York, Scribners, 1975.

Jackson, Carlton, *J. I. Rodale: Apostle of Nonconformity*, New York, Pyramid Books, 1974.

Jane Brody's Nutrition Book, New York, Bantam, 1982.

Johnston, James P., *A Hundred Years' Eating*, Dublin, Gill and Macmillan, and Montreal, McGill-Queens University Press, 1977.

Longh, J. L. de, *The Three Kinds of Cod Liver Oil*, London, Taylor, Walton & Maberley, 1849.

Kellogg, J. H., *The Home Hand-Book of Domestic Hygiene and Rational Medicine*, London, International Tract Society, 1896.

King, C. G., *A Good Idea: The History of the Nutrition Foundation*, New York, The Nutrition Foundation, 1976.

Lear, Martha Weinman, *Heart Sounds*, London, Arrow, 1981.

Lesser, Michael, *Nutrition and Vitamin Therapy*, New York, Bantam Books, 1981.

Liebig, Justus von, *Organic Chemistry in its Application to Agriculture and Physiology*, ed. Webster, Cambridge.

Lindlahr, Henry, *Natural Therapeutics, III: Dietetics*, Saffron Walden, C. W. Daniel, 1983.

Longmate, Norman, *How We Lived Then*, London, Hutchinson, 1971.

McCance, R. A., and **Widdowson**, E. M., *Breads White and Brown*, London, Pitman, 1956.

McCann, Alfred W., *The Science of Eating*, New York, Garden City Publishing Co., 1919.

McCarrison, Sir Robert, *Nutrition and Health*, London, The McCarrison Society, 1982.

   Studies in Deficiency Disease, London, Oxford Medical Publications, 1921.

McCollum, E. V., *The Newer Knowledge of Nutrition*, New York, Macmillan Co., 1939.

MacFadden, Mary, *Dumb-bells and Carrot-strips*, London, Victor Gollancz, 1956.

Mackarness, Richard, *Chemical Victims*, London, Pan Books, 1980.

   Not All in the Mind, London, Pan Books, 1976.

McLester, James S., *Nutrition and Diet in Health and Disease*, Philadelphia, W. B. Saunders Co., 1944.

McLaughlin, Terence, *Diet of Tripe*, Newton Abbott, David & Charles, 1978.

Mandell, Dr Marshall, and **Scanlon**, Lynne Waller, *Dr. Mandell's 5-Day Allergy Relief System*, London, Arrow Books, 1983.

Matthews, Wendy, and **Wells**, Dilys, *Second Book of Food and Nutrition*, London, The Flour Advisory Bureau, 1976.

Mauduit, Vicomte de, *They Can't Ration These*, London, Michael Joseph, 1940.

Medical Research Council, *Vitamins: A Survey of Present Knowledge*, London, HMSO, 1932.

Mental Health and Mental Development (*Diet Related to Killer Diseases*, V), 1980 update, Hearing before the Select Committee on Nutrition and Human Needs of the US Senate, 95th Congress, Berkeley, Ca., Parker House, 1980.

Morgan, Louise, *Inside Your Kitchen*, London, Hutchinson, 1956.

Mount, James Lambert, *The Food and Health of Western Man*, Marlow, Bucks, Precision Press, 1979.

Murray, Frank, with **Tarr**, Jon, *More Than One Slingshot*, Richmond, Va., Marlborough House Publishing Company, 1984.

Needham, J., Ed., *Hopkins and Biochemistry (1861–1947)*, Cambridge, W. Heffer, 1949.

Nissenbaum, Stephen, *Sex, Diet and Debility in Jacksonian America*, Westport, Conn., Greenwood Press, 1980.

Oddy, Derek J., and **Miller**, Derek S., *The Making of the Modern British Diet*, London, Croom Helm, 1976.

O'Hara-May, J., *Elizabethan Dyetary of Health*, Lawrence, Kan., Coronado Press, 1977.

Orr, Sir John Boyd, *Food and the People*, London, The Pilot Press, 1943.

and **Lubbock**, David, *Feeding the People in Wartime*, London, Macmillan, 1940.

Passwater, Richard, *Supernutrition for Healthy Hearts*, Wellingborough, Northants, Thorsons, 1981.

Pauling, Linus, *Vitamin C, the Common Cold and the Flu*, New York, Berkeley Books, 1981.

Pearse, Innes H., and **Crocker**, Lucy H., *The Peckham Experiment*, London, Allen & Unwin, 1947.

and **Williamson**, G. Scott, *The Case for Action*, Edinburgh, The Scottish Academic Press, 1982.

Pfeiffer, Carl C., *The Golden Pamphlet*, Princeton, The Princeton Brain Bio Center, 1982.

Zinc and other Micro-Nutrients, New Canaan, Conn., Keats Publishing Inc., 1978.

Picton, L. J., *Thoughts on Feeding*, London, Faber & Faber, 1946.

Plimmer, R. H. A. and Mrs V. G., *Vitamins and the Choice of Food*, London, Longmans, 1922.

Powell, Mrs Milton, *Eating for Perfect Health*, London, Athletic Publications Ltd, 1932.

Pritikin, Nathan, *The Pritikin Promise*, New York, Bantam Books, 1985.

Randolph, Theron G., and **Moss**, Ralph W., *Allergies: Your Hidden Enemy*, Wellingborough, Northants, Turnstone Press, 1981.

Rapport, S., and **Wright**, H., eds., *Great Adventures in Medicine*, New York, The Dial Press, 1956.

Saxon, Edgar J., *Sensible Food for All*, Ashingdon, Essex, C. W. Daniel, 1942.

Schauss, Alexander, *Diet, Crime and Delinquency*, Berkeley, Ca., Parker House, 1981.

Scott, Cyril, *Health, Diet and Commonsense*, London, The Homoeopathic Publishing Co., 1944.

Selye, Hans, *The Stress of Life*, New York, McGraw-Hill, 1978.

Shand, P. Morton, *A Book of Food*, London, Jonathan Cape, 1934.

Sheehy, E. J., *Animal Nutrition*, London, Macmillan, 1955.

Shelton, Herbert M., *Health for the Millions*, Chicago, The Natural Hygiene Press Inc., 1968.

Orthobionomics: The Hygienic System, San Antonio, Dr Shelton's Health School, 1953.

Rubies in the Sand, San Antonio, Dr Shelton's Health School, 1961.

Simeons, A. T. W., *Food: Facts, Foibles and Fables*, New York, Funk & Wagnalls, 1968.

Sinclair, H. M., ed., *The Work of Sir Robert McCarrison*, London, Faber & Faber, 1953.

Sloan, Sara, *Nutritional Parenting*, New Canaan, Conn., Keats Publishing Inc., 1982.

Stanway, Dr Andrew, *Taking the Rough with the Smooth*, London, Souvenir Press, 1976.

Swanson, Gloria, *Swanson on Swanson*, London, Michael Joseph, 1980.

Tannahill, Reay, *Food in History*, St Albans, Paladin, 1975.

Tilden, J. H., *Food: Its Influence as a Factor in Disease and Health*, New Canaan, Conn., Keats Publishing Inc., 1976.

Toxemia: The Basic Cause of Disease, Bridgeport, Conn., Natural Hygiene Press, 1982.

Waerland, Are, *In the Cauldron of Disease*, London, David Nutt, 1934.

Waerland, Ebba, *Rebuilding Health: The Waerland Method of Natural Therapy*, New York, Arco, 1972.

Walker, Caroline, and **Cannon**, Geoffrey, *The Food Scandal*, London, Century, 1984.

Whorton, James C., *Crusaders for Fitness*, Princeton, Princeton University Press, 1982.

Williams, Roger J., *Biochemical Individuality*, Austin, University of Texas Press, 1979.

Nutrition against Disease, New York, Bantam, 1981.

The Prevention of Alcoholism through Nutrition, New York, Bantam, 1981.

Williamson, G. Scott, and **Pearse**, I. H., *Biologists in Search of Material*, Edinburgh, The Scottish Academic Press, 1982.

Science, Synthesis and Sanity, Edinburgh, The Scottish Academic Press, 1980.

Wingate, Peter, *Penguin Medical Encyclopedia*, Harmondsworth, Penguin Books, 1972.

Wrench, G. T., *The Wheel of Health*, New York, Schocken Books, 1972.

Wright, Hannah, *Swallow It Whole*, Manchester, NS Press, 1981.

Yudkin, John, *Pure, White and Deadly*, London, Davis-Poynter, 1972.

Notes

References to books listed in the bibliography are given by author only, unless more than one work by the same author is listed, in which case the title is also given.

1. Animal and Vegetable

1. James Woodforde, *Diary of a Country Parson*, London, Oxford University Press, vol. 4, pp. 178–9.
2. *Hippocratic Writings*, p. 78.
3. Gershenfeld, 'Moses Maimonides', in *Medical Life*, 42, 1935, pp. 21–34 *passim*.
4. Ordronaux, 'The Medical School of Salernum', in Rapport and Wright, pp. 75–85.
5. T. Graham, pp. 154–68 *passim*.
6. Beaumont, *Experiments and Observations on the Gastric Juice and the Physiology of Digestion*, Pittsburg, NY, 1833, cit. Whorton, 'Tempest in a flesh-pot: the formulation of a physiological rationale for vegetarianism', *J. Hist. Med.*, 32, 1977, p. 128.
7. Aykroyd, p. 96.
8. Jongh, pp. 99–100.
9. ibid., p. 161.

2. The Chemistry of Life

1. Advertisement appearing in back pages of Jongh.
2. Liebig, pp. 188–9.
3. Victor Hugo, *Les Misérables*; passage translated by Mrs Rosalie N. Evans, in *Soil and Health*, 1, 4, p. 243.
4. Liebig, pp. 188–9.
5. McLaughlin, p. 65.
6. von Bunge, cit. McCann, p. 269.
7. ibid.
8. McCance and Widdowson, pp. 53–4.

3. Disease with a Minus Sign

1. Bernard Auzimour, *Résistance des Arabes*, Montpellier, 1905, cit. Hindhede, pp. 159–60.

2. Alfred McCann, *The Famishing World*, cit. Lindlahr, p. 55.
3. Hutchinson, *Food*, 3rd ed., London, 1911, pp. 25, 175, cit. Hindhede, p. 178.
4. Aykroyd, p. 195.
5. David, p. 194.
6. Vickery, *Biographical Memoir of Russell Henry Chittenden, 1856–1943*, p. 81, cit. Whorton, 'Physiological optimism: Horace Fletcher and Hygienic ideology in progressive America', *Bull. Hist. Medicine*, 55, 1981, p. 76.
7. Whorton, op. cit., p. 68.
8. ibid.
9. Horace Fletcher, *The A-B-Z of Our Own Nutrition*, New York, 1903, cit. Whorton, op. cit., p. 69.
10. Hindhede, p. 23.
11. ibid., p. 191.
12. ibid., p. 180.
13 Aykroyd, p. 26.
14. Wingate, p. 253.
15. Medical Research Council, p. 10.

4. A Certain Something

1. William Anderson, 'Kakke', in *St. Thomas Hospital Rep.*, 1876, pp. 5–30, cit. K. Codell Carter, 'The germ theory, beriberi and the deficiency diseases', *Med. Hist*, 21, 1977, p. 125.
2. *Lancet*, 1911, p. 843, cit. Carter, op. cit., p. 125.
3. C. A. Pekelharing, *Ned. Tijdschr. Geneesk.*, 70, 111, 1905.
4. Carl Voit, cit. *Hermann's Handbuch der Physiologie*, p. 19, cit. B. C. P. Hanssen, 'Early nutritional researches on beri-beri leading to the discovery of vitamin B₁', *Nut. Abs. & Rev.*, 26, 1, January 1956, p. 5.
5. F. G. Hopkins, Chandler Medal Address, 1922, cit. Needham, p. 67.
6. ibid., p. 65.
7. Aykroyd, p. 10.
8. C. Funk, 'The etiology of the deficiency diseases', *J. State Med.*, 20, p. 341.
9. F. G. Hopkins, *Daily Mail*, 28 Feb. 1911.

Also consulted:
Milton Lewis, 'The problem of infant feeding: the Australian experience from the mid-nineteenth century to the 1920s', *J. Hist. Med.*, 35, 1980, pp. 174–87.
Rima D. Apple, ' "To be used only under the direction of a physician": commercial infant feeding and medical practice 1870–1940', *Bull. Hist. Med.*, 54, 1980, pp. 402–17.

5. The Maize Mystery

1.   Lombroso, cit. Robert P. Parsons, 'Joseph Goldberger and pellagra', in Rapport and Wright, pp. 584–5.
2.   Rapport and Wright, p. 588.
3.   Mary Farrar Goldberger, 'Dr Joseph Goldberger', in Beeuwkes, p. 285.
4.   ibid., pp. 284–5.
5.   ibid., p. 285.
6.   ibid., p. 285.
7.   ibid., p. 286.
8.   Casimir Funk, 'Studies on Pellagra', *J. Physiol.*, 47, 1913, pp. 316–19, in Carpenter.
9.   ibid.
10.   Beeuwkes, p. 287.

6. The Science of Life

1.   McCann, *The Science of Eating*, pp. 192–215.
2.   ibid.
3.   Alfred McCann, *The Famishing World*, cit. Lindlahr, p. 55.
4.   Nissenbaum, p. 121.
5.   Shakespeare, William, *Twelfth Night*, II, iii.
6.   S. Graham, p. 537.
7.   S. Graham, cit. Nissenbaum, p. 32.
8.   S. Graham, vol. 2, p. 646.
9.   Shelton, *Orthobionomics*, pp. 220–21.
10.   Samuel Thomson, *Narrative of the Life and Medical Discoveries of Samuel Thomson*, Boston, 1825, p. 31.
11.   Nissenbaum, pp. 140–41.
12.   S. Graham, pp. 525–6.
13.   Alcott, *Tea and Coffee*, pp. 11–12.
14.   *Third Annual Report of the American Physiological Society*, Boston, 1 June 1839, cit. Hebbel E. Hoff and John F. Fulton, 'The centenary of the first American physiological society founded at Boston by William A. Alcott and Sylvester Graham', *Bull. Inst. Hist. Med.*, 5, 8, October 1937, p. 701.
15.   ibid.

7. Cold Water and Physical Culture

1.   Shelton, *Orthobionomics*, p. 381.
2.   ibid., p. 383.
3.   Trall, cit. Shelton, *Health for the Millions*, p. 171.
4.   Shelton, ibid., pp. 128–31.
5.   Trall, cit. Shelton, ibid., p. 280.
6.   *Graham Journal of Health and Longevity*, Boston, 1937, cit. Hoff and Fulton, 'The centenary of the first American physiological society . . .', *Bull. Inst. Hist. Med.*, 5, 8, October 1937.

7.   MacFadden, p. 64.
8.   ibid., p. 135.
9.   'Harvey Washington Wiley MD, 1844–1930: the *Health Quarterly* Hall of Fame', *The Health Quarterly Plus Two*, Nov/Dec 1981, p. 59.
10.   Dufty, pp. 163–4.
11.   ibid., p. 174.

8. The Vitamin Hypothesis

1.   Harry G. Day, 'The nutrition legacies of E. V. McCollum', *Nutrition Today*, January/February 1981, p. 27.
2.   ibid., p. 28.
3.   ibid.
4.   Aykroyd, p. 49.
5.   E. V. McCollum, 'The paths to the discovery of vitamins A & D', *J. of Nutrition*, 91, 1967, February Supplement 1, pp. 13–14.
6.   ibid., p. 14.
7.   John Parascandola and Aaron J. Ihde, 'Edward Mellanby and the antirachitic factor', *Bull. Hist. Med.*, 51, Winter 1977, p. 152.
8.   Charles Curtis, *An Account of the Diseases of India as They Appeared in the English Fleet*, Edinburgh, 1807, p. 41, cit. Medical Research Council, p. 189.

9. Eating for Health

1.   Orr and Lubbock, p. 16.
2.   ibid., p. 16.
3.   Robert McCarrison, *Studies in Deficiency Disease*, p. 9.
4.   Allinson, *Medical Essays*, Vol. 1, Foreword.
5.   ibid.
6.   ibid., p. 21.
7.   ibid., Foreword.
8.   T. R. Allinson, *The Advantages of Wholemeal Bread*, The London Natural Food Co., p. 11.
9.   Allinson, *Medical Essays*, Vol. 1, endpage.
10.   ibid., Foreword.
11.   Dr Ralph Bircher, 'Bircher-Benner's Life Force', in *Dr Bircher-Benner's Way to Positive Health and Vitality*, p. 11.

10. 'Mangez Vivant!'

1.   Bircher-Benner, *Food Energy*, p. 34.
2.   ibid.
3.   Bircher-Benner, *Food Energy*, *passim*.
5.   Dr Ralph Bircher, 'Bircher-Benner's Life Force', in *Dr Bircher-Benner's Way to Positive Health and Vitality*, p. 17.

6. ibid., pp. 31–3.

7. ibid., p. 23.

11. The North-West Frontier

1. Wrench, p. 13.

2. ibid., p. 18.

3. McCarrison, *Studies in Deficiency Disease*, p. 9.

4. ibid., p. 9.

5. ibid., *passim*.

6. Sir Robert McCarrison, 'Faulty food in relation to gastro-intestinal disorder', *Lancet*, 1, 208, 1922.

7. *Nutrition Reviews*, December 1943, p. 417.

8. Picton, p. 21.

9. The 'Medical Testament of the County Palatine of Chester Local Medical and Panel Committee', 1938, cit. Balfour, pp. 65–6.

10. McCarrison, *Nutrition and Health*, p. 15.

12. The Standard for Health

1. Orr, *Food and the People*, p. 12.

2. ibid., p. 24.

3. ibid., p. 12.

4. Hay, p. 15.

5. Sir Arbuthnot Lane, *The Operative Treatment of Chronic Intestinal Stasis*, p. 86, cit. A. Waerland, p. 199.

6. Sir Arbuthnot Lane, *The Prevention of the Diseases Peculiar to Civilisation*, p. 42, cit. A. Waerland, p. 199.

7. Lane, ibid., cit. A. Waerland, p. 154.

8. *Health for All*, June 1957, p. 9.

13. 'The Right Feeding of Our People'

1. A. Waerland, p. 110.

2. *Health for All*, July 1927, p. 41.

3. *Health for All*, June 1957, p. 23.

4. Advertisements appearing in early issues of *Health for All*.

5. Pearse and Williamson, p. 1.

6. Williamson and Pearse, p. 9.

7. ibid., p. 75.

8. Private communication.

9. 'Medical Testament of the Country Palatine of Chester Local Medical and Panel Committee', 1938, in Picton, pp. 22–30.

14. 'Food is Your Best Medicine'

1. Swanson, pp. 314–16.

2. Dufty, pp. 11–12.

3.   Bieler, pp. 49–50.
4.   ibid., p. 10.
5.   Tilden, *Toxemia*, p. 28.
6.   ibid., p. 39.
7.   Murray, pp. 43, 40–41.
8.   Advertisements appearing in US *Ladies' Home Journal* during the year 1926.
9.   Murray, p. 18.
10.   Hauser, *The New Diet Does It*, p. 1.
11.   ibid., pp.2–3.
12.   Hauser, *Look Younger, Live Longer*, p. 186.

15. The Kitchen Front in Wartime

1.   Orr and Lubbock, p. 10.
2.   Longmate, p. 153.
3.   Dr Charles Hill, *Wartime Food for Growing Children*, p. 9.
4.   Dr Charles Hill, *Wise Eating in Wartime*, p. 25.
5.   *BMJ*, 11 April 1942, pp. 479–80.
6.   McCance and Widdowson, p. 115.
7.   '85 per cent flour extraction', *Country Miller*, 1942, cit. McCance and Widdowson, p. 99.
8.   Picton, p. 126.
9.   McCance and Widdowson, pp. 103–4.
10.   *Woman*, 3 Nov. 1943, p. 11.
11.   Orr, *Food and the People*, p. 23.
12.   Report of the Hot Springs Conference, cit. Sir Robert McCarrison, 'Introductory remarks on nutrition today', *Nutrition*, 1947, p. 72.

16. The Growth of 'Faddism'

1.   King, p. 3.
2.   ibid., p. 18.
3.   ibid., p. 159.
4.   McLester, p. 335.
5.   ibid., p. 366.
6.   Council on Foods and Nutrition and the Council on Industrial Health, 'Indiscriminate administration of vitamins to workers in industry', *J. Amer. Med. Assn*, 21 Feb. 1942, p. 621.
7.   *J. Amer. Med. Assn*, 20 Feb. 1954, p. 693.
8.   King, p. 19.
9.   *New York Times*, 17 May 1951, p. 37.
10.   ibid.
11.   J. I. Rodale, *Pay Dirt: Farming and Gardening with Composts*, New York, The Devin-Adair Co., 1945, cit. review by Mark Fitzroy, in *Soil and Health*, vol. 1, no. 1, February 1946, p. 60.
12.   Hauser, *Look Younger, Live Longer, passim*.

13.   ibid., p. 18.

14.   Murray, p. 20.

15.   Davis, *Let's Eat Right to Keep Fit, passim.*

16.   Sally Beauman, 'How not to cook your own goose', *Daily Telegraph Magazine*, 16 Nov. 1976, pp. 37–43.

17.   Davis, op. cit., p. 28.

18.   ibid., p. 217.

19.   ibid., p. 203.

20.   George Urdang, 'Antibiotics and pharmacy', *J. Hist. Med.*, 6, 1951, pp. 402–3.

21.   Davis, op. cit., p. 166.

17. The National Health

1.   H. E. Magee, 'Application of nutrition to public health: some lessons of the war', *BMJ*, 30 March 1946, pp. 477 and 481.

2.   Sir Albert Howard, *Farming and Gardening for Health or Disease*, Faber & Faber, 1945, p. 81.

3.   Balfour, p. 21.

4.   G. V. Jacks, and R. O. Whyte, *The Rape of the Earth*, Faber & Faber, 1939, cit. Balfour, p. 50.

5.   Balfour, pp. 134–5.

6.   Adrian Bell, *Men and the Fields*, London, Batsford, 1937, p. 143.

7.   Eve Balfour in *Mother Earth*, July 1952, cit. Jorian Jenks, *The Stuff Man's Made Of*, Faber & Faber, 1959, p. 123.

8.   Unpublished material supplied by Mary Langman.

9.   J. Comerford, *The Healthy Unknown*, London, Hamish Hamilton, 1947, p. 12.

10.   Dr Kenneth Barlow, from a paper read at the Conference on Environmental Health organized by the Society for the Social History of Medicine at Bristol University, 7 July 1984.

11.   British Medical Association, pp. 11–12.

12.   ibid., p. 15.

13.   H. M. Sinclair, in a lecture given at the McCarrison Society's Annual Conference, 23 Sept. 1984.

14.   Bacharach, pp. 132 and 139.

15.   Dr Donald Acheson, Chief Medical Officer, Department of Health and Social Security, in the 10th Boyd Orr Lecture, given at the University of Aberdeen, 6 December 1984.

16.   H. M. Sinclair, in a lecture given at the McCarrison Society's Annual Conference, 23 September 1984.

17.   Fenelon, p. 42.

18.   Bacharach, Introduction, p. x.

19.   League of Nations, *Final Report on the Relation of Nutrition to Health, Agriculture and Economic Policy*, 1937 *passim*.

20.   Sir Robert McCarrison, 'Can Malnutrition be Prevented?' *The Listener*, 20 July 1939, p. 128.

21.   David, p. 23.

22.   *Lancet*, 4 Jan. 1947.

23.   *BMJ*, 1942, i, p. 393.

24.   Morgan, p. 92.

25.   Unpublished material supplied by Mary Langman.

26.   Ministry of Food, *Report of the Conference on the Postwar Loaf*, cit. McCance and Widdowson, p. 117.

27.   *Report of the Panel on the Composition and Nutritive Value of Flour (The Cohen Report)*, HMSO, 1956, cit. Kenneth Barlow, *The Law and the Loaf*, Marlow, Bucks, Precision Press, 1978, p. 45.

18. The Deadly Environment

1.   Scott, p. 151.

2.   M. Bircher-Benner, *The Hell of Ill-Health*, John Miles Publishers, 1940, cit. Chaitow, *An End to Cancer?*, Wellingborough, Northants, Thorsons, 1978, p. 47.

3.   Dr Ernest Tipper, *The Cradle of the World and Cancer*, cit. A. Waerland, p. 197.

4.   Scott, p. 154.

5.   Shand, p. 268.

5a.   Richard Passwater, *Beta-Carotene*, New Canaan, Conn., Keats Publishing Inc., 1984, p. 12.

6.   A. Waerland, p. 198.

7.   ibid.

8.   Gerson, *passim*.

9.   Gunther, pp. 59–60.

10.   Haught, p. 64.

11.   ibid., p. 21.

12.   Gunther, p. 59.

13.   Haught, p. 13.

14.   ibid., p. 15.

15.   Mackarness, *Not All in the Mind*, p. 60.

16.   Coca, p. 16.

17.   Randolph and Moss, p. 23.

18.   Mandell and Scanlon, p. 7.

19.   Carson, *passim*.

19. All in the Mind

1.   Dr Charles Mercier, 'Diet as a Factor in the Causation of Mental Disease', *Lancet*, 11 March 1916, p. 561.

2.   ibid., *passim*.

3.   F. Gowland Hopkins, Address, cit. Needham, p. 201.

4. Josef Brozek, "Nutrition and psyche, with special reference to experimental psychodietetics', *Amer. J. Clin. Nutrition*, vol. 3, no. 2, p. 106.

5. Pfeiffer, pp. 26–8.

6. Personal communication from Dr Hoffer.

7. Hoffer and Osmond, p. 57.

8. Dr Humphrey Osmond, 'Historical Aspects of Orthomolecular Psychiatry', a lecture delivered 5 April 1977 at a symposium organized by the Huxley Society of the USA.

9. Dr Jeffrey Bland, in a lecture at the Symposium on Nutrition organized by the British Naturopathic and Osteopathic Association in London, in October 1983.

10. Mandell and Scanlon, p. 98.

11. Abram Hoffer, Foreword to Mandell and Scanlon, p. x.

12. Randolph and Moss, p. 220.

13. Lesser, pp. 163–4.

14. P. Airola, *Hypoglycemia: A Better Approach*, Phoenix, Az., Health Plus, 1977, p. 66.

15. S. Freud, quoted by M. D. Sackler, *et al.* 'Recent advances in psychobiology and their impact on general practice', *Int. Record of Med.*, cit. Williams, *Nutrition against Disease*, pp. 154–5.

16. Williams, op. cit., p. 11.

20. Whole Food and Health Foods

1. *Daily Herald*, 1 May 1955.

2. Wright, p. 16.

3. Alan Lewis, 'The gentle persuader', *Natural Food Trader*, Jubilee issue, 1984.

4. Tony Osman, 'Health foods: how many of them really do you good?' *Sunday Times Magazine*, May 1971, p. 35.

5. ibid.

6. John Barr, 'The health foodists', *New Society*, 30 April 1970, p. 721.

7. *Woman*, 5 Jan. 1963, p. 9.

8. Kit Tulleken, 'The once and future face', *Queen*, October 1970, p. 56.

9. Magnus Pyke, 'Old wives in the kitchen', *Daily Telegraph Magazine*, 14 December 1976.

10. 'US diet termed poor in nutrition', *NY Times*, 31 Jan. 1956.

11. E. V. Askey, 'American public wasting millions on "vitamania" ', *J. Amer. Med. Assn*, 174, 1960, p. 1332, cit. Hunter, *Consumer Beware!*, p. 44.

12. *J. Amer. Med. Assn*, 17 Nov. 1962, p. 821.

13. Frederick J. Stare, *Eating for Good Health*, New York, Doubleday, 1964, p. 194, cit. Hunter, *Consumer Beware!*, p. 37.

14. Frederick J. Stare, 'Are there poisons in your food?', *Farm Journal*, Feb. 1961, cit. Hunter, op. cit., p. 37.

15.   G. Blix, ed., *Nutrition and Caries-Prevention*, Uppsala, The Swedish Nutrition Foundation, 1965.

16.   Joseph D. Beasley, Foreword to Beasley and Swift, p. iv.

17.   Sloan, p. 4.

18.   Carlton Fredericks, *Eat Well, Get Well, Stay Well*, New York, Putnam, 1980, p. 8.

19.   Williams, *Biochemical Individuality*, p. 203.

20.   Garrison.

21. Eating Hearty

1.   Lear, p. 11.

2.   Jack Challem, 'Vitamin E can save your life', *The Health Quarterly Plus Two*, July/August 1982, p. 63.

3.   Stefan Bechtel, 'Heart protection – the Mediterranean way', *Prevention*, January 1984, p. 25.

4.   Boots' advertisement, *You* magazine, 28 April 1985.

5.   Mark Bricklin, ed., *The Practical Encyclopedia of Natural Healing*, Emmaus, Pa., Rodale Press Inc., 1976, p. 436.

6.   Williams, *Nutrition against Disease*, p. 83.

7.   Stanway, p. 119.

8.   Yudkin, p. 99.

9.   Cleave, p. 98.

10.   ibid., p. 113.

11.   A. P. DeGroot, R. Luyken, and N. A. Pikaar, 'Cholesterol-lowering effects of rolled oats', *Lancet*, 1963, 2, 303.

12.   M. R. Malinow *et al.*, 'Effect of alfalfa meal on shrinkage (regression) of atherosclerotic plaques during cholesterol feeding in monkeys', *Atherosclerosis*, 30, 1978, pp. 27–43; M. R. Malinow, P. McLaughlin and P. Cheeke, 'Comparative effects of alfalfa saponins and alfalfa fiber on cholesterol absorption in rats', *Amer. J. Clin. Nutrition*, September 1979, pp. 1810–12; both cit. Bland, pp. 73–4.

13.   T. G. Kiehm, J. W. Anderson and K. Ward, 'Beneficial effects of a high carbohydrate, high fiber diet on hyperglycemic diabetic men', *Amer. J. Clin. Nutrition*, August 1976, pp. 895–9, cit. Bland, p. 159.

22. Capitol Concern

1.   Garrison, p. 200.

1a.   Murray, pp. 75–6.

2.   Garrison, p. 202.

3.   ibid., p. 214.

4.   Figures from the 1970 US Census; US National Center for Health Statistics; the American Heart Association; and other sources; quoted in Beasley and Swift; Passwater; Cheraskin, Ringsdorf and Clark.

5. *J. Amer. Med. Assn,* 9 May 1959, p. 154.

6. Davis, *Let's Eat Right to Keep Fit,* p. 220.

7. Dr Arnold Schaefer and Ogden C. Johnson, 'Are we well fed? . . . the search for the answer', *Nutrition Today,* Spring 1969, pp. 2–11.

8. Cortez F. Enloe, Jr, 'An idea whose time has come', *Nutrition Today,* Winter 1970, p. 14.

9. Williams, *Nutrition Against Disease,* p. 13.

10. ibid., p. 16.

11. Vance Packard, in a *Time* article in the Big Mac, quoted in Hess,, p. 198.

12. Pauling, p. 84.

13. Edward H. Rynearson, 'Americans love hogwash', supplement to *Nutrition Reviews,* July 1974, pp. 1–14.

14. The US National Dairy Council, 'Food faddism', ibid., pp. 48–52.

15. Ronald Deutsch, 'Where you should be shopping for your family', ibid., p. 52.

16. Deutsch, *The New Nuts among the Berries,* p. 8.

17. Simeons, pp. 108–9.

18. Herbert and Barrett, p. 57.

19. Esther S. Nelson, 'Nutrition instruction in medical schools – 1976'; reprinted from *J. Amer. Med. Assn,* (236, 29 Nov. 1976, p. 2534) in Hofmann, pp. 402–3.

20. Cortez F. Enloe, Jr, 'It might have been', *Nutrition Today,* Winter 1969/70, p. 21.

21. Hess, p. 7.

22. G. L. Blackburn *et al.,* 'Manual for nutritional/metabolic assessment of the hospitalized patient', presented at 62nd Annual Clinical Congress of the American College of Surgeons, 11–15 Oct. 1976, cit. A. E. Bender, 'Institutional malnutrition', *BMJ,* 14 Jan. 1984.

23. Benjamin Rosenthal, Michael Jacobson, and Marcy Bohm, *The Progressive,* November 1976, pp. 42–7, Hofmann, pp. 380–81.

24. Richard A. Ahrens, 'Out on the "range", it's credibility that counts', *Nutrition Today,* Jan./Feb. 1977, pp. 31–3.

25. Elizabeth M. Whelan, 'The fear of additives', in Herbert and Barrett, p. 48.

26. Harnik, pp. 3–7.

27. Murray, pp. 141–2.

28. *Jane Brody's Nutrition Book,* p. 12.

29. Keki Sidhwa in *J. Alternative Medicine,* June 1983, p. 8.30; personal communication from Keki Sidhwa.

23. EFAs, EPAs and All That

1.   H. M. Sinclair, 'Deficiency of essential fatty acids and athero-sclerosis etcetera', *Lancet*, 1, 1956, pp. 381–3.
2.   ibid.
3.   Quoted with the permission of Dr Donald Rudin from the MS of his as yet unpublished work 'The Omega Factor'.

24. Diet and Delinquency

1.   Personal communication from Schauss.
2.   ibid.
3.   Derek Bryce-Smith and H. A. Waldron: 'Lead, behaviour and criminality', *The Ecologist*, 4(10), December 1974.
4.   Statement of Mrs Barbara Reed, Probation Officer, Cuyahoga Falls, Ohio, *Mental Health and Mental Development*, p. 39.
5.   S. J. Schoenthaler, 'The effects of citrus on the treatment and control of antisocial behavior. A double-blind cross-over study of an incarcerated juvenile population', *Int. J. Biosocial Res.*, 5(2), 1983, pp. 107–17.
6.   S. J. Schoenthaler, 'The Los Angeles Probation Department diet-behavior program: an empirical evaluation of six institutional settings', *Int. J. Biosocial Res.*, 5(2), 1983, pp. 88–98.
7.   J. Egger *et al.*, 'Is migraine food allergy?', *Lancet*, 15 October 1983, pp. 865–8.

25. Self-help – and Self-interest

1.   Personal communication.
2.   Personal communication from Sally Bunday.
3.   Personal communication from Mrs Belinda Barnes.
4.   *US J. of Med. Educ.*, 50, 1975, pp. 888–92, cit. *Lancet*, 6 Aug. 1983, p. 333.
5.   *BMJ*, 29 Jan. 1972, 6; *J. Royal Soc. Med.*, vol. 77, May 1984, p. 436.
7.   Julian Freeman, *Arthritis: the New Treatments*, rev. ed., Chicago, Ill., Contemporary Books, Inc., 1981, p. 26.
8.   Dr Logan Clendening, *The Human Body*, cit. Bieler, p. 51.
9.   Personal communication from Dr Stephen Davies.
10.   Arnold Bender, *Health or Hoax?*, London, Sphere Books, 1986, p. 161.
11.   ibid., p. 30.
12.   ibid., pp. 147–8.
13.   ibid., p. 148.
14.   John Boyd Orr, 'The development of the science of nutrition in relation to disease', *BMJ*, 23 May 1931, p. 884.
15.   ibid.
16.   Medical Research Council, pp. 226–7.

17. Dr Ross Hume Hall, 'Is nutrition a stagnating science?', *New Scientist*, 2 January 1975, pp. 7–8.

18. Richard Bienia *et al.*, *J. Amer. Geriatrics Soc.*, 30 July 1982, pp. 433–6.

19. Script of Granada TV World in Action programme, 'The Great Food Scandal', screened on 7 October 1985.

20. COMA, *Nutritional Aspects of Bread and Flour*, HMSO, 1981.

21. ibid.

22. Sir Alan Marre, speech at the annual luncheon of the British Nutrition Foundation, 21 November 1984.

23. Norman J. Temple. in *Med. Hypotheses*, 10, 1983, pp. 411–24.

26. Food for the Future

1. *Woman*, 6 Oct. 1984, p. 18.

2. Jocasta Innes, 'Foodie Fare', *Sunday Times*, 9 December 1984.

3. *Woman*, 'The magnificent 20 families who got healthy with *Woman*, 10 Nov. 1984., pp. 16–19.

4. Brekhman and Nesterenko, pp. 16–18.

5. Friends of the Earth, *Report on PAN-UK*.

6. American Medical Association, *Let's Talk About Food*, cit. Wade Greene, 'Guru of the organic food cult', *New York Times Magazine*, 6 June 1971.

7. World Watch Institute, *Soil Erosion: Quiet Crisis in the World Economy*, cit. Steve Connor, 'Bad farming blamed for disappearing soil', *New Scientist*, 4 October 1984, p. 4.

8. HRH Prince Charles, speech to the British Medical Association on its 150th anniversary, *The Times*, 16 December 1982.

9. Claude Bernard, cit. Koretz, in *Digestive Diseases and Sci.*, 29, June 1984, pp. 577–88.

10. Anna Coote, 'Death to the working classes', *New Statesman*, 7 Sept. 1984, pp. 8–9.

11. Jean Golding, Mary Haslum and Anthony C. Morris, 'What do our ten-year-old children eat?' *Health Visitor*, June 1984, pp. 178–9.

12. Preface to Bircher-Benner, *Fruit Dishes and Raw Vegetables*.

Index